HEAVEN'S FURY

HEAVEN'S FURY

A NOVEL

Stephen Frey

ATRIA BOOKS

New York London Toronto Sydney

ATRIA BOOKS

A Division of Simon & Schuster, Inc.
1230 Avenue of the Americas
New York, NY 10020

First Atria Books hardcover edition September 2010

ATRIA BOOKS and colophon are trademarks of Simon & Schuster, Inc.

For information about special discounts for bulk purchases,
please contact Simon & Schuster Special Sales at 1-866-506-1949
or business@simonandschuster.com.

The Simon & Schuster Speakers Bureau can bring authors to your live event.
For more information or to book an event contact the Simon & Schuster Speakers Bureau at 1-866-248-3049 or visit our website at www.simonspeakers.com.

Designed by Brad Reina

Manufactured in the United States of America

10   9   8   7   6   5   4   3   2   1

Library of Congress Cataloging-in-Publication Data

Frey, Stephen W.
  Heaven's fury : a novel / Stephen Frey. — 1st Atria Books hardcover ed.
    p. cm.
  1. Sheriffs–Fiction.   2. Murder—Investigation—Fiction.
3. Wisconsin—Fiction.   4. Suspense fiction.   I. Title.
  PS3556.R4477H43 2010
  813'.54—dc22   2010026228

ISBN 978-1-4165-4967-3
ISBN 978-1-4391-7713-6 (ebook)

For Diana and our daughter, Elle.
I'll love you two forever.

HEAVEN'S FURY

1

S HE IS EXQUISITE, wonderfully responsive to my touch, and eager to please me any way she can. She is *Intrepid,* the canoe my father and I built twenty-four years ago during a long, hard Wisconsin winter.

Intrepid was a labor of love, assembled meticulously rib by rib in our drafty wooden barn because my father, John Summers, was a meticulous man. Joints had to be seamless; weight distribution exact; surfaces sanded silky smooth; and we had to use tools one at a time and return them to their designated hook or drawer before we could use the next one. My father allotted just one hour a day for the project, but during that time he allowed nothing to disturb us, not even my two younger brothers, who desperately wanted to be included. During that hour we were completely alone in a world dominated by the sweet smell of freshly cut birch and maple and the soothing sounds of jazz drifting softly from my father's dust-covered eight-track player.

It seemed like it took forever to build *Intrepid,* but in the end it didn't take long enough. We became father and son that winter despite what we both knew he'd done. Then, suddenly, he was gone. It was what he wanted, what I assume finally brought peace to his soul, but I still haven't forgiven him.

The sun's late-afternoon rays are captured by the river, transforming its glittering silver surface to burnt orange as *Intrepid* glides into the flames. Her smooth hull and sharp keel guide me downstream past the dense pine forest that surrounds the river on both sides, isolating me from the outside world. I inhale the warm summer air as I paddle. Wrapped inside it are the pleasant scents of pine, honeysuckle, wildflowers, and the water—scents that don't last long in north-country.

My daydream is shattered by the hollow ring of an old rotary phone that sits on my desk, and I'm thrust back into reality. Back to my small office and the gray Wisconsin winter laying siege to the territory outside my precinct.

The old phone hides among a stack of pending misdemeanor reports, unsolved crossword puzzles, and Styrofoam cups half-full of stale coffee. Over its ring I hear my assistant, Mrs. Erickson, gossiping on her phone. She and I are alone in this bush-league excuse for a precinct. It has just a small reception area, my office, a file room, a single jail cell, and a cramped conference room that's barely big enough for my four deputies and me at our weekly Monday afternoon meetings. It doesn't intimidate people the way it should—the way my barracks in Madison did and the way my precinct in Minneapolis did before that.

"Mrs. Erickson."

Mrs. Erickson is deep into her conversation and she ignores me. She's the lightning rod of a well-organized information web that's especially active in northern Wisconsin during the winter and encompasses several hundred square miles. North the short distance to Lake Superior, also called the Big Lake around here; west to Minnesota's port city of Duluth; south to the tiny town of Hayward; and east into Michigan's Upper Peninsula. Mrs. Erickson constantly relays lies, rumors, and sometimes even a little truth to her inner circle, who pass on the information to others, who pass it on to still others. Like concentric waves forced outward by the impact of a falling stone in a pond, the information spreads quickly into the community until it seems like everyone knows everyone else's business. I don't like the idea of everyone knowing my business; I don't think it's good for the community in general for everything to be so transparent. But my opinion doesn't matter.

When I became sheriff of Dakota County four years ago, I tried to sweep away Mrs. Erickson's web. Mostly because I wanted her focused on being my assistant, but a little, I have to admit, because I wanted to control the flow of information around here. I had a stern talk with her about it one morning a few weeks after I took over, and that afternoon I was called into a quickly convened, closed-door session of the Bruner town council. The meeting was held in the storage room of Cam Riley's hardware store, which is a few doors down from the precinct. There I was told in no uncertain terms to stop interfering.

I've never spoken to Mrs. Erickson again about how much time she wastes on the phone, because I need this job. Being sheriff of Dakota County is basically the end of the line for a lawman. Still, it's frustrating not to be completely in charge.

"Mrs. Erickson, answer that call!"

Her chair rolls heavily across the wooden floor beneath her sturdy form, then my door slams shut. She won't be answering the call. She understands the leverage she has around here and isn't afraid to use it.

I grab the receiver. "This is Sheriff Summers," I mutter angrily.

"Hello, Paul."

A familiar voice races to my ear. Gentle but powerful, it sets my nerves on fire. "Hi."

"I'm so glad you're there."

It's Cindy Prescott Harrison. She's beautiful, rich, and married—to someone else. She's a member of one of the River Families, as the locals call them. Wealthy outsiders who own estates south of town where they summer, the River Families usually only mix with locals when they need something.

"Why are you so glad I'm here?" I ask, trying too hard to sound casual.

"Relax, Paul."

Cindy heard it right away. "I am relaxed, damn it."

She laughs an easy laugh that's haunted me for years. "I'm on my way up there for the weekend," she explains, "but I want to fill my car up before I go to the estate so I'm going to Bat's Exxon station first. Then I'll drop by the precinct. I'll be there in a little while, so you stay put," she orders in a firm but friendly tone. "I can't wait to see you."

I lean back in my creaky chair, push up a slat of the dusty blind behind me, and peer out through a grimy pane into the half-light of the late afternoon. Big, puffy flakes are beginning to fall from the leading edge of a storm that's bearing down on us. It isn't even four o'clock, but it'll be dark in less than thirty minutes. By then there'll be an inch or two of new snow on the ground and I need to get home before things get bad, home to the other woman who haunts me.

"Cindy, I've got to—"

"I swear they're following me," she interrupts. Her voice turns faint as she looks over her shoulder. "I'm scared."

"What?" I lean forward over my desk and press the receiver tightly to my ear. "Scared? Why?"

"This blue van's been behind me ever since I left Hayward," she says, her voice back at full volume. "When I slow down, it slows down. When I speed up, it speeds up."

Hayward is the next town south of here. It's twenty miles away through the pine forest that isolates Bruner from the rest of the world. It isn't quite as remote an outpost as Bruner, but almost.

"They're following me, Paul, I know they are."

Panic and anger knife through me. I'd kill anyone who touched her. "They?"

"I can see two in the front, and there's probably a gang of them in the back. I've waved for them to pass me a couple of times, but they won't. It's creepy, I—"

Suddenly I'm picking up only garbled syllables. "Cindy?" The gibberish continues for what seems like an eternity. Finally, her voice blares through the phone again.

"Paul, Paul are you there? I hate cell phones," she mutters.

"Cindy." I can hear her, but apparently she can't hear me. "*Cindy!*"

"Paul, *Paul!* God, the reception's terrible out here. I hope these guys don't try to—"

The connection dies and I'm left to wonder if the blue van is real or just a ploy. Cindy can manipulate things so easily.

She's been able to manipulate me ever since I've known her. Ever since our first encounter that early summer afternoon so long ago on the Boulder River when I came around a bend and found her skinny-dipping alone. She was standing there knee-deep in the water as I paddled *Intrepid* downstream, smiling coyly at me, arms at her sides, not trying to hide anything. Water from her long blond hair was dripping down her beautiful, tanned body and her eyes were flashing. I was embarrassed and spellbound at the same time. I tried to seem like I wasn't looking at her, like I didn't notice her, when it must have been obvious I did. Then, out of the corner of my eye, I caught her signaling for me to stop.

After she got a towel from the riverbank and wrapped it loosely around herself, we talked for an hour. She did most of the talking, because I could barely put together a coherent sentence. I was sixteen, my hormones were raging, and I couldn't stop sneaking sidelong glances at this gorgeous girl. It turned out she was staying at her family's estate for the summer, assuming she was going to be bored out of her mind. It ended up being the best summer of her life, she told me years later.

It was the best summer of my life, too. Until her family found out she was seeing me and suddenly she was gone with no warning. Whisked back to the family compound in Minneapolis by her father before we were supposed to meet at her family's gate out on State Road 681 one August night. I waited there until midnight, hoping she'd show up, but she never did. Then it turned into the worst summer of my life. Not just because Cindy was gone, but because I suddenly figured out how the world really worked and which color my collar was. Then I lost my father.

I try calling Cindy's cell phone three times but it goes straight to her voicemail. Finally, I put the phone back down, the image of her standing there naked knee-deep in the river that summer afternoon vivid in my mind. As vivid as it's ever been.

I take a deep breath, aware that I should be getting home, but I can't shake the fear I heard in Cindy's voice. It sounded real. Maybe the blue van wasn't a figment of her imagination, and maybe the men inside just made their move, which is why my calls keep going straight to her voicemail. It's not far-fetched to think that. There are strange men who do strange things in the north-country when it's dark sixteen hours a day and gray the other eight. I've come face-to-face with that grim reality a few times.

I should go make sure Cindy's safe. The road between here and Hayward is desolate. It's a perfect place for a group of men with a bad case of cabin fever to do an evil deed. It would be official police business for me to check on her, my wife couldn't argue with that.

I shake my head. That's stupid. My wife can argue with anything—and often does.

I turn around and peer out the window again, trying to make a decision. The snow is falling faster and the flakes are turning smaller.

The storm is here.

The town of Bruner is tucked into the northern part of Dakota County. It's located five miles south of Lake Superior, at the intersection of Route 7 and State Road 681, which are the only two paved roads in the entire county. Just a forgotten dot on an upper Midwest map, Bruner's a place most travelers would politely term quaint but wouldn't stop in to visit if they didn't have business here. Along with the quaintness there's an eerie coarseness about it, too. A rough-around-the-edges, neglected quality that's obvious even to casual observers. Cars are old, rusty, and dented; buildings are peeling and rotting; and the people seem odd. It's as if they're hiding something and they don't want you stopping in because you might figure out what it is.

Bruner consists of a general store owned by Ike Mitchell and his live-in, Sara, a Chippewa woman who's been known to ride her ATV through town at two in the morning shouting at the top of her lungs about Washington and revenge after getting into the moonshine. There's a no-frills motel called the Friendly Mattress that's used mostly by hunters and fishermen from out of town, but, occasionally, by a few of Duluth's working girls, too. A tavern on the east side of town next to the Friendly Mattress called the Bruner Saloon, also owned by Ike and Sara, and their competition on the west side of town, the Kro-Bar. There's a Lutheran church with a rotting steeple; my precinct; Cam Riley's hardware store; Bat McCleary's Exxon station that still hangs an Esso sign from decades ago; a tiny branch of the Milwaukee Bank & Trust that only installed an ATM

two years ago; and a few rag-tag retail shops and businesses, including a washette where my wife works several days a week. All
of which is surrounded by a hundred or so small homes. They line
unpaved, rutted dirt roads that parallel Route 7 and SR 681 and
extend in all four directions away from the intersection for a few
hundred yards, then just kind of end in the weeds where the forest
begins.

Most of the locals work on the docks in Duluth or at the lumber
mill that's twenty miles east of Bruner on Route 7. It's low pay in
either direction, but, except for the shops in town, that's it for jobs
around here. You have to wonder why they do it, why they stick
around, because it's a no-frills existence. I've come up with all the
explanations I can think of, but I'll probably never come up with the
real one. See, I'm not a local. I moved here when I was fifteen, away
at eighteen, then back again in my midthirties. I had to move here
both times, so maybe I'll never really understand why the people
who were born here hang on. And maybe I'll always be a little jealous of them. They could leave if they really wanted to, but I can't.
Not if I want to stay a lawman.

Dakota County is bisected by a gin-clear, freestone river called
the Boulder that flows due north and stretches twenty-two miles
as the eagle flies. It begins its journey to Lake Superior in southern
Dakota County, in a place called the Meadows where it meanders
north for seven miles through high-grass marshes that are rimmed
by the pine forest. Then it narrows slightly and gathers strength,
running faster as it negotiates a series of steep canyons for another
ten miles and the forest closes in tightly around it. This section is
called the Gorges.

A short distance after the river passes beneath the Route 7 bridge
on the west side of town, it starts to roar. Canoeing the Meadows
and the Gorges isn't too dangerous, but making it from Bruner to
the mouth at the Big Lake without going over can be a real chal-
lenge, particularly in late spring when the snow pack is melting.

There are several Class IV rapids in the Falls and every few years we lose a teenager because, like all teenagers, he thinks he's bulletproof.

My father almost lost me to the Falls the spring after we built *Intrepid*, but I never told him what happened. I never told him how I was thrown into the frigid rapids and my right leg got wedged beneath a rock until it finally came free just before my lungs exploded. I never told him how I found *Intrepid* a few hundred yards downstream on a sand bar, miraculously without a scratch on it. He might have been more upset about losing *Intrepid* than me, which is why I didn't tell him. We got close that winter we built *Intrepid*, but my father had his emotional limits.

That middle section of the Boulder—the Gorges—is one of the most picturesque spots in all of the upper Midwest. Pine trees soar above the steep rock walls, which plunge in some places as much as four hundred feet straight down to the river on both sides. Each stretch of the Gorges seems more breathtaking than the last, until you make it around the next bend. It's in this section that the River Families have built their summer estates, rambling mansions, quaint guest cottages, and beautiful gardens that overlook the river from atop the western bluffs.

The Gorges roughly parallel SR 681 a mile west of the road. Every so often, as you drive south out of town, there's a gate on the right protecting a driveway that leads off into the forest toward the river and one of the estates. The River Families usually only come to town for supplies at Ike and Sara's store or to fill up at Bat's Exxon station. They don't come just to socialize at the Kro-Bar or the Bruner Saloon, at least not with the locals. And they keep their properties off limits to the locals. Strictly off limits.

When I come out of my office, Mrs. Erickson's finished with her call and she looks up from her dated issue of *Cosmo*. She's a stocky woman with white hair, a naturally tough expression, and a large mole on one cheek. We've had a tense truce ever since I was called into that emergency session of the town council four years ago, but it's still obvious we don't like each other.

"Are you going out to meet Cindy at the Prescott estate?" she asks with a smug smile.

"I'm just going down 681 to check on her, I'm not going to the estate." She knows who called because she has Caller ID on her phone. I don't because there isn't enough money in the budget, according to the town council. "She says she's being followed by some guys in a van."

A feigned look of deep concern comes to Mrs. Erickson's face. "Poor little rich girl. I do hope she's all right."

Mrs. Erickson doesn't give a fat rat's ass about Cindy. Like most of the locals, she despises the River Families. She despises their mansions and their expensive cars but most of all she despises their arrogance. I can't say I blame her but I'm caught in the middle on this one. During the long winters when the estates are vacant, my deputies and I patrol them to make sure no one breaks in. So the River Families treat us differently than the other locals. We get respectful nods from them and I get an off-the-books bonus. It's usually pretty healthy, too. At least a few thousand dollars in cash subtly slipped to me at the end of the season by whichever River Family was nominated to take care of me that year. A few thousand dollars goes a long way up here, and I count on that cash at the end of every summer.

"I'm going out there to make sure she's all right."

A knowing smile replaces Mrs. Erickson's look of concern. "I bet you are."

I know what she's thinking and it pisses me off, but I just change the subject. I've learned that it's the best thing to do. "Have you heard any news on the storm?"

"Yes."

She says nothing more, she just stares at me. I hate it when she plays this game. I spread my arms. *"Well?"*

"This one's not going to be too bad. A friend of mine talked to somebody up north near International Falls and it's already starting to taper off up there. Most of the heavy stuff is going south of us, down into Iowa and Illinois. We'll get a few inches, but that'll be it." She holds her hand up. "But there's a Clipper behind this one that's going to dump at least a foot and a half on us, maybe more."

One thing Mrs. Erickson is usually spot-on about is the weather. No rumors here. It's as if she knows she has to be straight up about something to make her lies seem more credible. "When?" I ask as I slip into my parka. It's a bone-chilling twelve degrees outside.

"It's supposed to start late Sunday night or early Monday morning."

"One hell of a way to start the week," I mutter, heading out without saying good-bye.

I hustle across the parking lot toward my white Jeep Cherokee that has DAKOTA COUNTY SHERIFF blazed down both sides in big, black letters. Ice and crusty snow crunch beneath my boots as I jog. At six-four and 230 pounds I crush things easily. I work out five days a week in my tiny home gym, so even at thirty-nine I'm still in decent shape.

At the stoplight in the middle of town I turn left off Route 7 and onto 681. Now I'm heading south toward Hayward. My wipers slap back and forth across the windshield as I pass a campground on my left that's run by Ike Mitchell's younger brother, Mickey, and just like that, the dense forest closes in around me and Bruner fades into my rearview mirror. The trees are so thick on both sides of the road you can't see more than a few feet back into them. I've often wondered what's lurking in there. Deer that will jump out in front of a vehicle with no warning and plow through the windshield, hooves flailing. Solitary black bears, wolf packs, and lots of coyotes, too. But I've always sensed that something else is lurking in there, too, something sinister that someday I'll have to face.

A mile down the road I pass the first River Family gate on my right. It's the Campbell estate. Old Bill Campbell is from St. Paul and owns a cable television network. I've heard he's worth over five hundred million dollars. That amount of money so boggles my mind I don't even bother thinking about it anymore. I used to wonder what it would be like to be that rich every night as I passed the Campbell entrance on my way home, but no more. It made me so bitter by the time I walked into my house a few minutes later I could hardly stand it. It was really starting to get to me, so I learned to let it go.

The thing is, for all of his money old Bill's a pretty unpleasant guy. He doesn't just keep his distance from the locals, he can be downright nasty to them even when he needs something. Last summer he had Bat McCleary do some work on one of his cars, his favorite Cadillac he keeps at his estate, but he argued about the charge when he came to pick it up, and he was an arrogant son of a bitch about it, too, I heard. So Bat took 20 percent off the tab just to get the guy out of his station. Apparently, old Bill was laughing about the whole deal with his son as they got into the car and drove off and that *really* got to Bat.

Bill's wife lost both of her prized poodles later that summer. No one knows for sure what happened, but we've all got a pretty good idea. Getting even is very important to people around here. Even to a good-natured guy like Bat.

I pass three more estates on the right, then my house on the left. My place is one of only two homes on the east side of 681 outside the town limits of Bruner and Hayward. It's composed of a four-bedroom log house and that drafty old barn across the yard my father and I built *Intrepid* in. Both the house and the barn are set back from the road on a slight rise. All in all it's twenty acres, only two of which are cleared. It's the place my father bought for our family when he moved us here from Los Angeles the autumn I turned fifteen, and the place I bought when I came back here four years ago. My family had long since moved away when I became sheriff of Dakota County, and at that time it was owned by an older man whose wife had just died.

I don't bother to look up the driveway to see if my wife's home as I race past. I figure if I don't see Vivian's car, she won't see mine.

I'm wrong. My cell phone rings right away and it's our home number flashing on the tiny screen. Vivian must have been looking out for me from the window in our second-floor bedroom, expecting me, since I told her I'd be home a little after four and it's now four-fifteen. She can only see about fifty feet of 681 through the trees from our bedroom, but the Cherokee is pretty recognizable with that black, block lettering down the sides.

I don't answer her call and I can't tell her later it's because of bad reception. My cell phone antenna still gets one bar here and Vivian knows that. So I'll have to come up with another excuse for ignoring her. Otherwise not answering could explode into an all-night war. I just hope she doesn't call Mrs. Erickson. Mrs. Erickson won't call her, but if Vivian calls in, Mrs. Erickson will be happy to tell her what she thinks is going on. She likes my wife even less than she likes me.

Vivian calls me four times in a row. I'll have to come up with a damn good excuse for why I didn't answer now.

I catch my reflection in the rearview mirror as I check to make sure Vivian hasn't jumped in her car and come after me. I've got dark hair with a few silver flecks, gray eyes, thin straight brows, faint crow's feet, full lips, and a three-day growth because I hate shaving.

Just as I refocus on the road, a doe leaps in front of me and I have to whip the Cherokee into the oncoming lane to avoid her, but there's no danger. She's the only creature I've seen since I left town. I haven't passed a single car coming the other way.

A few miles farther south I spot Cindy's car ahead on the left. It's a new BMW 7 Series. It's off the road in the snow in front of the tree line at a strange angle. I'm sure it's hers because there's no chance anyone else in Dakota County would be driving such an expensive car at this time of year. There's a blue van parked near it with its right tires in the snow and its left tires still on the pavement.

I swing the Cherokee around 180 degrees and come to a skidding stop behind the van. Then I flip on the emergency lights, reach into the glove compartment, grab my 9mm pistol, chamber the first round, hop out, holster the gun, and move carefully ahead, one hand over my eyes to shield them from the falling snow. I give the rusty van a wide berth as I move past it, aware that there might be more men inside. I should have called for backup, but I didn't want my deputies to know that what I was doing involved Cindy. It seems like everyone in Dakota County suspects Cindy and me of being more than just friends—including Vivian.

Four men are milling around the BMW, two on either side. The man by the driver's door is leaning down with his hands in his pockets. His face is just inches from the window. We've only got a few minutes of daylight left so it's hard to tell for sure, but it looks like the window is open a little. The men eye me with contempt, like I've spoiled their party.

"What's going on here?" I call loudly from the road. "What's the trouble?"

The man standing by the driver's door straightens up. "No trouble, officer," he answers in a friendly voice. "We got everything under control."

The men are rough looking. They're gaunt beneath their threadbare jeans and old jackets and they have long stringy hair, unshaven faces, and hungry looks in their eyes. Hungry looks that tell me they've never come close to touching a woman as beautiful as Cindy Prescott. I press my arm against my body, feeling for the pistol in my shoulder holster, feeling for exactly how the holster is positioned against my side. "Anyone inside the car?" I call, watching them glance at each other uneasily.

"Yeah," the guy by the driver's door answers.

This one is clearly the leader, the one I'll have to take down first if things suddenly go wrong. I've shot men before, I don't have a problem with it. Some people might even say I like it and that it's one reason I'm sheriff of Dakota County and no longer a lawman in a more important place. "How many?"

"Just one."

"Man? Woman?"

"Lady."

"She all right?"

The leader looks around at the other men like he's stalling for time, like he's hoping one of them will come up with a good answer because he can't. "Yeah, yeah," he finally says. "She spun off, you know? Slipped on a patch of ice, I guess. We're gonna help her get her car back on the road. We got the situation under control. You can get going."

"Great, thanks." I take a few steps toward the Cherokee, then turn back. "Before I go, why don't you do me a favor and open the driver's door?" The leader straightens up quickly and his head snaps back around. He had been leaning down toward the glass again, thinking he'd gotten rid of me. "Open the door," I demand, my voice turning steely. "Now."

"I told you," the man answers defiantly, "we got everything under control."

One of the guys on the passenger side of the BMW starts to reach into his jacket, but before he can make his move I've got my pistol leveled at him. I don't know why but I've always been able to draw like chain-blue lightning, and hit what I'm aiming at. See, that's the key. A lot of people can draw fast, but they miss. I don't.

"Don't be stupid," I advise the guy. He throws his hands in the air without even being told to. God, I hate a coward. I almost wish he'd gone for his gun. I swing the pistol to the left, at the leader, and he throws his hands up, too. "Open the damn door."

When he does, Cindy comes tumbling out of the car like some-thing stored in an overhead bin that's shifted in flight. She sobs as she scrambles to her feet, then races toward me and throws her arms around my neck.

"They told me they'd hurt me if I yelled, if I tried to get out of the car," she whispers. "They told me they'd kill you, then drag me into the van and . . . well . . . I can't even think about that." She pulls me even closer. "Thank God you came, Paul."

"It's all right," I assure her. "You're safe now."

"What are you going to do?" she asks, her voice trembling.

"Run 'em in."

She gasps. "Oh, God, no, I don't want to press charges."

"You don't have to. I will."

"But I'll have to testify."

I nod, keeping a sharp eye on the men. "Yes, you will."

"Then they'll *really* come after me," she says. "Just get them out of here, Paul. Please!"

She's not thinking straight, but I understand. "Okay, okay. Go get in the truck." She bounds away like that scared doe I almost hit a few miles back. When I hear the passenger door of the Cherokee slam shut, I nod at the leader. "Where are you boys from?"

"Hayward," he answers, looking like a hyena who's missed a scavenge. His head's down and there's a frustrated look on his face.

"Well, you guys better get on back there," I say forcefully, keep-ing the pistol trained on the leader. "Right now."

"Yes, sir," they all mumble with their heads down.

All of them except the leader. He stares at me sullenly.

"You got a problem, son?" I say "son" but he's probably my age, if not a little older. He needs to understand that I have no fear of him at all. "Well, do you?"

"Nope." He gestures at the rest of the gang as he saunters past. "I guess they don't appreciate Good Samaritans up here in Dakota County, boys."

I ought to check his ID, but I don't want to rile him up any more than I already have. During my two decades as a lawman I've learned to evaluate people quickly and my analysis tells me he's dangerous. I'm outnumbered four to one and even for a lawman who's as good with a gun as I am, those are terrible odds. Not in the movies, but here in the real world of northern Wisconsin I could quickly find myself in real trouble. And I don't want to end up in the Superior morgue tonight wearing a toe-tag.

So I just watch them get in the van, turn around, and roar off. Like I said, getting revenge is very important to people around here.

2

THE PRESCOTT MANSION is huge. It's three floors and ten thousand square feet, not including a finished basement it seems like you could park a 747 in. Also on the grounds are two guest houses, two tennis courts, a par-three golf hole, a heated pool and spa, a squash court, and a garden with a hedge maze that's big enough to get lost in.

I know because I did. It was the summer I was sixteen, the summer I met Cindy on the river. One moment she was standing beside me in the maze, the next she was gone and I was alone with just the ten-foot-high hedges towering over me. They were so thick I could barely see through them, much less pry them apart. She let me wander around in there for fifteen minutes before magically reappearing, and she thought the whole thing was hysterical. There were tears running down her face, she was laughing so hard when she finally came around a corner, clicking her camera at me over and over. I actually disliked her in those moments for making such a fool of me, for making me yell her name over and over like a lost child in a department store calling for his mother. I wanted to get back at her, but I never did. I didn't even give her a cold shoulder. I was too scared she'd turn her back on me and I'd never see her again.

My cell phone rings as I ease the Cherokee to a stop in front of the mansion's main entrance. Vivian's calling and it's the tenth time she's tried to get me since I sped past our house on my way out here. She's alone in our house and she tells me all the time that it scares her to death to be there by herself, especially after dark. She has this recurring nightmare that she's going to be murdered in the house. I feel guilty but I'm still not going to pick up. She'd be yelling at me before I could even say hello. I might as well wait as long as I can to face that storm.

One of the mansion's double doors swings open and Cindy appears, beckoning for me to come inside. After I got her car back on the road, I followed her here. She peeled off to the right back down the driveway where it splits, and she headed to the garages on the lower level as she stabbed her hand out the window pointing for me to go straight and come here. I won't stay long. I told myself that a hundred times on the way over.

I hop out of the truck without cutting the engine and jog toward her through the falling snow. Her smile widens as I move past her through the tall door, as though she's won some kind of victory. I smell oil burning. She's already turned up the heat from the fifty degrees her father keeps it on during the winter to keep the pipes from freezing.

I look around as I step into the foyer. The place is amazing, just as I remember it. Huge rooms full of expensive-looking furniture. It drips with wealth. Cindy's great-grandfather founded a commodities trading company a century ago that the family still owns. It's one of the biggest in the country, so this place has everything imaginable, just like their compound in Minneapolis does. From June to early September family and friends come to the estate here on the Boulder, but Cindy's father shuts the place down after Labor Day and they go back to the city ahead of the first cold wave, which usually hits before month end. Occasionally they use the mansion for Thanksgiving or Christmas, to celebrate an old-fashioned holiday if the weather forecast isn't too bleak for those few days. And sometimes family members come up on weekends by themselves to get away from the city, like Cindy has this weekend. Otherwise, the mansion stays empty until late spring.

Cindy gazes at me like she's a love-struck princess and I'm her knight in shining armor. She's so beautiful. She's thirty-eight but she looks ten years younger. She has long blond hair, sculpted cheeks, and a comely shape that's apparent despite the frumpy sweater and baggy jeans she's wearing. And she has dark blue eyes that seem innocent and mysterious all at once, along with a smile that seems like it could light up the Twin Cities by itself.

She's married to a United States congressman named Jack Harrison who joined the Prescott family business just after their wedding a decade ago, then went into politics last year. Harrison's family owned another big commodities company, which merged into Prescott Trading a month after he and Cindy were married. I've never figured out which was the dowry: Harrison's company— or Cindy.

Harrison's one of those can't-miss guys. He's got dashing good looks and a light-up-the-room charisma about him. Even though he's only a first-term congressman, he's already being mentioned in the Midwest as a potential presidential candidate.

Cindy hasn't had children and neither have I. We haven't because Vivian can't. I don't know why Cindy and Jack haven't.

"You want me to look around?" I ask.

She shakes her head and moves toward me until she's so close I can feel her warm breath on my face. "No."

"Then I better get going."

"You're not going anywhere," she says firmly, slipping her fingers into mine.

"I'm not?"

"No. Those guys in the van might come looking for me. We both know what they wanted." She shakes her head hard. "Oh, no, I wouldn't feel safe out here by myself tonight."

I hesitate. It looked to me like Cindy slid off the road because of the snow. I assumed it happened that way because the van was parked slightly behind the BMW, as if the men had pulled off when they saw what happened in front of them. If they'd run her off the road, the van should have been farther down the road than the car. Of course, they could have pulled back to make it look like she'd run off the road but they didn't seem that smart.

"You didn't want to press charges," I remind her. They still could have threatened her even if she did slide off the road. Which is what I figured happened. It's just that I've been trained to notice inconsistencies like that in people's stories and it makes me suspicious when I hear them say things that don't add up. "If you thought they might come after you, why didn't you want them locked up?"

"What could you have locked them up for?"

"I would have figured out something."

Cindy looks at me like she doesn't know what to say. I understand what she's going through. I've seen that same expression on women's faces before in Dakota County after their husbands have beaten them. It's a look that tells me they're caught in the middle. They want to do something but they don't want their husbands being even bigger bastards the next time because they had to spend the night on the cold cement floor of a jail cell. The middle is a bad place to be.

"Why didn't you want me to do that?" I press. "Why didn't you want me to lock them up?"

"I don't know."

I shake my head. "They aren't coming here, Cindy. I called Sheriff Wilson down in Hayward while I was following you here. He sent one of his deputies to the county line to see who they were and to make sure they didn't turn around. He'll find out who the driver was. Everything's taken care of. He and his crew won't bother you again."

"Thanks," she murmurs.

It's almost as if she's disappointed. "You'll be fine," I say confidently.

She squeezes my hand hard. "At least stay for dinner. I'll fix something good. It'll be fun."

Cindy doesn't know the first thing about cooking. What she means is that she'll take me to Duluth and *buy* me something good to eat. She's saying whatever she thinks will get me to stay because she has something important to tell me. I know her so well. "Why'd you come up here by yourself?"

"I needed to get away, I needed time to think." She bows her head. "It's just that . . . well, Jack's been . . . he's been, oh, God, I—"

The rest of her sentence is swallowed up by several sharp sobs. She thrusts her arms around my neck and squeezes hard. It feels good. The same way it did when she ran up to me out on 681.

"Please don't go," she begs. "Please don't."

"What's Jack been doing?" I demand. This could just be today's feature presentation, I remind myself. "What were you going to say?"

She takes a deep breath, pulls back a little, and gathers herself. "Jack's been hitting me."

"*What?*" She hikes her sweater up to her neck and I see that her left side is bruised. I grit my teeth as she lets the sweater fall back down. "Son of a bitch," I hiss. "How long's this been going on?"

"A while, but it's getting worse. And it's happening more often."

"Have you told your father?"

"I tried," she whispers, "but he didn't want to listen. He doesn't want anything to get in the way of Jack's future. I think he's looking forward to spending nights at the White House more than he is to having grandchildren."

I wouldn't believe her except I know that Cindy's father is one of the coldest men on earth. "You need to call the Minneapolis police. I still have friends on the force down there. I'll give you the name of one of the guys who I used to—"

"I can't call the police."

"Why not?"

"I just can't."

"Of course, you can. If you don't, I'll call them for you."

She shakes her head. "I told you. If I ever did anything that might put Jack's political future in jeopardy, I'd probably have a bigger problem than getting hit."

"What do you mean?" I ask suspiciously.

"Nothing."

"Cindy, I can't just sit here and let—"

"Kiss me, Paul." She rises up on her tiptoes and presses her lips to mine, then runs her long fingernails down the sides of my neck. "Please."

Her hand slides down my arm to my leg and I feel her fingertips moving across the top of my thigh and it all comes rushing back to me. But somehow I'm finally able to pry myself away. If I let her touch me like this for too long, there's no telling where it would end up.

She looks up at me like I'm crazy. "What's wrong with you?"

"Nothing."

"Then make love to me. We've got the place to ourselves. It's perfect."

"I can't."

"Why not?"

"I'm married. Jesus, come on, Cindy. Vivian's waiting for me."

"You hate Vivian," Cindy snaps. Suddenly she's cold and impersonal, focused on making her point. "Everyone does. She's a bitch and a little off." Cindy twirls her finger round and round by her right ear. "A *lot* off, actually."

"I don't hate her. Don't say that."

"Scrape her off," Cindy says callously.

Down deep Cindy has a lot of her father in her.

"She'll drag you down if you don't. Get rid of her, Paul. Seriously."

"Why?" I ask, spreading my arms wide. "So you can toy with me any time you want?" I point at her. "Why don't you get rid of Jack?"

"It's not the same," she says condescendingly.

Like her world is so much more important than mine. I'm the sheriff of an insignificant county at the northern edge of Wisconsin. She's a member of one of the richest and most powerful families in the Midwest. The situations are entirely different and I should understand that.

"Why did you come on to me like that?" I ask.

She gazes straight into my eyes. "Because I love you, because I've always loved you."

It's my turn to take her hand. "Then divorce Jack and marry me."

She jerks her hand from mine, like she's been hit by a violent shock. "My father would never approve of that."

I figured that was how she'd react. "Do you really care?" Which is exactly why I said what I said; I wanted to get her on the defensive. She would never seriously consider marrying me. We both know that. "How could you? He doesn't care about Jack beating you."

"Would you really get rid of Vivian?"

"Maybe." I'm playing the game because I want to see how far Cindy would go. Or how far she'd say she'd go.

"How?"

"I'd figure it out."

"You know she's not going to give you a divorce."

"Why do you say that?"

Cindy rolls her eyes. "She might be a nut job, but she isn't stupid. She knows she'll never catch anyone as good as you again."

I look down and kick at something on the rug. "Well, I—"

"How far would you go, Paul?"

"Huh?"

"How far would you go to get rid of her?"

My eyes move back to Cindy's. I see a strange gleam in them I've never seen before, and I can't believe she just asked me that question. I can't believe she'd even think it. Now I'm wishing I hadn't pushed. "Cindy, you can't be—"

"*See,*" she snaps. "You aren't serious."

"Hey, I can't just—"

"Enough!" She closes her eyes tightly for several moments, as if she's really considering everything. Finally she exhales heavily and leads me into the living room, to a big comfortable couch. The mansion's already warming up and it feels good. "Sit," she orders gently.

I do, like I'm that sixteen-year-old kid on the Boulder River all over again, instantly willing to do whatever she commands. She straddles me and gazes down at me seductively. It's going to take every ounce of willpower I have to resist her.

3

THERE'S NO REASON to sneak around when I come into the house, no reason to think I can avoid a confrontation. By the time I left the Prescott mansion there were *fourteen* unheard messages on my cell phone. Vivian's been watching from our bedroom window for two hours like a hawk, counting every set of headlights that passes from the south, and fuming when they don't turn into our driveway. So I act normal. I make a little more noise than usual to throw her off, to make her think I don't think it's a big deal that I'm late.

I pull my boots off on our back porch and kick them to a corner, then pad into the kitchen. Sure enough, she's standing in front of the stove, arms crossed over her chest, glaring at me with that look on her face. The one that means it's going to be a long night and the only way to avoid the fight is to leave. But this is my house, too.

Middle age is coming on fast, but Viv's still pretty. She has delicate facial features, a slim, pretty figure, and her body's stayed well toned into her thirties despite the fact that she never works out. Faint lines have come to the corners of her eyes and mouth and she's always been self-conscious about her lower teeth, which are a little crooked and slightly discolored after years of smoking. But, over-all, she's still very pretty. She's not on Cindy's level, but then most women aren't. And I honestly don't care, I really don't compare them. I'm still very attracted to Vivian. But, of course, she doesn't believe me.

I made the mistake of saying that to her one night a few years ago when we were arguing—that I didn't think she was as pretty as Cindy. It was a stupid and inconsiderate thing to say, but I was exhausted because my deputies and I had been up for three straight days looking for two kids who'd gotten lost in the woods while they were camping. After we finally found them I went home and Vivian started in on me before I could even take my jacket off. She didn't give me a kiss, she didn't congratulate me for finding the kids, she didn't even have a hot meal waiting for me. She just started right in on me, accusing me of being gone because I'd been with Cindy, which was ridiculous because Cindy was in Europe. So I said it even though I didn't really mean it. At least, I didn't mean that it mattered to me. But Vivian's never let me live it down. Every time we fight she makes it sound like I said it to her the week before, even though I've only ever said it once and that was a long time ago.

For several months she's been dyeing her brown hair midnight black, parting it in the middle of her head and letting it fall straight down both sides. It's kind of creepy, but I haven't asked her about it yet because I don't want to start anything. She's taken to wearing no make-up, too. A couple of weeks ago I suggested that she go to one of the nice places in Duluth and spend some money on herself. She took my suggestion to mean that I thought she was looking old and we didn't speak for two days. On top of that we haven't been intimate in two months and it's the longest we've ever gone without sex. I miss it, but I'm starting not to miss her.

"Where've you been?" she demands.

She loves candles and she's lighted lots of them here in the kitchen. This will be the battleground. I can tell they've been burning for a while because there's a buildup of melted wax on the plates she's set them on.

"We had a problem with some guys from Hayward."

"What kind of problem?"

She seems pretty composed, which isn't necessarily a good thing, because it's probably just the calm before the storm. "They were harassing some folks on 681 south of here," I explain, jerking my thumb over my shoulder. "A couple of people from one of the River Families who were heading to their estate. Sorry I was late," I mutter as I move to the refrigerator. "I'm starving. Is there anything to eat?"

"Which estate were the people going to?"

She's not going to let me off the hook that easily. "Why?"

"Which one was it?" she repeats, her irritation growing. "Which River Family?"

"Uh, the Campbells," I answer, reaching into the fridge for what's left of last night's lasagna. Vivian's a better cook than Cindy—everybody is—but the lasagna's still not great. The thing is I'm so hungry at this point I could eat anything. I wolfed down a Danish on my way into the precinct this morning, but that's all I've had today. "A couple of older women in the family were driving up together and these guys started following them as they were leaving Hayward," I explain, putting the plastic container down on the table. "They slid off the road a few miles south of here when it started snowing. I'm glad they called the precinct when they did. I got there just in time. After I ran the guys off, I followed the women back to the estate and helped them settle in. They were upset. You can understand that."

"What time did you get to the women?"

"Around four-fifteen."

"Then you followed them back to the Campbell estate. Is that what you're saying?"

Damn it. In my attempt to seem casual about everything I screwed up. "Yes," I respond quietly.

Vivian's expression sours. "That's ridiculous, Paul. Can't you come up with anything better than that?"

I've been spooning lasagna onto a paper plate so I can stick it in the microwave. I stop and stare at her, hand poised over the container. "What do you mean?" I ask, trying to sound innocent.

"You said the women ran off the road south of here, but the Campbell estate is north of us."

She caught my mistake right away. It was so basic, too. "So?"

"I was watching for your SUV." She nods toward our driveway. "I saw you go south around four-fifteen, but I never saw you go north. If you'd followed the women back to the Campbell estate, I would have seen you pass by. You're lying, Paul."

I exhale heavily. Why can't life ever be easy?

"Where were you?" she demands, heels clicking on the floor as she moves toward me with her arms still crossed tightly over her chest. "Don't lie this time."

I can't tell her the truth, not when she's in this state. That would be suicide. "It was police business." In fact, when it comes to Cindy, I can never tell Vivian anything.

She grabs her hair, shuts her eyes tightly, and shrieks at the top of her lungs. *"Damn it, tell me where you were!"* But she springs at me without waiting for my answer, nails clawing at my face.

I grab her wrists hard and force her back. I've had enough. There's only so much a man can take.

As she tumbles back against the refrigerator I think about how angry I was at Jack Harrison for beating Cindy. How all I wanted to do was kill him when I saw the bruises on Cindy's body. And here I am doing this.

Vivian steadies herself, then hunches down and forward like a cat getting ready to pounce. *"You bastard!"* she screams, leaping at me again. *"I hate you!"*

This time I reach out with my left hand and grab her slender neck before she can get to me. She flails violently, but it's no use. I'm much too strong for her—she's a foot shorter than me and more than a hundred pounds lighter. The soft flesh of her throat feels vulnerable and good and suddenly I understand how wild animals feel when they kill.

"Get off me, let me go!"

She kicks me in the shin with the sharp toe of her shoe and pain knifes through my leg. I remind myself that she's out of her mind with jealousy because somehow she's found out that Cindy's in town. That's the only explanation. Someone's told her. But my leg's killing me and I feel myself losing control. She tries kicking me again but I squeeze hard and her knees buckle.

"I hate you," she gasps, her fingers prying desperately at mine. "I hate you for lying to me. You're awful."

My right hand slips inside my jacket and I smoothly draw the pistol from its holster. I can't believe it but I force her down on her knees and press the end of the barrel to her forehead. She drops her hands to her sides submissively and lets out a pathetic moan as the gun touches her skin. I chambered the first round after I pulled the pistol from the glove compartment on 681, but I never removed the bullet. The gun's ready to fire and my finger's on the trigger.

4

Billy Brock is one of my deputies—and my best friend. His nickname is "Bear" because he reminds people of the black bears that roam the dense pine forests of Dakota County. I'm a big man but I look average-sized standing beside Billy. He's six feet seven inches tall and weighs 280 pounds. Probably even more than that lately, thanks to his steady diet of cheeseburgers and fries. His wife, Karen, left him a little less than two months ago, on Christmas Eve, after he'd passed out in his lumpy old easy chair watching some college bowl game. He's eaten almost every meal since Christmas at the Kro-Bar or the Saloon.

No one knows where Karen went. All she left was a note Bear woke up to around noon on Christmas Day. It was pinned to his old gray fleece and it said she couldn't take living with him anymore. It warned him not to come looking for her, that there'd be trouble if he did. Of course, she didn't say where she went in the note, so it would have been tough for him to find her even if he'd wanted to.

He hasn't mentioned Karen once since he came to our house on New Year's Day and he doesn't seem bothered by suddenly being alone. Of course, Bear doesn't share his feelings very often, even with me. Living with my father was a walk in the park compared to living with Bear's dad. Bear's dad beat him constantly, though he never bitched about it. But I saw the bruises in the locker room, everyone did. And they weren't from football, believe me. It left some deep scars inside him, though he'd never admit it.

Bear never works out, so he isn't cut like me, he doesn't have the six-pack abs I'm so proud of. In fact, he's developing a decent-sized gut. But he's still the strongest man I've ever known. I saw him pick up the front end of a car off a guy out on Route 7 last year just as I got to the accident scene. He did it by himself and the paramedics said the guy would have died if he hadn't. They were right behind me and they saw him do it, too.

No one in town believes my story about Bear lifting the car off the guy, but he doesn't seem to care. He hasn't tried to get the paramedics or the guy he saved to back up my story, so it's turned into one of those north-country legends. It just makes him happy that the guy sent him a Christmas card with a picture of all his grandchildren sitting around him on his sofa. He told me he looked at that card for a long time on Christmas Day after he found the "Dear Bear" note from Karen. He's never cared much about getting credit for things. He just wants to help whoever needs it.

Bear has dirty blond hair he wears long over his collar in the back, a curly, unkempt beard, a long, thin nose, and hazel eyes. He's a sloppy eater, so it seems like his uniform always has food stains on it even if he's just picked it up from the cleaners. He used to be a big hunter and fisherman, but a few years ago, instead of trekking into the woods to shoot a deer or snag a trout, he started watching football. Now he's a big fan of the University of Wisconsin and the Green Bay Packers. The morning after a Badger or Packer game you can tell if they won by his mood. Bear's a pretty simple man. Cheeseburgers, fries, vodka, and a Badger or a Packer game and he's pretty happy.

Bear and I were teammates on Wabash County High's football team because Dakota County's always been too small to have its own high school. So we had to ride the bus fifteen miles west toward Superior every morning. I was the tailback of the team and Bear was the fullback. He blocked for me, pulverizing linebackers into submission so I could gain all those yards, score all those touchdowns, and get all the glory, and we were state champs our senior year. In fact, the press in the area tabbed us one of the greatest Wisconsin high school football teams of the decade. I got a lot of ink, even more than the quarterback, but Bear's name hardly ever made it into the newspapers.

I wouldn't have gained half those yards or scored half those touchdowns with an average fullback blocking for me, but none of the reporters cared about Bear's blocking. I always asked them to give him some ink but they rarely did. Despite hardly ever getting his name in the papers, he never showed me any bitterness, never showed he was jealous of me or resented me in any way for my star status. He just gave me a bone-crushing hug the day I got a football scholarship to the University of Minnesota. Bear's always been the best friend a guy could have.

I pull to a stop at mile marker fifty-one on Route 7. There's a public picnic area here that marks the start of a narrow, winding trail that leads off into the woods toward Silver Wolf Rapids. Silver Wolf Rapids is a gorgeous stretch of white water on the Granite River, which is the next major river east of the Boulder. Silver Wolf lies at the end of a lonely, six-mile hike. During the winter hardly anyone goes back there. But this morning Mrs. Erickson picked up a report that there was suspicious activity in the area last night.

Bear pulls up alongside me in his Cherokee as I haul my ass out of mine. He uses the SUV I drove before I got my new one a few months ago. I told him he could keep the DAKOTA COUNTY SHERIFF letters on the sides if he wanted to, but he sanded them off. He said it wasn't right for him to keep them on there because he wasn't the sheriff and the other deputies might get mad. That's the kind of person Bear is. He doesn't put on airs for anyone, including himself.

"Morning, Professor," he calls as he climbs out of the truck and heads toward me.

"Morning."

He calls me Professor because I'm one of the few non–River Family people in Dakota County who went to college. I went but I didn't graduate. It was clear to me on the first day of practice my freshman year I'd never play much football for the University of Minnesota. There were too many players who were a lot more talented than me on the team. It hit me hard that our Wabash High football team was pretty good for our Single A League, but that we weren't one of the greatest teams of the decade. That the stories were just a bunch of hype designed to sell newspapers and generate ad revenue.

After two years at the university and the loss of my football scholarship, I dropped out and joined the Minneapolis City Police Force. My biggest disappointment in leaving school wasn't that I couldn't play football anymore. It was that I couldn't take the English classes I'd loaded my schedule with. I liked English. I liked reading the classics the most, then writing about them. Just like my father did. I still read a lot, especially when it snows. I like sitting in front of the fireplace in my big easy chair and losing myself inside another world. Even if Vivian's sitting on the couch a few feet over, it still seems like she's a thousand miles away.

Bear joined the Dakota County Police Force right after school and he's never had another job. Technically, he didn't graduate from Wabash High, but some people in town pulled some strings to make it look like he did so he could join the force. Officially, the Dakota County force requires all officers to have at least a high school diploma.

"How you doing?" Bear asks as he saunters up to me.

He's munching on a Milky Way Bar he probably grabbed on his

way out of the Kro-Bar from the rack beside the old NCR manual cash register. He was sitting there eating his cheeseburger and fries breakfast when I called to tell him to come out here. I wonder if he paid for the Milky Way. He's an honest guy but he's not above taking advantage of being a cop.

"I'm doing all right, Billy." I'm probably the only one in Bruner who doesn't call him Bear, and he appreciates that. He likes his nickname fine, but it's the fact that I call him something else that's important to him. "Were you by yourself when I called?"

"Nah, me and Davy was having breakfast together. He comes in while I was sitting there and sits right down next to me without even asking if he could. Kind of ticked me off."

Davy Johnson is another one of my deputies. He's a local boy who's only ever been out of Wisconsin to go to the Mall of America in the Twin Cities with his wife and three kids. Davy's thirty-two and he's locked into his life but he seems all right with that. "It's not me and Davy," I say loudly, "it's Davy and *I*." I don't know why but sometimes I correct Bear's grammar. I tell myself it's to help him improve, but I'm not sure he really wants to improve. Like Davy, he seems comfortable with who he is. "And it's *were* having breakfast, not *was*."

Bear stuffs the rest of the chocolate bar in his mouth and shakes his head as a couple of crumbs fall. "The Professor," he mumbles, chuckling. "So when you called, where was you at?"

"Don't end a sentence with a preposition, Billy." He butchered the conjugation of the verb again but I don't bother mentioning that.

He nods as he swallows what's left in his mouth. "Okay, where was you at, *asshole*?" He breaks into a wide grin, as if he'd been practicing this exchange all the way out here and it worked exactly as he'd hoped it would. Like the whole thing was a setup.

I grin back. I love the guy, I really do. He might as well be my brother. "I was leaving the house."

"Oh, yeah? How's Viv?"

Bear always asks about Vivian, and it's not as though he's just being polite. I think he actually likes her, and I think she likes him, too. He's the one local in all of Dakota County she seems to tolerate. It's this strange surface affection they have for each other. Maybe it goes deeper than the surface, I don't know, maybe I'm being naive. I shake that thought out of my head right away. Bear would never do that to me, he's too good a person. I would have said the same thing about Vivian until a few years ago, until we found out that she couldn't have children. Now I'm not sure. Not being able to have children seems to have driven a stake through the heart of our relationship.

"Well, you know," I hedge.

His ears perk up. "Trouble in paradise last night?"

He can tell by my tone there was. "Yeah, paradise."

"What about this morning? Was she still in her mood?"

"No, she was out of it. We had an okay conversation before I left."

I didn't have a conversation with Vivian before I left this morning. She took off from the house last night around eight and didn't come home. But it wasn't like she ran off right after I holstered the gun, then helped her to her feet as I apologized to her over and over. I told her I didn't know what had come over me, and I really didn't. I was just so mad. I literally had to peel Cindy off me out at the estate to get out of the mansion and get to my truck, but Vivian still assumed I was guilty of cheating as soon as I walked in the door to our house. So I paid the price even though I'm completely innocent, even though all I did was my job. I resisted the temptation of a beautiful woman who was telling me she'd give me anything I wanted and that there'd be no strings attached, but I was still crucified for it even though I didn't do it. I just wish I could find out who told Vivian that Cindy was in town.

After I finished apologizing, she heated up the lasagna in the microwave and fixed a nice side-salad to go along with it. I woke up from a nap in front of the television in the living room around eight and that's when I realized she was gone. I'm pretty sure she went to her cousin Heather's house, which is down in Gatlin. Gatlin's south and east of Bruner on Loon Lake. It's a tiny town of three hundred people about ten miles the other side of Hayward, set on the banks of the state's tenth-largest inland lake. Vivian's been spending the night down there a lot lately, at least two nights a week. Unfortunately, I can't be sure she went there. Heather and I got into it during Thanksgiving dinner a few years ago about something I can't even remember now and she hasn't spoken to me since. According to Vivian, Heather wouldn't take a call from me if her life depended on it. Neither would her husband, Marty. Marty and I always liked each other, but he can't go against his wife. He has to live in the same house with Heather, so that's just the way it is. I completely understand.

"Viv must be pissed off that Cindy's in town without smiling Jack Harrison," Bear says. "Which leaves her all alone out there at the Prescott estate waiting for you."

I'm searching the sky as Bear makes his crack. It's dark gray. The weather people aren't calling for snow—they're predicting a clear day—but it sure looks like we're going to get some powder. Smells like it, too. You know, that pleasant, faint scent of smoke. My eyes flicker to Bear's. "How would Vivian know Cindy was in town without Jack?" Bear knows Cindy's in town because it was his turn to make rounds at the estates last night. I called him while I was following her home yesterday to tell him she was at the estate so he wouldn't be surprised to see the place lighted up.

Bear shrugs. "She's got ESP. We both know that."

A big truck roars past, heading for the lumber mill with a cargo of logs, and I watch it until it disappears around the bend. Maybe it isn't ESP at all. Maybe I should just be more concerned with Vivian and Bear's relationship than I am. "Uh huh." I nod toward the trail-head. "Come on, let's go." I take one more sip of the coffee I picked up at Ike and Sara's, then toss the Styrofoam cup in a trash can as we pass a snow-covered picnic table.

As we reach the trailhead, Bear points at all the footprints in the snow. "Jesus, it looks like somebody had a convention out here last night. I was up here last week and there was only one set of snow-shoe tracks heading in. Think it's the cult?"

For the last few months there's been a rumor going around that we have a cult of devil worshipers in Dakota County, but there's never been any proof of it. Not that I've seen anyway. "There's no cult." It's the first time I've heard Bear mention anything about it and I don't like it. I make a mental note to say something at our Monday afternoon meeting—if the storm doesn't cancel the meeting—so all of my deputies are clear about where I am on the matter. So they're clear on the force's official position on the matter. "Understand?"

"Well, old Mel Hopkins had a goat stolen last week," Bear vol-unteers as we move along the trail and the pine forest closes in around us.

It gets quiet in here very fast. The trees seems to absorb all sounds. "So what?"

"He thinks the cult took it because they wanted to sacrifice it."

Mel Hopkins is the only person in Dakota County other than me who has a home on the east side of 681. It's a fifty-acre farm with a picturesque red barn, a corn crib, and a few big fields cleared out of the woods. He mostly manages dairy cattle but he has a few other kinds of animals hanging around the barnyard, too. Like most farm-ers do. Mel's place is south of mine, a little farther down the road from where Cindy had her run-in with those guys from Hayward.

"Christ," I mutter.

"What's wrong, Professor?"

"I don't want people getting all hyped up about some cult when there's nothing to get hyped up about. Everybody's been cooped up inside all winter and they're itching for something juicy to sink their teeth into. Damn it, they'll be sleeping with their shotguns if they think people are stealing livestock. They'll shoot at anything that moves at this point." I glance back at Bear. "You know how people get in February. We don't need that, Billy."

Bear nods. "Yeah, I hear you. Cabin fever usually does set in about now. Any other county sheriffs heard about a cult up here?"

I haven't asked around and I'm embarrassed that I left that stone unturned. "Call around when you get back to the precinct, will you?"

"Sure."

I stop short. We've gone less than a quarter of a mile into the forest and the footprints are breaking away from the path and leading off into a dense pocket of trees. I point in the direction they're headed. "This way."

A hundred feet off the path three deer burst out from behind some thick brush, surprising both of us. We stumble backward and grin nervously at each other as they bound away with their white tails pointed at the sky, embarrassed at how startled we were. It's eerie back here, eerie enough to put two experienced police officers on edge. I'm glad I've got my gun. Bear is, too. I can tell.

The footprints end at what's left of a bonfire that's encircled by large stones. The circle is ten feet in diameter, but the snow is melted for another twenty feet outside the stones and the branches above the area are seared black. I move inside the stones, squat down, and poke around with a stick. I hit something hard right away and scrape at the ashes until it emerges. I reach down, slip my finger through one of the holes, and pull it up. It's a skull. There's still charred flesh and hair on it.

"That's Mel Hopkins's goat," Bear says quietly.

I hate to admit it but he's probably right. A goat skull is pretty easy to identify by the horns and this sure looks like one. Then I spot something else and drop the skull. I brush away the ashes from the object and a chill runs up my spine. It's a steak knife, one I think I recognize.

My cell phone rings as I'm staring at the blade. I pull out the phone and check the number. It's Cindy.

5

I CAN'T BELIEVE I'm barreling south down 681 to help Cindy again, but she swore it was an emergency—again. This time it's a burst pipe on the second floor of the mansion and she doesn't know how to turn off the torrent or who else to call. She was frantic because she said there was water going everywhere.

Fortunately, Vivian was supposed to be at work at the Bruner Washette by nine o'clock this morning. It's after ten now so she shouldn't see me flash by the house this time. If she does, last night will seem like a lovefest when I get home this evening.

As I turned left at the lone stoplight in town a few minutes ago, I peered down the block at the spots in front of the washette where Vivian usually parks. I didn't see her rusty old Toyota sitting there, but that's not the end of the story. Sometimes she parks in the back, because the owner, Charlie Wagner, is hung over and feeling mean and makes her park back there because he says he wants his customers to be able to use the spots on the street right in front of the washette—even though those spots are rarely all taken. Vivian doesn't like parking behind the store, because it's dark and lonely back there when she leaves in the winter and it scares her, but sometimes she doesn't have a choice. Cabin fever gets to everyone around here long about this time of the winter. Charlie's no exception.

I tried calling Heather's house last night to see if Vivian was around, because I thought there was a chance Marty might pick up and I could reason with him, but I got no answer. Heather and Marty don't make much money but apparently it's enough to have Caller ID. I didn't bother trying Vivian's cell phone. I knew she wouldn't answer.

Once I'm past Mickey's campground, I jam the accelerator to the floor and quickly hit seventy. Just as the forecasters predicted, it's turning into one of the few crystal-clear days we'll have up here all winter and I'm forced to squint. I'm driving directly into the sun's blazing rays, directly into the southern fire. I'm donning my sunglasses when I spot a vehicle ahead of me through the glare. It's a van, a blue van, and it looks familiar.

I catch up to it quickly and check the license tag. It's the same one as yesterday, hanging by red and green electrical wires from the back bumper. This is the van that was following Cindy. Broken pipe at the Prescott mansion or not, I'm pulling the guy over. Sheriff Wilson told him to stay out of Dakota County and he meant it. I flip on the cherries and the van veers off onto the snowy shoulder immediately.

My pistol's already in my shoulder holster so I don't have to pull it out of the glove compartment. I chamber the first round after I hop out of the Cherokee—that scraping sound is always comforting—then I move cautiously toward the driver's side door. It's the same guy as yesterday, sitting calmly behind the wheel. He's smiling serenely at me from beneath the brim of a filthy green John Deere cap with his thin lips and his buck teeth. His long stringy hair falls to the shoulders of his White Snake jean jacket.

"Good morning, officer."

"What are you doing up here again?" I don't bother asking for his license; I already know his name. It's Caleb Jenkins. Sheriff Wilson from down in Hayward told me that yesterday. "You're supposed to stay out of Dakota County from now on."

"I had business in Duluth. I didn't actually stop in your county. Not until now, anyway," he adds. "And you made me stop."

I check my watch. "You've already been to Duluth this morning?" I glance past him into the van. It doesn't look like anyone's back there.

"Yup."

"It's only ten-fifteen, Mr. Jenkins."

He does a double-take when he hears his name, but he doesn't say anything. "Well, I'm an early riser."

"What were you doing in Duluth?"

The guy rolls his eyes. "Look, I'm an electrician, been one for a long time. I had a job up there." He motions behind him. "I got my stuff in the back. Check it out if you want."

"I'll check out whatever I want to, Mr. Jenkins. You can be sure of that. How long have you had this van?"

He looks at me like I'm nuts. "A few years, but it's older than that. I bought it used. What the hell's that got to do with anything?"

"Careful how you talk to me, son."

"Yeah, yeah."

"When did you buy this thing?"

"Last fall. Why?"

"I never saw it before yesterday." Cops in small towns are trained to notice things like who drives what. Even people who live in other counties close by. "I'd remember if I did."

"I don't get many jobs in Duluth, Sheriff. Most of my work is in Hayward or south. And when I do get work in Duluth, I usually take I-35 up there. I cut across Route 91 to get to it."

Interstate 35 heads north from Minneapolis to Duluth and goes all the way south to Texas. Route 91 goes west out of Hayward and intersects I-35 about twenty miles from town. "Why didn't you take it today?"

"There was a big accident on it between the 91 interchange and Duluth. The traffic people on the radio said to avoid it at all costs."

I'll check that out in a minute, on my way to Cindy's. "From now on take the interstate to Duluth all the time. Even if it's closed," I say with a wry smile. "Got it?"

He hesitates. "Yeah, I got it."

"Good, now get out of here." I wave him on and he wastes no time moving out. Ninety seconds later I roar past him as I continue to the Prescott estate. A quick check with Mrs. Erickson confirms the pileup on I-35. It was massive, caused by a sheet of black ice that formed out of nowhere. The state boys are only now getting traffic back to normal.

As I speed past my house I don't see Vivian's car beneath the big pine tree where she usually parks it, which is a relief. I don't get an immediate call on my cell phone, either, which is another good sign.

When I pull up to the Prescott mansion ten minutes later, I notice a second set of tire tracks in the circle in front of the front door. Another one in addition to the half-covered set I made yesterday. They're the tracks Bear made on his rounds last night. They must be.

I hesitate a moment inside the truck and stare out the windshield at the crystal-clear morning, awestruck by the view. I've come only a quarter of the way around the circle in front of the mansion, so I'm facing west toward Superior and Duluth as I sit here in front of the main entrance. The mansion is built atop a ridge, and from up here I get a real appreciation for the north-country's beauty and for how isolated Dakota County is. The sea of pine trees seems to stretch on forever below me like an unbroken carpet. Though I've never actually checked records, I've heard that Cindy's father is one of the largest owners of the vast tract of forest I'm gazing out over. I've heard that at the bottom of the ridge his land spreads north and south for miles behind all of the other River Family estates.

I hop out and move to the big front door, which is ajar. I slip into the foyer, straining to hear the sound of rushing water. Even in a place this big I ought to be able to tell quickly where the emergency is if the flood's as bad as Cindy claimed. But I don't hear anything, it's like a tomb in here.

"Cindy!"

I move into the kitchen and smell coffee, then spot a half-eaten croissant on the island counter. Past the island one of the drawers beside the dishwasher hangs open. Silverware is scattered all over the tile floor and there are a couple of broken dishes in amongst the knives, spoons, and forks. I back off a few steps, then whip around and go for my gun when I think I hear something behind me. But it's nothing, just my imagination.

Then I hear something upstairs, someone moaning, and I race up the left side of the dual main staircase. This time it's not my imagination.

I hear the moan again when I reach the second floor. It's loud this time, coming from a room down the long corridor. I tear down the hallway and stop just outside one of the rooms when I hear the sound again. My gun is pinned against my heaving chest with its barrel pointed toward the ceiling. The door's cracked, like the front door was, and I hesitate a moment, then burst inside.

Almost instantly the door slams shut behind me. I swing my gun at the figure standing there and nearly fire. But at the last moment I manage to slip my finger from the trigger and pull the gun up in front of my face.

It's Cindy, I realize, and I let the gun fall to my side. She's wearing nothing but a tiny black teddy and baby-doll heels. My God, I could have killed her. I think about how the bullet would have ripped through her chest; how she would have fallen; how her final

few gasps would have haunted me forever; how her blood would
have been on my hands.

I'm a wreck but she's not fazed at all by her near-death experience. She moves to where I'm standing, slips her hands around my
neck, and kisses my cheek. "I'm not going to be denied this time,
Sheriff Summers," she whispers seductively.

As she presses her body to mine I inhale that perfume she always wears. God, I love it. I was able to resist her yesterday when
she tried to seduce me on the couch, but this time it will be infinitely
more challenging to keep her at bay. My senses are aroused, my
adrenaline's pumping, and I'm oh so vulnerable. She's so damn good
at getting her way and she's relentless about it. She'll do whatever it
takes. That's one of her gifts, one of her special qualities. Besides, resisting Cindy yesterday afternoon didn't do me any good last night.
Vivian's sure Cindy and I had sex and nothing in the world's going
to convince her otherwise.

"Take me, Paul. Please."

The snow is six inches deep in the hedge maze, so it's slow going.
The good thing is I'll be able to find my way back out this time if she
deserts me. I'll just follow our tracks.

"You hated me for what I did to you in here that summer, didn't
you?" Cindy asks.

It's as if she can read my mind. "No." Usually it's Vivian who can
do that.

"Yes, you did. I could see it all over your face when I was snapping those stupid pictures. It was an awful thing to do but you never
said a word. You were so good about it, such a good sport."

Being a good sport had nothing to do with it, and I suppose
down deep she knows that, but she's being polite. "I guess," I mumble, glancing over at her. She looks incredible, like a movie star. She's

wearing a sexy pair of sunglasses, cowgirl boots, a pair of designer jeans, and a knee-length white coat with fur around the neck that fits her body like a glove.

"God, if I'd been you I would have strangled me, but then you're always in control. I don't know how you do it."

She might not have said that if she'd seen what I did to Vivian last night.

We reach the center of the maze. It didn't seem to take as long to get here as I remember. "It's nice in here."

She giggles. "Especially when you know you aren't going to get ditched."

I laugh. It feels so right with her, it always does. I make the mistake of checking my watch. It's getting late and Bear will be wondering. Worse, so will Mrs. Erickson. "I've gotta go." I wish like hell I didn't, but it would be stupid to stay any longer.

"No you don't."

"Yeah, I really do."

"I understand . . . I guess." She slips her arm in mine as we start to retrace our steps, toes in heels. "I'll be here all weekend, so come over whenever you want. You don't even have to call." She gets a faraway look in her eyes as we trudge through the snow. "Remember when I drove over to Madison to watch you play in the state championship game?"

Remember? Christ, I'll never forget it, not to my dying day. Not if I live to be a hundred and I've forgotten everything else that ever happened to me in my life. I couldn't concentrate for the first few minutes of the game. I kept looking up in the stands at her—and all the boys who were sitting around her trying to get her attention. I only gained fifteen yards in the first quarter and I fumbled twice. Finally Bear grabbed my face mask in the huddle, shook it violently, and yelled bloody murder at me in front of the whole team.

I gained over two hundred yards and scored four touchdowns after that. I was the star of the game, and it felt like we'd won the

Super Bowl. It's the only time Bear ever yelled at me, but I was glad he did, because I deserved it. As time ran out I hugged him harder than I've ever hugged anyone in my life and shouted thanks at him over and over for getting me focused. If he hadn't yelled at me, I never would have gotten my head in the game and we probably would have lost. And I wouldn't have gotten to experience an emotional high most people never do.

"You were incredible, Paul. The guys all around me in the stands were shouting your name."

Cindy went with me to the party the parents threw for us in the ballroom of the Drake Hotel in Madison after the game, and it was the best night of my life. I was the man of the hour, the one everyone in the crowd wanted to talk to, the one everyone wanted to touch on the arm just so they could say they had the next day. And I had this gorgeous girl draped all over me like I was some kind of rock star. Somehow she got away without her father knowing. I don't know how she did it and I never asked.

Bear got me a room upstairs so Cindy and I could be alone at the end of the night. He had a friend who was a bellman and we didn't even have to pay for the room. It was our first time and just the thought of it still sends shivers up my spine. Like I said, Bear's the best friend a guy could have.

Reality set in the next morning. Cindy went back to her world and I went back to mine. But at least I had that night, that one night. Most people don't, but I wish they could. Even though it's brutal when you realize how fleeting fame is, it's still awesome while you're in the middle of it.

"How's your house?" she asks.

She asks innocently enough, but it's hardly an innocent question. When I moved back to Bruner a few years ago, I didn't have a lot of money in the bank, nowhere near enough for the down payment on my house. So Cindy loaned it to me. She brought me forty thousand dollars in cash in a suitcase one day, and I drove all the way to Superior with it to open a new account at a new bank because I didn't want anyone in town knowing I'd deposited that kind of cash in the local branch of the bank in town. When I walked out of that bank in Superior, I went and had a beer at the closest bar I could find, because I was still shaking at having all that money on me. And because I felt like the guy who helped me open the new account was looking at me suspiciously the whole time.

Every year I mean to take that autumn bonus I get and repay her at least a little bit, but it seems like there's always something else I have to use it for. She never asks me for it, she just asks how the house is. It's her way of reminding me what she did and it's much more effective than actually asking for money back that she doesn't need. I think she had an ulterior motive for lending me the money; I think she likes my being close to the estate. But, any way you look at it, what she did was incredibly kind. And all she's ever asked for in return is my friendship.

"It's great, thanks. Look, Cindy, I'm really going to try to get you some money this—"

"It's okay, Paul, don't worry about it. I just wanted to make sure everything was all right."

"Okay."

Cindy and I are silent for a while as we continue to walk through the maze.

Finally she takes a deep breath. "My father's stealing money from Prescott Trading," she says, "from the family company."

My head snaps to the left. *"What?"* Maybe she needs the money back after all.

"Yeah. I can't believe it."

I knew it. I knew her coming up here wasn't just about Jack beating her or trying to get me into bed. I've always been her sounding board, I've always been the one she's confided in. I probably know more about the Prescott family than any outsider, probably more than most insiders. Which is because she knows I'll never tell anyone, she knows I'm that naturally and completely discreet. Maybe that's *my* most outstanding quality.

"How can he be stealing from himself?" I don't understand much about high finance, which has never been a problem for me, since I don't have much money. My thoughts flash back to that view from the driveway of all that land he owns here in Dakota County behind all the other estates. And though I'm no cash flow wiz, I can't help but wonder how in the world he could have money problems. "Doesn't he own the company?"

"Yes, but remember, he has three sisters. They each own 25 percent of the company, too."

"So what's going on?"

"He's taking money out of the company and putting it in his own account without telling them," Cindy explains, "without giving them their share of the distributions. He's telling them he's reinvesting the money the company's making into other things, but Prescott Trading isn't making money, it's *losing* money. I overheard him and Jack talking about how the company might not make it, how it might go under."

"Don't his sisters look at the books or have people who do that for them?"

"I think so, but Daddy's too smart. They'd never figure out what's going on."

"How did you figure it out? Why are you so smart?" She gives me a raised eyebrow, like she doesn't appreciate the remark, but she doesn't say anything.

"I stopped by to see Mom at the compound in Minneapolis a couple of weeks ago, and she asked me to look for something in Daddy's study. While I was in there I heard him coming and I didn't want him to think I was snooping so I hid in this little anteroom off to the side. Like I said, I heard him talking to Jack on the phone about it. When he left, I found some papers on his desk. It's terrible."

"So Jack's involved, too?"

She looks over at me. "Huh?"

"Well, Jack must know what your father's doing. He must know about the money being stolen. You said you heard them talking about it on the phone."

She hesitates. "Yeah, I guess he does."

"Jesus."

"I mean, I thought it was him that Daddy was talking to, but maybe it wasn't."

It seems like she's backpedaling, like she forgot that by telling me all of what she just told me that she was implicating Jack in the fraud, too. She's so damn concerned about ruining her husband's political career, and I don't think it's because she's worried about being First Lady. I think it has more to do with staying alive. "But you said—"

Cindy sobs out of nowhere. "I hate Daddy." It's a showstopper sob you'd swear was absolutely sincere, which it could be. It's just that I've known her long enough to know that I have to question it. "And he hates me."

I stop and pull her close. "Your father doesn't hate you." The tears are really flowing now.

"Yes, he does."

"And you don't hate him."

She sniffles into my jacket. "You're right, I don't," she admits softly. "Even with all the things he's done to me."

I hold her for a few minutes, until she stops crying. Then, reluctantly, I pull her gently ahead. There's so much I want to say but we're almost out of the hedges and I'm late. Then, from nowhere, I find the courage. "Could you be with me, Cindy?"

She smiles sweetly as we emerge from the maze. "You know I think about that all the—Oh, God."

I follow her gaze. A black Porsche is motoring carefully up the driveway, staying in the tracks Bear and I made. It's Jack Harrison. I'd recognize his car anywhere.

Cindy breaks away and starts trotting toward the mansion as Jack pulls the Porsche to a stop behind my Cherokee. She's to him right away and she slips her arms around his neck the same way she slipped them around my neck in the guest room a while ago. It makes me want to kill him. It doesn't make me feel great about her, either, but I figure she's just doing it so he won't get angry and beat her later.

"Hello, Jack," I say politely when I reach them.

He looks over at me with a curious expression. "I'm sorry," he says with his killer smile, "do I know you?"

We've met several times so this not-knowing-me thing is total crap. And I know Cindy's told him all about me, if only to make him jealous when he gets back from one of his trips to Europe, during which she's convinced he's been cheating on her. She's told me all about that, too. "I'm Sheriff—"

"Come on, Jack," Cindy interrupts, stepping back from their embrace. "Don't be rude."

"Oh, right, right," he says, like he finally remembers me but wishes he hadn't. "You're Summers, Sheriff Summers. But I can't remember your first name."

"Paul." I hate the guy, his half-million-dollar Porsche, his dashing good looks, and his path to the Oval Office.

"Okay, Paul. Well, what are you doing here?"

"I thought there was a problem with the plumbing," Cindy answers for me, "so I called him."

Jack smiles slyly, like he's enjoying this psychological cat-and-mouse. "So you called the *sheriff*? I would think you'd call a—"

"You know Paul's always helped us with things like that. His whole department's always been helpful to us that way."

Jack gestures toward the maze. "Why would he take care of a plumbing problem out there?"

"We were just catching up," she says guiltily. "We haven't seen each other in so long. I was telling him how you're going to be running for that Senate seat next year."

Jack swells up like a peacock on the prowl.

Cindy's so good.

He glances at me with a superior expression. "Yes, I am."

She looks up at him. Jack's a couple of inches taller than her but several inches shorter than me. "Why didn't you call?" she asks. "Why didn't you tell me you were coming?"

"I wanted to surprise you." He smiles at me. "I thought it might be . . . well, fun."

"Are you still going to Europe tomorrow morning?"

"Yes."

There's an uncomfortable silence.

"Well," I finally say, "I better get going."

"Oh, too bad," Jack says. "Well, ciao."

"Yeah, ciao."

He chuckles. "If we have any more plumbing problems, we'll be sure to call."

"Yeah, okay." I'd love to have five minutes alone with him in a place where money has nothing to do with anything and I wouldn't be hauled off to jail after the outcome. "Bye, Cindy," I mutter as I pass her.

I'm seething as I steer the Cherokee down the hill, over the river, and out the long Prescott driveway toward 681. Jack Harrison was having too much fun back there at my blue-collar expense.

My cell phone rings. It's Cindy.

"What?"

"Sorry about that," she whispers. "I had no idea he was coming. I don't think he's even staying the night. He's got a 9:00 A.M. flight to

London tomorrow. He won't want to drive four hours to the airport in the morning. He'd have to get up at three o'clock and he hates doing that."

"Why do you make him think you love him?" I demand.

"What do you mean?"

"Why do you hug him like that?"

"I have to, he's suspicious of me. He might think something's up if I don't. And I don't want to get beaten," she says, her voice turning indignant.

As if I'm the bad person for not understanding. "Leave him, Cindy." My head's spinning. I can't believe I'm saying this, but our walk intoxicated me. It made me realize how wonderful it would be with her. Somehow I managed to resist Cindy's attempt to seduce me again, but now I'm regretting being such a good husband again. "Tell him right now." There's ten seconds of dead air. "I'll turn around and come back," I offer. "I'll protect you." More silence. "Cindy?"

"I can't, Paul," she finally answers. "I just can't. You and I both know that." She pauses for a few seconds. "Maybe you shouldn't come over here anymore this weekend. Okay? Now good-bye."

6

I'M IN THE living room reading *Moby-Dick* and Vivian's in the kitchen washing dishes. In the "miracles never cease" category, she's being nice, incredibly nice. Which is truly amazing after what happened last night, coupled with the fact that Cindy's in town.

It turns out Vivian did go to Heather's place down in Gatlin last night, then got up this morning and drove straight from there to work at the washette. At least, that's the story I'm getting. I told her when I got home that she should have called to say she was all right, because I was worried about her. She hugged me tightly and almost cried. I felt bad. It's been a long time since I've said that to her and everyone needs to hear it once in a while, even Vivian. Then I told her I loved her and that I was sorry, too—which made her cry harder.

She spent an hour fixing what turned out to be a pretty decent meatloaf along with mashed potatoes and creamed spinach—which are my two favorite sides. During dinner she sat close to me and asked me about my day, something she hardly ever does.

"Here, honey," she says, breezing into the living room. "I got these for you, too."

She puts a plate down in my lap and on it are two chocolate-covered doughnuts, which are my favorite dessert in the world. She runs her fingers through my hair as I take the first delicious bite, and her touch feels good. She leans down and kisses me, then turns to go.

I catch her hand and pull her back. "Hey, what's gotten into you?"

She smiles and puts a hand to her chest. "Why what do you mean, Sheriff Summers?"

God, if she were just like this all the time. "You're being so . . . so nice tonight."

"Why shouldn't I be nice? I live in a nice house with a nice man who takes very nice care of me."

Guilt surges through me and I take a deep breath. "I really am sorry about last night, Viv. That was so awful. I don't know why I—"

"Shhh." She puts her fingers to my lips. "Let's not talk about it."

I caress her hand for a moment. "Where were you today?" I shouldn't ask this right now, but I can't help it. That's just how I am. I'm always trying to fit the pieces together even when I shouldn't.

"What do you mean?"

"Well, when I got home you weren't here. In fact, you didn't get home until after seven-thirty." It's almost ten o'clock now. We didn't finish dinner until nine-thirty. "The washette closes at four on Fridays in the winter, right?"

"Yeah," she says hesitantly.

It's not like she's got a lot of places to go in Bruner other than the washette. She's certainly not going to the Kro-Bar or the Bruner Saloon for a beer by herself. Maybe she was picking up what she needed for dinner and maybe she had to go all the way over to Superior to get it. Ike runs out of things a lot at his store. "Well?"

"I was just, I was just, um . . ." Her voice trails off when the phone rings.

I don't want to answer, but I have to, because that's part of the covenant that comes along with being the county sheriff. Picking up a phone even when you don't want to. "Hello," I say curtly.

"Sheriff! Sheriff, it's me Davy! Oh, God, oh, God, you gotta get out here right away."

It's my deputy Davy Johnson and he sounds like he's having a complete breakdown. "What's the matter?" I snap, sitting straight up in my chair. "What's wrong?"

"Get out here, Sheriff. Get out here *fast!*"

"Where?"

"The Prescott estate. *Hurry!*"

I don't tell Vivian where I'm going. I just grab my coat and gun and race for the door. The drive to the Prescott estate seems to go on forever but it actually takes less than ten minutes.

When I get there I skid to a stop in front of the main entrance, behind Davy's squad car. I jump out and take two quick steps for the door, then come to a sudden, slippery stop. In the Cherokee headlights I spot a strange-looking pair of footsteps leading toward the entrance. They start right about where I jumped out, now that I look back. They weren't here this afternoon, I'm sure of it. They aren't Davy's, either, because I can see exactly where he got out of his car up ahead. And in the light coming from the mansion's entrance and my headlights I can see where his footprints and this strange pair collide on the way to the door. They're strange because they're deep, wide, don't seem to have defined toes or heels, and in some places they don't even look like footprints—just deep depressions in the snow. It's as though two or three people, maybe more, walked carefully in the same spots. It's as if they were trying to disguise their numbers.

Davy's on his hands and knees in the foyer, waves of sickness overtaking him as I rush through the main door. He manages to gesture toward the living room, then another tremor shakes his stomach. I sprint past him, then freeze when I see Cindy. She's on her back, naked, eyes wide open. Her arms and legs are spread wide, her hands and feet are nailed to the floor, her throat is slashed from ear to ear, and blood is pooled around her beautiful, terrified face. There's a ring of extinguished candles encircling her body and what looks like a crude pentagram carved into her forehead. I sink to my knees and bring my hands to my mouth. As I do, I notice a crumpled piece of paper on the floor under a chair near her body, at the edge of the blood pool.

I crawl to the paper, pick it up and slowly unfold it. It's a dry-cleaning ticket from the Bruner Washette.

7

I CALLED THE state's crime scene investigation team in Superior as soon as I could think straight, as soon as I could calm my trembling fingers enough to accurately push the buttons on my cell phone, as soon as I could turn my back on the grizzly scene on the living room floor: Cindy's body splayed out before me crucifixion-style on the floor, outstretched hands and feet nailed to the stained hardwood slats, a pentagram carved into her forehead.

They came roaring up to the house a few minutes before midnight and even they were shocked at what they saw. I could tell by their expressions. I could tell by the way they didn't look straight at her body at first but glanced at it sidelong while they put on their latex gloves and blue paper masks. That told me volumes because they see a lot.

I called Bear right after I called the CSI guys. He rolled out of bed immediately and came straight to the mansion. I told him he didn't have to but he did. I'd like to think it was mainly to give me support, not only with the investigation but emotionally as well. He knows more about Cindy and me than anyone. Of course, he also came because he wants to be in the middle of things. He wants to be able to say he was at the crime scene so he has more credibility with the locals when he doles out the details he'll undoubtedly dole out—even though he shouldn't.

Cindy's murder is by far the biggest thing that's ever happened in Dakota County, and Bear spreads rumors almost as indiscriminately as Mrs. Erickson does. In subtler ways, of course, but he does. And, like I said, this is Bruner's case of the century. We've had murders here before—three in the last fifteen years—but they've always involved locals killing locals. This one involves a River Family. People will be dying to get any detail about what happened, especially because it's February and they're thirsting for anything that will distract them from their cabin fever.

The coroner took Cindy's body away at ten o'clock this morning. I left the estate shortly after that but the crime scene people are still out there. They're still scouring the mansion and the grounds for clues. I had to get to the precinct, so I left Bear in charge. He hung around for another hour, then he had one of the other deputies come out and take over for him. It isn't official, but Bear's the number-two guy on the force and the other deputies don't seem to have a problem with that. At least, none of them have ever said anything to me about it.

I stopped by the house on my way into town to shower and change, and Vivian couldn't have been nicer or more helpful. She had a crisply pressed uniform laid out for me on the bed when I came out of the shower and a thermos of fresh coffee waiting for me downstairs on the kitchen table. She never once asked what had happened and I didn't say. But she knew, I could tell.

"So what are you doing, Paul?" Lewis Prescott asks in a low monotone. "I want a full rundown."

Cindy's father sits in front of my office desk at the precinct. He's a thin, wiry man of average height. Sixty-three years old with straight white hair, he's got perfectly trimmed salt-and-pepper eyebrows, piercing blue eyes, and a patrician nose that's spiderwebbed with tiny blue veins after years of drinking scotch. He's dressed in sharp, preppy clothes, and there's a dark plaid scarf draped around his neck with a Brooks Brothers tag staring me in the face.

Prescott took a helicopter up here from Minneapolis after I called him to break the news about Cindy at around nine-thirty this morning, a half hour before they took her body away. The chopper landed in a vacant lot up the street, much to the fascination of a crowd of locals. Prescott's eyes are red-rimmed and he seems devastated. Maybe he's not as cold a man as I thought he was, but you never know. It could all be an act.

"We're doing everything we can," I answer. Prescott and I are alone in my office. "The crime scene people are still out at the estate. You can't go out there until they're done." I take a deep breath. It's past one in the afternoon and I've been awake for more than thirty hours. "They're good people," I continue. "They'll find anything the killer—" I interrupt myself because "killer" sounds so awful. "Anything that's there to be found," I finish. Why do I have compassion for this man? He's never had any for me. "Have you spoken to Jack?"

Prescott shakes his head. "He left for London early this morning on business. As you know, he came up here yesterday, then drove back to the Twin Cities in the afternoon so he could catch his flight. I haven't been able to reach him yet, but I'm sure he'll take the first plane back when I do." Prescott's voice had been soft and subdued since he sat down in the chair on the other side of my desk, but now it grows stronger.

There's something more Prescott wants to say, something important. It's obvious by the way he's fidgeting.

He checks his watch. "He should be back in Minneapolis by tomorrow at some point."

That wasn't it. That was just filler. He's still fidgeting.

He glances at my closed office door, then at me. "Paul, is there anything you want to tell me while we're alone?"

I'm taking a sip of Vivian's coffee. Most of the time I throw it away the few days a month she makes it for me, because it's basically undrinkable. I take it with me in the truck to make her feel good, but most mornings I end up pouring it in the office sink because it's so bad. This morning it's okay, though. I'm on my second cup.

I look up over the Styrofoam through the steam. "What do you mean?"

"You know what I mean."

I put the cup down. "No, I don't," I say firmly.

Prescott grinds his teeth, like he didn't think it was going to be this hard to get me to say what he wants me to say. Like he doesn't have this problem with his multitude of subordinates at the trading company and he's irritated that I'm not as tuned in to him as they are. "You were at the estate yesterday. You were the last person to see Cindy alive."

"Her killer was the last person to see her alive."

"You know what I mean, Paul. You were at the estate yesterday afternoon."

I stare into Prescott's eyes, fighting the urge to look away. "I was there yesterday morning. She called me and begged me to go out there," I continue. "When she called me I was with Billy Brock. He's one of my—"

"I know who that moron is, for Christ—"

"I was out east on Route 7," I interrupt right back. "We were in the middle of a routine traffic stop." I don't want to tell him about the bonfire, the burned goat skull, or the knife. He'll find out about the pentagram carved into Cindy's forehead soon enough, but I don't want him jumping to conclusions about a cult when the investigation's only a few hours old. "I went to the mansion because she asked me to go there, because she told me there was a broken pipe."

"A broken pipe," Prescott echoes under his breath, spitting the words out like they're last week's sour milk. "I spoke to Jack yesterday afternoon and he told me that you and Cindy were going at it outside the mansion when he got there. He said she was crying, that she was very upset. He said it was a good thing he got there when he did because it looked like you might have done something to her."

"*What?*" This is ridiculous. "She called me on my cell phone to—"

"Am I going to find a broken pipe when I go out there, Paul?"

Jack must have told Prescott there was nothing wrong. The problem here is that Prescott will never let himself think that Cindy would ever initiate anything intimate between us. He never has. That would be beneath her, in his mind. "Check my cell phone," I say confidently, pulling it out of my pocket. I lean forward and put it down in front of him. "Check the list of received calls. She called me, I didn't call her. She called me from a land line at the mansion. The call's there. You'll see it, you'll recognize the number."

He puts on his reading glasses, snatches the cell phone off my desk, and scrolls through the menu. "Don't see it," he announces triumphantly, tossing the phone back down on my desk so it disappears into a pile of papers.

I grab it and scroll through the list myself. Jesus, I got so many calls last night that Cindy's is gone from the memory. I'm so tired I forgot that it only shows the last twenty calls. "I'll get the records. You'll see it."

"What were you doing at the estate?" Prescott asks accusingly. "What were you really doing there?"

"I told you why I went out there," I answer evenly. "I was there when he got to the place all right, but Cindy and I weren't arguing. He's making all that up. He's the one who's lying."

"Sure he is," Prescott snaps, raising an eyebrow. "Okay, that was your morning trip. I'll give you the benefit of the doubt on that one. But why'd you go back in the afternoon? Did Cindy call you then, too? What was the emergency the second time?"

Prescott must see that he's caught me off guard, and, to make matters worse, that I'm struggling with what to say. "She was upset.

She and Jack argued after I left and I was afraid he'd hit her." How could Prescott know I went back out there? "She needed me. I wasn't there for very long."

"Long enough."

"What's that supposed to mean?"

"Nothing," he mutters.

I don't want to get off point here. I want to make certain he knows what a bad guy his son-in-law is. "Did you hear what I said about Jack?"

"What?"

"About him beating Cindy."

Prescott stares at me for several seconds, then looks down and rubs his eyes. "I loved my daughter very much," he says sadly, "but she was prone to making up stories. And that's putting it mildly."

I saw those bruises on Cindy's side when I followed her back to the estate after rescuing her from Caleb Jenkins and his crew. The thought of telling Prescott about them flashes through my mind and it's very tempting, but I hold my tongue. I saw the bruises but there's no way for me to prove that Jack's the one who made them. And Prescott might draw some unintended conclusions from my admission that I saw such an intimate thing on such an intimate area of his daughter's body.

Prescott nods at my cell phone. "Can you show me her calling you and asking you to come out a second time in the afternoon? Can you get me a record of that call, too?"

The problem is I can't. I went the second time on my own, without a frantic plea from her—even though she told me not to. I was really worried about what Jack might have done to her. "What are you saying?" I ask. All I can do is hit this head-on.

"Who's leading this investigation?" Prescott asks, delaying the confrontation.

"I am."

He rolls his eyes. "Christ."

"I can handle it, Mr. Prescott," I say angrily. For some reason I still call him "Mister." Like I'm still that sixteen-year-old kid praying he'll accept the fact that Cindy and I want to be together. "I know what I'm doing."

"It's not that. It's—"

"I learned a lot before you had me run out of Minneapolis." It took a lot for me to say that, though I've wanted to for a long time. I'm pretty sure he didn't know I knew he had me kicked off the Minneapolis police force, but I've got to give him credit. He barely flinched when I dropped the bomb. He's got a hell of a poker face. "I learned a lot in Madison, too. I can handle this thing."

Prescott takes off his reading glasses, folds them up, and slides them back in his shirt pocket. "I know you've had a thing for Cindy ever since you were a teenager, Paul, ever since you met her that day on the river. I know you've carried a torch for her even though you knew nothing could ever come of it." He holds up a hand when I try to say something. "And I understand why. Cindy was a wonderful woman in many ways." He tilts his head forward. "There's so much more to her than that stripper you ended up with."

He says the words so snobbishly, like he's so much better than Vivian and me. Like his life is so much more important than mine. What a prick. He always has been and he always will be.

"I don't want you running this investigation," he continues. He's all business now. The red-rimmed eyes have cleared. "You're conflicted."

"Why?"

"You went out to my estate yesterday morning begging Cindy to be with you, telling her you'd do anything for her. That's what happened. Things got ugly when she said it would never happen. When she told you to leave you got rough with her. You started to—"

"You're crazy! Jack's feeding you lies so—"

"That's when you got physical with her!" he shouts. "But Jack drove up in the nick of time and you had to back off. You were mad at her, but there was nothing you could do, so you went back to the estate in the afternoon, after Jack left."

I slam my fist on the desk and shoot up out of the chair. Two half-empty Styrofoam coffee cups flip over, spilling mocha slag everywhere. "What the hell are you saying?" I can feel that vein in my neck, the one that bulges when I'm *really* pissed off.

"I'm saying that at the very least a part of you is glad she's dead," he snaps, "and no one who feels that way should be running this investigation."

I feel like I'm going to lose control in a second. "You're wrong!" My voice shakes with rage. "I cared about Cindy very much. I would never be glad that—"

"And, at worst you . . . well, you might have . . ." He looks away. "We don't want to go there. Not yet, anyway, not without the proof."

The blood's pounding in my head so hard his face is blurring in front of me with each beat. *"Get out,"* I order, pointing at the door. *"Get the hell out of my office!"*

8

"THE BASTARD," I mutter. "The *God damned* bastard."

"Calm down, Professor."

"*I'll kill him.*"

Bear's eyes flash around the place. "Easy, easy, let's not get crazy here. Just calm down and tell me what happened."

Bear and I sit across from each other in a booth at the back of the Bruner Saloon. It's ten after two and the lunch crowd's almost gone. Just a few grizzled old-timers are still hanging around chewing yesterday's fat along with the last of their burgers. No one seems to know about Cindy's murder yet. If they did the place would be swarmed with people and everybody would be speculating wildly about what happened.

Mrs. Erickson found out about Cindy's murder a few minutes ago, right before I kicked Lew Prescott out of my office. I tried to keep it from her, but apparently Davy Johnson was talking to one of the other deputies about it and she overheard him. She probably overheard me yelling at Prescott, too. It wouldn't have been hard. I cringe. I can feel those gossip waves racing out in concentric circles over the territory even as I sit here. The Saloon's going to be packed again in an hour or two and so will the Kro-Bar. Everyone will rush out to hear what happened and then the rumor mill will explode.

"Prescott basically accused me of being involved in Cindy's murder," I mutter, my voice still boiling with emotion.

Bear was about to gulp down a huge mouthful of Sara's specialty of the day, Chili del Fuego. But the spoon stops an inch from his lips. *"What?"*

He's interrupted his cheeseburger diet today because I wanted to meet here at the Saloon and Sara's cheeseburgers aren't very good. The Saloon's closer to the precinct but the burgers aren't fat and juicy like the Kro-Bar's. Ike and Sara are in it to make money while the Kro-Bar's changed hands three times in the last five years.

"Are you serious?" The steaming spoonful of chili remains poised before his lips.

"He didn't actually say those words," I answer carefully, taking a sip of some much-needed coffee, "but he implied them. Jack swore I was roughing Cindy up when he got there, too. He's such a liar."

"Is that where you went yesterday morning after she called you out on Silver Wolf Trail?" he asks, finally slipping the spoon into his mouth. "To the Prescott estate?"

"Yup."

"And Jack Harrison showed up while you were there?"

I hadn't told Bear all that. "Yup."

Bear dumps a small mountain of pepper on his chili, then stirs it in. It's like throwing jet fuel on a raging fire, but he's always had an iron stomach. "Well that explains it."

"What do you mean?"

"Prescott hates you. He has ever since he found out his daughter liked bad boys from Bruner, not blue-bloods from the Twin Cities. That's why he framed you for stealing drugs from the evidence room in Minneapolis. You know that. We all do." Bear devours another steaming spoonful of chili. "Jack Harrison was never real fond of you, either, Professor. He knows Cindy loved you."

It makes me feel good to know that my best friend understands exactly what's really going on and doesn't question anything at all. "Prescott told me I shouldn't be running the investigation. He says he's going to get somebody from Madison to take over, some ex–state cop."

"He can't do that," Bear says confidently. "Not even with all his money. It's your jurisdiction."

"I don't know," I answer hesitantly. "Seems like Lew Prescott can do just about anything he wants."

I spot Ike Mitchell talking on the wall phone at the end of the bar. Around six feet tall, he has blond hair that's cut page-boy style so it frames his round face on three sides. Like most men up here he's got a paunch that always seems bigger in the winter months. He hangs up the phone and heads purposefully toward the booth Bear and I are sitting in.

"Hi, Sheriff," he says, smacking his gum. He chews a lot of it. He says it keeps him off the two-pack-a-day Camel habit he supposedly quit a year ago.

"Hello, Ike."

Ike glances at Bear. "Hi, Bear."

Bear grunts but doesn't look up. He just keeps methodically spooning chili into his mouth like his arm and the spoon are integral parts of a well-oiled machine. Bear doesn't care much for Ike, which is the other reason he prefers the Kro-Bar. Before Karen left Bear on Christmas Eve the rumor around Bruner was that she and Ike were having an affair. Ike denied it up and down, he still does, but everyone around town more or less assumes it was true. Not because Ike's a lady's man. He's not, far from it. More because people figured Karen was so tired of getting no attention from Bear that she was willing to hang out with just about anyone who would give her some. They figured she needed a distraction or she might have killed him, and there weren't any rumors about her messing around with anyone else.

"What's up, Ike?" I ask him.

Ike's the talkative one of the couple. Sara never says much. In fact, she rarely socializes at all. She mostly hangs out in the kitchen during the day concocting her recipes and prefers to come out at night when everyone else has gone to bed. She's attractive, though, I'll give her that. In her midthirties, she's the prettiest local around.

One thing that doesn't jive with the rumors about Ike's affair with Karen is that Sara never did anything to Ike for being unfaithful to her, she never took it out on him. She tends to take revenge into her own hands, and when she does, it's swift and brutal.

When I first became sheriff of Dakota County four years ago, Sara was living with a guy named Toby Sims in an old place in the woods out east of town on Route 7, a few miles from the lumberyard. The story goes that Toby started running around with a woman down in Hayward. He spent a lot of his time in the Kro-Bar, but in the beginning of June that year the regulars noticed he wasn't coming in anymore and nobody ever saw him after that. Bear and I went to talk to Sara one day, but she said she hadn't seen him since the beginning of June, either. Then, in the middle of August, some fisherman from Michigan discovered a skeleton in some reeds near the mouth of the Boulder, down at the Big Lake. The state boys in Superior identified the skeleton as Toby's. I'm sure Sara killed him, sure as I can be. She probably threw him in the river off the Route 7 bridge late one night after beating him unconscious, but there wasn't any proof. The state boys and I combed the place they lived in and Sara's pickup truck for clues, but we couldn't find anything. So there was nothing we could do.

Sara beat the hell out of Ike two weeks after they moved in together. She beat him with a tire iron when he tried to have sex with her one night and she didn't want to. At least, that was the rumor Mrs. Erickson picked up off her web. Ike had a black eye and a swollen nose, but he never pressed charges. He never even admitted it was Sara who did it to him. Sara's face was scratched up pretty good, too, and nobody else in town had bruises or scratches on them. I know what happened, but it isn't about what I know, it's about what I can prove.

But Sara never touched Ike for the rumor about Bear's wife and him. Not that I know of anyway, and I don't miss things like that. Even though I'm not a true local, I'm still tied in, I still have a damn good information network of my own—much to Mrs. Erickson's chagrin. What's strange is that Ike doesn't lie very well, and the few times I've mentioned Karen having an affair with someone to him, he sure looks guilty.

You've got to watch out for Sara, you've got to deal with her cautiously no matter who you are. She's like something out of Greek mythology. She's like one of those sirens who lured sailors in so they dashed their ship on the rocks. She's beautiful and feminine, but she'll take you down in a heartbeat if she even suspects you've done her wrong. I wonder if she knows anything about a devil worship cult in Dakota County. It seems like she might.

Ike sits down next to me so I'm forced to slide over, and a heavy whiff of cigarette smoke drifts to my nostrils despite the spearmint-flavored gum he's chomping on. "I just heard about Cindy Harrison," he says in a hushed voice, glancing around.

Bear and I look up in unison. Mrs. Erickson's web must be hard at work, because Ike isn't one of her direct reports. He's separated from the center of her web by at least one degree, probably two. The concentric waves must be moving out at tsunami speed.

"What the hell happened?" he demands, like it's his right to know.

I can't tell him anything but I want to see what he knows. "What did you hear?" I ask, like I really intend to tell him what happened after I hear his side.

Ike folds his hands on the table, takes a deep breath, and shakes his head. "It was that devil cult," he says. "They killed her out at the mansion. They crucified her. She was hanging from the wall like Jesus on the cross when Davy found her. She had knives stuck in her all over." He gazes straight ahead with a horrified expression, as if he's picturing her hanging on the wall across from the booth we're sitting in. "People are scared, Sheriff, *really* scared. They think the cult's gotten tired of animal killings and now they're going after people."

"It was nothing like that," I say firmly. "It wasn't a cult. There's nothing to all that stuff." I can feel Bear's eyes boring into me. As soon as he saw Cindy's body he said the same thing. That the cult must have gotten tired of sacrificing animals, that they must have gotten thirsty for human blood. "She wasn't hanging from the wall, she didn't have knives in her, she didn't have five pentagrams carved in her body. You can't listen to the crap Mrs. Erickson puts out, Ike, you know that. We've talked about it before. There's no damn cult here in Dakota County."

"Sure there isn't," a female voice says sarcastically.

I glance up past Ike, right into Sara's big burning brown eyes. She's standing there, staring down at me hard. She's heard every word I said and it seems like she isn't buying any of it. I wonder why.

After a few moments she breaks into a grin. Then she turns and walks away. Her long black pigtail sways sexily from side to side across her back as she goes.

9

A ROUND SIX O'CLOCK I go back out to the Prescott estate because Peter Schmidt, the man who's leading the crime scene
investigation team, called me. One of his guys found footprints in the hedge maze and Schmidt wanted to talk to me about it,
like it was some big discovery that was going to break the case wide
open. He said he didn't want to get into specifics because he was on
his cell phone and he couldn't take the chance of someone picking
up our conversation over the airwaves, so he wanted me to go out
there. I was short with him, because driving all the way back out
there was about the last thing I wanted to do, and I felt bad about it
after I hung up, but it's been a terrible twenty hours. Plus, I'm still
pissed off at Lew Prescott.

It turns out that Schmidt's all up in arms about the footprints in
the maze because he's positive one set was made by boots he found
in the mansion. Cindy's boots. He figures the other set might be the
killer's. The enthusiasm drains from his face when I tell him that
the other set is mine. What I don't tell him about are those strange-
looking footprints I found when I pulled up to the estate last night.

But he and his team would have a tough time determining that they were of any significance at this point anyway because so many people have been in and out of the mansion in the last eighteen hours that those prints have been all but obliterated. I don't tell him about the Bruner Washette ticket I found near Cindy's body, either. Or the knife I found out on the trail to the Silver Wolf Rapids in the ashes of the fire. This is my investigation and I've got to be careful about the flow of information with Lew Prescott breathing down my neck.

I've known Schmidt for years, from my days in Madison, and he's basically a good guy. He's in his late fifties and he's usually much more concerned about his pension than he is about who gets credit for solving a case. But this is different. The Prescott family is a high-profile name in the entire Midwest, not just in the Twin Cities and Bruner. So Schmidt wants to be the man who figures out what happened, because it'll be one of the most publicized cases of the year and he'll want to see his name in lights. No matter how old people get, they still enjoy that fifteen minutes of fame. It's one of those irrefutable laws of nature.

I tell Schmidt how I came out to the mansion yesterday morning because Cindy called me for help, and I promise to get him the damn phone records so he can confirm it. I could have told him that over the phone, but I wanted to see the look in his eyes when I said it. I don't tell him about my second visit, and I feel guilty, but it isn't the right time to tell him about that.

With a frustrated wave, Schmidt says he won't need the records. At least someone believes me.

The team packs up at nine o'clock and I'm left alone in the mansion. It's eerie in here as I stare at the dried blood pool on the floor where Cindy's body was. I glance across the room at an antique table beside a Chippendale chair. On it is a beautiful headshot of Cindy inside a tasteful gold frame. She was only twenty years old when the picture was taken, and it's my favorite one of her. I move across the floor, carefully avoiding the blood as I stare down at her, at that beautiful face I'll never see alive again. Finally, I grab the picture and head for the door. I have to have something to remember her by.

On my way out I make certain the place is locked up. I won't call Prescott to let him know he can get back into his mansion until tomorrow morning. The thought of him spending a night in a drafty room at the Friendly Mattress doesn't bother me at all.

I head to my truck. It's parked halfway around the circle because when I got here all the crime scene vehicles were in front of the mansion.

It's really cold under a crystal-clear, star-studded sky. Eight degrees, and to help stay warm I bang my arms to my chest as I jog. The frigid air burns my lungs and the dampness inside my nostrils freezes with every breath. The weather's supposed to turn ugly tomorrow night. The storm's supposed to start as freezing rain and sleet, then dump as much as two feet of snow on us, maybe more. It's a monster and it's still growing. We always get at least one of these a year.

I was inside the mansion for less than thirty minutes, but the truck's already freezing and the air blowing out of the vents is ice-cold when I start the engine. I slide the picture of Cindy under my seat, rev the engine a couple of times, then get going.

The Prescott driveway is almost two miles long. From the ridge the mansion is built on, the driveway twists and turns down the hill to an old wooden bridge where it crosses the Boulder, then straightens out and heads toward 681. Once the driveway straightens out, the pine trees rise up on both sides of it, cathedral-like, closing me in. I understand why Cindy kept so many lights on. I breathe a heavy sigh of relief when I get to 681 and make the turn for home. I always like coming back out of this forest, but I don't know why.

When I come into the house I'm in for a shock. Vivian's waiting for me wearing a little schoolgirl outfit. A white cotton shirt unbuttoned all the way, no bra, a skimpy plaid skirt cut way high on one thigh, and those five-inch heels she used to wear when she worked at the club on the outskirts of Madison. Amazingly, she's done something with her hair, too. It's combed to one side, styled, and looks incredible. It changes her whole face, her whole *demeanor.* She seems like a completely different person.

"Come on, Sheriff Summers," she says in a sexy voice, taking me by the hand and leading me into the living room. "Let's have some fun."

"Vivian," I say softly as we reach the lumpy couch. "It's okay."

"I want to."

I'm so damned tired I can barely keep my eyes open, and that image of Cindy lying on the floor in the pool of blood is still stark in my mind. I'm not in the mood despite how long it's been since we made love and how good she looks and I don't understand how Vivian wouldn't understand that. "Viv, please, I—"

"Don't embarrass me, Paul. I tried so hard tonight to look good for you. Don't you find me attractive anymore?"

I gaze deeply into those dark eyes. "It's not that." I'm not in the mood, but she certainly is. "You look very pretty."

At three o'clock in the morning I wake up to take my nightly trek to the bathroom, but when I'm finished I don't go straight back to bed. Instead, I pad softly downstairs to the kitchen. One thing about Vivian, she keeps the kitchen very neat. She's like my father was in that way. Everything has its place and has to be put back in that place before she goes to bed at night.

I hesitate for a moment at the doorway after I switch on the overhead light, staring across the room at the drawer where she keeps that set of six steak knives we bought at the Wal-Mart over in Duluth a couple of months ago. They have black handles and thin pointy tips with an inch of serration starting just below the tips.

Just like the one I dug out of the bonfire ashes up on the Silver Wolf Trail has.

I pull the drawer out slowly and gaze down, feeling my breath go short. Only four steak knives are in their designated spots. I shake my head. We don't have a dishwasher and the sink is empty.

"What are you doing?"

I whip around. Vivian is standing in the doorway, wearing nothing at all. "I was just, well, I . . ." My voice fades as she moves seductively toward me. "Viv, I don't—"

"Shush," she whispers, putting a finger to my lips.

She slips her hands to my cheeks and gives me a passionate kiss. I feel very guilty. Cindy's lying in the morgue in Superior and here I am doing this. But if I turn Viv down, it might turn into a war—like it did the other night—because she'd think I was too distracted by Cindy's death. She doesn't even want me to think about Cindy, not even in death. She told me that in no uncertain terms when I wasn't in the mood earlier.

10

I PATIENTLY WAIT my turn to greet Father Hannah after Sunday services at the Lutheran church down Main Street from the precinct—we call Route 7 Main Street from the Bruner Saloon over to the Kro-Bar. In summertime, after following the choir back down the narrow center aisle of our small church with the rotting steeple, Father Hannah greets his congregation outside, beneath an old oak tree that's been around as long as the old-timers who spend their days chewing the fat at the Saloon's counter can remember. It's nice to stand out there on a warm summer morning while you wait for him, enjoying the precious few Sundays a year you can. It makes you feel glad to be alive.

It warmed up last night, all the way to thirty-seven degrees by six o'clock this morning. But it's still too cold for an outside holy greeting, so the line stretches down the center aisle as Father Hannah dutifully says hello to everyone at the church door. Most people strike up conversations with friends while they wait, but I keep to myself. That's one of the downsides of being sheriff in a small town, especially after something like Cindy's murder. The entire town hangs on your every word, so it's best to stay off by myself and not socialize. That way nothing can be misconstrued and I can't be blamed for a rumor later.

Father Hannah makes everyone in his flock feel as if he really cares about them. He always knows about something that happened to you during the week so you feel like he takes a special interest in you. He got close to Mrs. Erickson right after he moved to Bruner two years ago to replace Father Pettigrew, who finally couldn't hide his Alzheimer's any longer—one morning the old padre showed up to lead Sunday services in his pajamas and slippers and we all had to admit what we'd suspected for a while. Father Hannah quickly recognized how valuable a resource Mrs. Erickson would be, so he made her the church choir director a month after he took over, and he has dinner with her every Monday night to go over the hymns they'll use that Sunday. At least, that's why he tells her he has dinner with her. I doubt Mrs. Erickson has any idea how she's being used, but so what if she doesn't. Father Hannah uses the information he gets out of her at dinner in good ways, and people up here can use any kind of help they can get, especially in the winter.

I glance out through a pane of glass that isn't stained and watch crystal-clear drops fall from the icicles clinging to the church's eaves. This wave of sun and warmth for the north-country is just a wolf in sheep's clothing. Something sent to fool the uninitiated and the stupid. The swing in temperature could allow a sheet of black ice to coat the territory before we're pounded by the snow. A buried layer of black ice can be ten times more dangerous than the piles of snow.

"Sheriff."

I glance over my shoulder. It's Maggie Van Dyke, Karen's younger sister. Bear's ex-Karen. Maggie's short, wide, and thirty-two years old. She's not very attractive, even by Bruner standards, but a sweeter woman was never born. She's never been married and she's lived in a little trailer over on Tunlaw Street ever since her parents died in a nasty car wreck last Thanksgiving weekend on Route 7.

Gus and Trudy were on their way to Superior and Duluth on Black Friday to go Christmas shopping when they ran off the road and hurtled into a thick grove of white pines. As far as we could tell, they were dead on impact. The old Impala was so badly mangled it took us an hour to cut their bodies out of it.

Everything about that crash was strange. It happened in the middle of the day, the weather was clear, and there wasn't a single skid mark on the road. And Gus—who was driving—hadn't had a heart attack or a stroke, according to the coroner's office.

The one thing that really hit me hard at the funeral was that Bear cried. He and Gus were close, almost like father and son. It isn't usually like that up here, because everybody knows everybody else's business. The father-in-law knows when his son-in-law is hanging out late at the Kro-Bar or the Saloon, he knows when his son-in-law is running around with another woman. Ironically, there's a lot of hostility *because* of that closeness, which is one reason I tried to stamp out Mrs. Erickson's web.

Bear didn't hang out at bars drinking and didn't have affairs, and I would know. His vices were the same as Gus's: vodka, cheese-burgers, and football on TV. So the two of them watched a lot of football together and that bond blinded Gus to how Bear wasn't giving Karen what she needed, what every human being needs: companionship. I remember thinking to myself at the funeral how I'd never seen Bear cry. It scared me a little, and I don't scare easily.

"Sheriff."

"Yes, Maggie." I'm only half-listening, which is rude, but I assume she's going to ask me about Cindy's murder just like everybody else in this musty old church wants to do. And I can't say anything. "What is it?"

"Can I talk to you in private after this?" she asks quietly. "After we're out of church."

I turn to face her and see a lost, helpless look in her eyes. "What's it about?"

"I'd rather not say here." Her voice turns meek. She motions for me to keep up as the line shuffles forward. "It's not about Cindy," she whispers. "Promise."

I glance toward the front. We're only five people away from Father Hannah. "Where then?"

"How about the precinct?"

"Is this something you want to keep just between us?" It seems obvious that it is.

"Yes."

Then the precinct won't work because Mrs. Erickson will be there. She almost always works after Sunday service, and not because I make her. She goes in because she's usually picked up a lot of gossip from the choir and she wants to get it out over her web right away so she gets credit for it. That way she can charge me up for a few hours of overtime, too. "The precinct's no good. How about we talk at your place?"

"You sure you don't mind coming over?"

"It's no problem, Maggie, really."

"Hello, Sheriff." Father Hannah has a deep, booming voice for such a small man.

"Hello, Father."

He leans in close. "You okay?" he whispers. The blood of Christ hangs heavy on his breath and it's probably a nice merlot. That's what he always brings to our house when he comes to dinner every few months—two bottles, too. "A terrible thing about Cindy Prescott."

I like the way most people around here call her by her maiden name. I never liked to think of her as Cindy Harrison; it doesn't seem right. I'll admit it has a ring to it. But to my ears it was always the *wrong* ring. "Yes, it is."

His expression grows even darker. "How is Vivian?"

Vivian never comes to church. I probably wouldn't, either, if I wasn't the sheriff. Since my father committed suicide that September I was sixteen, I haven't believed in God. But I have to come to church, all the town leaders do. It wouldn't look right if we didn't.

"She's fine." She's at home asleep. At least, she was when I left. "Thanks for asking."

He gazes at me, starts to say something, stops, then starts again. "Will you wait a minute while I finish up here?"

Suddenly it seems like everyone wants to talk to me offline. "Sure."

When everyone's gone, Father Hannah leads me to a little room off to the right of the pulpit. He shuts the door, puts one hand to his mouth, looks down at the slate floor, and knits his eyebrows together. "Paul, it's come to my attention that there's a cult in Dakota County. A cult of devil worshipers."

Not him, too. "Father, everyone's jumping to conclusions about Cindy's—"

"This isn't about Cindy's murder. I don't believe in all that crap Mrs. Erickson's feeding everyone about pentagrams carved into Cindy's body everywhere or her hanging from the wall like she was crucified. I know she's just selling herself."

Father Hannah's a sharp guy. "Then what's it about?"

"My counterpart down in Hayward, Father Marshall, called me. He told me a teenage girl came to him while he was praying alone at the altar in his church yesterday morning and started telling him how someone she knew was in the cult. How they'd done some bad things and how they were about to do some *very* bad things. She was very nervous while she was talking to him. She told him that there are some people from Hayward in the cult, but that the important people, the ones who run it, are from Dakota County.

"Before she could get too far into things," he continues, "before she could name names, there was a noise at the back of the church. Father Marshall didn't see anyone, but it spooked the girl and she ran out." He hesitates, looks heavenward, and crosses himself. "She hasn't been seen or heard from since and her parents are going crazy. He told me they were going to call the Hayward sheriff right after they got off the phone with him."

I run my hands through my hair. I feel like the walls are closing in around me. I'm going to have to accept that the cult really exists, and that maybe these people are getting tired of killing animals and maybe they want more. Maybe they've already taken more.

I wish those two steak knives weren't missing from my kitchen drawer. And I wish I hadn't found that ticket from the Bruner Washette beside Cindy's body.

11

As I tap on the storm door of the pastel-pink mobile home, I gaze up through the thick pine tree branches above me. I drove to church this morning beneath a clear sky, but now high clouds are rolling in and the temperature's dropped back to thirty-three degrees. That's still warm for this time of year in the north-country, but those changes the weather people have been predicting for the area are starting to move in. Freezing rain is supposed to begin late this afternoon or early evening, then change to snow around ten o'clock tonight. Now they're calling for up to two and a half feet of the white stuff. The storm keeps getting bigger and bigger.

"Hi, Sheriff," Maggie says as she opens the door. "Would you like some coffee?"

I wipe my boots on the cement stoop before coming in. The path to the door through a few inches of old snow has turned muddy because of the sudden temperature change. "No thanks," I say as I move past her.

"Tea?"

I shake my head.

"Pop?"

"No, Maggie."

"How about something to eat? I could fix you some eggs and bacon, or maybe a sandwich."

"I'm fine," I say firmly, trying to let her know that we need to get down to business sometime before the start of baseball season. "Thank you."

"I feel bad that you came all the way over here," she says, pointing to an old sofa. "Please sit down."

The tiny trailer isn't far from the church. It's not like coming over here was a big deal.

I'm about to sit down when a snake comes slithering out from beneath the couch, tongue flickering. *Christ Almighty!* I shout, taking three panicked steps backward. "What the hell?"

Maggie looks at me like I'm crazy, then sees the snake and smiles. "Oh, that's just Charlie," she says, like it's some doddering old uncle that wouldn't hurt a flea. "He's my little Burmese python. Come here, you bad boy." She bends down, grabs it roughly behind the head, and starts pulling. Four thick feet later the wriggling tail appears. "I'll be back in a sec, Sheriff. Make yourself comfortable."

Instead of the couch I pick a wooden chair in the corner of the room to sit in. It isn't as comfortable as the couch, but I can see beneath it and nothing's going to sneak up on me from behind. I swear I'll never get used to this place—or its people.

"I feel so guilty for putting you out," she says, huffing as she comes back into the room. "I want to get you something."

"It's fine, really. What did you want to talk about?"

She relaxes onto the couch and catches her breath. "I . . . I wanted to talk to you about Karen."

I figured that was it when she said it wasn't about Cindy's murder.

"I'm real worried. I haven't heard from her since Christmas Eve, since she left Bear. I thought I'd hear something from her by now."

I shrug my shoulders. "The note your sister left Bear said she was going away, way away. It said she didn't want him to come looking for her, either." And, as far as I know, Bear's complied with her request. He hasn't lifted a finger to find her. I guess he's that pissed off, or he felt the same way she did. "It said all that twice."

She reaches inside her top and pulls a wadded Kleenex from her bra. Maggie's emotional to begin with and in the last few months she's lost her parents and, apparently, her sister. Maggie and Karen were close and it does surprise me that Karen hasn't at least called. "I know."

"I showed you the note," I remind her.

"I remember."

"You told me it was her handwriting, her signature at the bottom."

She lets out a little sob. "It was. I recognized it."

"You can file a missing person report," I say. "Then I can call the state police and put things into motion. If that's what you want to do."

She looks up at me. "Do you think I should?"

I stare at her for a few seconds, then finally nod. Regretfully, because right now I don't need another high-profile investigation in Dakota County. I don't have much in the way of resources and I don't want her to get frustrated with me when Karen doesn't turn up right away. "Probably," I say quietly.

I like Maggie. She's a sweet girl and I've always had a soft spot in my heart for vulnerable women. That's what I thought Vivian was when I met her at that club in Madison. She caught my eye the first time I saw her, when I was in there doing a routine check one Friday afternoon before things got going. I found out she was from somewhere down near Illinois and that she'd been through a long line of foster homes and didn't have any idea who her parents were.

I hate those kinds of stories, and she looked so pretty and sweet. I know, I know, the stripper-with-a-heart story, but all I could think about as I stared at her was getting her out of that awful place. And she always thanked me for getting her out of that place, she was always so sweet to me—until she found out for sure she couldn't have children.

Then she turned into someone I didn't know for a few months, then into someone I didn't want to know.

"Do I have to fill out paperwork?" she asks.

"I'll do it. You'll just sign it. Come by the precinct after the storm's passed through, okay? On Tuesday or Wednesday morning."

"Okay," she agrees, her voice cracking. Two streams of tears run down her puffy cheeks to the corners of her mouth. Taking this step is admitting to herself that there's a big problem. "It's just that I—"

My cell phone goes off and it's the precinct calling. "Hello." I hold my hand up, letting Maggie know this won't take long.

"Sheriff?"

"Yes, Mrs. Erickson."

"You need to get over here. There's someone to see you."

"Who?"

"He says his name's Darrow Clements. He says Mr. Prescott sent him."

Darrow Clements. Jesus, Lew Prescott doesn't screw around. And, of course, Mrs. Erickson would have to be there when Clements showed up. I consider telling him to pound salt, to come back after the storm, but that'll only delay the inevitable and get us off on the wrong foot. "Tell him I'll be there in fifteen minutes."

"All rightee."

I shove the phone back in my pocket. "You were going to say something, Maggie?"

"I'm scared."

"Why?" I ask, standing up.

"I keep hearing about this devil cult," she says, standing up, too.

"I keep thinking maybe that's what happened to Karen, that maybe they got her." She looks up at me and her tears start flowing even harder. "Are we safe, Sheriff?"

I move slowly to where she stands and put my hand on her shoulder. I can tell she needs to be held, but I shouldn't do that. It wouldn't be appropriate. Here, alone in the trailer with her. "Yes, Maggie, you're safe. Don't worry."

She starts sobbing and presses her cheek against my chest. Against my better judgment I wrap my arms around her and comfort her for a few minutes before I finally step back and bid her a gentle good-bye.

12

I EASE INTO my office chair at the precinct to the sound of its familiar creak, the way I always do when there's someone I don't trust sitting on the other side of my desk. I sit slowly and deliberately, never taking my eyes off the person, letting him know that I don't trust him and that I'm watching everything he does.

Darrow Clements retired from the Wisconsin State Police Force two years ago. Like Peter Schmidt, Clements was someone I knew while I was a trooper stationed in the barracks on the outskirts of Madison, which was only two miles from that club Vivian danced in. Unlike Schmidt, Clements was someone I never got along with. Lew Prescott probably knows that, too. That's probably the main reason Clements is sitting in front of me right now and not someone else who's smarter. Prescott figures he needs a bulldog for this assignment, someone who can get under my skin, make me vulnerable, and get me to drop my guard. He has lots of other people who can sift through the clues and make assessments.

Clements always reminded me of a drill sergeant because of his build and because he has absolutely no people skills whatsoever.

He has broad shoulders, a flat stomach, and not an ounce of fat on him, though he's got to be in his midfifties by now. He's completely no-nonsense except that he's half an inch shy of six feet tall but tells anyone who'll listen he's an even six. He has little eyes and talks in rapid bursts, like an automatic weapon going off. His failing as a police officer is that he's absolutely black and white. There's no gray area for him, no interpreting the statutes, which is why we never saw eye to eye.

Say you're doing eighty in a forty. He'd write you up for reckless driving even though your wife's lying passed out and cold beside you and she's eight months pregnant. He doesn't care that there wasn't time to call an ambulance or that you'll lose your license for six months if you're convicted. Or that you'll lose your job on top of that because you can't drive to work. He doesn't care that he'll ruin your life. Worst of all, he doesn't care that your wife and baby might die while he writes up the ticket. I know how that sounds, like it couldn't *possibly* be true, but it is. I heard he was forced to retire because the judges couldn't take him anymore.

See, he always figured that interpretation and compassion were for the courts. He always figured it was his job to haul as many people in front of the bench as he could and let the robes decide what to do with them. He believes most people are inherently bad and ought to be in jail anyway and that's our fundamental difference. Even though I'm a police officer, despite all the awful things I've seen over the years, I still believe most people are inherently good.

"How have you been, Darrow?" I haven't seen him in four years, not since I came to Bruner. "How's your wife?" I ask when he doesn't reply. I'm trying to start this thing off in a friendly way even if it kills me.

"She's dead." He stares at me impassively. "Ovarian cancer last summer."

"I'm sorry to hear that."

"What about you? How's that stripper you married?"

I grit my teeth so hard I feel like I'm going to crack one. "Fine, Darrow, Vivian's fine," I answer, somehow keeping my temper in check.

"I remember running her in one night for soliciting in front of the Drake Hotel in downtown Madison. It was a few weeks before you two got married."

He's such a prick. He arrested Vivian in front of the Drake that night with no cause whatsoever. She was just walking down the street, minding her own business. Okay, she was dressed provocatively, but that was how she always dressed back then, even nights she wasn't working. He only arrested her so he could tell all the boys at the barracks she was a hooker, too, not just a stripper. That was his idea of fun, to make it look like I was marrying a prostitute. I'd never done anything to him; in fact, we barely knew each other at that point, but he didn't care. It was a chance to really hurt someone else and he wasn't going to pass that up.

He gives me a snide chuckle. "That was interesting. She wasn't convicted, but I know she was trying to—"

"Why are you here, Darrow?" I ask coldly, trying to make him understand that in a minute I'm going to jack him up against the wall and make him wish he'd never come.

It did bother me that Vivian never gave me a good explanation for what happened. She never really came clean about what she was doing down there in front of the Drake so far from her apartment at one o'clock in the morning the week I was working a graveyard shift. I only asked her about it once, and she dodged the arrow, but I've always wondered if there was more to the story.

"How the hell did you get mixed up with that woman?"

I want to bang him back about the semi-truck he married but I can't. I wouldn't even if she hadn't died, it's not in me. "Why are you here?" I ask again in the same gruff tone as I clench my fists tightly. He finally gets the message. I can tell by the way he crosses his arms over his chest and pushes his chin down.

"Lewis Prescott wants me to consult with him about his daughter's murder."

"Consult? What does that mean?"

"He wants me to make sure this investigation's run right."

Well, at least Prescott and his congressman son-in-law couldn't have me replaced. If they could have, Clements wouldn't be sitting in my office now. Bear was right on target with that one. "You're a citizen now, Darrow," I remind him, leaning forward over the desk. "You were fired."

"I resigned."

"Not according to people who—"

"I want everything on this case, Paul," Clements interrupts. "I want access to all the records, all the reports, and all the evidence. Don't try to stonewall me, either."

I give him my best did-I-really-hear-what-you-just-said look. "I couldn't give you anything having to do with this case even if I wanted to, Darrow. You know that. All the information I have has to stay absolutely confidential. I shouldn't even need to say that."

"You play it that way and you'll be sorry. Prescott thinks you know a lot more than you're saying about what happened to Cindy, and I agree with him."

"Screw him *and* you."

Clements points at me angrily. "Listen, I've still got friends in Madison, friends who can bring the hammer down on you, people who can climb inside your life and see if there really is a conflict with you leading this investigation. People who can have you suspended from duty, maybe even fired." He spears at me again with his index finger. "You lose this job, Paul, and you're flipping burgers at one of the bars in town. There won't be anything left in law enforcement for you. Not after Minneapolis *and* Madison."

I can feel that vein in my neck bulging. "I was framed."

"Not in Madison," he counters.

I wasn't ready for that. Prescott must have told him what I said about being set up on that trumped-up evidence-stealing charge in Minneapolis. I mean, everyone knew it was a complete joke. But Prescott had that precinct completely under his thumb and I went down. Of course, if I'd really stolen evidence from that room I never would have gotten the job in Madison. But the trooper gig was all set up for me as long as I agreed to leave Minneapolis without any trouble, as long as I agreed to put that distance between Cindy and me immediately.

"Nothing was ever proven."

"We gave you a break, Paul. They were running drugs out of that club your wife was stripping in. You were the one who was calling over there to warn the bouncers on nights we sent the undercover guys in. We had proof, Paul, we had phone records."

"You're out of your mind. You didn't have anything." They didn't, either. This was all just part of his bluster intended to get under my skin. "If you had, you'd have pushed me harder."

"You had that itchy trigger finger, too," Clements keeps going, raising one eyebrow as he leans back in the chair. "There were those two incidents," he says, forming quotation marks with his fingers when he says the word "incidents." "Those two people who got shot on routine traffic stops in less than a year."

"They pulled guns on me. I was cleared both times."

Clements breaks into a smug smile. "Then why'd you take the deal, Paul?" He makes a sweeping gesture with both arms. "Why'd you trade Madison in for all of this."

My eyes narrow as I stare at him. I hate him almost as much as I hate Lewis Prescott. These two men could destroy my life, maybe even put me behind bars for the rest of my days without the slightest shred of evidence. I need to remember that. The law isn't always fair, and no one knows that better than me.

• • •

After Clements leaves, I pull out the missing-person paperwork on Karen Brock. I really don't want to start the process, but I don't have a choice. Karen could be in real trouble. I'm convinced the handwriting on the "Dear Bear" note was hers, but you never know about these things. Maybe she hasn't been able to handle life outside Bruner as well as she thought she could. My experience is that sisters have an incredible and inexplicable bond. It's almost like ESP, like they can tell when the other one's in trouble even if they're on opposite sides of the world.

As far as ESP goes I know it's irrational to believe in it, but I've seen Vivian pick some pretty crazy things out of thin air. She had a vision that Gus and Trudy Van Dyke were going to die two weeks before they did. She even called them on the phone and begged them to be careful, which was odd because they'd never been very nice to her. Gus gave her a real insincere thank you and laughed it off as Vivian just being Vivian. Bear told me how Gus and Trudy described the call in detail to a couple of friends over dinner at the Kro-Bar one night a few days after Vivian phoned them. He told me how the two couples got a big laugh out of it and called her nuts. How he almost went over to the table and told Gus off but he couldn't because after all Gus was his father-in-law. I bet Gus and Trudy wished they'd listened to Vivian as they were hurtling toward that grove of white pine trees at sixty miles an hour screaming for their lives.

I stare down at the missing-person forms, wondering if Bear was the one who told Vivian about Cindy's being in town by herself. It bothers me so much to think like that, but I can't help it. I've been wondering a lot about their relationship over the last twenty-four hours.

When I'm finished with the paperwork I drive over to the trailer so Maggie can sign everything. I know she didn't want to wait until after the storm, and, now that the weather people are saying this monster could dump so much snow on us, it might be the end of the week before things get back to normal. Even though 681 is technically a state road, it usually takes a while for the plows to get this far north. We just aren't that important to the people in Madison.

Maggie starts to cry when I show up. She tells me I should be home with Vivian as she signs the forms with a shaking hand at the cheap table in the trailer's kitchen. If Maggie only knew how I've stayed awake at night staring at the bedroom ceiling, worried that I haven't done my job in this case, she might not be thanking me so much. But then she'd understand my conflict and I can't have anyone understand that.

Vivian couldn't have been nicer about my deciding to go into the precinct after church. She told me just to get home as soon as I could and that she'd have something good waiting for me. I know there's a connection between her new attitude and Cindy's murder. I just pray it isn't direct. When I get back to the precinct with the signed papers, Mrs. Erickson is beside herself. She's banging desk drawers, stamping her feet and muttering.

"This has got to be illegal," she fusses as I pass her desk.

I don't say anything at first.

"It's just got to be!" she shouts even louder.

I hesitate. I should walk straight into my office and pay no attention, but my curiosity gets the better of me. "What's the problem?"

She nods at her computer. "There's a damn chat room on this website that's dedicated to Cindy Prescott's murder. Some woman down in Hayward's put it together already. Everybody's on it."

Even Mrs. Erickson can't fight technology and I have to admit it makes me happy to see her so irritated. "Do me a favor, will you?"

"What?"

"Call all the deputies and tell them we won't be having our weekly meeting tomorrow afternoon because of the storm." I close the door to my office without waiting for an answer.

I spend fifteen minutes sending Karen's information out to the other contiguous county police forces and to the state boys in Superior and Madison, then pack it in for the day. I'll think about widening the search if we don't hear something after the storm is gone.

By the time I come back out of my office it's a few minutes before three and Mrs. Erickson's gone. She didn't even stick her head in to say good-bye. The thing is, she wouldn't have said good-bye even if I had been more compassionate about that website infringing on her territory. I'll have to call the deputies myself to make sure they know about the meeting being canceled. I doubt she followed up.

Davy comes into the precinct just as I'm leaving. He's the deputy on duty tonight but I tell him to leave when the snow starts. I don't want him getting stuck here away from his wife and three kids.

Finally, I head home down SR 681 beneath a threatening sky. The gray clouds are so thick it's almost dark even though technically it's another hour to sundown. It's like we're experiencing a solar eclipse or something and everyone's gone for their burrows. Hardly anyone's on the road. I only have to dim my high beams once for an oncoming car.

I spot that first flake as I'm passing the campground. It's small, not like the big fat flakes the storm a few days ago started with. This storm is serious. At least it isn't starting with the freezing rain and sleet the weathermen had predicted it would. Fortunately, the temperature dropped this afternoon more quickly than they anticipated. It was twenty-three degrees when I left the precinct and the temperature was still falling fast.

I race past the Campbell estate on the right, then past two more gates. I'm only a couple of miles from home when a lone figure darts out from the tree line up ahead of me on the left. Then two more figures appear, apparently chasing the first one. It's difficult to see much through the gloom, but the first one looks like a teenage girl and the second two look like men. Then all three of them are gone, swallowed up by the forest on the west side of 681. What's so crazy is that the girl didn't look like she had much on. In fact, it looked like she wasn't wearing anything at all.

I skid to a stop at the spot where I figure they ran into the woods, grab my gun from the glove compartment, chamber the first round, hop out of the truck, and lock it. Then I race ahead until I pick up the tracks in the snow: three clear sets of prints heading off into the trees and the underbrush. Suddenly I hear a scream and I sprint ahead, holding my arms in front of my face to protect against the low-hanging branches swatting me.

The trees and brush are so thick I can barely see more than a few feet ahead of me. I'm trying to follow the tracks, trying not to get my eyes poked out by a branch, and trying not to get killed by whoever's chasing this poor girl. Like I said before, people do crazy things up here when cabin fever sets in. You can't understand how bad it is until you live here, until you physically experience the cold and gloom that stifle this territory day after day for months and months.

I grab my cell phone from my pocket and try Bear, but he doesn't answer. Then I start pushing the precinct number but there isn't time to finish the call. There's no telling what these guys might do to the girl. I've got to get to her as soon as possible, so I shove the phone back in my pocket and move on.

A quarter of a mile into the woods I reach a clearing about an acre in size and right away I spot the men on the other side of it. They're pinning the girl facedown in the snow and I can see that she's definitely naked. It looks like they're trying to tie her hands behind her back but she's putting up one hell of a fight.

"Dakota County Police!" I yell loudly across the open ground, aiming my gun at them. Adrenaline is raging through my system and my voice is even louder than I expected it to be. "Put your hands up!"

The two men hit the ground even before my voice fades into the trees and roll away from the girl, then start shooting blindly at me. I dive behind a stump as bullets zip nastily through the branches above me. The men are so shocked right now they couldn't drop a rock over the side of a boat on Lake Superior and hit water.

The girl scrambles to her feet and takes off into the trees, snow falling from her body as she goes. She must be very cold.

One of the men jumps to his feet and chases her. For a moment it looks like Caleb Jenkins, the ringleader of the group that was harassing Cindy the other day. I blow a warning shot across his bow and he does a one-eighty and takes off in the other direction, following his buddy into the woods. Now I'm not completely sure it's Jenkins.

I rise and move through the trees rimming the clearing, in the direction the girl went, my gun leading the way. I'm going after her and not the men because I have no idea how long she's been out in the elements and hypothermia could be setting in. As soon as her adrenaline rush dies she could pass out and I'd probably never find her. Or she might get lost. It's easy to do out here, to go round and round in circles when you think you're going in a straight line. She'd die before morning.

And going after the men under these circumstances would be stupid, bordering on insane. They've got a major advantage because there are so many places to hide and it's almost dark. They could lure me into an ambush and shoot me very easily.

I find the girl's tracks right away. The good thing is she's heading straight for the Boulder River. The drop from the forest floor to the river in the Gorges section at that point is over three hundred feet almost straight down on both sides of the river. If I haven't caught up to her by the time she reaches it, she'll have to turn and she'll probably turn north, downstream toward town and Lake Superior, because that would keep her heading away from the last point she knew the men were. I'll call somebody and get them to wait for her at the Route 7 bridge while I follow her.

I kneel behind a couple of trees and case the area, gun still out in front of me, peering through my breath as it mists before my face.

I don't see any sign of the men and my guess is that they're long gone. They'd love to pop me at this point, but sticking around is a bigger risk. They probably figure that I have backup on the way and all they want to do is get out of the area.

Just as I'm about to rise and go after her, I spot something moving out there in the woods. It's a gray shape moving from tree to tree, but it doesn't look like the girl. Whatever it is sends an eerie shiver up my spine. If it isn't her, she's putting a lot of distance between us, and I'm worried that I'll lose her tracks in the fading light. I just have to hope it was some kind of animal.

I pull out my phone again and call the precinct but Davy doesn't answer. Maybe he's already gone home because of the storm. I dial his cell phone but he doesn't answer that, either, which is strange. He's usually pretty good about picking up right away when he's on duty, even if he's been called away from the precinct. I start dialing Bear's number again but I'm losing too much time. I've got to get going. Once again I shove the phone back in my pocket and race after the girl.

I sprint several hundred yards through the snow, then stop suddenly. I swear I heard footsteps behind me. They stopped, too, a second after I did. It could be my imagination or it could be just the echo of my footsteps. I start running again, then stop quickly, but I don't hear anything this time.

I start moving ahead again, following the tracks, trying to catch up. It's obvious that she's bleeding because red traces rim the edges of her tracks. The old snow is six inches deep and the top layer is frozen because the temperature went up and down so fast. It's sharp and it's slashing her ankles as she crashes through it. God, she must be scared.

I finally catch a glimpse of her moving through the trees. The trees aren't quite as thick in here because the topsoil gets rockier near the river. I see her stop and lean against a large tree up ahead, shoulders heaving from exertion. It's odd to see this girl standing in front of me in the middle of the woods. Even odder than it was to come around a bend on the river and see Cindy standing naked in the water. It's the dead of winter, for Christ sake. Nobody should be out here like this. I'll give the girl my Dakota County Police jacket as soon as I catch up to her.

As I watch her, I realize that this might be the girl from Hayward that Father Hannah was talking about this morning. The girl who told the minister down there she knew someone who was involved with the cult, then got spooked and ran. She hasn't been seen or heard from since. The tearful reunion with her parents flashes through my mind. I hope she'll be able to shed a lot of light on the cult, too. Starting with who the leaders are.

I move slowly through the trees because I don't want to scare her. The girl's head finally snaps around. She gazes toward the tree I'm standing behind for a few moments, then runs. I race after her. I don't want to shout in case the men are still close. I wish she understood that I'm a friend, not a foe.

Finally I take a chance and call out to her. "I'm Sheriff Summers of the Dakota County Police Force! I'm here to help you!" My voice echoes through the trees. "I'm here to help you!" I shout again, louder this time. I stay still for a few moments, listening for her—and the men. "I'm the one they were shooting at!"

But she takes off crashing through the snow again, screaming in pain with each bloody step. I holster my pistol and race after her.

As we reach the crest of the cliff overlooking the Boulder, I'm only fifteen feet behind her. She's plodding along almost out of energy, bent over at the waist against the driving snow, breathing hard. "Stop! Please!" I yell. We're moving along the edge of the cliff. A few inches to our left it's three hundred feet straight down to the river, and there are only a few places where I can still see dark water running. Otherwise, the surface is frozen solid and covered with snow. "Stop!"

Amazingly, she does. She turns and stares at me, hands at her sides, sobbing pitifully, bloody gashes in her ankles and lower legs, scratches all over her body. We're less than ten feet apart and I make certain to keep my eyes focused on hers. I don't want her to lose faith in me; I don't want her to think I might be with the men who were chasing her.

"Everything's going to be all right," I say softly, peeling off my jacket. It's very cold out here. How can she have survived without anything on for so long? "I promise." She's standing ten feet from me and a foot from certain death. But in her fractured mental state she may not realize how close she is to the edge. I'm worried that she's slipping into shock and may not even know where she is, so I stay still. Instead of moving closer, I hold my jacket out for her like you'd hold a piece of food out for a squirrel in a park. "Here, come on, take it."

She takes one step toward me, then her knees buckle and she collapses.

I dive for her and I'm just able to grab one slender wrist as her body tumbles over the side. Then I lunge for the closest tree. There's a small one growing close to the edge of the cliff—its trunk is barely bigger than the girl's wrist—and I clutch it as tightly as I clutch the girl.

Now I'm in danger of going over the edge, too. I'm lying flat on my stomach with one arm over the edge holding on to her while she dangles three hundred feet in the air, screaming like a maniac, begging me to do something. The little tree I'm clutching is doing its best to hold our combined weight, but it could snap at any second.

It's after nine o'clock before I finally pull into my driveway and the snow's coming down hard. Six inches of fresh powder already cover the ground and the roads are getting bad. I had the Cherokee in four-wheel-drive low on the way home from the precinct, so driving wasn't a problem, but anyone out there tonight who doesn't have four-wheel drive is risking his life. I know it's hard to believe, but not everybody up here does. It's mostly because they can't afford to.

By tomorrow morning even the Cherokee won't be much good for getting around. Now the weather people are saying the storm is going to stall over the upper Midwest and spin for a day and a half thanks to another front to the east that's coming up out of the Gulf. It'll dump snow on us until early Tuesday and we could get three feet, maybe more. This could be the storm of the decade, maybe even the century.

Somehow I was able to save that girl. That little tree held and I was able to pull the girl back up to safety. God, I was happy, and thankful that I work out as hard as I do. I couldn't lift a car off someone like Bear did, but I don't think an average-sized guy could have done what I did, either.

As I wrapped my coat around her, Davy Johnson called me on my cell to tell me he was speeding out 681 to where my SUV was parked—I'd left a message on his cell phone the time I'd called him. After we hung up, he called the paramedics, and by the time I got the girl back to the road, they were there waiting for us. I had a lot of questions I wanted to ask her, but I held off. She needed to get to the hospital as fast as possible, and I probably couldn't have relied on the answers she'd have given me in the state she was in anyway.

In my high beams I notice a squirrel struggling through the blizzard to make it to that big pine tree in our front yard Vivian always parks her car beneath. He moves forward in great leaps, hurtling two or three feet in the air and disappearing beneath the snow for a few seconds on impact. Then he reappears with a flaky white cap on his head, which he quickly shakes off before leaping forward again. Finally, he makes it to the tree and scampers up the trunk.

I take a deep breath and slowly let my head fall to the steering wheel, feeling heat building at the corners of my eyes. Why, I don't know. It's been a long time since I cried. Since a day ten years ago when I was walking in the woods outside Madison by myself, and I realized I might have made a mistake marrying Vivian. But I'd made promises to her at that altar in front of everyone, and I couldn't go back on them. That wouldn't have been fair, that wouldn't have been right.

I knew why I was upset then, but I'm not sure now. Maybe it's because I haven't had time to really think about the fact that Cindy's gone forever and it's finally sinking in. Despite the fact that Viv hated her so much, she was a good person and she was a big part of my life for a long time. Or maybe it's the look I saw on that poor girl's face just before she fell off the cliff. Sheer terror as she reached for me during that fraction of a second she teetered on the brink. She was hoping against hope I could save her—but I did.

I just wish I could have saved Cindy.

13

"I LOVE YOU, PAUL."

I gaze up at Vivian from the kitchen chair, taken completely off guard. It's been a long time since she's said that to me without my saying it first. I'd taken her to Minneapolis for a big New Year's Eve party a few years ago and we were staying at a four-star hotel downtown where we were spending a good chunk of my off-the-books bonus from that year. Everybody in the main ballroom had just finished a raucous countdown led by a tuxedo-clad master of ceremonies, and we were kissing to the orchestra's soulful rendition of auld lang syne. When the song ended and we pulled back she stared into my eyes and murmured the words, "I love you, Paul." Almost inaudibly, but she did. That was the last time she had said it to me first.

At that point we were still desperately trying to have children. She was taking all kinds of fertility drugs, and it seemed like we were having sex all the time. In fact, we had to rush back down from our room to make the countdown in the ballroom. It seemed like we'd reignited that infatuation passion we had for each other at the beginning of our relationship. The one that lasts for a few months, then vanishes like a morning fog. And you can't put your finger on exactly when it burned off, but you know it did, because you don't have that burning desire to see the other person anymore. And your heart doesn't beat any differently than it does when you see anyone else.

We were kissing in the hotel elevator like two teenagers on prom night. It was a passionate kiss that went on in front of an elderly couple during the entire trip down to the lobby. The old couple was appalled, and rightfully so, though we couldn't have cared less. We were feeling good from the wine and champagne we'd been drinking. We were enjoying a great time, swept up in the conviction that soon we'd finally find out we were having the baby we both wanted so much, certain that modern technology was going to win the battle for us.

But it didn't. A month later Vivian got the definitive word from her doctor in Madison that she couldn't have children no matter how many drugs she tried, and that incredible passion we'd managed to reignite had a heart attack and died in front of us before it even hit the floor.

"I . . . I love you, too," I mumble.

She's cooking a western omelet for me. It's my favorite kind and she's dressed in nothing but a little teddy while she cooks.

It's ten o'clock in the morning and we only got up fifteen minutes ago. It's the first time I've slept this late since last year's blizzard dumped two feet on us, and I feel refreshed despite all that's going on. I checked the lawn from the back porch window right after we came downstairs, and it looks like we've already gotten at least a foot and a half. Just a few random flakes are spiraling down from the sky now, but, according to the Weather Channel, this is simply the storm taking a break. Sometime early this afternoon the barrage is supposed to reform and rev up again. The weather people are predicting at least another foot for the north-country.

Vivian sways seductively across the floor when she's finished making the omelet. She puts the plate down in front of me on the wooden table, then sits on my lap and feeds me.

"Good?" she asks.

It's incredible. It's better than the omelet I had at that four-star hotel in Minneapolis for New Year's Day brunch as I was fighting a bad hangover. "Oh, yeah."

In the last few days it's as if she's gone from short-order cook to Wolfgang Puck, from matron to runway model. Well, maybe that's pushing it, but any way I look at it the change is dramatic. She's wearing just the right amount of makeup, she's still doing that thing I like with her hair, and, most important, she's being nice. The transformation has been immediate and amazing, but there's a double-edged sword to it. Suddenly I'm living with that person I've always wanted to live with, but it seems obvious why, and that could have a dark side to it.

She cuts another bite with the fork, wiggles on my lap and smiles suggestively as she slides the tines past my lips. But she doesn't pull the fork out right away. She hesitates, then tilts her head back and gets a wild look in her eyes. Then she forces it farther into my mouth so the tips of the tines touch the back of my throat.

I gag and push her off me. *"What the hell are you doing?"*

She doesn't answer. She just drops the fork to the floor, straddles me, kisses me, and grinds herself against me. "Make love to me," she whispers as she pulls the teddy over her head. "I want you so badly."

By three o'clock in the afternoon twenty-seven inches of fresh snow cover the territory, and the storm doesn't show any signs of letting up. We lost the satellite again an hour ago but it doesn't matter. This time Vivian and I do it on the couch, breaking one of its wooden legs in the process. This time I started it. Apparently, I'm over my problem of last night.

"I'm so happy, Paul."

"Me, too."

It's after ten and we're lying on the couch naked beneath two heavy blankets watching a late movie on TV. It's been a hell of a day. It reminded me of those first few months when we were intimate so long ago, and that period when we were trying so hard to conceive. Even when we weren't making love today we were touching each other and smiling knowingly when we passed each other in a room or in the hallway and we were giving each other lots of kisses. I couldn't believe how good it was.

"I feel like we're finally getting everything back on track," she says. "Know what I mean?"

"Yeah, I do." I'm not just saying that, either. It wasn't just the sex for me today. I felt good about her for the first time in a long time. And us.

"It's been so long." She looks up at me and smiles sweetly. "You've been a pretty tough man to live with for a while. I know it's tough to be the sheriff, but sometimes I think it's tougher to be the woman who lives with the sheriff."

I don't like the sound of that. She's the one who's been hard to live with, but I'll let it go in the interest of keeping the peace and keeping the good momentum going. "Yeah, well . . ."

"And I forgive you."

She's trying to get under my skin. I can tell she is because I've known her for so long, but for the life of me I can't figure out why. "Forgive me for what?"

"You know."

"No I don't."

"Forget it," she says. "I love you so much."

We're silent for a while and then I can't help myself. If she just hadn't started it with the little verbal jabs, I'd be fine. But when she does that, it gets me going. "What's going on, Vivian?"

"What do you mean?"

"You know what I mean," I say gently. I'm her husband, but, as she said, I'm also the sheriff. I have a huge responsibility on my shoulders, and I can't get the connection between the immediate change in her attitude and the timing of Cindy's murder out of my head. "Why are you acting so different? Why are you being so nice to me all of a sudden?" She rolls her eyes and snuggles even closer to me. I don't actually see her roll her eyes, but I know she does because I know her so well. She does it all the time when I say something she doesn't like. "Come on, talk to me."

"It's been such a good day, Paul," she murmurs as she strokes my chest with her fingernails. "Why are you trying to ruin it?"

"I'm not trying to ruin anything, Viv." My voice rises with conviction this time. "I just want to know what's going on."

She takes a deep breath and I can hear the angst tangled up inside it. She leans a little away from me, too, and stops stroking my chest. "Are you trying to get me to say that I'm glad Cindy was murdered?"

"Well, are you?"

"Well, are you sad about it?" she snaps, moving to the other side of the couch and crossing her arms over her breasts.

I hear that tone in her voice. It's the same one I heard the other night before she came at me in the kitchen. "I think it's terrible any time anyone's murdered."

She turns to look at me. "Oh, really?" she asks sarcastically.

"Of course." My eyes narrow. "What's that supposed to—"

"You didn't think it was terrible when you shot those people over in Madison."

"*What?*" She can be so damn mean sometimes. "Are you talking about what happened during those traffic stops? Are you talking about those guys I shot in self-defense?"

She rolls her eyes again, but this time I see it. "Self-defense?" she scoffs. "That's not what I heard. I heard it was something else."

"Oh, yeah?" Now I'm getting angry. "Who'd you hear that from?"

"A friend of mine on the police force over there."

"You mean that same rat bastard who ran you in for soliciting in front of the Drake Hotel that night?"

She jumps off the couch and points down at me with a shaking finger. "I told you a long time ago never to bring that night up again."

I rise off the couch slowly and straighten up to my full height, so I'm towering over her. "Too bad." I always heard about this one guy who came into the club every once in a while and took up all her time when he did. I never met him but I heard about him from two of the other girls who wanted me to get Viv out of that place so badly. Maybe he was taking up her time that night but it wasn't at the club. "I want to hear the truth; I'm tired of wondering. What the hell were you doing down there in front of the Drake that night?"

"You're such an ass sometimes, Paul." Her eyes are on fire as she glares at me. "I was minding my own business, and that's all I'm going to say about it."

"What kind of business were you minding?" I don't come right out and say it, but we both know exactly what I'm talking about.

"I can't believe you said that. *I can't believe you!*" she shouts.

She leaps at me exactly the way she did the other night, clawing at my face with her fingernails. I push her back and she falls onto the couch, but she's up again and at me in a heartbeat. This time I hurl her down when her nails rake my chest, then fall on top of her. I spin her over so she's face-down, straddle her, grab the sash from her robe that's lying on the arm of the couch in front of me, bring her hands behind her back roughly and start to tie her up. She's screaming bloody murder but I'm not going to take this tonight. And I'm going to finally find out what happened that night Clements ran her in, no matter what. I suddenly realize how crazy it's been driving me all these years. Maybe she wasn't just a stripper.

As I'm tying the knot, there's a pounding on the back porch door that almost shocks me out of my skin. It sounds like someone's trying to break down the door, it's so loud, and I swear my heart stops for a few beats. I freeze like an ice statue at Bruner's winter carnival as I stare into the darkness beyond the window over our couch. The curtains are pulled back so anyone out there could have looked in here and seen me tying Vivian up. Maybe some idiot who was trying to drive on 681 through the storm spun off the road and came up here looking for help. Christ, just my luck. I was just keeping her away from me, just trying to keep her from scratching me, but it might not look like that to someone outside. It might look like something very different.

I lunge for the wall and flip off the lights, then fumble for my sweatpants and T-shirt that are on a chair across the room from the couch. When I've got my clothes on I feel my way back to Vivian, who's gone quiet, and I quickly untie her.

"Get upstairs," I hiss over my shoulder as I head through the darkness toward the kitchen and the banging that keeps on going. "Go on!"

When she's gone I slink to the back porch window. I can actually feel the sound waves blasting into the room right beside me, see the door depress with each blow in the dull glow from the stove light. I pull the curtain back slightly with one finger, press my face to the glass, and flip on the outside lights. Christ, it's Bear. I'd recognize that hulking six-foot-seven-inch frame anywhere, even beneath his red down parka and orange ski mask.

I twist the knob open and pull back the door. "What the hell are you doing here?" He smiles at me from inside the mouth hole of the mask.

"Are you going to ask me in or what, Professor?"

"I ought to let you freeze," I mutter, moving out of the way so he can come in from the cold. "How'd you get here?" I ask, shivering as he moves past. But I know before he answers by the kind of boots he's wearing.

"I skied." He stamps his boots, then jabs a thumb over his shoulder. "They're beside the door."

"You skied seven miles?" Bear lives in one of those little boxes at the edge of town. *"In a blizzard?"* It seems strange to me that a guy who's become a dedicated couch potato would suddenly cross-country ski seven miles at night through this weather. "What's wrong with you?"

"I was bored," he answers cheerfully. "And lonely," he adds with a searing shot of honesty. He peels off his boots, then three layers of warmth—parka, wool vest, and sweater—and tosses everything to the floor. Now he's down to his turtleneck and his spare tire is obvious. "Seemed like the thing to do at the time," he says, heading through the kitchen. "The satellite was out."

I follow him into the living room. "Billy, I—"

"Hello, Viv," Bear says loudly. "How are you?"

"Fine, thanks."

She's coming downstairs in a short lace robe I didn't even know she had. This outfit's almost as revealing as the teddy she cooked in for me this morning and my mind boils with suspicion. She must have heard me say his name, so why would she come down looking like this? In fact, why would she come down looking like this no matter who was at the door? She ought to be wearing her old terry-cloth robe with the patches on the elbows, or maybe a pair of jeans and a baggy sweater.

Then she and Bear hug. She usually gives him a hug when he

comes over but she's not usually dressed like this and their hug doesn't usually last this long. Maybe it's my imagination, but it seems too passionate.

"You look great," he says to her with a big smile. "Really great."

She flashes me a coy look, then smiles back at him. "Want some coffee?"

"Sure. Love some."

I wake up and it's pitch black in our bedroom except for the clock on the nightstand that says 4:47 with its red LCD numbers. I slip my hand across the sheet to Vivian's side of the bed but it's empty. So I swing my feet to the floor, to the rug we bought cheap at a garage sale in Hayward when we first moved here. Then I move cautiously across the bedroom like a blind man, waving my hands out in front of me, searching for the chair I laid my clothes on when Vivian and I came to bed last night. Bear decided to spend the night after eating a whole sixteen-inch pizza by himself as Vivian and I sat at the kitchen table watching in awe, and it was still snowing when we all came upstairs.

I find the chair and my sweatpants and I step into them cautiously, careful not to fall. Then I steal to the door and down the short hallway to the guest room. In the moonlight coming through the window on this side of the house I can see that Bear isn't in bed, either. As I creep down the stairs I hear them moaning in the kitchen. I knew it, damn it, I've always known it. This is the reason Vivian doesn't mind Bear coming around. I can't believe I was so stupid.

I lean around the kitchen doorway and in the dim rays coming from the stove's light I see my wife and my best friend going at it like animals in the woods. She's bent over the kitchen table and I can't handle it. I've brought my gun downstairs with me and

I lift it slowly until it's pointed directly at Bear. "Get off her!" I shout.

His head snaps up and he stumbles backward against the refrigerator. "Paul!"

Vivian screams and puts her hands to her face.

My finger curls around the trigger and constricts. "You *bastard*."

"Paul, Paul, *Paul!*"

Darkness, nothing but darkness, then I have that strange lost feeling l always have when I'm coming out of a dream, especially a nightmare. That's followed by a few seconds of no-man's-land while I'm still not sure where I am or who I am, then a towering wave of relief surges through me when I realize what's really going on.

"Paul, Paul."

"I'm all right, I'm all right." I sit up and run a hand through my hair, feeling perspiration coursing down both sides of my face. "I'm okay," I say, more to myself than to Vivian.

"What were you dreaming about, honey?" she asks, taking my hand and rubbing it gently. "Tell me."

"Nothing," I mutter, getting up and moving to the window to look outside. The storm clouds are gone and they've been replaced by a clear sky filled with stars and a full moon. It's almost bright outside with so much snow on the ground and the heavens so clear. Jesus, I'm still shaking from the dream. "Nothing, honey," I whisper, easing back onto the bed. I feel her hands come around me and her lips on my back. It feels good. But I can't shake the nasty realization of how terrible it would have been to really find my wife and my best friend going at it. So I have the answer to whether I'd care if she was having an affair. I actually thought I'd be more indifferent, but I was dead wrong. "Sorry I woke you up."

"Don't worry about it," she whispers, pulling me even closer. "Come here and hold me."

When she's in my arms I nuzzle her ear, then kiss it softly. "I'm sorry for what happened tonight, I really am."

"I know you are. I'm sorry, too."

I gaze up at the ceiling through the darkness. I'm sorry, but I still wonder what happened that night Clements ran her in. It still bothers the hell out of me. But at this point, I guess I'll never know.

Vivian's fixing Bear and me a big breakfast of eggs, bacon, and hash browns in that same little robe she was wearing last night, and I'm pretty sure I catch Bear sneaking a long, lustful look at her. At my wife, for Christ sake. He's not a subtle guy to begin with, but I'm still pissed.

She sets my plate down and as the aroma reaches my nostrils I realize how hungry I am. I reach for the salt and pepper, and out of the corner of my eye watch her put Bear's plate down in front of him, then catch her fingers running gently along his broad shoulders as she heads back toward the stove to clean up.

The dream still haunts me. As do my suspicions.

14

I HAVE TWO pairs of extra-large Atlas snowshoes on the back porch and it's a good thing I do. Otherwise, Bear and I wouldn't be able to make it down my driveway to 681. The storm dropped almost three feet of snow on top of what was already on the ground, and, in places, it looks like it's ten feet deep out there because this morning's gusts blew up some monster drifts. Without the snowshoes we'd be up to our waists or higher in the white stuff with every step.

We're leaving the warmth for the frigid temperatures outside because I thought I heard something grind past the house a few minutes ago. Vivian and Bear think it was just my imagination, but I want to see if one of those big state plows that can go through almost anything actually made it to Bruner already. The snow only tapered off a few hours ago and the state boys usually take a day or two to get here after a storm blows through. That's with just half the accumulation this monster dumped on us.

The stone foundation of my house rises four feet from the ground so the first floor is elevated, but, when I try to push open the back porch door, it barely budges. I have to give it a firm shoulder-shove to wedge it open wide enough to get out. The stoop and the wooden stairs leading to the ground are completely covered and it's amazing, I've never seen anything like this. Not in Bruner, not anywhere. I step out into the frozen landscape gingerly, wary that, despite my specialized shoes, I might disappear into the snow as if it were quicksand. But I don't, I only sink a few inches.

When I'm almost to the end of the driveway I can tell we've gotten lucky, that a plow did go past. The towering snowbank it created is on my side of the road so it must have come from the south, because plows always push or throw snow to the right. Bear's already well behind me and struggling because, despite the snowshoes, the fresh powder rises to at least his knees with every step. He's just too heavy for them to support him the right way.

I don't wait for Bear to catch up. When I reach the snowbank I climb it, then slide down the other side to the road. A few inches of packed snow still cover the asphalt and the path the plow cleared isn't wide enough for two cars to pass each other. But that's fine, I'm not complaining. It's better than the alternative. It'll take Bear and me a few hours to shovel my driveway and clear the wall of snow created by the plow. But by nightfall I should be able to make it out of here. Then the Dakota County Police Force will be back in business, and I'll be able to get to the hospital and interview that girl I grabbed before she tumbled off the cliff. She could be the key to everything.

I glance over my shoulder and watch Bear tumble clumsily down the wall of snow to the road.

"Yeehaa!" he shouts as he rolls down the face of the slope onto the roadway. "Yeehaa!"

I chuckle. He's still got a lot of kid in him, but he's a hell of a man, too, a damn brave man. I just wish I hadn't had that dream about Vivian and him last night, or seen that touch she gave him at breakfast.

"One monster storm," he yells as he picks himself up and trudges toward me, brushing snow off.

"You ever seen anything like this before?" I ask.

"Not in a long time," he says when he makes it to where I'm standing. "I remember this one we had when I was a kid. It was a few years before you moved here. I was eleven or twelve and it was bad, real bad. I think it dumped more snow on us than this one but I could be wrong." He breaks into a wide grin. "Everything always seems bigger when you're a kid, you know? And sometimes your memory—"

Fifty yards down the road a huge branch halfway up a tall pine tree suddenly gives way, unable to hold up against the weight of all the snow. It tears off with a sharp crack, leaving a long yellow-orange scar on the trunk as it tumbles down through the lower branches and crashes onto the roadway. Right in the middle of what the plow cleared.

"We better move that thing," Bear says.

"Yeah, let's go."

"Hey, that's one hell of a game you and Vivian play," Bear says out of nowhere as we start for the fallen branch. "I was shocked, and I don't get shocked much anymore."

My head snaps around and I don't know what to say. I'm hoping to God he's talking about something other than what I think he is. "Game?" My heart's thumping in my throat so hard I can barely breathe. "What do you mean?"

"You know what I mean, Professor."

"No, I don't."

Bear chuckles and shakes his head. "I didn't think you had it in you. I didn't think you were into ropes and bondage and making a woman do those kinds of things, even your wife. And I've known you for what, twenty-five years?"

Christ, Bear saw it. And instantly my suspicions about Vivian and him jump to a new, even more dangerous level. Maybe that's why Vivian came at me so hard last night. Maybe she knew Bear was coming over and she wanted him to look through that window and see what I was doing to her. Maybe the whole thing was a setup. Maybe they had it all scripted out. I mean, why else would she start slinging the verbal jabs at me after such a great day? And why would Bear cross-country ski to our house in the middle of a blizzard? He doesn't have that kind of Lewis and Clark fire in his belly anymore. He used to, but his nose for adventure went the way of the couch.

"Billy," I begin as calmly as I can, "I think you—"

"Hey," he says, putting his hands up and out in front of him like he's really not trying to embarrass me. "It's none of my business."

I'm going to hear about this for a long time if I don't do something right away. Even worse, the town might hear about it. Sometimes when Bear drinks beer his mouth runs faster than the steelhead trout run up the Boulder to their spawning grounds in the spring. The last thing I need, the last thing any small-town sheriff needs, is a rumor like this one going around.

I shudder as the image of Mrs. Erickson's smug smile appears before me like the Cheshire Cat's when I think about how she might hear Bear blather on about this. I can't stand to think of how embarrassing it would be to have to explain what happened in my living room last night to the town council as they sit there with their arms crossed over their chests smoking cheap cigars in the storage room of Cam Riley's hardware store. As they nod to each other like they knew all the time that I wasn't the man for the job. Sorry that they'd relented and given me the job because they felt bad for an old high school football hero who was down on his luck a few years ago.

"What husbands and wives does in their own homes," Bear continues, chuckling, "is their business, not mine. As long as no one gets hurt and it's consensual. But I do think you ought to pull the curtains across the window next time you get the urge to tie Vivian up and to—"

"There's something I need to tell you," I interrupt, "something you need to know." The thought of Bear watching me tie Viv up is too much for me. I just can't deal with it. "Maggie came to me after church on Sunday and asked me to look for Karen." Bear stares at me blankly for a few seconds as his smirk evaporates, as the realization of what I'm saying sets in. I wonder if he understands what's going on here. I feel bad but I've got to change the subject. "She's worried."

"That note Karen left me on Christmas Eve said she didn't want anyone to come looking for her," Bear reminds me in a low voice. "*Anyone*," he repeats. "She was real clear about that."

"I know."

"Maggie's just butting in where she doesn't belong."

"She's worried about her sister, Billy. That's understandable."

Bear stares at me for a long time. "Well?"

"Well what?"

"Well, did you fill out the paperwork? Are you still going to try to find Karen even though she doesn't want you to?"

"I have to."

"No, you don't."

"Yes, I do. You know that."

"Damn it, Paul!"

Bear called me by my first name and that's a sure sign he's getting riled up. And when he gets riled up, it doesn't matter who you are. Best friend or sworn enemy, the situation's the same. You're in mortal danger. You either do what he says or you get out of his way. Those are your two options and there are no others. There's another outcome but it isn't your choice and I don't want to think about it. In hand-to-hand combat with Bear, I'd lose. Just about anyone would. And what you have to understand about Bear is that when he really comes unglued, when he gets past the riled-up stage, when you manage to finally knock down those load-bearing walls of his inner psyche—whether by chance or by choice—once he's got you down he won't let you up. He'll keep fighting until he's too tired to throw another punch or something he can't overpower finally gets in his way.

I saw it happen at a drive-in movie theater a few nights before I left for freshman football practice at the University of Minnesota all those years ago. Thank God there were nine of us to get in the way. The bastard Bear attacked is still eating through a straw, but nobody ever ratted on Bear for what happened. The guy deserved what he got, really deserved it. He was that bad a guy, and the rape of the nine-year-old mentally challenged girl he'd committed two days before was that terrible. The point is, even if what the guy had done wasn't that terrible, no one would have ever ratted on Bear. No one wanted to be on the end of what they saw him do that night and they figured if they ratted on him, they'd get it, too.

One of the few times Bear ever called me "Paul," one of the few times I saw him really riled up, was that night he grabbed my face mask in the huddle during the first quarter of our high school championship game in Madison. After that I did what he told me to do and I'm glad I did, for a lot of reasons. It all worked out for the best and I need to keep that in mind, for a lot of reasons.

"What's the problem?" I ask carefully. "Why are you so nervous?"

"I'm not nervous," Bear growls. "I just don't want to drag it all up again. I don't want to think about how she left me for another guy and what I really don't want to do is meet him. If you find her I don't want her feeling like it's okay to come back here to Bruner and bring him with her, even if it's only to visit. I don't want her thinking she can come walking down Main Street and run into me coming the other way and everything will be cool." Bear points a gloved finger at me. "Because it won't be cool. I'll beat the hell out of the guy, Paul."

"Easy, easy." I could see Bear going ballistic faced with that situation, in the middle of town with everyone watching. And the guy's face quickly turning into a bloody mess. "Is that really what you think happened? That she left you for another man, I mean?"

"I don't *think* that's what's happened," he answers emphatically. "I *know* that's what happened."

I never thought about the possibility that Karen left Bear for someone else. He never said anything about it, he never mentioned that another man was involved. Maggie hasn't either, not in the nearly two months it's been since Karen left. I never figured it happened like that because I figured I would have heard something about who the other guy was. Even though Mrs. Erickson does her best to carve me out of her web, I still hear about most everything that goes on in Dakota County. Maybe not as fast in some situations, but I get it.

I trust Bear like a brother but I'm still a little skeptical about his saying Karen left him for another guy because I can't figure out how she would have met anyone without my hearing. As far as I know there aren't any men missing from Dakota County or not being heard from lately. And believe me, any guy who'd taken Bear's girl wouldn't have stuck around Dakota County. He would have run as far away as he could as fast as he could.

"Was it someone from around here?" I ask.

"Nah. It was some guy from Duluth."

"How did he meet her?"

Bear looks down and kicks at the snow. "She was on a shopping trip over there."

That's strange. Bear and Karen didn't do much together, but he always made sure he went with her when she left Dakota County— which wasn't very often. He always said he wouldn't feel right if she was far away from home without him, and she was a real timid person on her own. So he'd complain the whole time they were gone— according to Karen—then ignore her again when they got home. But he rarely let her leave by herself, and it sounded like she always wanted him to go with her despite all his complaints. But maybe she couldn't take it anymore and she told him she was going to the store in Bruner one time when she actually went off to Duluth instead.

"She left me," Bear continues. "I mean she walked out on me on Christmas Eve for another man. How awful is that?" He grimaces and blinks several times quickly. "I never felt so alone in all my life as that morning," he whispers. "It's the first time I ever, the first time, well . . ." His voice trails off.

"The first time you ever what, Billy?"

"Nothing."

"Come on, tell me."

"Don't say anything to anybody. Okay, Professor?"

He's calling me Professor again. That's good. "I won't." He knows I won't tell a soul no matter what it is he's about to say and he knows he didn't have to ask me not to. So now I know this is going to be important, really important. I just hope it's not what I think it is. Because once someone starts taking mental trips down that road, it's pretty likely that one day they won't come back. I should know. "You didn't even have to say anything."

"I guess not. I mean, I *know* not."

I wait a few seconds. "So?"

"So after I wake up on Christmas and read Karen's note, I look over at the bookcase, at the top shelf." His voice is hushed. "That's where I keep my gun when I'm home, before I take it with me into the bedroom at night." Bear swallows hard and his eyes mist up. "You know?"

Like I said, the only other time I've seen Bear cry was at Gus and Trudy's funeral, not that it's the Mississippi River coursing down his cheeks right now. It isn't, it's barely a stream. It's just that he doesn't cry. He wouldn't even cry when he'd tell me what it was like to have his father beat him all the time as a kid. That's why the stream seems more like a torrent. "Yeah, I know." That's where Bear's gun has been whenever I've been to his house—on the top shelf of the bookcase in its holster.

"So I put Karen's note down, I get up out of my chair, I get my gun, and I look at it for a long time. I just stare at it as I keep turning it over and over in my hands. I think about how Karen and me had some pretty good times and how this must be some kind of nightmare I'm having. I can't understand how she could possibly leave me like this."

"You should have called me, Billy. I should have been there to—"

"Then I chambered the first round." He raises his right hand, extends his index finger, and puts the tip of it to his head. "And I put the gun to my head."

I figured this was coming. But now that Bear's actually said it, the image of his brain splattered across the bookcase and the wall becomes horribly clear in my mind. It hits me almost as hard as the sight of Cindy actually lying on the floor in her pool of blood. "You should have called me, Billy. You should have called me right away. I would have been to your house in ten minutes."

"I didn't want to bother you. It was Christmas."

"That's ridiculous. You've always been there for me. It's the least I could have done."

Bear brings his hand down from the side of his head and his eyes flash. "Here's the thing, Professor," he says, gazing at me intently. "Mrs. Erickson is telling some people around town that Darrow Clements was in Bruner to help Lew Prescott prove you killed Cindy. That Clements is gonna be back to town over and over until he wears you down enough to get a confession out of you. She isn't blaring it out there over her loudspeaker like she usually does. She's just dropping the word to a couple of people she thinks won't let it out that she's behind the rumor."

Like I said, Bear's a pretty smart guy. He knew I started the Maggie-looking-for-Karen thing as a way to distract him, as a way to turn the conversation away from how he'd seen what I was doing to Vivian through the window. So he took the long way around the barn to return fire, to let me know he knew what I was doing and to shift the focus back on me. It was the long way around it all right, but it certainly was effective. There's always been a simmering unease between us about what really happened to Karen, but I've never investigated the incident as diligently as I should have. Like I said before, I've stayed awake nights, lots of nights, staring up at the bedroom ceiling thinking about it. Listening to Vivian's deep breathing as she slept, wondering if I'd ever come to grips with what I haven't done. With what I could still do.

The problem is that Bear saved my life—twice. The first time was when we were kids. It was that summer after my father and I built *Intrepid* and I was canoeing the Falls. It was that summer I was sixteen and I wasn't alone when the canoe went over—which was another reason I didn't tell my father what had happened, because he would have been very angry that I had someone else in the canoe without telling him. He was damn strict about that. I made a bad choice on which current to follow into one of the toughest rapids, and boom, before I knew it I went over the gunnels, into the white-water. So did my passenger.

Which was Bear. He was in the front of the canoe and he went over, too. It was stupid for us to be going through the Falls in the first place, doubly stupid because we each weighed so much, and triply stupid for Bear to be in front. The bigger person should always sit in the back of a canoe. But I had to be in back, I had to be the one steering and in control because my ego told me I did. I told Bear it was because my father had warned me not to let anyone else steer but that wasn't true. It was just my ego telling me I was the better paddler and it was my canoe. I almost died in those rapids with my leg wedged beneath that rock, but Bear got me out with a Herculean heave.

The second time Bear saved my life was three years ago. I was in the Kro-Bar by myself breaking up a fight late one Saturday night and Bear shot a guy who was just about to shoot me. He got to the

Kro-Bar in the nick of time and blew the guy's knee apart with a well-aimed bullet just before the guy pulled his trigger.

So that's two times Bear's saved my life and the score's two-to-nothing. I've never returned either favor. Not that I've ever had the opportunity to, but the bottom line is this: I owe him. Man, do I owe him. If you've never been trapped underwater with about three seconds to go before your body takes that first uncontrollable gulp, if you've never felt that incredible panic, you can't understand how much I owe him. Or if you've never had an angry drunk aim a gun at you. And therein lies my dilemma.

I don't really believe Bear did anything to Karen. It's just that I haven't followed up the way I should have because of that sliver of a chance that there was foul play and Bear was somehow involved or knows more about what happened than he's ever let on. He's my best friend and he saved my life twice. How could I ever do something that might land him behind bars for the rest of his life? On the other hand, how can I not do my job?

"Mrs. Erickson's telling those same people," Bear continues, "that you went out to the Prescott estate at least twice on the day of Cindy's murder. Once in the morning after Cindy called you when we were out on the trail to Silver Wolf Rapids, then again after lunch. But she's telling people Cindy didn't call you that second time. That you went out there on your own the second time and there's lots of unanswered questions about why you went and what you did while you were out there."

I stare at Bear for a long time, trying to figure out how Mrs. Erickson's getting her information. It must be coming from Lew Prescott or Darrow Clements. It wouldn't surprise me if Prescott or Clements recruited Mrs. Erickson to help them in this matter, but it could be coming from someone else, too.

"Answer one question for me, Billy."

He nods.

15

AFTER BEAR ANSWERED that question I asked him, I told him I needed some time to myself, some time to think. Then I told him to get back to the house and start shoveling my driveway. I was demanding about it, too. I said I wanted to see a lot of progress by the time I got home, and I said it in a tone that couldn't be taken as anything but a boss giving orders to a subordinate, certainly not a friend talking to a friend. He agreed to get started right away and that he understood about me needing time to myself. He also swore he'd never tell anyone what he saw through my living room window last night.

I believe him; I believe he'll never tell a soul what he saw, despite my concern about what could happen when he gets drunk. What bothers me is that I think I know *why* he's willing to keep my secret. And *why* he didn't seem put out at having to shovel my driveway by himself on my orders. He didn't even give me that exaggerated exhalation and glance to the sky he usually does when he feels like I'm being a jerk. Which was a warning signal about as subtle as a freight train whistle at a crossing that something strange is going on.

I hope Bear's being so easy to deal with because of everything we've been through together, because we're best friends, and because he understands that a sheriff needs to get to his precinct as soon as possible after a storm like this. But there's this nagging voice in the back of my head that's telling me he's willing to maintain his silence and start shoveling the driveway alone at my specific orders for another, darker reason. A voice that's telling me we executed a fragile but crucial treaty before we lugged that branch off the road, dotting the I's and crossing the T's of our unwritten armistice without any obvious negotiation. I'm concerned that he was so quick to agree to the treaty because he assumes I no longer care how he saved my life twice, because he's worried that my dedication to duty might override my mortal loyalty. So he took out an insurance policy and he'll never say anything as long as the premiums are paid.

I've always wondered if Bear had something to do with Karen's disappearance. I've never said anything that would even subtly suggest a whiff of my suspicion to him or anyone else around here, but Bear knew where I was headed when I told him about Maggie wanting to follow up on Karen's disappearance. He knew I could have stopped Maggie dead in her tracks as soon as she brought up the search if I'd chosen to. He knew I could have told her right then and there in a firm voice that it was a waste of time because there wasn't anything to investigate, given the note Karen left for Bear on Christmas Eve. And that would have been that.

After all, who's Maggie going to complain to? Her parents are lying side by side six feet down in the frozen Wisconsin ground, her sister's disappeared, and if there's one thing most Dakota County residents don't want to do it's get sideways with the sheriff's office. Especially when a woman's just been murdered in her home a few miles from town and Mrs. Erickson's telling anyone who'll listen that the victim had multiple pentagrams carved in her nearly decapitated body. Getting sideways with us has nothing to do with me personally. The citizens don't want to be at odds with the sheriff's office in general because it's simply not smart. A police force has too many ways to hassle or not help troublemakers. Throw on top of all that the fact that Maggie's a meek soul to begin with and it's game over.

I could have roadblocked Maggie easily, but I didn't. And that one simple fact has Bear as nervous as a coyote at a wolf kill.

I'm sure he's always suspected that I haven't completely closed the book on Karen's disappearance. I'm sure the dark recesses of his active imagination wonder if I think he put the barrel of his Dakota County pistol to her head—literally—and forced her to write that note on Christmas Eve telling him she didn't want to be found, then did away with her in some cold-blooded way because he was drunk and in that state he couldn't take her constant nagging and bitching and the awful arguments that followed anymore. But our interaction of an hour ago beside that fallen branch must have absolutely confirmed any suspicion he had.

I'm not sure it's ever crossed Bear's mind before today that I might also suspect him of having something to do with Gus and Trudy's deaths, with their hurtling into that grove of pine trees at sixty miles an hour because they were suspicious of his doing something to their daughter, too, but I bet he's thinking about it now. I bet his brain's spinning with possibilities and suspicions as he hurls shovelful after shovelful of fresh powder from my driveway. Maybe all that's the real reason he's willing to keep my secret. Maybe he figures if he promises to keep his mouth shut about last night and not tell anyone else what his answer to my question of a little while ago was, I'll just go through the motions with Maggie, that I won't be diligent about my search for Karen because it's a search that could end up very close to home—his home.

Vivian could tell people what I did to her last night, but no one would ever believe her, not for a second. Like they wouldn't believe that I put my gun to her head the night I saved Cindy from Caleb Jenkins and his crew on 681. But if Bear backed up her story in front of the town council and added a few juicy spitballs of exaggeration to it, I'd be in trouble, real trouble. I wouldn't be sheriff for long. In fact, I'd probably be ordered to give up my badge and gun on the spot.

In turn, I could open the spigot about Karen and her parents, about Bear's involvement in their deaths.

So what we have here is an old-fashioned game of chicken— except we aren't playing for some stupid car title. The stakes are much higher.

Bear knows full well that if I'm fired as sheriff of Dakota County I don't have anywhere else to go, not as a cop, anyway. We talk about it every once in a while, usually after he's been drinking. He knows I'm at the last station stop on the law enforcement line. He knows I really would have to flip burgers to earn a living after that and I probably wouldn't even be able to do it in Bruner. That I might end up doing exactly what I'm trying desperately to avoid: following my father's footsteps out of this world by putting a bullet through my head.

At least I won't do it in front of my son the way my father did.

Experienced people always warn friends never to go into business together, but I didn't understand why they did it so adamantly— until a few minutes ago, until I suddenly found myself up to my neck in alligators with my best friend. But now I get it, God, do I get it.

I slog through the trees, thinking about Bear and Karen as I check the branches above me every so often for the avalanche that could come tumbling down on me at any moment. Karen was a tough woman to get along with. As nice as Maggie is, Karen was a constant whiner and sometimes she was worse than that. I saw a lot of that side of her during the last couple of years. For a while she kept up that fake, polite facade when I was at their house. But then one day I heard the beast inside her roar when she didn't know I was in the kitchen making quick work of a turkey leg I'd lifted from their refrigerator. Bear yelled at her that I was in the house and she quieted right down. But after that she didn't hold back when she got mad and I was around.

Not that Bear sported a halo in their marriage, either—far from it. I don't think he always asked for sex, I don't think it was always a mutual roll in the hay for those two, especially on cold winter nights after he got into the vodka. I never saw any marks on her, but that doesn't mean things were always consensual.

I lean against a tree, breathing hard. Walking in snowshoes is tough. The snow isn't as deep here as it is on my driveway, because the canopy of needles arching cathedral-like over my head has temporarily intercepted some of the blizzard. But I still sink in a few inches with each step, and going up and down these hills has me huffing and puffing.

I push off the tree and start plodding through the woods again, wondering what's going on with my driveway. Perhaps there was another, darker reason Bear was so quick to head home. Maybe instead of clearing my driveway he and Vivian are going at it the way she and I did yesterday. Well, I ought to be able to tell what's happened by how much of the driveway has—or hasn't—been cleared when I get home.

Then there's that video camera I set up in the bedroom closet. I'm not stupid and I'd rather be paranoid than naive, even if my suspicions involve my best friend and my wife.

"Hi."

I spin around, shocked by the sound of a voice from nowhere. I'm forced to grab a low-hanging branch to keep my balance when my snowshoes get crossed, I'm so surprised. "Jesus," I gasp when I recognize the face, "what are you doing out here?"

I've just reached the edge of a clearing that's bathed in sunlight and Sara is standing twenty feet away. My first instinct is that she's been following me, but then I spot her tracks coming from the other side of the clearing. Along with a tan parka and snow pants, she's wearing snowshoes as well, but hers look like something the first pair ever made probably looked like. In fact, they look like antique tennis racquets, catgut strings and all. They wouldn't support me for a second, but Sara doesn't weigh much. At five-seven she's tall and wispy thin, unlike her Chippewa ancestors. Maybe she's not as pure as she claims to be.

She isn't wearing a hat and her long, jet-black hair is perched on the back of her head in a wild bun. She looks very pretty, even more so than usual. Exotic, too, which I've always found fascinating. Of course, I've never been subjected to that crazy, wolverine temper of hers. I've only heard about it. Experiencing that kind of rage can change the way a man looks at a woman. It's certainly changed the way I look at Vivian. And Vivian just talks a big game when it really comes down to it. Sara actually goes for it—hard.

"What are you doing out here?" My heart's still thumping from the shock of hearing her voice.

"It seemed like a nice morning to take a walk in the woods. I like being out here after a big storm." She hesitates. "And Ike was being a jerk."

"What do you mean?" I ask quickly, slipping into what the locals call my "precinct tone."

She shakes her head and that bun of long, silky, jet-black hair tumbles down her back like the frothy water of the Boulder River tumbles down a rocky set of rapids. The move's enough to take a man's breath away and I'm sure it has. More than once, because it just stole mine.

"It's nothing like that, Sheriff," she assures me, "but thanks for asking. So, what are *you* doing out here?"

"I don't know," I answer lamely. "I really don't."

"I figured things in your house had gotten better," Sara says, "after what happened to Cindy Harrison the other day."

I put up one hand. "I can't talk about—"

"I figured you and Vivian would have spent yesterday and today rechristening every room in the house," she interrupts as she cuts the distance between us in half with a few agile steps on her snow-shoes. "Frankly, it surprises me that you're out here in the middle of the woods when there's a willing woman at home and three feet of new snow on the ground."

I grin self-consciously. I can't help it. Ever since I moved back here four years ago Sara and I have had this sexual tension shim-mering between us like the air above a blistering-hot pavement shimmers on a summer day. I've known enough women to recog-nize it's there for her, too. It's not just me feeling it. "You would think that, wouldn't you?"

Sara takes two more steps toward me. Now the tips of our snow-shoes are touching. "Am I wrong?"

"Well, I—"

"Maybe Vivian's not so willing."

"Oh, she's willing."

"Or is she still as cold as ever? Even with her competition dead." Sara's eyes flash. "At least, the woman she *thinks* was her competition."

This is crazy. "Sara—"

"Or maybe you're tired of Vivian," Sara keeps going, "maybe you need someone else, someone more exciting."

Despite a flash of guilt, the image of Sara and me entwined in a naked embrace races through my mind. It's a mesmerizing image, and we stare at each other for what seems like forever. Finally I manage to push my pesky male curiosity to the side.

"This is a long way for you to walk," I finally say.

"Does it make you uncomfortable to talk about sex with an-other woman?" she asks slyly.

I can't tell if Sara means talking about sex in a general way with a woman other than my wife, or actually having sex with another woman. That male curiosity's back, but still I manage to resist it. "My house is seven miles from town," I say, ignoring her right back.

Now I've sparked her interest in something else, I can tell. She likes distances and topography. She always has.

"So what?"

"Seven miles is a long way to walk." I point down at her snow-shoes. "Especially in those."

"What makes you think we're seven miles from town?"

"I've been going east since I left my house, straight away from 681, and Bruner's seven miles from my house." I shrug. "I'm no ge-ometry whiz, but, hey, maybe that makes us even farther than seven miles from town."

Sara laughs. "You've been going mostly north since you left your house, Sheriff." She points to her right. "Six-eighty-one's not far that way. We're actually about halfway between your house and town."

I don't argue because I'm sure she's right. She knows these woods a lot better than I do. I meant to go straight back into the woods from 681, I meant to go east. But, as I've been walking, whenever I haven't been sure of which side of a tree to take, I've always gone left of it because that seemed like the safest thing to do. It seemed like the best way to make sure I didn't get too lost.

"It's easy to get turned around out here, especially with all this snow." She laughs again. "Especially for you palefaces."

I don't know about everybody else but she's right about this pale-face. Without a trail it's slip-slide easy for me to get turned around out here. Back when we were kids, Bear and I got lost one summer for several days. Ben Sanderson, the Bruner sheriff back then, had to call in the state boys with their K-9 teams and choppers. They finally found us five miles northeast of Hayward, but it wasn't like we were hurting. Bear shot a deer on the third morning out, then quartered it, started a fire, and cooked it. It was delicious and we were actually surviving pretty well when the troopers found us.

In fact, I'm not sure Bear was ever really lost. Like Sara, he knows these woods damn well, and it's occurred to me over the years that he might have been just having a good time. Maybe he didn't want to go home because being lost was a lot better than being beaten by his dad. Maybe he felt more lost at home than he did in the woods. Maybe he liked seeing me scared, too. At that age guys like to see other guys scared, even their best friend.

"Is this Lewis Prescott's land?" I ask. The question's out of left field but I can't think of anything else to say. Sara's looking at me all doe-eyed, like she wants something to happen. I'm trying to think of anything to keep the conversation going. "I heard he's the biggest landowner in Dakota County."

"He is," she confirms, "other than the Feds," she adds with a curl of her upper lip, like she's just sucked on a lemon wedge. "They've stolen a lot more of my forest than Lew Prescott has."

That was stupid of me. She hates the federal government very much. I should have remembered that and anticipated how my question would lead her right to them. Sometimes I can be pretty insensitive. I don't mean to be but I can. But then Sara can turn almost any conversation into a bash on Washington.

"Of course," she keeps going, "that's where you and I have a major difference of opinion. You probably think Lewis Prescott's a bigger jerk than the Feds by a long shot."

"Why do you say that?"

"Come on, Sheriff. Everybody knows how you felt about Cindy, and how her father feels about you."

"Yeah, well, I—"

"I want to show you something," she interrupts. She points east, the way I had originally meant to go. "It's something you need to see."

"What is it?"

"Just trust me."

"Sara, I don't want to—"

"*Trust me.*"

"How far is it?"

"We've got plenty of time to get there and back before dark."

That dream I had last night about Bear and Vivian flickers through my mind again. Maybe it was actually a premonition and not a dream. Maybe I should turn around and get back to my house to protect what's mine. Or maybe it's too late and I should go with Sara.

"Let's go." Sara moves beside me and touches her glove to mine. "Come on."

I gaze into her mahogany eyes with the gold flecks, hoping to decode the degree of her desire and therefore the truth of her intent. Finally, I nod. "Okay, but this better be good."

With Sara in the lead, we hug the edge of the clearing for a short distance, then turn into the woods going east. At least, that's the direction she tells me we're going. I wouldn't know at this point because even when we can see it, the sun's in the middle of its arc across the sky. Without being able to use it as an indicator I've got no idea where we are or which way we're going. I think Sara senses that I'm lost and it wouldn't surprise me if she likes that. The same way Bear probably did all those years ago.

We climb up and down four ridges and it's a lot of work. At least, it is for me. Near the top of the fifth ridge she stops, turns around, and puts a finger to her lips. "Stay here and be quiet. I'll be right back."

She'll get no argument from me. I was about to tell her I needed a break anyway, and I'm glad I didn't have to so I can save a little of my male pride. I nod, then glance around uneasily as she moves off. I start feeling like Custer must have felt on that Montana hillside. Why do I need to be quiet?

Sara vanishes among the trees at the crest of the ridge, then reappears a few minutes later. "Come on," she calls in a low voice, waving for me to come up. "Hurry up."

I expect her to be smirking at how I'm plodding up the slope, but she isn't. Her expression's grave and her eyes keep darting around. "What's the matter?"

"Just come on."

We retrace her steps of a few minutes ago, grabbing low branches to keep from falling as we head down the other side of the hill and the going gets treacherous. As I'm about to ask her again what this is all about, I spot something through the pines at the base of the slope. It's a log cabin, and if I wasn't looking for something to begin with, I doubt I would have noticed it. One side of it is tucked into a cut in the hillside and it's set in amongst some big trees. I assume it's a hunting cabin, but it's awfully big to be that. Hunting cabins in these woods are usually like ice-fishing houses on the lakes, only large enough to squeeze a few people and a stove inside. Mostly just places to get warm and cook something. This place looks like it might be big enough to have a couple of rooms.

"Is that what you brought me out here to see?"

"Yes."

"What's so special about it?"

"I'm pretty sure this is federal land, not Prescott's," she says, not answering my question. "Prescott doesn't own that much land on this side of 681. Most of his is over on the west side of the road, across the river and back behind the other estates." She points at the cabin. "And that isn't a Forest Service building."

"How do you know?" The Feds never tell me what they're doing in my woods. Hell, they rarely tell the state so why would they tell me?

"There'd be something on it identifying it as federal government property," she answers. "They tag everything with some sort of ID number. I looked all around the last time I was out here, but I didn't find anything."

She's right about that. The Feds usually do tag their assets with ID numbers no matter what they are. I guess that directive comes from the General Accountability Office. "Big deal. People build hunting cabins all over these woods without getting the landowner's okay."

People up here in the north-country figure it's their God-given right to hunt or fish wherever they want to no matter whose land or water it is. The Gorges is the only place in Dakota County where I'm able to really enforce no-trespassing laws, and that's only because the River Families can snap pictures from up on the bluffs and email them to the precinct. And because there's no place for the offender to take his canoe out of the water other than the Route 7 bridge where we can lie in wait.

"You know that," I add.

"But as big as this one?" she asks as we near the place. "I don't think so."

"It is bigger than the ones I usually see, I'll give you that. But I still don't get why I slogged all the way out here."

She's quiet for a few moments, then she points at the cabin again. "There were bones on the ground last time I was out here and they were all over the place. Mostly on the other side of the cabin from here where there's a clearing. You'll see when we get down there. And, yeah, they were animal bones. And, no, I didn't see anything human," she says, anticipating what I'm thinking. "But they were everywhere. Some of them were chopped up and burned bad and it was crazy, I'll tell you. You won't be able to see them now because of the new snow, but they're all around. I wasn't out here that long ago, either. A month maybe, that's all." She hesitates. "Some of them were on top of the snow that was here then. On top of the snow," she repeats. "That's what made me think it wasn't that long ago when the bones were burned. It wasn't last summer or anything."

As she's talking I get this peculiar feeling, and the tiny hairs on the back of my neck stand straight up against the inside of my parka collar. The sensation sends a chill streaking up my spine and I grab Sara's arm and pull her to a stop. We stand there for a few seconds, frozen in our tracks, holding our breath. Then there's a loud rustling and a sharp crack from above and Sara thrusts her arms around my neck. My eyes snap to the noises, over her left shoulder, just as a ton of snow and a large branch tumble to the ground only a few feet in front of us, causing a blast of cold air to rush past and dust us with powder. Vivian's ESP must be rubbing off on me.

Sara heaves an audible sigh of relief but doesn't pull back right away. Instead, she hesitates and stares up into my eyes as the pleasant, flowery scent of her shampoo drifts to my nostrils. Finally, she slides her gloves from around my neck and down the front of my jacket, slowly backs her snowshoes off mine and shakes the dusting of snow from her hair and shoulders.

Sara's a strong woman. I can't imagine much scares her, so the way she threw her arms around me and grabbed me so tightly seems odd. I mean, the avalanche took me by surprise, too, but her reaction seemed overdone. "Did you go inside the last time you were here?" I ask.

"No. I saw the bones and I got out of here fast."

"Okay, let's go."

When we reach the cabin I check around for tracks, but, other than ours, there aren't any. I didn't expect to find any, since the blizzard only ended twelve hours ago and this place is deep in the woods. But after everything that's happened in the last few days I'm taking no chances. There aren't any windows, so I can't see if anyone's inside, and the only door to the place is locked tight, though it doesn't feel like it would be hard to bust it down when I lean against it.

When I turn away from the entrance I notice what looks like a path going off into the woods, basically following the valley floor. It's clear that the lower limbs up to about seven feet off the ground have been chopped off leading away from the place. Also, as Sara described, an area on the other side of the cabin is clear of trees. It's pretty sizable and it seems logical to assume that the trees cleared from this area were used to build the cabin. As I gaze up, I notice that the branches of the trees at the edge of the clearing look charred. The same way the branches above the smoldering bonfire off the trail to Silver Wolf Rapids did when Bear and I went out there to check on Mrs. Erickson's tip. I don't feel a hundred percent positive about what I'm about to do. This is someone's private property, and I really don't have reasonable cause to break in. But sometimes you have to go with your instincts, and since I'm here, I figure it might be a good idea to poke around inside just to see what's what.

"The bones were mostly over there, right?" I ask, pointing toward the clearing. Sara doesn't answer and I glance over at her. She's ten feet away and she's staring in the direction of the path. "What's the matter?"

"I thought I heard something," she whispers.

I watch her for a few seconds, conscious of staying calm while I process what's happening, then I shift my gaze to the trailhead. I brought my gun. I never go anywhere without it. Bear had his gun on this morning, too. I saw it hanging from his shoulder holster before he put on his parka. He never goes anywhere without his, either. That's just the way it goes up here. On duty or off you carry it because you never know.

"What is it?"

"I don't know, but it's about a hundred yards out that way." She points slightly left of the trailhead. "And it's big."

Sara's a hell of a hunting guide, as anyone around here will tell you, and she works for the River Families in the fall during deer season. Like most rich people, the River Families seem to be obsessed with trophies, and for a decent day's pay she'll track down big whitetail bucks. I know Bill Campbell and Lew Prescott used her this past autumn and both parties bagged big bucks that were nearly Dakota County records. The deer up here have gotten pretty wily since the comeback of the wolf, but Sara's parties always end up satisfied while most of the other guides have had a tough go of it with their clients over the last few seasons. So when Sara says she hears something big moving out in the woods, I ought to listen.

We stand still for thirty seconds, but I don't hear anything. As my eyes flicker back and forth between her and the direction in which she's looking, I think about how I figured she'd be involved with any cult that was operating in Dakota County. But she's the one who brought me out here, so that involvement seems unlikely now. Even if she's decided she no longer wants to be in the cult, it's crazy to think she'd rat on them after what happened to Cindy Prescott and that poor girl who almost fell off the cliff. It's not like Sara's got anywhere to go. She's lived all her life in Dakota County, and as far as I know, she's got no relatives anywhere else. And as mean as I've heard she can be, she'd be no match for whoever killed Cindy. I can say that with certainty after having seen the condition Cindy's body was in at the estate.

"We should get out of here," she whispers.

"I don't hear anything."

She's still staring in the direction she pointed a few moments ago. "Something's out there. I know it."

"It's probably just an animal."

She takes two steps toward me, still gazing at the trailhead. "I've got a bad feeling, Sheriff."

"Well, I'm going inside."

Her eyes race to mine. *"What?"*

I nod at the door. "I'm going in. I didn't come all the way out here not to take a look inside. Especially if these people are burning animals like you said. Especially with the way Cindy was—" I interrupt myself in the nick of time. That was almost a big mistake. If I'd confirmed the ritual way in which Cindy was killed, Sara might have sent the information out into the county almost as quickly and indiscriminately as Mrs. Erickson would. Sara isn't usually much of a talker, but this would be *huge* news in Bruner, and that would make it tough for even her to resist talking. People are people no matter who their ancestors are. Folks in Dakota County like to hear what Mrs. Erickson has to say, but most of them don't really listen to her. With me as the source the news would be taken very differently.

"The way Cindy was *what*, Sheriff?"

Details of the murder will get out soon enough, but I want to keep them under wraps as long as I can. "Nothing."

"Sheriff?"

"I can't say anything," I snap as I turn back to the door, squat, and grab the handle. "I already told you that."

"Sheriff!"

"No! That's the end of it."

I push the door a few times, but the handle's only a foot above the snow, so it's tough to get much leverage. I need to hit it as close to the lock as possible with as much force as I can if I'm going to get in. So I spend several minutes clearing a space in front of the door. All the while Sara gazes into the woods.

It doesn't take long to get the snow out of the way. I grab the handle, coil myself up, and slam my side against the wood. The door doesn't give way completely on my first try, but almost. Another shoulder and a hip to it and the lock busts, the door swings back on its shiny new hinges, and I stumble inside, falling to my hands and knees on the dirt floor. After I struggle back to my feet and my eyes adjust to the dim light, a chill snakes up my spine. Like that one did a few minutes ago a split second before the snow cascaded down in front of Sara and me. Except that this one is ten times as powerful and my body actually contorts involuntarily when the spark reaches the base of my neck.

Dark curtains cover the walls; animal skulls—mostly rams and goats—hang suspended from the ceiling; half-burned unlit candles line the walls on the dirt floor, and there is what appears to be an altar at the far end of the room in front of several rows of crude pews. As I come before the altar I see that it's covered with a dark purple cloth. On the cloth are two crossed, gleaming sabers with what look like ivory handles; a human skull with a black pentagram painted on the forehead with one of its points going straight down toward the nose; a pentagram with one point going straight down knitted into the cloth at the skull's chin; two tall white candles rising from two ornate silver candle holders; and a blood-stained knife lying beneath the pentagram.

My pulse takes another jolt at the sight of the knife. It's a steak knife with a black handle and a serrated tip. It looks exactly like the one I found up on the trail to Silver Wolf Rapids—and exactly like the two that are missing from my kitchen drawer.

"Sheriff Summers!"

I whip around, shocked by Sara's voice for the second time today. "*Jesus*, what is it?" She's standing in the entrance.

"Let's get out of—" She stops herself as she glances around the room. "What is this place?" She catches her breath. "My God, it's the cult," she blurts out, answering her own question in a hushed voice. "This must be where they get together. It's probably their headquarters or something."

There's nothing I can say, no way I can protest anymore. The weight of the evidence is too great. "You can't say anything to anyone about this, Sara," I warn her. "You understand?"

But before she answers she shrieks and turns away to look outside.

Just as I hear someone moan softly. At least, I think I did. It sounded as if it was coming from behind the altar, and I hustle around it as fast as I can on my snowshoes. Behind it there's a door, and I unzip my parka, yank my gun out, and move to the left side of the door, barrel pointed at the ceiling. I glance back at the entrance but Sara's gone.

I hesitate beside the door, straining to hear anything from behind it, staring at the empty entrance, straining to hear anything from outside. But I don't, I don't hear a thing except the sound of my own shallow breathing. I reach for the knob with my left hand and turn it slowly, then push the door open, bring the gun down in front of me, and back off a step.

When there's no reaction from within I lean slowly around the side of the doorway. It's tough to see much in the dim light but I can tell this is a much smaller room than the main room. I have a tiny, four-inch silver flashlight attached to my holster and I pull it out quickly, flip it on, and scan the room. The beam shakes in front of me as I focus on certain objects. Past the doorway two chests are stacked one on top of the other directly in front of me against the far wall, and to the right there's what looks like a curtain spanning the width of the narrow room. But when I look at it more closely I see that it's not a curtain. It's actually a row of about ten black robes hanging from a silver rod, and three of the robes have purple stripes across the upper arms.

Then I hear the moan again. It's coming from the left and it's louder this time. I whip the flashlight beam around and it illuminates a sack on the floor. I rush to the sack, kneel, lay the gun beside me on the dirt, throw off my gloves, and start fighting the knot of the drawstring that's keeping it tightly closed. Finally, I get the knot undone, pull open the string, and yank the sack back. Inside is a hog-tied young boy clad in just a dirty white T-shirt and jockey shorts. He can't be more than seven years old. His eyes are closed and the skin of his arm feels like ice. He's barely alive. I don't need a doctor to tell me that.

There's a noise behind me and I grab my gun, hustle to the left side of the door—so I can fire more easily with my right hand—and peer out into the main room. Two figures stand just inside the entrance. I can't make out their faces and I can't tell if they're armed.

"Who's there?" one of them yells.

"Police!" I yell back. "Put your hands up!"

They duck down and suddenly there's a hail of bullets coming at me. They're medium caliber, probably 9mm like mine, judging by the sounds they make as they smack nastily into the wood all around me and plow into the chests against the far wall. I've got another clip in my pocket so I respond heavy with five shots of my own as I hold just my hand around the doorway.

"I'm hit, I'm hit!" I hear somebody scream. "Jeeesus Christ! I took one in the shoulder. God, it hurts like—"

What sounds like a cannon shot drowns out the guy's voice. It had to have come from a shotgun, probably a twelve gauge because of how loud the report was and because the shell blew a hole in one of the chests the size of a beach ball. Two more blasts blow into the small room in rapid succession and one of them disintegrates part of the door frame above me on its way through. Whoever's shooting must have an over-and-under model, so he's probably got two more rounds in the gun. I hunch beside the door as kindling sprinkles down on me like ticker tape in one of those old newsreel parades. I stick my hand around the doorway and blow five more shots into the altar room, then it's quiet after the sounds of my shots fade away. I lean hesitantly around the side of the doorway and strain to hear anything. I can't let them sneak up close, then rush me. That would be the end of Sheriff Paul Summers. At least I wouldn't have to worry about following in my father's footsteps.

I lean a little farther out, exposing myself to gunfire, searching the makeshift pews in front of me for any movement, but I don't see anything. I've got four shots left, and I reach into my snow pants pocket for the spare clip, quickly lean far enough out of the room to check left and right outside the door, see no one, then empty what's left of the clip in the gun into the altar in case one of the men managed to crawl up behind it. But there's no indication that anyone's on the other side of the altar and I have no doubt that my bullets went straight through it. If there'd been someone behind it, I'd have hit him.

I take a deep breath, unclasp my snowshoes, make it to my feet, and move into the main room. It's empty. It's not like there's anyplace to hide in here, and now that I'm in the room I can see everything pretty clearly in the light from the entrance. I'd see someone lying in the pew area or standing behind the curtains covering the walls. I steal quickly to the front door and, again, flatten myself against the wall to the left of the doorway. After a few seconds I lean around the side, squint, and peer outside. In the snow I see two sets of tracks coming to the front door directly from the trailhead, then two sets leading away. And there are drops of red alongside the footprints—what I assume is blood.

I stare at the trailhead for thirty seconds, quickly going through my options. I have to get this boy out of here as fast as possible. He's in bad shape. But I don't want to stumble into an ambush, either. It looks like whoever those people were ran in the opposite direction to the one I'd take, but you never know. They might swing around a ridge and lie in wait for me.

I assume Sara ran, too—I see her tracks leading off into the woods as well. I grit my teeth and curse under my breath. Was this all a setup? But how could she possibly have known I'd be out in the woods this morning? And, if she did know, even if Bear called her on her cell phone to tell her, how could she have possibly found me out there? It would have been like finding a needle in a *field* of haystacks even if she knew the general area I was going to be in, and I would have had to have mistakenly turned north for her to have any chance of running into me. How could she have known I'd do that? She couldn't have. Plus, she was the one who tried to get me to leave a few minutes ago; she was the one who heard them coming. No, that's all way too much coincidence. I bet she knows more about the cult than she's telling me, because I always figure she knows more than she's telling me about anything, but I don't think she and Bear set me up. I don't mind a good conspiracy, but it's got to have some legs to it.

I rush back to the small room, grabbing the bloody steak knife off the altar on my way. Then I put my snowshoes back on, untie the boy, wrap him in my parka, hoist him over my shoulder, retrace my steps to the entrance, and lay him down gently on the floor. I take another long look at the trailhead, then slip outside and make a quick lap of the cabin, gun out in front of me. When I'm back at the entrance I scoop up the boy and head out. He probably only weighs sixty or seventy pounds, but the extra few inches I'm sinking into the snow sets my leg muscles on fire right away. It's going to be a long trek home, but I've got to keep pushing, I've got to get there as fast as I possibly can.

This boy's life is in my hands.

16

To my amazement, when I finally make it home the entire driveway is clear of snow except for a thin layer of slush. Bear even dug a path leading from the top of the driveway to the back porch, and he cleaned off both cars. He must have spent most of the time I was gone outside, shoveling. That's the only way even he could have finished the job so fast by himself.

I finally broke out of the pine trees and onto 681 a half mile north of my house—I've done the drive between the house and town enough times that I recognize every inch of that seven miles, even when it's snow-covered. Then I hustled south in the cold and the fading light of the late afternoon with what little strength I had left after climbing up and down those ridges carrying the boy, paranoid that someone was closing in on me from behind.

I don't know what happened to Sara. I half-expected her to slip out from behind a tree like a phantom or hear her voice out of nowhere again as I was slogging through the woods, but I never heard or saw her. As I lurched along with my human cargo I convinced myself once and for all that she couldn't have set me up at the cabin, that there was no conspiracy. At least, that she isn't part of one. It seems awfully odd that those two guys showed up out there at the exact same time we did, but I can't think on that now. I have to do all I can to save this boy, and not because he could be a vitally important factor in terms of shedding light on the cult and, potentially, on Cindy's murder. I have to do it because he's an innocent young kid who's been through a horrible ordeal.

As I turn off the driveway and onto the path Bear bursts through the back porch door. "What happened?" he demands, hurrying down the cleared steps and grabbing the boy off my shoulder like he's a twig. I've known Bear for many years, but every time I see him do something like that it's still incredible.

As Bear disappears inside I collapse on the steps, gasping for breath.

He's only gone for a few moments, then he's back. "What happened?" he asks again, helping me up off the stairs and into the house. "Who's that kid?"

I stagger through the back porch into the kitchen and there's Vivian. She's standing by the stove and she's got one of those guilty looks on her face that only I would recognize after having lived with her for so many years. Did she and Bear still find a few minutes to be together despite how long it must have taken to clear the driveway? Or did she recognize the boy? I just wish I'd had the strength to carry the little guy those last few paces so I could have seen her face when she first saw him. That would have told me what I needed to know.

The paramedics get to our house in fifteen minutes, which is a miracle considering the fact that the roads are still so bad. They work on the kid feverishly in the living room for a little while, then they slide him into the ambulance and tear off for Superior Hospital, siren wailing. The boy didn't regain consciousness while he was at the house and I could tell by the paramedics' expressions that they were pretty pessimistic about his chances, despite their confident words. They told me I was a hero, and so did Bear a couple of times. But I won't feel good about anything until the kid opens his eyes and the doctors say he's going to be all right.

Nobody recognized the boy, so I don't think he's from around here. I know he's not from Dakota County and I'm pretty sure he's not from Brower or Wabash, either. My guess is that the cult's going to kidnap people from far away and do their dirty work away from the spotlight. I doubt there'll be another incident like the one at the Prescott estate, but you never know, especially around here. Hell, at this point I can't even be sure Cindy was murdered by the cult. Maybe somebody killed her and made it look like the cult's work. And what's the cult going to do if that's the case? Come out and disclaim responsibility? I don't think so.

One thing I know for sure is that whoever built the cabin was going to do something awful to that little boy. I mean, they already had by leaving him out there tied up in the sack freezing to death. But I shudder to think what they would have ultimately done to him if the storm hadn't gotten in the way. Bottom line: Somebody's acquired a desire to see human blood run red and the killing isn't going to stop until whoever's doing the killing is caught.

After the EMTs leave, I offer to give Bear a ride home and he takes me up on it immediately. Apparently he's satisfied his exercise fix. He has no desire to ski home.

"So what the hell happened out there?" he asks before we're even out of the driveway. "What's the deal?"

He asked me that question several times at the house before the paramedics showed up, but I waved him off because I didn't want to talk about it in front of Vivian. I saw her catch my subtle head shake to him, but she didn't say anything about it before I left.

"I ran into Sara out in the woods after I left you."

"Really? That's weird."

I look over at him. "Why?"

Bear shrugs. "I don't know much about probabilities, Professor,

I'll admit. I never paid much attention in math class, but it seems like a long shot to run into somebody in a forest as big as the one we've got up here a few hours after a storm like the one we just had quits." He chuckles. "Then again it's Sara so maybe it's not such a long shot after all. She's out in the woods a lot, and they say that squaw can track a deer across bare rock, so it wasn't going to be real tough for her to track you down in the snow. Yeah, that's probably what happened," he says, like he's trying to convince himself. "She probably crossed over your footprints out there, then tracked you down." He chuckles again, louder this time. "She's got a thing for you. I don't know whether it's because she really likes you or because she really hates Vivian, but she's got a thing for you. I hear even Ike admits it."

I don't tell him how Sara's prints were coming from the opposite side of the clearing where we ran into each other, and I have no intention of getting into a discussion about some "thing" Sara may or may not have for me. "Well, anyway, she said she wanted to show me something and it turned out it was this cabin east of here a few miles."

"And the kid was in the cabin," Bear says, anticipating what I'm going to say.

"Yeah. Sara said she found the place a few weeks ago when she was taking a walk."

Bear pushes out his lower lip. "Huh," he says in a noncommittal way.

I take a deep breath. I don't know if I want to tell him the rest, but it'll come out at some point and he'll wonder why I held back on him and that's something I can't have. I need him to be as loyal to me as ever right now. But I've got to be careful. I hate to say it, but I can't trust anyone a hundred percent right now. That's how I feel, anyway, and it's terrible to live like that. Even for a short time.

"Was anyone around out there?"

"No." I hold back on what happened, about the shootout.

"Was the place locked up?"

"Yeah, tight."

"But you broke in and found the boy."

"Yes."

He shakes his head. "It's got to be a hunting cabin somebody put up. Illegally, too, because I think that's federal land back in there. And there aren't any logging roads going through those woods that I know of. Not anymore." He glances over at me. "So was that it? Was it a hunting cabin?"

"That's what I—"

"But why'd Sara want to take you back there so bad?" Bear interrupts. "I don't get it. People put up hunting cabins all the time around here on other people's land."

I hesitate. "She saw burned bones in the yard, and some of them were chopped up."

His eyes flash to mine. "My God, were they—"

"She said they were just animal bones."

"Oh."

"But it looked like a place the cult could be using." I tell him what I saw inside the cabin's main room and he slams the dashboard. "The kid was tied up in the back room," I finish.

"These people have lost it!" Bear shouts. "First Cindy, then that girl you saved from going off the cliff, now this kid. Christ!"

"We've gotta keep this quiet, Billy."

Bear sneers. "Good luck. Davy called me this afternoon while you were gone and he told me that Mrs. Erickson found out about that girl in the Gorges. He says she's already broadcasting it all over the place.

It's my turn to slam the dashboard. *"How the hell did she find out about that?"*

"Nobody around here can keep their mouth shut about anything. You know that, Professor."

If Lew Prescott and Darrow Clements hear about the girl and

about how she said she knew someone in the cult and what the cult was doing, I could have a disaster on my hands. Pretty soon they're going to find out about the pentagram carved into Cindy's forehead. Peter Schmidt, the head of the CSI team, told me he can't hold on to Cindy's body for long, not with Prescott banging on the morgue door. Then Prescott and Clements might put two and two together and start suspecting that there's a cult up here after Clements does some digging. A little more digging and they'll confirm the rumor and I probably won't be in charge of the case after that. At the very least I'll be shoved onto a siding, because then they'll be able to get the state guys or the Feds to take it over on some kind of technicality.

I've just got to keep Schmidt from telling Clements and Prescott the specific circumstances surrounding Cindy's death for a little while longer. How she was nailed to the floor, how the candles were around her body and that it seems obvious that there were at least a few people present at the murder. If I can keep that under wraps for a few more days, I just might have enough time to solve this thing before Prescott and Clements can take over.

I curse out loud and shake my head. There's just too much going on at this point.

Bear pats my shoulder. "It'll be all right, Professor. And you know I'm here for you."

"Thanks, Billy." I take a deep breath. "I just feel so bad for that little kid."

"That's why you're a good sheriff. You do care, it isn't just a job for you. These people around here are like your children, all of them. I just wish they understood that." He gazes into the pitch dark out the passenger side of the truck. "I don't think that kid you brought home today was from around here. I mean, I know he isn't from Dakota County."

I know what Bear's thinking. We've had this discussion many times. "I don't think so, either."

He waits a few moments before he starts up again. "They're gonna start taking people from far away, so it's harder for us to solve the case. You just got lucky stumbling onto that cabin with Crazy and finding the boy. Hell, that kid could be from Minnesota or Iowa for all we know, maybe even farther away than that. He's probably from a poor family nobody gives a damn about, too. We might never find out who he is."

"I know," I agree quietly.

"I meant to tell you," Bear speaks up when we're almost to town, "Davy called to tell me that Route 7's cleared east and west of town now. We'll be able to get to everybody now."

"Good."

"And here's another good thing," Bear says enthusiastically. "The temperature's supposed to get pretty warm over the next few days, up into the forties, I think." He shoves me on the arm in a friendly way when I don't say anything, like he used to do when we were teenagers. "What's wrong with you?" he asks as the Bruner stoplight appears in the distance, when we're just about out of the woods. "Come on, lighten up. Everything will be all right."

But I just keep gazing out the window into the darkness of the dense pine forest closing in on me on both sides, wondering if I've finally met that sinister element I always figured was waiting for me in there—or if this is just the beginning.

When I come through the back porch door Vivian is standing by the stove with her arms crossed tightly over her chest.

"Hi."

"Hello," she answers coldly.

"What's wrong?"

"What took you so long?" she demands.

I shrug. "What are you talking about?"

"You left two hours ago. It shouldn't have taken more than thirty minutes to get Bear home."

"The roads are icy."

"Still."

I stare into her steely eyes. "Okay, I stopped by the precinct, then I went to the Saloon with Bear." I was hoping we'd made some permanent progress over the last few days, despite what happened right before Bear started pounding on the back porch door, but apparently we hadn't. "I was hungry and I got a bite to eat. That okay with you?"

"Do you expect me to believe anything was open tonight?"

"Call up there yourself." I nod at the wall phone. "Ike's probably still around. Ask him if I was in there. He'll tell you." Ike and Sara were both there, though I didn't talk to her. She stood behind the counter and never took her eyes off me. It made me uneasy because Ike caught her staring at me a couple of times and I could tell that he was wondering what was going on. "I had chili." I nod at the phone again. "Go on, call."

She takes two steps toward me, arms still crossed over her chest. "I don't need to call. It doesn't matter."

"Then what in the—"

"Why are you taping me?"

I swallow hard. The video camera I set up in the bedroom before I left this morning. She must have found it. "What, um, what do you—"

"In our bedroom closet, no less."

Deny, deny, deny. That's what my father always told me, even when you've been caught red-handed. "I don't know what you're talking about."

Her eyes narrow to slits. "You know *exactly* what I'm talking about," she hisses, reaching for something on the counter beside her. "And what about *this*?" she demands, holding up the picture of Cindy I took from the mansion after she was murdered. "What was this doing in your truck under the driver's seat?"

The kitchen blurs before me. How can I possibly deny knowing what the picture was doing in my truck? I have to go on the offensive, I have no choice. "What were you doing going through my truck?" I yell. She must have gone through it while I was out in the woods. "You had no right to do that."

"I had *every* right!" she shouts back.

She puts the picture down, then snatches a piece of paper and holds it out for me to see. "And I printed this off your computer, off your email."

I have a computer upstairs in the guest room, but she's never asked to use it and she has no idea what my password is. At least, I didn't think she did. "What's that?"

"Take a look. I think you'll find it interesting. I know I did."

I grab the paper from her and my eyes open wide as I read. It's an email from Cindy's account that was sent some time after I left the Prescott estate that morning, after Jack showed up out of nowhere. In it she begs me not to do anything to Vivian, not to do away with her like Cindy says I promised I would. Which is ridiculous. I never said that. I was the one who couldn't believe Cindy would even suggest something like that. But that's going to be awfully hard to prove now.

My eyes rise slowly to hers. "I don't know what to—"

"So, you two were going to kill me?"

"Of course not. She was trying to get me in trouble with you by sending this. She was trying to frame me." Another thought flashes through my mind. "Or someone else was."

"Do you really expect me to believe that, Paul?"

"It's the truth."

"Well, I forwarded that email to my own account for safe-keeping." She shakes her head and pushes her chin out. "And I forwarded the naked picture Cindy sent of herself along with the email."

"*What?* I swear I don't know anything about a picture . . ."

My voice trails off as Vivian turns and stalks out of the kitchen, leaving me to wonder how she could have gotten the password to my computer.

17

WHEN I COME upstairs an hour later, our bedroom door is locked. It's easy to jimmy the thing open. I know from experience, but I don't bother. I don't even knock or call to Vivian, I just turn and head down the short hallway to the guest room where my shaving kit and a rumpled uniform are tossed on the bed. She hasn't put my sleeping pills in the kit—probably on purpose because she knows how badly I need them—so I figure I'll have trouble falling asleep, but I'm so tired I'm out almost as soon as my head hits the pillow. Before I know it the sun's blazing through the guest room window because I forgot to pull the shade down. It's a good thing I did or I might still be sleeping. I guess I was that worn out, physically and emotionally.

I wake up at seven-thirty, an hour and a half late, but Vivian isn't up yet. Our door is still shut when I come out of the guest room and I don't bother trying to mend fences. Despite the long night's sleep, I don't have the strength to deal with her and I'm still shocked that she got my password and that Cindy—or whoever—sent that email to me. Before I crawled into bed last night, I checked my computer and, sure enough, the email from Cindy was there, sent about an hour after I left the estate that morning. There wasn't a racy picture attached to it, and I'm sure that was just a lie intended to make the story seem even worse. But it's not like it matters much, it's not like that's much of a relief. The incriminating piece is the insane email. I can't believe Cindy sent that, or that Vivian went through my truck and found that picture of her I took from the mansion.

At least there's one thing to cheer about as I head toward town. Bear was right about the temperature. When I pull into Bat Mc-Cleary's Exxon station, it's already well above freezing, according to the digital readout in the upper right-hand corner of the SUV's rearview mirror. And, despite the fact that the strong rays from a clear blue sky are streaming down at a winter angle from the south, the thick white blanket of snow is beginning to turn to liquid. If the mercury continues to climb, the Boulder River's going to become a raging torrent and bust its ice cover in the Gorges and the Meadows. That almost never happens in February.

"Hi, Sheriff," Bat calls from the other side of the pumps as I step out of the SUV. "Good morning."

He's just finished topping off the tank of an old red Chevy pickup truck. It's owned by an older couple who live out east on Route 7 past the lumberyard. I'm glad to see they've made it to town and I wave to them. I've gotta give the people in Madison credit. They came through for us this time with the plows.

"Hi, Bat."

Bat's a short, bowlegged guy with thick, black hair that sticks up at an angle over his big, pointy ears, making them seem even bigger and pointier. His hair's forced up like that over his ears by a grimy Milwaukee Brewers hat he keeps pulled down over his scalp as tightly as he can. I've never seen him wear anything else on his head, even when the temperature drops into single digits. He's almost always in a good mood and he's always willing to help. Maybe it's the hat.

"Glad to see you're open."

"Yeah, my sons and I were over here yesterday with shovels and the IH tractor first thing in the morning. It took us a while but we got things cleared out pretty good." He gestures around the station proudly with one hand while he opens the gas tank flap on my truck with the other. Then he deftly unscrews the cap and shoves the nozzle in with a clatter. Like he's done a million times before. It's like he could do it in his sleep, you can tell. "These warm temps keep up and the snow'll be gone in a few days. Three feet of snow gone that quick, now that would be incredible." He chuckles. "Maybe all that whining those commie liberals do about global warming really has some teeth to it." He shakes his head like he can't believe he just said that. "Those idiots. It's all just nature going through its cycles."

I don't waste my breath trying to convince him how wrong he is. His grandkids will figure that out soon enough. Of course, they probably won't be able to do much about it at that point. "Yeah, idiots," I say, taking a deep breath of the gas station fumes. I like the smell of petroleum, sweat, and sawdust all mixing together. It reminds me of being in the barn with my dad while we built *Intrepid*. I like that Bat's never taken down his Esso sign, too, even though it's been blasted full of buckshot over the years. "So how long is it supposed to stay warm?"

"For at least a few days. Up into at least the forties every day. Maybe even the fifties," Bat adds, looking up at the sky. "Sure are a lot of out-of-towners and River Families coming through Bruner lately."

He's in a talkative mood, and, when he is, he changes subjects on a dime.

"There was a fellow in here the other day," he keeps going. "He was asking a lot of real sticky questions."

My eyes flash up from my wallet at this new piece of information. I'd been trying to decide if I was going to pay cash or give Bat a credit card. "You get his name?"

Bat scratches his head. "I'm trying to remember, Sheriff. I think he said he was working for Lew Prescott."

"Was it Darrow Clements?"

Bat snaps his fingers. "Yeah, that's it. Darrow Clements. Like I said, he was asking all kinds of questions and they were," Bat hesitates, "well, they were mostly about you. About if I'd ever seen you hanging around with Prescott's daughter. You know, that poor Cindy girl." Bat grits his teeth and inhales quickly so the air whistles through them, like he's suddenly worried he's said something wrong. "But I didn't say anything he could use, Sheriff. Don't worry, I didn't say anything wrong, I didn't get you in any trouble. You're a good man and we need you here in Bruner."

"Thanks." I pat Bat on the shoulder. I appreciate that he doesn't want to get me in trouble. What bothers me is that he thinks he might. "You answer questions like those however you feel you should."

Bat shakes his head. "Bill Campbell was in here, too. The old mule."

My ears perk up again. "Bill Campbell?"

"Uh huh. God, I hate that guy. Worse than any of the other River Family people."

"When was he here?"

Bat scrunches up his face as he tries to remember. "Sunday. The morning the storm hit. The same day Clements was here."

Normally the River Families call me or Mrs. Erickson to let us know they're going to be at their estates—the way Cindy did—so my deputies and I aren't surprised on our rounds when we see lights turned on in the mansions. Despite his perpetual crankiness, Bill Campbell's always been pretty good about doing that, but I never got a call from him or any of his family last week. Maybe Mrs. Erickson took his call but didn't tell me, though that doesn't add up, either. She's a professional, at least when it comes to police work.

If we didn't know Campbell was at his place, one of the deputies or I might go into the mansion to investigate and get shot when we surprise him—or shoot him. Everyone up here has guns in the house, including the River Families, and that can mean trouble fast, especially with what happened last week. Everybody's going to have their fingers on their triggers at all times. Mrs. Erickson might not like me much, but I don't think she wants to see me get killed. And I know she doesn't want to see the other guys get killed. Since she never had kids of her own she pretty much looks at the deputies as her boys.

"Was anyone with Campbell?" I ask.

"Nah, he was by himself."

"Did you talk to him?"

"Not too much. I don't have much to say to him since he stiffed me on that job he had me do on his Cadillac last summer."

I gaze at Bat, wondering if he knows where those poodles are. The ones Mrs. Campbell lost a few weeks after her husband stiffed Bat last summer. I bet he does. "Was he going to his estate or leaving?"

Bat scrunches up his face again. "I don't know. I didn't ask. He's such a prick. He actually made a joke about Cindy, about her murder."

I was about to pull my credit card out. *"What?"*

"Yeah, he said it was such a nice family it was too bad it wasn't both of them. He said it real sarcastically."

I've never had any problems with Bill Campbell, but then I've never had much of an opportunity to get into it with him, either. During the four years I've been sheriff of Dakota County, we've managed to stay out of each other's way. So, except for the fact that he's filthy rich, I've never had any reason to hate him—until now. "What did Campbell say?" I need to hear it again because it's hard to believe anyone would say such a terrible thing.

"He said it was too bad both of them didn't get it."

"Both of them," I repeat. "Was he talking about Chelsea, too?" Lew Prescott has another daughter, named Chelsea. She's younger than Cindy was. "Is that what he meant?"

"I don't think that's what he was saying. I think he was talking about Cindy and her father."

"But why would he say that?"

Bat nods like now he understands something. "I guess you never heard about what happened."

"Guess not." I thought I'd heard about everything, even everything that happened before I got here. "Fill me in."

"Well, I think it was about seven or eight years ago when all this happened. Apparently, Campbell's wife ended up over at the Prescott estate after a cocktail party one of the other River Families threw. It was during the middle of the week in July and Bill was back in St. Paul working and Lew's wife was on the West Coast with Chelsea doing something. Anyway, the story goes that Bill's son showed up at the Prescott estate looking for her and caught his mom and Lew in a pretty compromising position. She swore she'd just gone over there to look at some artwork, but the kid was in the Saloon later that night with his brother and they were drunk and they were talking like it wasn't that way at all. A couple of the locals heard them. I think Sara was one of them. The next day everybody clammed up about it, but Bill and Lew haven't spoken since. At least, that's what I heard."

"Jesus, I never heard anything about that."

Bat raises both eyebrows. "Everybody figured Bill was gonna go after Lew, but he never did. As far as I know anyway." He points at me in a friendly way. "Then there was this other guy who came by in the middle of last week," he says, changing subjects again like he's pulling the trigger of a gun. "Nice fellow but a real gearhead," he says, rolling his eyes. "You know, the pocket protector type. I don't relate much to those kind." Bat smiles and swells up with pride. "Even though I'm in the energy business myself."

If you're a good local sheriff you learn to listen to how people are talking to you, not just what they're saying. You know, inflections in their voice, the way they look at you when they speak, how often they touch you on the arm to get your attention. That's why I went with Sara to the cabin. I could tell she really wanted me to go with her by how she was talking, not just by what she was saying, but by how she was getting animated with her arms, because she rarely does that. It's the same with Bat. I can tell Bat really wants me to hear what he's saying now because he's leaning on a few words, emphasizing them hard, and he doesn't usually do that.

"Was this guy just passing through town or was he here on business?"

"He said he was here on business. He said he was back in the woods behind the estates doing some work for a couple of days. He said he was working off the River Road."

The River Road is a dirt and gravel road that runs north and south through the forest about five miles west of the estates on the other side of the Boulder from 681. There isn't anything on it. No homes, no nothing. It's just another way to get north and south around here and it parallels 681 all the way down to Route 91. Then it cuts across 91 and keeps going another few miles south before the pavement begins and homes start to come up along it. The entrance to the River Road up here on Route 7 is six miles west of town and that's where it ends. It doesn't go the last five miles to Lake Superior. The spot where it dead-ends into Route 7 is right about where Gus and Trudy slammed into that grove of white pines that day they were going Christmas shopping. It's actually a state road even though it doesn't have an official designation, but they don't plow it. And I'm not sure why we call it the River Road. Six-eighty-one is closer to the Boulder than the River Road is.

"Did he tell you what he was doing back there?"

"Nope. But he had this smirk on his face the whole time I was filling his truck up. It was the only thing about him I didn't like. I felt like he was keeping something from me, something important, too."

I gaze at the grimy glove insignia on Bat's Brewers cap. I don't want to alarm him, I don't want to get any more rumors started—especially right now—but I don't want to miss the chance to pick up some valuable information, either. "How did he pay?"

Bat smiles. "Credit card."

He's obviously proud of himself for some reason that's not immediately obvious to me.

"I always remember how everybody pays me," he explains. "Most of the time how much they paid me, too. It's like those pro golfers who can tell you what club they used on every hole in a tournament twenty years after they—"

"You still got that receipt?" Bat seems miffed at my interruption, but I don't have time for this and I don't like golf very much. It's a sport I could never get into. "It'd be helpful if you did."

He nods. "Yeah, I think I got it."

"Can I look at it?"

"Sure."

I follow him into his cramped office, which is off the two-bay garage. He picks up a pair of scratched reading glasses that are lying beside the cash register and puts them on, then pulls an old shoe box out from beneath the counter. He runs through the receipts for a few moments, then stops, digs one out with his grease-stained fingers, and hands it to me.

The name on the receipt is Henry Steinbach, and, just as I'd hoped, Steinbach used a corporate card to pay. The company name on the card is Edina Engineering and, according to the receipt, it's based in Minneapolis.

"Is that what you needed, Sheriff?"

"We'll see, Bat, we'll see." I manage a quick, noncommittal response even though I'm suddenly wondering if there's a hell of a lot more going on in Dakota County than I thought there was. I hope Bat didn't see that look hit my face. He's more perceptive than people who don't know him very well take him to be. I thought he was kind of slow the first time I met him, too, but over the years I've learned. "One more question, Bat."

"Sure, Sheriff. Fire away."

"Was Jack Harrison in here last week? He drives that black—"

"I know his car," Bat says. "He's such a jerk. He's not as bad as Bill Campbell, but almost." Bat takes off his reading glasses. "Nah, Harrison wasn't in here. I'd remember if he was. I mean, he is a congressman and all." Bat chuckles snidely. "You know, I might pour some sugar in his tank when he wasn't looking if he ever does come in here with that Porsche."

I chuckle back, letting Bat know that there wouldn't be any investigation by the Dakota County Police Force if he did.

I end up parking the truck off to the side of Bat's lot, then walking over to the precinct. The temperature may be up and the sun may be out but there's still a tremendous amount of snow on the ground, and I noticed on my way to Bat's that our lot at the precinct wasn't cleared yet. Charlie Wagner, the owner of the washette where Vivian works, gets twenty-five bucks a storm to clear it. But he's feeling his age these days and he doesn't get up as early as he used to after drinking himself to sleep most nights on bourbon since losing his wife last year. Bat's probably not real happy about my truck taking up space at his gas station, but people around here are generally pretty accommodating to my deputies and me.

"Hello," I say evenly to Mrs. Erickson as I come through the precinct door. One thing about her, she's always at her post when she's supposed to be. I don't think she's taken a sick day since I've been here and she gets colds and flu just like the rest of us do. "You should have called me." Her old pale green and white Skylark isn't outside anywhere so she must have walked over. Her trailer isn't far from the one Maggie lives in on Tunlaw behind the washette, so it's not too bad a hike to get here. Still, she's no spring chicken anymore. "I would have come and picked you up."

She's filing reports in the metal cabinets that line the file room. We still file things the old-fashioned way in Bruner. "That's all right. I wore my snowshoes and I was just fine," she answers without looking up. "Just because I'm a little older doesn't make me an invalid, Sheriff."

"Oh, I know." I take a step into my office, then lean back out. "Any of the River Families call in lately to let us know they were coming into town?"

Now she looks up and raises an eyebrow. "You mean other than Cindy?"

I grimace. It's been thirty minutes since I've thought about Cindy lying there dead on that floor, which is a decent stretch of time, all things considered. Yesterday it was every ten minutes. Of course, Mrs. Erickson would have to remind me. "Yeah," I say in a low voice, "other than Cindy."

She shakes her head. "No. You would have told me if they had, just like I would have told you."

"Okay, thanks."

"Who were you thinking might have called?" she asks before I can duck back into my office.

Mrs. Erickson's good. She smells a story. "Nobody in particular." I don't want her to know I'm talking about Bill Campbell. "I was just checking."

With that I head into my office and close the door. I want to rake her over the coals for blabbing to everyone about that poor girl who almost fell off the cliff in the Gorges and how she was running from the cult, but I don't. Instead, I call Sheriff Wilson down in Brower County to give him an account of what happened to the girl, then make an appointment to see him later in person in Hayward. We've got a lot to talk about and I volunteer to drive to him because I've got some other people I want to see down that way, too.

My next call is to the Superior Hospital. I know a couple of nurses over there pretty well, and I make sure I get one of them on the phone before I ask about the kid I carried back from the cabin yesterday. Nurses aren't supposed to give out information concerning a patient to non–family members—I think Superior's even gone to a specific list of preapproved call-ins ever since the government crackdown on patient privacy a few years ago. But since this woman knows me and knows what I do, she tells me what's going on right away. She says the kid hasn't come out of his coma and isn't doing well. She tells me that his vital signs aren't improving and the doctors are worried. And that's all there is to hear. Nobody's claimed him and nobody seems to be trying to.

Then I ask her about the girl who I pulled off that cliff. She's in the same hospital—at least, she's supposed to be. But it turns out she's gone and nobody knows where she went. She wasn't discharged, apparently she just walked out—and her parents are going crazy.

As I hang up slowly, wondering whether the girl walked out or was carried, Mrs. Erickson knocks on my door. I can tell it's her because she always does it the same way—three heavy times with those thick knuckles of hers.

"Sheriff?"

"Yes?"

"Mr. Clements is here to see you."

Jesus Christ. This is Clements's MO. He isn't the sharpest blade in the drawer, but he's a bulldog and he hits you hardest when you're least expecting it. He won't ever outsmart you, but his endurance is legendary, and that's how he gets you. "Just a minute." I take a few seconds to pick up some files off the chair he'll be sitting in, then I open the door. "Hey." I hold my hand out to shake his but he doesn't respond. I don't know why but I'm still trying to be civil to the guy.

"We need to talk," he says gruffly.

"Sit down." I point at the chair, then head back to mine.

"What's this about a girl almost going off a cliff into the Boulder River on Sunday?" he demands, launching his attack with no warning. "What's this about her running from a devil worship cult you've got up here? And what were you doing out at the Prescott estate a second time on the day Cindy was murdered? *What the hell's going on in Dakota County, Sheriff?*"

At least he doesn't mention the pentagrams Mrs. Erickson has been going on and on about or any of the other specific circumstances surrounding Cindy's murder. But it won't be long before he hears about all that, too. I'm running out of time. "Darrow," I say as calmly as I can, "like I told you before, I can't say anything about what's happening." I'm trying to keep my composure, but it's tough. I can hear the aggravation simmering in my voice. I can hear all those nasty comments he made about my wife the last time he was here, too. "We've got several investigations ongoing."

"I don't care what you said before and I don't care how many investigations you've got ongoing. This is Cindy Harrison we're talking about, the wife of a United States congressman and the daughter of Lew Prescott. Not some damn local woman," he snaps, rising out of his chair and coming around the desk. "Her investigation takes precedence over anything else you're working on right now."

I stand up, too, and suddenly we're toe to toe. "Get out of here," I tell him. "Now."

"Never could make it on a big-city police force, could you, Paul?"

My eyes narrow. "Never wanted to, Darrow."

"Always let women get in your way, didn't you?"

I can smell his brand of chewing gum, he's so close. It's Big Red. "Get out of here, Darrow, while you still can."

"First it was Cindy, then it was that whore you call a wife!" he shouts.

I don't think I've ever hated anyone as much as I hate Darrow Clements right now. Not even Lew Prescott. "I'll give you one more chance to get out of my office," I say with my teeth clenched, "then I'm locking you up for interfering with a police investigation."

"You've always hated women, haven't you?"

"What?"

"Hell, I bet you push your wife around whenever you get the chance."

Clements's face blurs before me. *"Are you out of your mind?"*

Then he does something a civilian absolutely cannot do, even an ex-cop. He makes physical contact with a law officer. He shoves me with both hands. Then he does it again—harder.

I grab him by his wool sweater and toss him over the desk like he's a rag doll. He crashes off the chair he was sitting on and onto the floor and I hear Mrs. Erickson shriek as I haul my ass around the desk and grab him again by his sweater as he's just starting to scramble to his feet. I hear the door fly open as I jack Clements up against the wall. Clements's eyes are as big as saucers as I cock my fist and I can tell he's scared out of his mind. My God, I can't wait to slam his face, I can't wait to split that nose wide open and send a few teeth down his throat. They say revenge doesn't taste sweet. Well, it tastes like I'm eating a warm, chocolate-covered doughnut right now, let me tell you.

I grab Clements by his throat and pull my clenched right hand back a few inches farther, then let go. But my arm's not moving, there's something holding it back.

It's Bear.

He throws me back against the far wall with one quick extension of his massive right arm, then he points at Clements. "Get out, Darrow, before I tear you apart with my bare hands."

The man doesn't wait to be told again. He dashes out of my office, grabs his coat, and sprints for the precinct door.

I gaze at Bear, breathing hard. "You should have let me kill him," I gasp, adrenaline still coursing through me so hard my hands are shaking like cans in a paint-mixing machine.

He shakes his head slowly. "Just thank God I got in here when I did."

I keep staring at him. I know I shouldn't start this but I can't help it. "Is that what you think of Vivian?"

"What are you talking about?"

Clements shouted it so loudly that Bear and Mrs. Erickson had to hear him even with the door closed. There's no way they couldn't have. "Do you think she's a whore, Billy? Like he does?"

"I don't know what you're on, but—"

"You heard him, you heard what he yelled. Don't try to tell me you didn't."

"The guy's just a giant prick and we both know it," Bear says, like it's as obvious as the fact that he's tall. "He's just trying to get into your grill any way he can, Professor, and it looks like he's doing a pretty good job of it. I care about Vivian very much. I don't think of her that way at all. You know that."

I flex the fingers of both of my hands, flex them into tight fists. "Yeah, maybe you care about her a little too much."

"What?"

"You heard me, Billy."

18

A FTER BEAR RAN Clements to his car faster than a bloodhound runs a rabbit to his hole, I figured I had two choices:
get back to the cabin or get going south. The obvious
choice was to get back to the cabin because there's probably a ton
of evidence out there waiting for me, but I also had a duty to get to
Hayward to give Sheriff Wilson an accurate account of what happened to the girl in the Gorges. To tell him about the two men who
were chasing her and how one of them looked like Caleb Jenkins,
though I can't be absolutely sure it was him. Wilson's got a firestorm
on his hands now that the girl took off from the hospital—or was
taken from it. Her parents are hysterical—they never even got to see
her before she went missing—and I want to help him any way I can.
Plus, I've got a couple other important things I need to get to right
away that are farther south of Hayward.

So I sent Davy and Chugger McDowell—another of my
deputies—out into the woods for me. I thought about telling Davy
to recruit Sara to guide them to the cabin, but then I thought better of it. She's unpredictable and not always the most helpful soul

around. I don't want her to start popping off about everything in the middle of the Saloon when they go get her and suddenly send the town into an uproar because people are at the counter having a late breakfast and they hear her ranting. And I'm still not sure about her motives; I'm still worried that there was something else going on yesterday when we "happened" to meet in the woods and those two guys "happened" to come to the cabin at the same time we did. Bear got me thinking about how she could have easily made it seem like it was a coincidence that we ran into each other out there.

I told Davy what happened at the cabin—except for the part about the shootout—then I gave him the best directions I could. I told him to look for my footprints coming out of the woods on the east side of 681 north of my house and to follow them over the ridges. My tracks should still be obvious despite the warm-up in the north-country overnight. They'll find the cabin, I'm confident they will. Chugger McDowell is the second-best tracker in Dakota County behind Sara.

Right before I hung up with Davy, I told him to bring back anything that looked important, then I warned him to be extra careful. I told him in no uncertain terms that he and Chugger needed to have their guns chambered and ready at all times. Then I told him twice not to tell anyone what they were doing. I hope Davy understood what I was saying. That I meant for Chugger and him not to tell *anyone*.

After I hung up with him I ordered Bear and Frank Holmes—my fourth and, at twenty-three, my youngest deputy—to go out and make sure everyone's accounted for in both directions on Route 7. I didn't tell Bear about Davy and Chugger heading to the cabin. Even though it's Bear, I'm trying to keep things as compartmentalized as I can.

As I speed past the house my cell phone rings. I assume it's Vivian but it isn't. A number I don't recognize flashes on the screen. Most people I know wouldn't answer a ring from an unknown num-

ber or a private caller, but I have to. Again, that's part of being sheriff, part of the covenant I made with the people of Dakota County
when I swore to protect them.

"Hello."

"Paul?"

"Yes."

"Paul, it's Peter Schmidt over in Superior."

As in the Peter Schmidt who headed the CSI team at the Prescott
estate the other night. "Hi, Peter."

"You survive the storm okay?"

"We're fine. Madison came through for us this time. They've already got 681 and 7 passable. We're still digging out around town
but we'll be all right. Thanks for asking."

"Well, they had the resources. They damn well should have gotten to you fast."

"What do you mean?"

"South of Hayward only got a foot."

I never thought about checking on that. I figured everybody
in Wisconsin and Minnesota ended up getting hammered by the
storm as badly as we did. That was the prediction.

"And Madison barely got a dusting. Just a few inches," Schmidt
adds.

He takes a labored breath, like he doesn't really want to get into
whatever it is he called about. There's something bad coming, I
know it. For some reason people always feel like they have to work
themselves up to telling me something bad. More than they do with
most other people. Cindy always told me it was because I was naturally intimidating, but she was never specific about what she meant
by that.

"Paul, we've been working overtime on this thing because of
who's involved."

"Of course, I understand that."

"I hate to admit it," Schmidt goes on in a guilty tone. "I mean we work hard on every case, but when it's the Prescott family the whole thing gets elevated in terms of priority. And then there's the whole Jack Harrison factor on top of that."

"*Believe me,* I get it."

"Anyway, I wanted to tell you about something we found." Schmidt's voice grows serious. "It's something that has to do with Cindy's body."

"You mean that thing that was carved into her forehead?"

"No, it's something else." He takes an even longer breath than he did before. "We found two different semen samples inside her."

It seems like every gasp of breath is sucked out of my lungs instantly. And my palms start sweating right away. I can feel the perspiration on the steering wheel immediately. "Two?" Schmidt must hear that tension in my voice. I do.

"Yeah, I know," he says slowly, subtly acknowledging that he did, "we've got to be delicate about this. I know Harrison was up there at the estate the day Cindy was murdered. I'm assuming one of the samples is his. But, like I said, there's another one. The lab just called and told me about it."

I can hear Schmidt struggling. He doesn't want to be the one to tell Lewis Prescott or Jack Harrison that Cindy was a cheater. He doesn't want to be the messenger because often times the messenger gets shot in situations like these. And Lewis Prescott can aim a damn big gun at you in this neck of the woods.

"My guess," he goes on, "is that she had sex with someone down in Minneapolis before she drove up to the estate, probably the morning of or the night before. Then she had sex with Harrison after he surprised her at the estate the next day. He took off that afternoon, right?"

"That's what I understand."

"He was going to Europe early the following morning."

"Yeah, London."

My mind's spinning. One of those semen samples is mine, from when Cindy and I had sex the afternoon of her murder. When I went back the second time that day without her calling me. When I got there she was crying because she said Jack had roughed her up again before he left, and I was holding her and consoling her and it just kind of happened. She said she was so glad I'd come back even though she told me not to, and we started kissing and my defenses crumbled when she told me she wanted me so badly and that we were meant to be together and it was stupid that we weren't. Then, when it was over, she took everything back and told me she'd just been caught up in the moment. I couldn't believe how easily she could lie to me about wanting me forever just to get me to be close to her.

"At least, that's what Prescott told me."

"Have you confirmed that Harrison left the estate that afternoon?" Schmidt asks. "And that he went to London the next morning?"

"Not yet, but I will."

There wouldn't be anyone on the planet more excited to find out that Jack Harrison wasn't on that early flight to London the morning after the murder. But I'm pretty sure I won't turn up anything like that. Besides, what motive could he possibly have for killing Cindy? She already assumed he was cheating on her in Europe, she had for a long time. And it wasn't like he was afraid his father-in-law was going to do anything about that. She'd told me several times how she'd tried to convince her father that Jack was cheating on her but that Lew wouldn't listen. Like he wouldn't listen to how the guy was beating her, either. She made the comment about his being more excited to spend nights at the White House than to have grandchildren. I mean, what kind of father is that?

But now I'm wondering if maybe those were just things she was telling me to make herself feel better about our relationship, about us having our affair. I'm wondering if they were just props in the drama. Maybe those bruises on her side were self-inflicted, maybe Jack never touched her. What a fool I've been.

"Peter, I hate to even ask you this question because I hate to think of Cindy going through it, but is it possible that she was raped by the person or persons who murdered her at the estate? Could that have been what happened? Could that be why there were two samples."

"I thought about that and of course it's a possibility," Schmidt agrees. "But there weren't any bruises or scratches on her thighs and there usually are in cases like this. Either because the victim is resisting so hard or because the attacker has so much adrenaline in his system he's basically out of control. And," Schmidt continues, his voice going low as though he doesn't want someone at his office to overhear him, "her vaginal walls showed no signs of trauma, either. Now," he says, his voice growing stronger again, "that's not proof positive of what did or didn't happen in that house. I'm just telling you that in my years of being a police officer, if it's a rape situation, I almost always see some kind of trauma to that area of the victim's body. Again, as easily caused because of the attacker's heightened state of agitation as by the victim trying to defend herself."

"Okay."

"She did have a few bruises on her left side but they were faded. They didn't look like they'd been made on the day she was murdered." He pauses. "The fact that two samples showed up could be helpful for you in terms of your investigation," Schmidt volunteers. "You ought to try to find out if Cindy was having an affair down in the Twin Cities. Maybe she broke it off and that's what happened. Maybe whoever she was seeing couldn't take being tossed aside so he followed her up to Bruner and killed her. Then made it look like a cult killing to send you in the wrong direction. I've had three or four other cases like that over the years. Where the killer tried to make it look like a cult or a gang did it."

I'm pretty sure I know who the two samples came from: Jack and me. But I've got to play along, I can't have him getting suspicious. "That's a good idea, Peter, and I'm going to the Twin Cities later today. Maybe I'll stop in and see Cindy's sister, Chelsea. They were close. Maybe Chelsea will have something to tell me."

"Why are you going down there?"

"It's not related to this case," I lie.

"Oh," he says slowly, like he's not convinced.

There's silence at the other end of the line for a few moments. "Well," Schmidt finally says, "I'd leave it up to you in terms of what you want to do with this information about the two samples, but that prick Darrow Clements who's working for Prescott on this thing keeps calling me every ten minutes. He keeps demanding information. I haven't given him much, just enough to get him off the phone each time he calls. But sooner or later and one way or another Clements is going to get the details, I can tell you that, Paul. I've already gotten two calls from Madison, from people way up the chain in the department. And I'm going to have to turn Cindy's body over to Prescott here soon," he says. "That's gonna cause you a lot of problems, too, because then they'll see that pentagram carved in her forehead. I can't cover that up. I'm not supposed to let her body be materially altered while I have it, other than things we have to do specific to the autopsy, and I'm not going to risk my career. Sorry, but I'm too close to my pension." He hesitates again. "I'm assuming you'd like to keep that pentagram thing quiet."

My first thought is that somehow he knows about the Bruner Washette ticket and the two bloody steak knives I've got locked in my strongbox at home and that's why he thinks I desperately want to keep news of the pentagram quiet. Because he figures—like I do—that there's a connection. Then a wave of relief rolls over me and I understand what he's getting at. He's saying it in a general way. I'm being too paranoid, but I have to keep it going. I can't let my guard down for a second.

"I think that might cause a lot of panic you don't need to deal with," Schmidt says. "You don't want people thinking there's a cult hunting people down in Dakota County. God, you'll have a vigilante situation on your hands. And we all know what happens then, don't we? Accidents," he keeps going, answering his own question. "Bad accidents."

The word's out with the locals that we've got a cult in Dakota County, but Schmidt doesn't understand how efficient the information web is and I'm not going to tell him. But he's exactly right. I do want him to keep Cindy's body as long as he can so I can buy time with Prescott and Clements. "Peter, will you call me before you release Cindy's body to the family?" The entrance to the Prescott estate flashes by on the right. No one's been there to plow it yet. The driveway's still covered by a deep blanket of snow.

"I'm going to try to delay that until Friday but I might have to do it late tomorrow. Either way, I'll give you a heads-up at least a few hours before it happens."

"I appreciate that."

"Well, good luck over there."

"Thanks, I—"

"Oh, oh," Schmidt breaks in, "I meant to tell you one more thing."

"What's that?"

He takes a deep breath and suddenly I realize he's about to tell me what he's wanted to tell me the entire call but couldn't bring himself to say.

"Every time I talk to Darrow Clements he mentions that you were at the Prescott estate twice on the day of the murder. Once in the morning right before Jack Harrison got there, and once in the afternoon, probably after Harrison left. Clements keeps telling me that Lew Prescott doesn't understand why you went there twice that day." Schmidt hesitates. "I thought you should know that, Paul. I don't know why Clements keeps bringing it up, but it's getting kind of annoying. I mean, he seems to remember everything else he tells me." Schmidt hesitates again, longer this time. "Well, like I said, Paul. I thought you should know."

I swallow hard, trying to figure out how Prescott could possibly have known about my second visit to his estate that day. The only answer I can come up with is that he and Cindy spoke that afternoon and she told him about it, but that doesn't make sense. Cindy's always wanted to keep our relationship away from her father.

After I hang up with Schmidt I call home but there's no answer. I can't remember if Vivian was supposed to work today or not. I figured the washette would be closed at least another day because of the storm but maybe not. By the time I left for Hayward a few minutes ago, Main Street was clear and there were narrow paths from the street to most of the shop entrances. Life gets back to normal pretty fast in the north-country, even after three feet of snow.

My next call is to Bill Campbell's office in St. Paul. I have at least two numbers in the Twin Cities for each estate so I can get in touch with somebody quickly if I need to. I get his secretary first. She tries to stonewall me—that's her job and I understand what she's trying to do—but I use an official voice and make what I have to say sound urgent.

"Hello," Campbell says, coming on the line in his crusty, all-business voice. "Sheriff Summers?"

I always feel like I need to talk quickly when I'm speaking to Campbell, like I'm already taking up too much of his precious day by the time I've finished saying "hello" and he can't wait to get me off the phone. Like even if I was calling to tell him he'd just won three billion bucks in the Powerball Lottery, he'd still be impatient and hang up on me the second he felt like I was dragging the call out. It's the same way I felt whenever I called my father at his office in Los Angeles, before we fled to Bruner.

"Yes, Mr. Campbell, this is Sheriff Summers."

"What's the problem? Why are you calling me?"

Campbell's got a reputation as a tungsten-tough businessman who isn't afraid to use tactics that aren't necessarily within the law. In his early days as an entrepreneur he was supposed to have employed a crew of guys who could have given Bear a run for his money. Campbell was supposed to have paid those guys a lot of cash to help him build his cable television empire. There were rumors that a few regulators in St. Paul and Washington got some unexpected, late-night visits from them, but nothing was ever proven. He built a national company in less than five years, though. I understand that's pretty damn fast in the cable television industry.

"Damn it, Sheriff, are you there?"

"Yes, sir, sorry. I've got just one question. Were you up here in Bruner last week?" There's a long pause at the other end of the phone. "Mr. Campbell?"

"Why?" he finally asks.

What I really want to do is ask him about that thing that happened with his wife and Lew Prescott, but I can't. Even if I did, he wouldn't tell me anything important and then I'd probably have another enemy on my hands. "I heard you were here."

"So?"

I always deal with Campbell like I'd deal with the occasional porcupine I find in my barn—carefully and respectfully—but I want an answer. My deputies have hard and fast orders to immediately investigate anything unusual at the estates when we haven't been alerted to the fact that someone from the family is coming to town. I don't want to put my guys in any kind of danger I don't have to, but at the same time I want them in those mansions right away if someone who shouldn't be there is. If Campbell was here and he didn't warn us, he needs a slap on the wrist.

"Sir, I don't mean to be—"

"Okay, okay, I was there and I should have called you."

"You usually do, Mr. Campbell. All of your folks are usually very good about calling us. That's why I'm a little surprised."

"Hey, I said I was sorry. I'll remember next time. It won't happen again. Is that all?"

"Yes, sir."

The phone clicks in my ear and I'm left alone in the middle of the forest.

19

SHERIFF WILSON AND I end up meeting at a spot two miles north of Hayward instead of at his precinct where we'd originally agreed we would. At the entrance to a campground on 681 that one of the locals must have plowed, because I can't imagine a state guy taking time to clear it. They just clear the main roads and that's it. Wilson called me right after I hung up with Bill Campbell, but he wouldn't tell why he wanted to switch meeting places. He acted kind of strange about it on the call, too, real tight-lipped, and he's not usually like that. Despite what happened to him a few years ago, he's still pretty laid-back and easy to deal with. A lot of cops aren't.

Wilson's in his midfifties and he's been around Brower County for a while, though he's not originally a local. He's like me in that he moved here from the West with his family when he was a teenager, so we've always had that bond between us. He was a deputy for nearly two decades before he became the sheriff eleven years ago. The entire time he was a deputy and for the first six years he was sheriff he didn't carry a gun. He kept his cool on his sleeve and his county-issue Beretta 9mm in his desk drawer and he was famous for it.

But one winter night Wilson got shot during a routine traffic stop out on Route 91 east of Hayward. It happened a year before I became sheriff of Dakota County and Wilson was lucky to survive. The guy who shot him was just passing through town, but he was hopped-up on crystal meth when Wilson pulled him over. Wilson just walked up to the car and asked for the guy's license and registration after pulling him over for speeding and suddenly all hell broke loose. Apparently the guy had a lot of drugs in his car and he was worried Wilson would see how hopped-up he was and search the car. So he just started shooting.

Because of the drugs plowing through his system the guy couldn't tell for sure if he'd finished Wilson off, but he figured he better get out of there when he didn't hear any more shots coming from the clip. Fortunately, neither of the two bullets that found their mark hit any of Wilson's major organs and the guy peeled away after the trigger just started clicking over and over. Then he ran off an embankment a mile down the road doing ninety-five and killed himself. It was good riddance, too. I don't say that very often, but in this guy's case, it was, and the cops in Chicago where he was from agreed.

Now Wilson carries a .44 Magnum with him at all times and walks with a distinct limp. He paid for the gun himself but at least the county bought the knee brace he'll wear for the rest of his life.

He wears that cannon of a .44 on his hip at all times like a Vegas billboard so everybody sees it right away, so there's no mistaking what you'll be dealing with if you want a fight. I'll give him credit, though. He went to the gun—something he swore he'd never do—but he was back on duty six weeks after his knee was blown apart. He wasn't out patrolling, but he was back in his office protecting his county. A month later he was on patrol again. Now that's a tough man.

Wilson's waiting for me when I pull up to the campground. He's leaning back against his black SUV with Brower County Police painted down the side in white block letters, smoking a cigarette. He never smoked until he got shot. I hear he smokes all the time now. Two to three packs a day.

"Hi, Roy," I call as I step down onto packed snow. I notice right away that Peter Schmidt was spot-on with his weather report. Brower County didn't get nearly as much snow as we did. "How are you?"

"Fine, Paul. How about you?"

"Good. Uh, why are we meeting out here?" I ask, getting straight to the point. There's a guy sitting in the passenger seat of Wilson's SUV and I want to know who he is. I get the feeling he has something to do with why we're meeting outside at a snowy campground instead of inside a warm office. "And who's that in your truck?"

Wilson takes one more puff off his cigarette, then flicks it into the snow and jabs a thumb over his shoulder. "That's Justin Gates, and he's got something I want you to hear. Something that sounds important," he says ominously.

Christ, it seems like I'm getting hit with things out of left field all the time now.

"It has to do with Lew Prescott's daughter," Wilson continues, "and I thought it'd be better if you heard it where we can't be bothered. If you get my drift," Wilson adds under his breath. "We'll talk about that girl up in the Gorges after we finish with Justin."

Wilson seems kind of standoffish today, not his usual friendly self. "Okay." And I definitely don't get his drift.

Wilson raps on the driver's side window with his thick, gold wedding band, then waves for Justin to get out. I recognize the guy as soon as he comes around the side of the SUV. He's one of the men who was harassing Cindy that day out on SR 681, one of the men in Caleb Jenkins's crew. He's still got that gaunt, hungry look about him.

"Go on, Justin," Wilson orders without any introductions. "Tell him what you told me."

Justin peers around a tree and checks 681 in both directions, like he's scared, then he asks for a cigarette. He takes a long drag off the Camel as Wilson lights up another one, too. "The thing is," he says in a gravelly voice advertising what's clearly been a lengthy relationship with tobacco, "it wasn't any chance meeting we had with that lady in the Beamer up north of here last week on SR 681."

I don't like Justin right away. He's got a smugness about him that makes me want to smack the smirk off his skinny face with a quick right cross. "What are you talking about?"

"It was all a setup."

"A setup?"

"Yeeup." He takes a long drag from the cigarette. "That lady wanted to make damn sure you left your office to come see her that afternoon. So she got Caleb to round up me and some of the other guys to follow her past the county line into Dakota. Then she drove her car off into the snow on purpose. We met up with her right here, right in this very spot the day last week when she was coming up from Minneapolis. Then we followed her past the Brower line in Caleb's van and we watched her go off the road and it wasn't because she slipped on ice or we ran her off the road like she probably told you we did. She drove that car straight off the road. Yup, it was right here where we met her." Justin points down at the snowy ground, then puts the same finger he just pointed with to his chin and looks up at the sky. "Thursday, I think it was," he says after a long pause. "Yeah, that's right, it was definitely Thursday because the next day was the day she was murdered and that was Friday. I remember seeing her picture in the papers and reading the articles on Sunday morning and thinking the whole thing was crazy. I saved the papers and I remember how it said Sunday on all the covers the day she was murdered and how in the articles it said she'd been killed Friday night but it had happened too late on Friday to get the story into the

Saturday papers. How the police beat reporters didn't find out till Saturday afternoon what happened." His eyes get big. "That woman sure wanted to make it look like we were gonna do something terrible to her beside the road so you'd be sure to stay with her that night at her mansion." Justin chuckles loudly, like he finds what he's about to say really amusing. "I guess she liked you a whole, whole lot, Sheriff Summers."

"I don't believe you," I snap, sneaking a quick glance in Wilson's direction so I can try to gauge what he's thinking about all of this. What worries me about what Justin said is that it sounds exactly like something Cindy would do. What also worries me about this is that Sheriff Wilson's getting an inside look at my relationship with Cindy. He's probably heard a lot of things second- and third-hand, but now he's got a front-row seat. "Come on, how would she ever meet Caleb Jenkins?"

"She—"

"She met Jenkins at that bar on the south side of town a couple of weeks ago," Wilson interrupts. Justin's a slow talker and it was obviously bothering Wilson.

"You mean the Steelhead Saloon?" I ask.

Wilson nods. "Yeah, that's it. Jenkins lives about a mile from there, back in the woods in an old shack."

"Yeah, I remember you telling me that." I talked to him after I left the Prescott estate the day I went out 681 to help her. "Cindy would never go into a place like that."

Wilson shrugs. "Well, one of the bartenders at the Steelhead is an old guy named Hank Brown and he's pretty sure of what he saw. I showed him a picture of Cindy earlier today, that newspaper photo of her that was in Sunday's papers, and he ID'd her right away. Said he knew Cindy obviously wasn't a local the second he laid eyes on her a couple of weeks ago and it raised his antenna. Said she and Jenkins weren't in the bar for more than a few minutes before they went outside to talk. Hank said he went to the window and saw them standing by Cindy's Beamer for a while, too. Then he said it looked like she handed Jenkins some money and took off. Sounds to me like Cindy went into the Steelhead looking for recruits, Sheriff Summers. It sounds to me," Wilson says confidently, "like she really did set the whole thing up. And I've known Hank a long time. He wouldn't make all that up."

"He didn't make any of it up," Justin says evenly. "She gave Caleb five hundred bucks to do it and he gave us each a hundred and kept two for himself. He claimed she wanted six of us out there when you came by, Sheriff Summers, but Caleb wouldn't split the money that far." Justin smiles widely and I get a close-up look at his crooked teeth. "Guess four of us worked out fine, though," he says, pointing at me, "because you sure got heated up when you saw us crowding around her car."

"What are you talking about?"

"You drew your gun," Justin says loudly. "And I was a little worried there for a few seconds. I thought Caleb might have gotten us in over our heads. I thought you might actually start shooting at us and I hear you mostly hit what you aim at. I was ready to take off into the woods at one point." He chuckles like he's proud of himself. "I guess we did a pretty good acting job. Maybe I should think about a new career."

I feel Wilson's eyes drift to me after Justin says what he says in a snide and, even worse, accusatory tone. "Why are you telling us this?" I ask as I glance in Wilson's direction and meet his stare. "What he's saying isn't going to do him any favors with Caleb Jenkins," I point out. "I can't understand why he'd make all this up other than to get his name in the newspapers."

"I'm not making it up and that's the last thing I'd—"

"Justin's got a problem with me," Wilson explains. "Last night he got drunk and one of my deputies pulled him over while he was trying but failing to find his way home." The sheriff points at Justin and frowns. "He was twice the legal limit. When he woke up in his cell this morning he mumbled that he had something he wanted to tell me. He said he thought maybe it might help him cut a deal with me so he wouldn't lose his license. After I heard what he said, I called you to change our meeting spot. I didn't want him going through his story again where a lot of people could hear him. This is your case so I figured I'd give you a chance to hear it with just him and me around." Wilson nods at him. "So, what do you think?"

"I think I want to talk to Caleb Jenkins," I say quickly, still unnerved by what I've heard. "I think I want to hear what he has to say about all this."

"Okay." Wilson waves for Justin to get back into the SUV and warns him not to call anyone while he's in there. As I turn to go back to my truck, Wilson grabs my arm. "Wait a second, Paul."

Jesus. Is something else about to come screaming at me from out of left field? "Yeah?"

Wilson waits for Justin to go around the front of the cruiser and climb inside, then he walks me to my door. "You know a guy named Darrow Clements?"

I shut my eyes tightly and shake my head. "Jesus," I mutter.

"I take it," Wilson says sympathetically, "you do."

"Yup."

"I figured you knew him when you were with the state boys down in Madison, but I wasn't sure."

"I knew him all right." Christ, Clements is calling *everyone*. He really is going to get me arrested for Cindy's murder if he isn't careful.

"He called me yesterday to tell me he's working for Lewis Prescott on the case," Wilson says in an even tone.

"I figured."

"Said he's calling all the sheriffs in the area to let them know he's working for Prescott on the chance that they turn up anything related to the murder that could be of interest. He's telling us to call him first, before you."

"*Jesus Christ!*" I hiss under my breath.

"You could probably get him arrested for interfering with your investigation at this point," Wilson says. "Of course, that might not look so good. It might be exactly what Lewis Prescott wants you to do." Wilson takes a long, careful look around the woods, as though he actually thinks someone might be out there listening to our conversation. "I've known Darrow Clements for a long time, Paul, even longer than you have. Which makes me dislike him even more than you do just for the simple reason that I've had more experience with him than you have. He's such a jerk you can't help but hate him more each time you deal with him. He's one of those guys." Wilson points a paternal finger at me. "And as much as I've always hated Clements, I've always liked you. I've heard about your itchy trigger finger and how you got drummed out of Minneapolis and Madison, but I always form my opinion of another law officer based on how that person treats me, not based on what other people say about him. And you've always treated me really well, Paul, I've got no complaints. You're one of those guys I'd want going back to back with me if I ever got caught in a dark alley by a gang of thugs, you know? And a couple of little birds told me how you've been manipulated by the powers that be for things you shouldn't have been manipulated for. They told me how you haven't always put yourself in the best situations, but how down deep you're a good cop and that Dakota County's lucky to have you. And I agree." His eyes narrow. "So listen when I tell you this and listen hard. It's my opinion that Darrow Clements has been instructed to do anything he can to implicate you in Cindy Harrison's murder. And I bet there's a big fat bonus waiting for him if he does. That's what I take from my conversation with him yesterday." Wilson hesitates as he goes for his pack of Camels. "You got a lot of trouble on your hands, son. Watch out."

• • •

As soon as we pull up in front of Caleb Jenkins's place the bullets start to fly. They blaze from two broken front windows of the falling-down, one-story, middle-of-the-woods shack Caleb Jenkins apparently calls home. I hear the pop-pop-pops, see the fire flashes spit from the barrels, and half-hear, half-feel those eerie zings that bullets always make as they knife through the air around you.

I jump from my truck and dash across the snowy, junk-littered yard as fast as I can, then tumble behind an old railroad car that's thirty feet from the shack's front door. It's a perfectly good Soo Line boxcar that's probably storing something illicit. The closest rail line is five miles away, but around here it isn't uncommon to see cars like this one in people's yards even farther away from a railroad line. I don't know how people get them. It seems like a dumb thing to steal if you ask me, because it would be pretty easy for the railroad to point out that it was theirs, but then we've got people around here who couldn't spell IQ if their lives depended on it.

"Hold your fire!" Wilson shouts at the top of his lungs from behind his truck. He raced back there and took up a defensive position as fast as his bad knee would carry him. Justin ran off into the woods and is probably long gone. "Now! Or I shoot back!"

Wilson's already got that .44 Magnum out and God it's a big gun. It's hard to get a real appreciation for how imposing the thing is when it's nestled in its leather holster on his hip, and I find myself thinking about getting one for myself even in the middle of the chaos. Just then a shot ricochets off the boxcar above my head with a nasty ping and my attention snaps back to the house.

"Caleb, it's me!" Wilson yells. "What in the hell's wrong with you?"

I pull out my pistol, lean cautiously around the side of the railcar, and spot somebody moving inside the shack. It doesn't look like Jenkins; in fact, it looks like a young guy, a kid in his midteens maybe. Whoever he is he's holding a revolver that looks like it's aimed right at Wilson. I can't let him pop off a shot at my fellow lawman so I fire. There's a surprised yelp and a howl as the sound of my bullet echoes away, then a second later there's a shotgun blast from the window next to the one I just shot into.

Wilson curses at the rude response and unloads four ear-splitting rounds through the window the shotgun blast just came from. His bullets shatter what's left of the glass and most of the wooden frames and that does it for the guys inside. They've had enough that fast and it's a good thing for them they have.

"Okay, okay!" somebody yells from inside. "We give, we give!"

"Then get out with your hands up," Wilson orders. "Throw those guns through the windows first, then move out the front door with your hands as far above your head as you can get 'em. Understand?"

"Yes, sir."

A pistol and a shotgun come sailing through the broken windows and bury in the snow, but I don't bring my gun down yet, not like Wilson does. A moment later he's out from behind his SUV holstering that monstrosity of a weapon, but I'm still tight behind the railcar with my barrel aimed squarely on the front door. In my humble opinion, Sheriff Wilson's too damn trusting. You'd think he would have learned after what happened to him.

Two boys stumble out of the shack with their arms raised, and I notice right away that the first one has a bloody hand. It looks like I nailed him in the thumb. I didn't take kill aim like we're trained to in these situations. I just wanted to scare the hell out of him. I just wanted to get that pistol out of his hand so he didn't hurt Wilson—or me.

"Down on your knees, boys," Wilson yells, "and lock your fingers behind your heads. Is there anybody else inside?"

"No, sir."

When they're down in the snow with their hands behind their heads, I move out from behind the boxcar, gun out in front of me as I move cautiously across the yard. Am I really supposed to believe that there isn't anyone else inside the shack just because the older-looking of the two kids said so? Wilson's limping quickly toward them and he hasn't even gone for his cuffs yet. He's either dumb as dirt, suffering from a bad case of an invincibility complex, or he's crazy brave. It's probably a combination of all three, but I think most of it's the crazy brave thing. So does everyone else.

"What in the hell are you boys shooting at me like that for?" he snaps. "These are Caleb's kids," he explains as I get close. "Mitch is the older one on the right and Grady's the one you nailed in the thumb. Nice shot, by the way."

"Not really," I admit.

"What are you talking about?"

"I was aiming for his wrist."

"Oh." He looks back at Mitch. "Where's your dad, Mitch?" he asks the older boy.

"Gone, but we don't know where he went. He wasn't here Sunday morning when we woke up and we haven't seen him since."

"Well, why'd you start shooting when we drove up?"

"Um, we uh . . . it's because we—"

"You boys got drugs in there?" I interrupt, pointing at the shack. They seem doped up to me. I saw a lot of this in downtown Minneapolis so I recognize it fast. "Come on, boys, come clean."

"No," Mitch says indignantly, starting to stand up, "we don't have anything in there."

He kneels back down again quickly when I take two steps forward and press the barrel of my gun to his nose. "I'm gonna go look around inside, Sheriff," I say, seizing an opportunity that just dawned on me. "You watch them."

"Okay," Wilson answers deliberately, like he's not sure how to react to my taking control of the situation in his county. Then he shrugs. "Have at it." He looks back at the boys and starts delivering a good old-fashioned tongue-lashing.

Wilson's voice fades as I head inside the shack, gun leading the way. It smells like dry dog food in here and I'm ready to shoot right away if I come face to face with an angry mutt—most of these back-woods guys have some kind of dog for hunting and protection. But nothing takes a leap or a growl at me.

The first room past the front door—a door that hangs at a tilt by one bent hinge—is the kitchen and the sink's piled high with dirty dishes. It's disgusting, even worse than a normal bachelor pad, which I suspect this is, because I can't imagine a woman would live here. But I don't see anything out of the ordinary, at least, nothing illegal.

There's a cluttered living room beyond the kitchen, and, thanks to a roaring fire in the hearth that's spitting embers onto a tattered rug, it's actually warm in here despite the blown-out windows and wide-open front door behind me. At least ten cellophane bags are spread out on a table in front of an old leather couch that's in terrible shape. They're the size of small Fritos bags and they're full of what looks like dried grass. I pick one up and sniff. Pot, no doubt, and probably why Wilson and I got the bullet-riddled reception. I'm pretty sure those kids outside weren't planning on smoking all this stuff. In fact, I'd wager that they were going to sell most of it. They're probably the last link in the chain to people who do smoke it, the last link of a chain that at this time of year started in Florida or California or even farther away, then somehow made its way through Chicago and ended up in Hayward. Bags delivered by somebody like the guy who shot Sheriff Wilson out on Route 91 that winter night.

When I drop the bag beside the others I notice some smaller bags filled with pills. I pick one up and see through the thin plastic that there's a design imprinted on each pill. It has to be XTC, the drug that makes everyone want to get naked wherever they are and with whoever they're with. I shake my head. I heard that stuff was getting into the north-country, but I haven't seen any yet in Dakota County. XTC is dangerous. Not necessarily because of the sex-inducing effect it has but because it makes the user hallucinate, too. As a state trooper I've seen the kind of traffic wrecks this thing can cause and what it can do to the innocent driver coming the other way. Now I definitely know why we were fired on when we pulled up. Possession of this stuff means serious jail time.

I make my way through the clutter toward the hallway on the other side of the living room after repositioning the screen in front of the fireplace so the place won't burn down while I'm in here. Based on the wall posters of mostly naked girls and rock bands, the first room on the right in the hallway is either Mitch or Grady's room. But the first room on the left seems more likely to be Caleb's, which is the room I'm looking for. There's an unmade king-size bed that takes up most of the room, no posters at all on the wooden walls, three rifles standing in one corner, and a small desk positioned in another. On the desktop are about fifty empty shotgun and rifle casings lining one of the walls the desk is pushed up against and two small videotapes. On the corner of the mattress nearest the desk is a small video camera. It's probably stolen, because it's the most expensive item in the room by far except for the rifles. Which are probably stolen, too. Based on the state of the house, I don't see how Caleb would have the money to buy much of anything. I don't think his electrician business can be doing very well.

"Paul! You all right?"

Wilson's voice takes me by surprise. It sounds like he's in the living room and heading this way. I scoop up the two tapes, stick them in my pocket, and head back out just as he appears in the doorway.

"What are you doing?" he asks.

"Looking for anyone who might be hiding in here." I grab him by the upper arm and pull him back down the hall toward the living room. The damn tapes feel like they're going to fall out of my jacket. "Did you see what was on the table in the living room?"

"No, what?"

I point at the table as we come through the doorway. "That's at least five to ten years for each of those kids in the front yard. On top of whatever they get for shooting at us."

After I showed him the bags of pot and pills, Sheriff Wilson reluctantly took Mitch and Grady into custody. I helped him cuff them and load them into the back of his truck, then I followed him to his precinct in Hayward where two of his deputies met him. I took off with a wave once I saw his deputies come out of the precinct and trot down the steps toward the truck. I didn't want a lot of people to notice me and I needed to get south to Minneapolis, anyway. I've been in Brower County a lot longer than I wanted to be.

It's strange to say, but I don't think Wilson would have given those kids anything but a warning and a pat on the back if we hadn't found drugs in the house. I almost think he wouldn't have arrested them for the drugs if he'd found the stuff and not me. He told me the kids weren't really trying to hit us when they were shooting. He tried to convince me that they were just scared and that the bullets and shells didn't come anywhere near us or damage anything so where was the harm. I didn't tell him how that one bullet hit the railcar right above me, no more than a few inches away from my head.

I'm worried about Sheriff Wilson. I'm worried he's gone soft again since that incident out on 91 a few years ago. He's too good a man to lose to a couple of punks like Mitch and Grady—or their supplier. I tried to warn him as we were loading the kids into the truck to be more careful, but he told me to mind my own business.

So I will.

This is a long shot, I realize, as I pull into the second filling station, but what the hell. I know Jack Harrison didn't fill up in Bruner after surprising Cindy at the estate last week. Bat remembers everyone who comes in and, even if he didn't, he'd remember that Porsche. You don't see many shiny black Porsches in Dakota County, especially in February. But Bat didn't remember a Porsche coming in last week when I asked him this morning and Jack would have had to refill his tank somewhere after his three-hour trip up from the Twin Cities. I don't think he could have done a round trip without a pit stop and he certainly wouldn't have wanted to push his luck between towns. It was cold and it could have been a long walk if his engine had stalled.

Hayward has two gas stations, a Chevron in town I stopped into after leaving the precinct and an old independent station out near the Steelhead Saloon. I didn't get much out of the guy at the Chevron—he grunted that he hadn't seen any black Porsches and he certainly hadn't seen a Minnesota congressman—and I'm not expecting much more than that from this short, gray-haired old guy I'm staring down at right now. He's the only person here at the independent station.

"Hi."

"Hello." He nods back at me from behind the counter, then glances at the Dakota County Sheriff block letters on the side of my truck. "What can I do you for?"

"You the owner?" I ask.

"Yep."

The guy has no lower teeth and I think that grit beneath his fingernails must be permanent, it's so black. Like Bat's, this guy's station has a two-bay service garage. Unlike Bat's, there's only one lift in use and no cars waiting for service in the lot. Bat's place is almost always busy. It was busy this morning even though the storm hadn't been gone for long. "Are you here most of the time?"

"Yep."

"Were you here last Friday?"

His eyes narrow. "Why?"

Chances are he knows that Cindy was murdered. He doesn't

impress me as a man who reads much in the newspaper other than the sports and the used-car sections, but most retail owners hear everything that's going on in the area from their customers. So chances are good that either he heard about Cindy's murder from a customer or he's connected to Mrs. Erickson. He's wearing a scratched-up wedding band and it's a better than fifty-fifty shot that Mrs. Erickson gets into a home in these parts if there's a woman in the house. Way better, and it's more likely that I'll get help from him if I'm open, so I'll lay out what happened.

"My name's Sheriff Summers. I'm sheriff of Dakota County."

"Okay."

"We had a murder outside Bruner last week. Maybe you heard about it."

"Involved one of the River Families, didn't it?"

"That's right."

"So why do you want to know if I was here last Friday?"

"Well, were you?"

"Maybe."

Sometimes it can be a real struggle to get people in the north-country to talk. "Look, I want to know if you saw a Porsche that day. I want to know if a black Porsche came in here and filled up."

"Maybe."

My eyes race to his. I'd been looking over at his vintage soda machine thinking about how thirsty I am and how good a Pepsi in a tall glass bottle would taste. "Oh, yeah?"

The old man nods. "It was a real flashy car. We don't get many cars like that in here." He pauses. "I couldn't see much of the guy who was driving it, though. He was wearing his hat pulled way down over his eyes and the collar of his coat was pulled up."

"What time was he here, sir? Do you remember? Do you have a receipt, maybe?"

"I don't have a receipt because he paid cash, but I can still tell you what time he was here on Friday because he was my last customer of the day and I always shut down at eight o'clock on Friday nights. He filled up at around quarter to eight. Rude son of a bitch he was. Real rude, so I don't mind telling you anything you want to know about him. Like I said, I figured he was with one of those River Families."

My heart skips a beat. *Quarter to eight.* I was gone from the Prescott estate Friday afternoon by five o'clock, but I didn't see Jack Harrison anywhere around the place while I was there. I didn't see his car, either, so I figured he'd already headed back to Minneapolis. Cindy acted like he was long gone when I drove up to the estate the second time around four o'clock. It wouldn't take more than thirty minutes to get from the estate to this guy's filling station, so where was Jack for those three-plus hours?

"Do you remember which direction he went when he left?" I ask.

The old guy points south. "That way, toward Minneapolis."

20

E DINA IS AN old-money neighborhood located a few miles southwest of downtown Minneapolis. It's got all the typical trappings of a blue-blood neighborhood with its three-story stone homes, sprawling oak trees, expensive cars, and quiet, shaded streets. It also includes Lake Calhoun and Lake Harriet, two of the largest inland lakes in North America that lie less than ten miles from the center of a major city. These beautiful lakes—a couple of hundred acres each—provide the wealthy families with lots of outdoor activities, including swimming, sailing, skating, and fishing just a few feet from their front doors and only a few miles from the city's soaring skyscrapers. It's a wonderful place to live—and it's where Lewis Prescott built his compound.

Prescott owns what were once three separate mansions occupied by three different families near the center of Edina on its most desirable street. The Prescott clan originally lived farther south of Minneapolis in Bloomington. But, when Lewis was named CEO of Prescott Trading at the relatively young age of thirty-eight, he decided it was time to move the family closer to its downtown business headquarters and upgrade its home address.

The rumor was that Prescott bought his first Edina mansion on the up-and-up with every intention of forcing the families on either side of his new home to sell to him as soon as possible using pretty much any means necessary. Whether the rumor was true or not, he owned the other two mansions within a year. Then he connected the places with tunnels and skyways and built a fifteen-foot-high brick wall around all three homes despite major objections from his neighbors and the community association. Any way you look at it, building the wall was an amazing accomplishment, because, as Cindy told me, the community association had the legal right to stop him—but didn't.

The story didn't end there. A few years later another rich guy bought two homes next door to each other a half mile away from the Prescott compound and tried to put up his own wall around his properties—but couldn't. The police showed up and stopped construction literally as the first brick was being laid and that was that. Prescott was going to see the wall every day from his limousine on his way into Minneapolis and he didn't like that. He wanted to know he had the only compound in Edina, not just the biggest.

Ever since, Cindy's told me, Prescott brags that, in fact, he was a nice guy to his neighbor for stopping construction when he did. After all, he tells people at cocktail parties after a few scotches, he could have sent the police in when the wall was almost finished and made the guy pay to tear it down, too. The story's become a legend in Minneapolis over the years.

It's three o'clock in the afternoon and I don't know why I came to the Prescott compound. It seemed like I was on I-35 one minute coming south from Hayward and the next minute I was gazing at the ivied wall, my mind filled with the same envy and bitter memories I felt years ago. It was almost like the SUV went on autopilot for a few minutes and drove itself here. I've got two important things to do in Minneapolis, but for some reason I wanted to see this ivory tower I was never allowed into before I get to what I really came for.

Cindy tried to sneak me in here one time back when I was a cop at the Plymouth precinct, which is northwest of the downtown, after I'd dropped out of the University of Minnesota. But her father found out I was coming over and he called the private security force he uses and warned the guard at the main gate not to let me in. It was one of the most embarrassing moments of my life. Several of Cindy's friends were with us and I was the only one who was turned away. Cindy apologized and gave me a sad little wave, but then she shrugged and went inside with her friends.

The whole thing was proof to me of how connected Lewis Prescott is, and how loyal people are to him. How loyal people are to money. I'd only talked about going to the Prescott compound with three people that night: Cindy, my partner on the force, and my sergeant. Though Cindy always loved drama and leaving me in the maze that time up at the estate was damn mean, I don't think she deliberately embarrassed me in front of her friends. I still talk to my ex-partner on the force every once in a while. He's a good guy and I trust him to this day. That leaves my sergeant, and he seemed like the kind of guy who could be bribed. He died a few years ago and though I didn't like him much, I still went to his funeral and paid my respects.

Not long after being barred from the compound, I was accused of sneaking several bags of cocaine out of my precinct's evidence room and was quickly packed off to Madison to become a Wisconsin state trooper. The whole thing stank like a five-day-old deer carcass on a hot summer day and it had Lewis Prescott's fingerprints all over it. But I didn't have a choice, so I took the job even though I knew what was going on. It was actually a step up, if you think about it. Being a state trooper carries more respect than being a city cop just about everywhere except New York. But that's Lewis

Prescott. He drummed me out, but he gave me an incentive to leave, too. In the end, he's a businessman but not much else. He's certainly not much of a father.

I gaze at the slate roof of the mansion to the left. It's Chelsea's place, given to her by her father as a wedding present. Chelsea is the younger Prescott daughter. Her husband, Tom, is an investment banker at a small firm in downtown St. Paul that wouldn't do much business if not for the crumbs Prescott and his friends throw in the firm's direction every once in a while. Tom's not very smart and he's never been allowed into the family business like Jack Harrison was at the beginning of his and Cindy's marriage. Of course, Tom didn't bring a huge commodities operation to bolt onto Prescott Trading along with him the way Jack did, either. Tom was baggage and Jack was upside. At least, that's how Prescott looked at it, according to Cindy.

Even though Chelsea and Tom lead a life anyone I know would gladly trade for, Chelsea hates her father. As much as Lewis Prescott wanted Cindy to be a boy, he wanted Chelsea to be a boy ten times more. He quit trying after Chelsea because he figured he'd always have girls and he didn't want to be disappointed each time. Then he spent three decades blaming Chelsea—and, though not as obviously, Cindy, too.

Despite his frustration at not having a boy, Prescott kept up appearances and did all the right fatherly things. He sent Chelsea to the right schools; gave her Minneapolis's second-best wedding of the decade after Cindy's; and presented her with the mansion as a wedding gift. But behind the ivied walls Chelsea constantly heard about how much her father had wanted a male heir and how she'd failed him before she was even born. It got so bad sometimes Cindy would cry to me on the phone about it. Well, maybe I can use all that pent-up bitterness, resentment, and rage to my advantage.

My eyes narrow as I stare at the incredible wealth rising up before me. What I wouldn't give to see a foreclosure sign hanging on it. If only Cindy's right about her father's financial problems. Maybe I should feel bad about wishing such misfortune on a family—but I don't.

My cell phone rings as I pull away from the curb and head to my first appointment. Well, I can't really call it an appointment. The other party has no idea I'm coming. If he did, he'd probably get out of his office as fast as he could.

It turns out it's Vivian who's calling.

"Hello," I say tentatively. I'm ready for her to still be angry at how I had the video camera turned on in the closet to try to catch Bear while I was gone in the woods.

"Hi, sweetheart."

But her voice is soft as cotton. I don't get it, but I'm not going to ask why.

"Where are you?" she wants to know.

"Minneapolis." If Cindy were still alive I wouldn't have told her, because I'd never hear the end of it. But how could she take issue with my being here now that Cindy's gone? "I've got some business down here."

"Oh," she says quietly.

"You okay?"

"I don't know."

I press the phone hard to my ear as I take a left at a stop sign. I know Vivian well. That was real fear I heard in her voice just then. No acting. "What's wrong?"

"I had a nightmare this morning, Paul. I can't shake it."

That's why she's being so nice to me. Fear is one hell of a motivator. "Tell me about it," I ask, but I'm pretty sure I already know which one.

"I don't want to bother you with it."

"Talk to me, Viv." I'm going to be as compassionate as I can. I want us to get back to getting along. I liked being lovers and friends again. I was starting to feel things I hadn't felt in a long time, and not just in the bedroom. I don't care what anyone says about her or me, I really did love her for the first few years of our marriage. Madly, I mean that head-over-heels stuff. I want that back. I *really* want it back. "Come on, honey."

"I had the one about being murdered in the house again."

It sounded like she sobbed but I couldn't tell for sure. It must have been really vivid this time to still be getting to her so badly, because it's three in the afternoon and I'm sure she's been up since right after I left. "It was just a dream, Viv." That sounds hollow. I wish I could think of something better to say. "Don't worry about it."

"I know, but it seemed so real. And it was that same one I always have. The people break in through the back porch door, tie me down on the living room floor, rip my clothes off, and cut my throat. I woke up this morning grabbing my neck so hard I thought I tasted blood." She sobs again. "I wanted you to be here but you were gone."

A chill snakes up my spine, but I tell myself that there's no way she could know the details of Cindy's murder—she isn't tied into Mrs. Erickson's web and really doesn't have any friends other than Bear. I catch my breath as an awful thought hits me. She couldn't know the details—unless, of course, she was there. I think about those two bloody knives and the dry-cleaning ticket that are stashed in my strongbox at home. Then I glance quickly to my right. The tapes I lifted from Caleb Jenkins's bedroom are on the Cherokee's passenger seat and I wonder what's on them. I'll have to watch them with no one else around.

"I'm sorry I was such a bitch last night, Paul. I can't believe how I get sometimes. I shouldn't have locked you out of the bedroom, I shouldn't have—"

"I shouldn't have put that camera in there," I interrupt firmly. "I'm the one who's sorry."

"But what were you trying to—"

"Nothing." I don't want to get into it. We both know what I was trying to do, and it's embarrassing to talk about it. I was just being very insecure. If she'd done that to me, I'd probably be twice as mad as she is. "I'm sorry," I mumble again. "And I never said anything about doing away with you to Cindy. I swear it. She was just trying to get me in trouble." I swallow hard. "She's always been jealous of you." That'll make her feel good. "You know that."

"Really?" she asks in a weak, hoping-to-God-I'm-telling-the-truth voice. "Jealous of me?"

"You know it. You've always known it."

"When will you be home?" she wants to know. "I'll fix you a nice meal and I'll wear something special for you."

This is going to tear her apart, but there's nothing I can do about it. "I might have to stay down here tonight."

"Oh, God, no. You can't do that."

"It all depends on whether I get in to see this one guy. If I can't see him until tomorrow morning, I'll have to get a motel room down here."

"Paul, please don't leave me in this house alone tonight. I've got such a bad feeling about it."

"Why don't you go to Heather's for the night?" I suggest. She's crying hard now and I feel really bad. "Go down to Gatlin. If you leave now you'll make it there before dark. I'll stop by on my way home tomorrow morning and we can convoy it back to Bruner together."

"I talked to Heather this morning. She and Marty won't be home tonight. They're going to his parents in La Crosse."

The problem is that even if I do get in to see the guy I'm headed for now, my second meeting isn't until eight o'clock tonight. Even if that only goes a few minutes and I drive straight back to Bruner when it's over, I still won't be home until after eleven, as slick as the roads will be.

"I'll call Billy and see if he can come over."

"What?" she asks, sniffling.

"I'll call Bear and tell him to stay with you until I get home."

"Why in the world would you want Bear here with me if you're hiding cameras in the house to try to catch us?"

"Look, I was just being stupid. Maybe it was because you and I were getting along so well again and I was feeling a little jealous myself—ah, shoot," I say. "I've gotta go, Viv. It's Davy Johnson on the other line. I've got to talk to him."

"Don't hang up on me, Paul."

I've been trying to reach Davy all afternoon. I've been worried that something happened to Chugger and him out in the woods. "Honey, I've got to take his call. I'm sorry."

"Please, Paul!"

"I'll call you right back, I promise." I cut her off in midshriek. I feel bad about it but we'll be on the phone for another hour if I don't hang up. "Davy?"

"Yeah, it's me, Sheriff. Hey, look, Chugger and I just got back to 681. We found the cabin all right, but it was burned to the ground. It was still smoking when we got there. It was a real mess."

My eyes narrow as I drive into Edina's small business area. "You're kidding me."

"No, I'm dead serious."

He is, too. Davy doesn't have much of a sense of humor to begin with, and if there's one thing he'd never joke about, it's police business.

"Sorry it took so long, Sheriff. We would have been back sooner, but I had to do something for Bear first. We were halfway to your house when he called me."

"Something for Bear? What?"

"He had me go east of town to check on the Kendrick family."

The Kendrick family lives back on a dirt road off Route 7. They're poor and they've got a couple of small kids, and it's legitimate to wonder if they're all right after the storm we had. But that detour gave somebody else time to get to the cabin, burn it down, and destroy any evidence. My God, I can't believe it. I really can't.

"He said he wanted to make sure they were okay."

"Since when do you take orders from Bear?" I demand. "Huh?" Vivian's calling back and the beeping in my ear is driving me nuts. Mostly because I thought I'd come to terms with Bear being my best friend, that I could always count on him and that he was above suspicion of *anything.* Now this. *"Well?"*

"Um," he starts nervously, "I, I guess I figured you told Bear to call me and tell me to do it. That's how it usually goes."

I take a deep breath as the beeping from Vivian's incoming call continues. Davy's right, of course. That is how it usually does happen. I tell Bear to tell the other guys what to do. "Sorry, kid, I shouldn't have snapped at you. But let's get one thing straight. You take orders from me, not Bear. I'll talk to him about it," I say, raising my voice as Davy tries to interrupt. I know what he's going to say. How the next time Bear tells him to do something and he doesn't do it, there's going to be hell to pay. It's my fault because I've let Bear become my unofficial second in command and I need to fix that. Otherwise I'll have a mutiny on my hands. Maybe I already do. "All right?"

"Yeah, okay."

"Thanks for going out there." At least the beeping from Vivian's call has stopped. "I know it was a pain in the ass."

"No problem, sir."

"And there was nothing left of the place?"

"Nothing."

Vivian's trying to get me *again.* I was hoping she'd give up, but no luck. The thing is I really am worried about her. It almost sounded like she had a premonition on top of her dream, and the last time she had a premonition Gus and Trudy ended up dead in a grove of pine trees.

I turn the phone off as I swing into a parking lot marked "Edina Engineering." I'm worried about Vivian but I can't listen to her right now. I'll call her back after I'm through talking to Henry Steinbach, the man who stopped in at the Exxon station last week and told Bat he was working on something out on River Road. I need to know what he was doing out there. I've got my suspicions, but I need to confirm them.

I can see the anxiety all over the poor receptionist's face as soon as I come through the inner glass doors of what turns out to be very nice offices. It's a facial expression you get accustomed to as a police officer.

"I'm here to see Henry Steinbach," I say in as friendly a tone as possible. "Is he available, Mrs. Driscoll?" That's her name, according to the plate on the front of the desk.

"Is there a problem?"

"I don't think so." There isn't, of course. Not with Steinbach. Not that I know of, anyway. But people seem to react more quickly when they think there is, so I leave the possibility open. "But I guess we'll see."

"And you are?"

"I'm Sheriff Paul Summers," I say, taking out my badge and giving her a good long look at it. "I'm from Dakota County, Wisconsin. That's up northeast of Duluth just off the Big Lake."

"I see. Well, Mr. Steinbach isn't in today. He's traveling in California. He won't be back in the office until Monday."

I stare at her hard for a few moments, giving her time to change her story if she needs to. She seems sweet and innocent and she probably is, but you never know. And if you give people that cold stare from above the uniform, most of them end up telling you the truth pretty quickly even when they've lied to you the first time.

"He really is," she speaks up, a trace of irritation inching into her voice.

She's figured out what I'm doing. If nothing else good, age brings experience and a little offhand impertinence. I smile despite my disappointment. She's a kick and, besides, my eight o'clock meeting may well end up being more important than seeing Steinbach. That meeting is the main reason I drove all the way down here. "Could you give me his cell phone number."

"I'm sorry, Sheriff, but I can't do that unless you have something official that I can look at. Something from a judge, maybe."

Someone's trained her very well. "Okay. Then I'd like you to leave him a message to call me. Could you do that for me, Mrs. Driscoll?" I want her to know that I'm making it a point to remember her name in case there's a next time and she hasn't been completely truthful with me this time.

"Certainly."

When I'm back in the Cherokee with my cell phone turned on, I see that I have seven messages. Five of them are from Vivian; one is from Darrow Clements, who tells me in no uncertain terms that he's going to be in my office at eight o'clock sharp tomorrow morning and I better be there; and the last message is from Peter Schmidt, who asks me to call him as soon as possible.

So I do. The hell with Darrow Clements. If I'm in my office at eight tomorrow morning, I'll see him. If I'm not, screw him.

"Hello."

"Peter, this is Paul Summers from Dakota County. I'm returning your call."

"Hi, Paul." Schmidt lets out a long, frustrated breath. "Look, I'm really sorry about this, but I had to give up Cindy's body. Darrow Clements showed up over here in Superior really making trouble for me and while he was here, *while he was in my God damn office, for Christ's sake,* I got a call from my boss's boss in Madison. I'm sorry, Paul. I told you I'd give you a heads-up before I did that, but there was nothing I could do." He hesitates. "And just so you know,

Clements looked at her body while he was here. He saw that penta-gram carved into her forehead."

Chelsea didn't get Cindy's looks. She's blond and she's clearly a Prescott but she's short and overweight—and not just a little bit fat, she borders on obese. She doesn't make up for her lack of looks with sweetness the way Maggie does, either. In fact, Chelsea can be a royal pain. I guess she figures she doesn't have to make up for anything because of all the money her family has. But I do know she's swallowed a lot of her bitterness about her father's wanting her to be a boy by constantly eating sweets. Cindy used to tell me about the cookies and cakes Chelsea would eat and it was pretty amazing.

We're sitting across a table from each other at a greasy spoon called the Lion's Tap. It's out past Chaska on a back road that over-looks the Minnesota River. When Chelsea called me yesterday to ask me to meet her she said she couldn't go anywhere she could be recognized, so I suggested this place. It's purely blue collar. My partner and I used to come here all the time for lunch during our shifts. The cheeseburgers are outstanding, even better than the Kro-Bar's and miles ahead of Sara's Saloon Burger. I'm hungry. I haven't eaten yet today.

"The stuff's in my car," Chelsea says. "It's in a box. I don't know what it is. I haven't looked at it, but Cindy told me to make sure you got it right away if anything happened to her. It's probably old love letters she never sent you." She shakes her head. "It's weird," she says in a soft voice. "She only gave it to me a few weeks ago."

Chelsea's eyes are red-rimmed and it seems obvious she's been crying. Coming to meet me must have brought the tragedy of Cin-dy's death rushing back to the surface. Chelsea isn't nice to many people, but she loved Cindy more than life itself. "Can I get you anything?" I ask. "Something to drink?" I don't want to insult her by offering her a cheeseburger.

She shakes her head. "No, I've got to go," she says, standing up. "I've got to get home."

The waitress is just putting a fat, juicy cheeseburger and fries down in front of me and it smells so good my stomach starts growling.

Chelsea's halfway to the door when she turns around, puts her hands on her hips and scowls at me. *"Damn it, Paul, let's go!"*

The waitress smiles down at me compassionately. "Don't worry. I'll wrap it up for you." She raises an eyebrow. "If your wife can wait thirty seconds."

I'm ten miles from home on a particularly lonely stretch of 681 north of Hayward when there's a loud bang and the Cherokee's front end pulls suddenly and sharply to the left. I wrench the steering wheel to the right and fight the truck for a hundred yards before I finally bring it to a sliding stop in the middle of the slippery road. A lot of snow melted today, but since nightfall the temperature's fallen below freezing and there are ice patches everywhere.

I reach into the glove compartment, grab my gun, chamber the first round, holster it, then open the door and climb cautiously out of the truck. I'm not sure, but that bang I heard sounded like a rifle shot. Not the tire exploding,

It's deathly quiet and pitch black outside the Cherokee. I shut the door and quickly move away from the vehicle. I'm a sitting duck out here and I figure I've got two choices. Walk home and dive into the woods on the way whenever I hear a car coming, in case I'm being stalked. Or change the tire and give anybody who's out there the opportunity to sneak up on me and get an easy shot.

The way I see it, both choices stink.

he would have found out I hadn't brought the thing in. If I'd told Davy the truth about having a flat tire, he would have asked me why I didn't fix it right away. And no matter what I'd said it would have gotten him to thinking, because he's just that kind of guy.

In fact, with a little training, I think he could have made detective on a small-city force like Duluth's. I encouraged him to think about doing that a few years ago because I knew a guy over there who could have helped him. It would have meant a solid bump in pay, but after he thanked me for having the confidence in him to suggest it, he told me he was satisfied with his life just the way it was. He told me he liked leaving work at work when he went home to his wife and three kids at the end of his shift. But he knew that if he were a detective he'd never be able to completely let go of the cases he was working on. After he explained the way he felt about it, I nodded and smiled, and I haven't bothered him about it since.

When I called Davy and asked him for the favor he was very curious about why I wanted him to stay with Vivian. He asked me several questions before he agreed to go over to the house and do it. Not because he felt put out, he didn't act that way at all. He's a decent man who became a cop because he likes to help people, not because he needs a power trip every time he walks out his front door like a lot of lawmen I know do. He just wanted to understand what the deal was because I'd never asked him to do it before. I told him Vivian had a death in her family and she needed company while I was in Minneapolis working on Cindy's case—a story she quickly agreed to go along with, because she was just happy I'd found someone to stay with her. A story Davy would have had no way of checking out as long as Vivian didn't crack. Which I knew she wouldn't, because it wasn't in her self-interest to do that, and we all have a way of acting in our self-interest most of the time. I could tell Davy wasn't completely satisfied with my answer, but he's a subordinate, and though he's not hesitant to ask probing questions, he usually knows when to stop. Unfortunately, that won't keep him from speculating with Chugger and Frankie Holmes about it, and that's what worries me.

I left three messages for Bear yesterday afternoon while I was in Minneapolis, but I didn't hear back from him until he pulled into the driveway this morning to take me down to the Cherokee—on the last message I told him I needed the ride, which was why he showed up at the house at seven. I never asked him why he didn't call back and he never gave me an explanation. I did talk to him about giving orders to the other guys on his own, but all he did was grunt when I asked him if we were clear on the matter. After that we didn't say anything to each other the whole rest of the trip to the Cherokee, and he didn't offer to help me change the tire, either. When we got to the truck he just dropped me off, turned around, and roared back to Bruner without so much as a wave. It was strange.

What's happened since last week has put a lot of pressure on our friendship, and I'm looking forward to getting things back to normal. I hate being at odds with Bear in any way. He's my damn best friend and it makes me feel really bad when we're like this. And I could really use his support right now. All of it.

I'm glad I decided to walk home last night—and hustle into the woods three times on the way when I heard vehicles coming. I can't be sure, because the tire was pretty chewed up all the way around after I fought the truck so hard for control, but it looked like the thing had been punctured through the side, not through the tread. Which I know doesn't rule out the possibility that a large, sharp object was lying on the road and it kicked up, causing the damage, instead of a gunshot. But I was coming around a tight curve—the tightest one between Bruner and Hayward—when the tire blew, at a point when I'd slowed down to less than twenty miles an hour on the road's slick surface. That slow a speed would have given a shooter a perfect chance to hit the tire.

And about a hundred yards back of where I finally got the truck under control after the tire blew, there were bootprints leading into the woods that stopped and turned around just inside the tree line, then headed deeper into the woods. After I put the spare on I drove back to where I figured the tire blew, and the tracks leading off into the forest were easy to spot. It was obvious that they were recent, too. They were sharply defined in the snow, not at all melted, so I could see the tread on the sole and even read the name of the boot's maker—which was Big Buck. I followed the tracks into the woods for a ways, but I turned around and headed back to the truck when I remembered my eight o'clock meeting with Clements and I realized it was already seven-forty-five.

The Cherokee had been broken into while it was sitting on the side of the road. The lock on the driver side door had been popped, which is easy to do for someone who knows what he's doing, so the break-in didn't really surprise me. In this part of the north-country even police vehicles are vulnerable to scavengers when they've been abandoned on lonely stretches. The thing is, it usually takes a few days for people to move in. The Cherokee had only been sitting there for a few hours when I got back to it. I'm just glad I grabbed the Jenkins tapes and the box Chelsea gave me off the passenger seat before I took off for home last night.

I'm fifteen minutes late for my meeting with Darrow Clements, and, predictably, he's not happy about it when I walk into my office. But then he's never happy about anything. I don't bother shaking hands with him when I come in and I notice him glance nervously at the door after I bang it shut. What happened last time left an indelible impression on him—which is fine with me.

"What do you want, Darrow?" I ask with a frustrated groan as I sink into my chair. With only a few hours' sleep last night and the stress of everything that's going on, I'm beat, and I've got no patience for this guy. I simply don't want to deal with him. "How can I get you out of here as quickly as possible?"

"Easy," he says, not at all sidetracked by my nasty remark, at least, not outwardly.

"Oh, yeah?"

"Yeah. Just agree to a blood test."

My eyes flash to his. *"What?"* I regret the emotion in my reaction instantly. He saw and heard my fear. We both know it.

"You heard me, Summers. Give me some blood so I can find out whether your semen is the other semen that was inside Cindy when she was murdered. Other than her husband's." He breaks into a cocky smile. "Or maybe you don't want to. Maybe I'll have to force you to do it." He leans forward in the chair. "I will, too. I'll get a court order if I have to."

How in the world did Clements find out about the two different semen samples? It had to be Peter Schmidt. That's the only way he could have found out, and I curse the guy under my breath. Schmidt didn't need to tell Clements about that. All he had to do was give up Cindy's body. At least he could have told me on the phone when we talked yesterday what he'd done so I would have been ready.

"Schmidt was real easy to deal with after his boss's boss called him from Madison while I was in the office. He got the message real quick when we started talking about his pension."

I shake my head. It's all about the money for most people.

"It's like I've been telling you, Summers," Clements keeps going. "Lew Prescott will call in any favor he needs to call in to bring his daughter's killer to justice as quickly as possible. Don't fight it. It'll be worse for you in the end if you do."

All I can do is try to stare Clements down, because I can't think of anything to say. I'm too tired. So that's what I do. I just stare back at him.

"Congressman Harrison told us that he and Cindy had sex the day he drove up to the estate," Clements continues. "That was Friday of last week, the day of her murder." He points at me. "The same day you went to the estate twice. The first time in the morning to fix a pipe you claimed was broken. Even though Mr. Prescott had a plumber from Superior go to the place to inspect the plumbing yesterday and the guy couldn't find a thing wrong with anything. And the second time you went there was in the afternoon. Cindy and her father actually spoke on the phone while you were there that time."

So that's how Prescott knew about my second visit. Cindy got out of bed and went downstairs to get a drink, and, now that I think about it, she was gone for a while, longer than it would have taken just to get something to drink. She must have called her father while she was down there, because I didn't hear a phone ring. But why the hell would she tell him I was at the estate? That doesn't seem right, it just doesn't add up. It's like Prescott and Clements are trying to fool me into saying something I shouldn't. I mean, she knew full well that he wouldn't want me to be there. Maybe they got into an argument while they were talking and she told her father in spite. But, as I think back on that day, she didn't seem upset when she slipped back into bed with me and kissed me.

"Yeah, you went there the second time. After Congressman Harrison left to go back to the Twin Cities." Clements's stupid smile morphs into an accusatory sneer. "We know about it."

I'm tempted to tell Clements what I know about Jack. How the congressman filled up his Porsche at the independent station just south of Hayward at seven-forty-five the night of the murder. How he didn't leave the area when he said he did. It's so tempting to blurt everything out—but I don't. I can't. That would give Prescott and Jack the chance to come up with an excuse or an alibi. Or time to get to the old guy who owns the gas station south of Hayward and convince him with money or threats that he was wrong about seeing Jack. I have to keep it all bottled up because, as shocking as it is to me, I'm starting to think Prescott and Jack are responsible for Cindy's murder. And I can't give them the chance to avoid the trap I'm setting for them.

After I sent Davy Johnson home to his wife at three o'clock this morning and made sure that Vivian was fast asleep, I opened that taped-up box Chelsea gave me in the Lion's Tap parking lot. I'm glad Chelsea thought it was full of old love letters, because she wouldn't have given it to me if she knew what was really inside it. As much as Chelsea hates her father, she loves the life she leads, and she'd be helpless without money. The box Cindy sent me from the grave was full of financial information that seems to prove what she told me about Prescott Trading. That it's on the brink of disaster. There's no way Chelsea would want that kind of information getting out.

I'm no financial guru—far from it—but it didn't take a genius to see the red numbers splashed all over the internal statements inside the box. Or to read about how the Minneapolis operation had made a lot of bad bets on oil prices right before the crude market crashed two years ago and that was why company accounts were suddenly pouring blood to the tune of something like a hundred million dollars a month. Or to read that hand-scrawled memo from Jack to Lewis Prescott that was in the box—dated just a month ago—indicating that the company would be lucky to stay solvent until spring. It said that the company's bankers were already starting to ask tough questions. It said that if the bankers called their margin loans due at the end of March, Prescott Trading would be forced into bankruptcy and that any monies that had been distributed to shareholders during the nine months before that would have to be repaid.

I'm going to make copies of the information in that box, then take one of the copies to a friend of mine in Minneapolis who's a CPA so he can confirm what it all seems to indicate. It scares me to death to think that somehow Prescott and Jack suspected Cindy of getting her hands on the information in the box and they killed her to keep her quiet while they pilfer what's left to pilfer of Prescott Trading, then hide the proceeds in overseas accounts where the Feds can't find it so it's there for them when they run. It scares me but it makes a lot of sense, too.

And what if they find out that Chelsea gave me a box full of something from Cindy? I doubt they'd believe me if I told them it was just old love letters she'd never sent me.

Then it hits me. Maybe Jack was at the estate last Friday when I went back there in the afternoon. Maybe he left—maybe they kissed good-bye and Cindy watched him motor down the driveway in the Porsche—then somehow he got back into the mansion without Cindy knowing. Maybe that's how Lewis Prescott knew I was there a second time; maybe Jack told him. Maybe that's why they think they can pin Cindy's murder on me like Sheriff Wilson said Clements was trying to do.

"You had sex with Cindy that afternoon, didn't you, Summers?" Clements jars me back into the moment.

"Or maybe it was even later than that," Clements adds ominously. "Maybe it was more toward evening when you forced yourself on her."

"Forced myself on her?"

"Okay, raped her."

I manage to keep my eyes locked on Clements as he makes these awful accusations, as he conjures up wild ideas in his head. My God, if he starts telling people about my raping Cindy on the day of her murder I'd be finished in Bruner. The town council wouldn't put up with that if they thought there was even a grain of truth to it. The last thing they want is trouble with the River Families, especially the Prescotts. Mrs. Erickson has been telling people for years that Cindy and I are more than just friends, but there's never been a sliver of proof, because it isn't true. We had our fling when we were young, but since I've been married, it's never happened. People around here whisper about us behind my back, but they all recognize who the source of the information is, so it's all taken with a pile of salt. But if Darrow Clements and Lew Prescott are the sources and they tell everyone they have proof to back up their claims, I'm done.

But what's even worse is that my marriage would be finished, too. I've never felt as guilty in all my life as I did when I left the

Prescott estate after Cindy and I had sex Friday afternoon. In all the years we've been married I've never been unfaithful to Vivian until that day, not with anyone, not at any time. For years and years Viv accused me of running around on her with Cindy, but we both understood that she was just using the accusation to try to make me feel bad. And I never did run around on her—until Friday.

"You don't know what you're talking about," I hiss, still glaring at him as hard as I can. "You're out of your mind."

"Am I? Am I really? Are you also going to try and tell me I'm imagining the fact that Dakota County has a cult of devil worshipers?"

"See. You don't know—"

"Or that I'm imagining how Cindy was nailed to the floor of the mansion crucifixion-style and her throat was slashed when Davy Johnson found her. Or that she had a pentagram carved into her forehead. Or that there were candles circling her body," he keeps going, his voice getting louder and more excited with each new fact. "Come on, Sheriff. That sure sounds like a ritual killing to me. It sure sounds to me like you've got a cult up here." Clements's eyes narrow and he takes a quick look at the door. Like he's gauging whether he can get to it before I get to him. "Are you involved with it, Sheriff? Are you in it?" He straightens up and sticks his chin out, gaining confidence with every second I don't charge around the desk at him. "My God, you're probably the leader of it."

"Shut up!" I yell, banging my fist on the desk. Trying to make it clear that if he pushes me any further I might come around the desk at him again. The problem is that I'd indict myself if I did. This is the nightmare scenario, the absolute worst outcome I could have. I think about threatening Clements with being locked up for interfering with a police investigation like Schmidt suggested—which Clements is clearly doing—but that would probably backfire on me at this point. I wouldn't be able to keep him behind bars long, and in the end locking him up would just make me look guilty. "Have you

told Lewis Prescott all this crap?" I ask, reining in my tone, keeping it tough but steady.

"All but the part about you having sex with Cindy," he replies, shifting uncomfortably in the chair, then leaning back into it. "I haven't decided if I want to do that yet."

Clements can't wait to tell Prescott I was having an affair with Cindy. It's just that he doesn't want to tell Prescott about Cindy having an affair with me. For the same reason Peter Schmidt didn't want to say anything. He doesn't want to be the messenger. But if Clements can prove it was my semen inside Cindy and get a rumor going that I'm involved with the cult, then he can tell Prescott I raped Cindy as part of some awful ritual murder. He can tell Prescott and Jack that I forced Cindy to have sex with me and that she isn't a cheater but a victim. I can see the wheels spinning in the bastard's brain as he gazes at me. Schmidt must be right. There must be a huge bonus in this for Clements if he can get me arrested. It would be such perfect cover for Prescott and Jack if they could frame me for the crime.

"I'm going to get you to take that blood test," Clements continues, "if it's the last thing I do, Sheriff Summers."

It dawns on me that I need to get that strongbox out of my house. The one that has the Bruner Washette ticket I found near Cindy's body and the bloody steak knives. If Clements got a search warrant to go through my house, he'd find the box very quickly and it wouldn't take him long to open it, even without a key.

"The very last thing," he says in a hushed voice. "I swear it."

I don't say anything for a few moments, I just stare at him. "Are you staying at the Friendly Mattress?" I finally ask.

He nods, obviously surprised by my question and probably even more so by my tone of resignation. "Yeah, why?"

"I've got a lot of things to do today so I don't have time to deal with this now. Come back tomorrow morning at nine o'clock. I'll give you my answer about the blood test then. Just give me twenty-four hours. Okay?"

He hesitates, thinking over my proposition. "Okay."

"One more thing," I say, leaning over my desk and putting the tips of the thumb and forefinger on my left hand into the exhausted corners of my eyes.

"What?"

"Don't say anything to anyone around here about what Schmidt told you until at least tomorrow morning. Don't say anything about Cindy's body or what the crime scene looked like. Can you at least do that for me?"

"Maybe."

"Look, you and I may not like each other, but you'll be doing the right thing if you listen to me. You understand?"

"Yeah, okay," Clements agrees after a few moments as he waves a warning finger at me. "But you better be here tomorrow morning, Sheriff. You better not be screwing with me, because you'll be sorry if you are. If you aren't here in the morning, if it's one minute past nine o'clock and you're not in this office with me, everyone in this part of the world is going to hear about what I've got on you."

I lean back in my chair and stare up at the ceiling through glassy eyes when Clements is gone. What the hell am I supposed to do now?

At ten-thirty Mrs. Erickson knocks on my office door. Her signature three heavy bangs startle me.

"Sheriff, Maggie Van Dyke is here to see you."

I take a deep breath. When it rains it pours. But I can't turn Maggie away, I have to see her. She has every right to ask me about what's going on with the search for her sister, Karen. The truth is I should have called her by now. She shouldn't have had to come here. The problem is that I don't have anything to tell her.

"Show her in," I call, standing up.

A moment later Maggie's chubby, smiling face fills my office doorway and I nod at the chair Darrow Clements has been sitting in lately more than anyone else. "Have a seat."

"You look so tired, Sheriff," she says softly. "Are you okay?"

"I'm fine, Maggie, but thanks for asking."

"Why don't I run home and make you something to eat? You're starting to look too thin." Her expression turns from happy to sadly compassionate. "Cindy's murder must be putting so much pressure on you. I'm sorry I—"

"It's all right, Maggie." I stare at her for a few moments. "Look, I'm sorry but I don't have anything to tell you." I don't even bother sitting down because I know how short this meeting is going to be. "The counties I sent the information to on Sunday haven't responded. I was just giving them some extra time because of the storm. But I promise I'm going to go wider with the search tomorrow."

She breaks down and starts crying out of nowhere. "Thank you, Sheriff," she sobs. "You're such a nice man." She buries her face in her hands. "I'm so worried about Karen. I'm so worried something terrible has happened to her."

22

"LET'S GO TO lunch."

I glance up from my desk, from a report I was filling out. Bear's in my office doorway with a very determined look on his face that has a glint of mischief in it, too. My eyes sweep to the wall clock. It's not even noon yet. "I'd like to, Billy, but—"

"Come on, Professor," he says, striding in and pulling me out of my chair by my elbow like a guy yank-starting a lawnmower, though he probably doesn't think he's being that rough about it. "Don't argue with me," he warns in a friendly way when I'm on my feet. "We'll call it a working lunch. Okay?"

He wants to get us out of this bad-karma thing we've fallen into, and he knows the best way for us to do that is to talk it through. Whenever we've had a problem in the past, that's what we've always done. Sometimes it's just a few words, some uh huhs and a couple of nods, but it usually works right away and it sets us back on a good course. I just hope it can today. There's more at stake right now than there's ever been. Much more.

I figure we're going to walk over to the Saloon after he pulls me out of my chair. When we climb into his Cherokee, I assume we're going to take a quick ride across town to the Kro-Bar because he wants better food than Sara's greasy stuff. But then we whip past the Kro-Bar, roll over the Boulder River bridge and we're headed west toward Superior.

"Where we going?"

"Somewhere the folks of Dakota County won't be able to bother us," Bear answers. "We're going to the Champlain Room."

"Oh, Christ." The Champlain Room could turn into an all-afternoon thing. It has before. "I don't have time for—"

"No arguing, Professor. I'll take you there by force if I have to," he teases.

I let my head fall back and smile despite everything that's going on. "You would, too, wouldn't you? You'd take me there by force."

"Of course."

"It might not even be open," I point out. "Shank might not have cleared the lane yet."

"It's cleared," Bear assures me. "I called him." He grins. "Don't worry. He's ready for us."

The Champlain Room is a tiny restaurant with incredible food that's out by Shawmut Lake, which is halfway between Bruner and Superior, and though it's only average-sized, it's deep and cold and home to some of the biggest walleye around. Fortunately, not many people know how big the fish there are, so Bear and I usually have it to ourselves. We've pulled some monsters out of this one particular cove on warm summer evenings. One gill-heaving example in particular last July that probably would have set a state record. But recording it with the state DNR would have given away our honey-hole to the general public, so we took some pictures and released it back into the dark waters without any other fanfare.

The Champlain Room is off Route 7 at the end of a narrow, winding, potholed road called Biskerstaff Lane. The owner and chef is a fifty-something Irishman named Shank McAllister who claims he moved from Vermont to Wisconsin a decade ago because he was "having lady troubles." I figure the real story is that he's wanted by a local jurisdiction somewhere in New England for something, but I haven't put his name and picture out on any of the lists those authorities could check because I like him too much, and he hasn't done anything wrong around here as far as I know. He gives Bear and me boating access to Shawmut Lake from his property, which has the only decent put-in on the entire shoreline, and he's a great cook with a good sense of humor.

Like I figured, Bickerstaff Lane isn't plowed. What Shank meant when he told Bear it was cleared was that he'd been able to get his Hummer out to Route 7 and back a few times so we have tire tracks to follow. But it turns out that's enough. It's amazing how much snow has melted thanks to the warm spell that's hung around since the storm hit. The temperature's going to climb into the upper fifties this afternoon, which is almost unheard-of around here in February. But the mercury is supposed to plunge again this weekend and the weather people are predicting another storm for the area. Nothing like the one we just had, but it'll probably dump another six to eight inches on us.

Shank's waiting for us when we pull to a stop beside his Hummer. He's leaning against the railing of the Champlain Room's open-air front porch with his arms crossed over his barrel chest smiling. He's a red-faced, silver-haired, overweight, middle-aged bachelor whose main goal at this point in life seems to be finding the next good time. He claims he starts each morning with a shot and a smoke, and that he's never been to a doctor in his life and doesn't see any reason to break that tradition now, even though he is starting to feel a few sharp pains in his chest every once in a while. He probably won't make it to his sixtieth birthday but he understands that and seems to have come to terms with it.

"Hello, gents," he calls out in a heavy Irish accent that's probably not a hundred percent authentic. "Good to see you."

"Hello, Shank," Bear calls as he climbs out of the truck. "Thanks for taking us on such short notice."

"No problem. Glad to have the company after all this weather."

It's like someone's home inside the Champlain Room because it is. After Shank moved here he converted his living room into a small restaurant with three very private, very comfortable booths all in a row along one wall. Each booth seats up to six people, and they all look out from behind floor-to-ceiling windows over what's still a frozen, snow-covered Shawmut Lake. Seating is by appointment only; he reserves the right not to accept your reservation if he doesn't know you or, worse, doesn't like you; some days he's open and some days he's not, and what you have to eat is entirely up to him. Sometimes it's pasta with a hearty salad and sometimes it's a sirloin steak dinner Morton's of Chicago would be proud of. The thing is, every meal I've ever had here was incredible.

"What'll it be to drink, gentlemen?" he asks as Bear and I slide onto opposite sides of the middle booth.

"Grey Goose and tonic," Bear orders, then he looks at me. "That okay, Professor? Just one?"

I nod. "As long as you let me drive back to town and you take the rest of the day off."

Bear breaks into a big grin. "There's a deal I don't have to think about too long."

"Sheriff?" Shank asks.

"Coke. Big glass with lots of ice."

"Come on, Professor," Bear says quietly as he leans across the table. "Have one beer. We've got a lot to talk about. It'll help."

"No, I can't."

I'm still thinking too much, my paranoia's still in high gear, and suddenly I'm sorry I agreed to come out here. What I should have done during lunch was go back to the house, get that strong-box that has the washette ticket and the knife inside it, and bury it somewhere back in the woods. Now that I'm thinking about it, I'm worried that Darrow Clements agreed to back off until tomorrow morning way too fast. I'm worried he's got a plan. I'm worried that while I'm all the way out here with Bear he'll show up at my house with something that looks like a search warrant and get inside because Vivian won't realize that what he's showing her is a forgery. Then he'll undoubtedly find what I'm trying so hard to hide.

"Come on," Bear pushes.

"No."

"Okay, okay," Bear says in a frustrated tone, glancing up at Shank as he leans back. "I'm still having my vodka and tonic."

Shank nods and starts whistling loudly as he heads off down a hallway toward the kitchen.

I gaze at Bear, suddenly suspicious that this is all part of a plan designed to keep me away from my house so Clements can get in and take a look around. Suddenly I wonder if he and Clements are working together.

I take a deep breath and gaze out at Shawmut Lake. Christ, Maggie's right. The stress of the past week has been too much for me. I must be losing my mind to think all that about my best friend. About a guy who's saved my life twice and wouldn't hesitate to put himself in harm's way to save me again.

"Look, I'm sorry about—" Bear stops himself when Shank comes back down the hallway still whistling the same tune.

"Here you are, gentlemen," he says, putting vodka down in front of Bear and a Coke in front of me. "To our health," he says, bringing a shot glass to his lips and turning it upside down. Then he's gone again.

"I'm sorry about this morning," Bear says after several gulps of his drink. "That was a crappy thing for me to do. I should have helped you change that tire. I don't know what got into me."

"You were pissed off at me for telling you not to give orders to the other guys," I say. "I know that and it's partly my fault because I—"

"Why do you think Shank calls this place the Champlain Room?" Bear asks, looking around.

I know why he's interrupting me so rudely. He made his apology and now he wants to move on. He's always had a hard time saying he's sorry, and once he's done it he doesn't like to dwell on it. "Is it some kind of play on words?" Bear asks. "Like strip clubs have champagne rooms? You know, the private rooms in the back where the girls—"

"He's from Vermont," I interrupt. "I'm guessing he lived in the western part of the state near Lake Champlain, which is a big lake for out East. Not for around here, of course, but for them it's huge."

"Oh, *I* get it," Bear says loudly. "I bet you and Shank didn't even talk about that. I bet you figured that out all on your own."

"Maybe."

"But I still wonder about that play on words because—"

"Naming it Champlain probably reminds him of the good times he left, Billy."

Bear chuckles. "The Professor. How'd you get so smart?"

Fortunately Shank's back with an appetizer. I'm as bad at accepting a compliment as Bear is at apologizing.

"Here's some venison sausage with brie cheese," Shank says, setting a big plate down on the middle of the table, then a basket of bread beside it. "This ought to tide you guys over until the main course. It's really good," he calls over his shoulder as he heads away again. "I'll be back with more drinks in a minute."

The scent of steaming sausage and melted brie is so powerful that the sides of my mouth actually ache. I pick up one of the sausages and wrap it inside a piece of the warm, butter-drenched sourdough bread, then shove the whole thing into my mouth. Suddenly, I'm in heaven. At this moment in time it's easily the best thing I've ever put into my mouth, and all my problems seem to fade away. Maggie was right again. I'm not eating enough and I need to pay more attention to the basics of life despite everything going on around me.

"I know you think I had something to do with Karen disappearing this past Christmas," Bear says quietly after finishing what's left of his drink. "I know you do."

I guess heaven can only last so long. Bear's shattered my beautiful moment, so I grab another piece of sausage and bread and put it into my mouth. But the second piece of sausage never tastes as good as the first one does, nowhere near as good. It's like a law of physics or something. "What are you talking about?" I grumble.

Before Bear can answer Shank's back with more drinks. But he doesn't stick around this time, he doesn't have a shot with us, he doesn't even say anything. He just puts the glasses down and goes.

"You know what I'm talking about," Bear snaps. "That's what you were getting at when we were outside your house, when we went to see if that snowplow had come by when the storm was over. When you told me about Maggie wanting you to start an investigation into Karen's disappearance. Come on."

"I don't want to talk about it." It's a flimsy answer but it's all I can think of to say. I wasn't ready for this. "I, I—"

"I don't blame you, Professor. If I were you I'd think I had something to do with it, too. I mean, of course I made her write down that note before she left."

I want to put my hands over my ears, but instead I take a long drink of soda. I can't believe what I'm hearing. What am I supposed to do now? Arrest my best friend?

"I'm going to have her come to Bruner tomorrow so you can see for yourself that she's alive."

I stop gulping in midswallow. "What?"

Bear grabs three sausages and two pieces of bread and makes a sandwich and the whole thing is gone in a few seconds. All except for a piece of bread stuck between his two front teeth. "I'm having Karen come to Bruner tomorrow. I figured we'd meet at my house."

"Are you serious?"

"Yup," he says, making another sandwich, this time with four pieces of sausage. "Let's make it ten o'clock at my house." He wags a finger at me. "Nobody else can know about this. Not even Maggie."

"But—"

"No," Bear says firmly. "This is the way Karen and I have it all worked out."

"Why?"

"I told you before. She ran off with another guy. This is how I want it. No questions."

"Karen will want to see Maggie," I say, still processing what I'm hearing as relief floods through me. "Don't blame me because I won't be able to stop her."

Bear smiles grimly. "Ten o'clock tomorrow morning at my house. Nobody else knows. Okay?"

I nod slowly.

"Swear to keep this absolutely between the two of us?"

It sounds silly for him to ask for my silence that way, but I agree. "Okay, I swear." It sounds like we're back in high school again, but I'm so glad about tomorrow and so relieved that he wasn't telling me what I thought he was telling me that I don't hesitate for a second.

"Okay." Bear nods and finishes his second vodka.

Just in time for Shank to deliver a third one along with two heaping salads.

"What did Darrow Clements want this morning?" Bear asks, starting to root through his salad like a wild boar roots around a field.

"He wanted me to take a test."

Bear stops going through the greens and glances up at me, eyebrows crunched, eyes narrowed. "Huh?"

I exhale heavily. I'm convinced I'm going to see Karen tomorrow morning and suddenly I feel terrible for all the things I've thought about Bear over the last few days. Hell, for the last month and a half, really. "Cindy and I had sex the afternoon she was murdered," I say in a low voice, swallowing hard. It's tough to admit, but it feels good to tell him. It feels good to talk about it, and he's the only person in the world I can talk to about it. "At the estate."

Bear's gaze drops to his plate. "Oh."

I shake my head. "I can't believe I actually did it with her."

"That's the first time, isn't it? I mean, since you got married."

I nod regretfully, but it feels good to know Bear believes that I've been faithful to Vivian all these years. "She just kept coming on so strong, and Viv and I had just had a terrible fight."

"That's the first time you've ever cheated on Viv, isn't it?"

I nod again. "Yeah."

"Well whatever you do, don't tell her what happened."

"I have to." I do, too. Not right now, but someday I'll have to admit to the awful thing I did. I have to be honest with her. Maybe she'll end up leaving me, but I can't live with the lie. "I do."

"No, you don't," he shoots back quickly. "Cindy's gone. That's all Vivian cares about."

It's shocking to actually hear him say that. "Do you really think she's glad that Cindy's gone?"

Bear rolls his eyes. "Come on, Professor." He glances out at Shawmut Lake. "But what does all of this have to do with Darrow Clements?"

Bear was exactly right to pull me out of my office chair and bring me out here. I'm glad he did now because we're back to normal, we're back to being best friends, and I can tell him anything. "When the coroner did the autopsy he found two different semen samples inside Cindy."

Bear grimaces. "Uh, oh."

"One of the samples belongs to Jack," I go on. "He told them he had sex with Cindy and somehow Lewis Prescott found out I was at the estate after Jack was supposed to have left. So now Clements wants to see if that other sample is mine. He's made the connection, which I guess wasn't real hard to make. He says he hasn't told Prescott yet but he will. He claims he told Prescott about the cult but not about the two semen samples. Nobody wants to tell Prescott his daughter was a cheater." I exhale heavily. "So he wants me to take a blood test so he can prove it's me."

Bear gazes at me for several seconds. "So what if it is yours? That doesn't prove anything except what a lot of people up here already assumed for years. That you and Cindy had a thing for each other. As screwed up a thing as it was for both of you," he adds under his breath.

"*So what?* I'll tell you so what. I think Prescott told Darrow Clements to do everything he can to implicate me in Cindy's murder. I think once Clements proves the semen is mine he's going to tell the world I raped and killed Cindy as part of a ritual. He's going to tell everyone I'm in the cult."

Bear shakes his head. "Even if you're right about what Prescott and Clements are trying to do, which I don't think you are, it would never stick. You don't have anything to worry about, Professor. You aren't in any cult and you didn't kill Cindy. We both know that."

"I wish I was as confident as you are."

I go silent when I hear Shank coming down the hallway pushing a cart loaded with food. He's fixed an amazing filet and lobster entrée with grilled vegetables and boiled potatoes all mixed together with the meat and seafood, and it's as good as any meal I've ever had. He's also brought three plates to the table, so the discussion immediately turns to sports and fishing when he sits down and digs in with us.

When the meal's over Shank reloads the cart with dead dishes, then heads off to the kitchen swerving from side to side along the hallway. It's a good thing he's driving the cart and not the Hummer. We offered to help him clean up but he wouldn't hear of it.

Bear leans over the table when Shank's gone. "So, how you feeling?" he asks me with a drunk chuckle.

I smile at him. "Fine. I think the better question is, how are *you* feeling?"

He takes a gulp of his fourth vodka without answering, then does something he's never done. He reaches across the table and touches my arm. It's a simple friendship tap but it's a first for him. This shocks me. "I got a question," he says, slurring the words as he pulls his arm slowly back across the table. "It's something I've wanted to ask you for a long time, Professor."

"What?"

"If I'm prying just tell me to shut up. Okay?"

"Okay." I will, too. Bear can ask some pretty crazy questions when he drinks.

Bear gathers himself up while he stares into his glass. "Why did your father move your family from Los Angeles to Bruner. What the hell did he do in L.A.?"

"He strangled a woman," I answer evenly. I've been waiting a long time to tell Bear that. I've been waiting a long time to tell anyone that. I haven't even told Vivian. "A woman he was having an affair with."

Bear's eyes streak to mine.

"He told me all that," I say in a low monotone, "right before he put the gun to his head and blew his brains out in front of me in our barn."

I like my Dakota County precinct at night when there's no one else around. It's quiet and it feels like a fortress I could defend by myself if I had to. There are always pros and cons to everything, there's always an upside and a downside to every issue. Maybe it doesn't intimidate people the way the ones I worked out of in Minneapolis and Madison did, but it's cozy. It's a precinct one man can control. Ought to be able to control, anyway. If Mrs. Erickson weren't around. Of course, if it wasn't her, it'd be someone else. So this is about the only time I can control it, completely, anyway. When I have it to myself.

After I made two copies of the financial data that was inside the taped-up box Chelsea gave me, I actually spent fifteen minutes checking around for listening devices despite how anxious I am to watch the Jenkins tapes. I didn't find any, but I still don't feel completely secure. That's how paranoid I am right now.

I put the first Jenkins tape into a TV I have in my office that also has a VCR built in it. Disk and DVD equipment is just starting to make it to the north-country on a widespread basis so a lot of us still use old technology. I stand beside the TV and keep the volume low in case anyone comes through the front door. Mrs. Erickson and all the guys have keys, but there's an alarm that'll chirp even if the person disarms the siren using the code on the pad by the door.

The first tape has nothing on it but Jenkins and his kids hunting deer. Illegally, too, because they're shooting does, and that's not allowed up here. The kids kill two of them while Jenkins handles the camera and whoops with pride when the knees of the deer buckle and the things staggers around for a few seconds before finally keeling over.

The second tape is very different. I catch my breath instantly because I can't believe what I'm seeing. On the screen in front of me are hooded figures huddled around the embers of a bonfire chanting something I can't understand. It looks exactly like that fire Bear and I were investigating out west on Route 7 when Cindy called me. It's hard to tell for sure because everything's so dark, but it sure looks the same.

Then the tiny hairs on the back of my neck stand straight up, and I almost feel as if I'm going to pass out. The hooded figure just to the right of the camera turned left to face the lens for a split second. But a split second was all I needed to recognize the face.

Why do people have this insatiable and stupid desire to record themselves doing stupid things? I'll never understand it.

23

I GAZE AT Karen without uttering a word for several moments
after I come through the front door of Bear's cluttered home.
It occurs to me that I haven't been here since she left, and the
place has definitely gone downhill since she did. "Hi," I finally manage. It's like seeing a ghost when you assumed the person you're
now looking at was dead. Which I did.

"Hello."

She looks good, better than I've ever seen her look. She's taken
off some weight, she's doing something different with her hair, and
she's wearing makeup. Not a lot, just the right amount—some mas-
cara and a little blush. Her clothes are edgier, too. She's wearing a
black leather jacket, a pair of snug jeans, and heels. Not the frumpy,
typical north-country stuff I've always seen her in. It's amazing how
much a person can change in seven weeks. Bear's explanation that
she left him for another man seems on target now that I see her, and
I feel bad all over again that I ever doubted him. This is what women
and men do to themselves when they're in that first few months of

a love affair, in that infatuation stage. They work hard to look good. Then it all goes downhill. Until they have another affair.

"I'm glad to see that—"

"Is this all you needed?" she asks, turning to Bear. "Can I go now?"

I guess a person can only change so much in that short a time. "Have you seen Maggie?" I ask her.

"Hey," Bear snaps, pushing himself off the wall he was leaning against. "You promised you wouldn't do this."

"I don't want to see her," Karen says in an irritated tone.

"But she—"

"Look, Paul," Karen snaps, interrupting me again, "I appreciate what you're trying to do. I'm sure she's telling you how worried she is about me and how she cries herself to sleep every night wondering what's happened to me."

"Well, yeah. I think it's natural for her to do that when she thinks you might be dead."

"She didn't seem worried about me at the table in Superior when the lawyer read the will after our parents died in that car accident. When they gave her fifty grand and me five."

Jesus. I had no idea Gus and Trudy Van Dyke even had that kind of money to give. The realization overwhelms me for a second because it makes it very clear to me that I'm way behind. Vivian and I have less than ten thousand dollars invested and that figure's gone down in the last few years thanks to Wall Street.

"It's not Maggie's fault your parents did that," I say quietly.

"She could have made it right."

"Maybe they figured you have a better chance to make it on your own than she does. If you know what I mean."

Karen's gaze drops to the floor. "Thanks, Paul," she says quietly. "That's nice of you to say."

I'm about to add to it when my cell phone rings. It's Davy Johnson. "Hello."

"Sheriff?"

His voice is shaking like it did the night he discovered Cindy's body. "What is it, Davy?"

"You got to get over to the motel right away." He can barely get the words out. "We've got another problem."

Bear and I make it to Room 10 of the Friendly Mattress in less than five minutes. Right away I understand why Darrow Clements didn't make our nine o'clock meeting this morning. He's faceup on the mattress, tied spread-eagle to the bed, his throat slashed from ear to ear. And there's a pentagram carved into his forehead with one of its points going directly down the bridge of his nose.

24

B Y THREE O'CLOCK I'm sitting in the storage room in the back of Cam Riley's hardware store with all of my deputies: Bear, Davy, Frank, and Chugger. I asked Cam if we could use his place because I didn't want Mrs. Erickson or any kind of listening device to overhear what's being said during our meeting. I didn't call the meeting, my deputies did. Davy, specifically, but he said he was doing it on behalf of Frank and Chugger, too. Peter Schmidt and his crime scene team are in Room 10 at the Friendly Mattress with Clements's body and since it's pretty straightforward to monitor who goes in and out of a single door, Schmidt was all right with the Dakota County force leaving the scene for a while. After all, there wasn't much we could do except stand around the door and get in the way.

I can tell Schmidt's getting real edgy about what's going on in Bruner. Hell, we all are. But what got to me was that he seemed different today. He was wearing an odd look when our eyes met and there wasn't any of that usual friendliness he has about him. He was all business; it almost seemed as if he didn't want to deal with me at all. Maybe it was just my imagination, but I don't think so.

Cam's got an unpainted picnic table and some spindly metal chairs set up in one corner of the chilly room—he only keeps it at sixty degrees in here. It's where the town council meets and he had no problem with us using it. He didn't even ask me why I wanted to meet here. I think he knew.

After Bear slowly eases his huge frame into the seat to the right of mine, I nod at Davy, who's sitting at the other end of the table. "Go ahead, Davy, say what you've got to say. And everyone keep your voices down," I add. At this point I don't trust anyone except my deputies—maybe not even all of them. "What's said in this meeting is for our ears only." For all I know the town council is huddled on the other side of the wall a few feet away from the table, trying to listen in. "Is that understood?"

Everyone mutters their agreement.

I nod at Davy again. "Go on."

After I give him the go-ahead, Davy looks down and unfolds a piece of paper that's in his lap. He stares at it for a few seconds, then crumples it up and curses. "We're scared, Sheriff," he says. "I had a big speech all ready for you, but I'm just going to lay it out for you in my own words. We think—"

"Scared?" Bear interrupts loudly, his expression twisting into one of irritation, then flat-out rage. "You called us together like this to say that you're *scared*? Well I don't know about the rest of you, but I don't have time to waste—"

"Keep your voice down, Billy," I snap. Christ, as loud as he is, people sitting across town at the Kro-Bar will hear him.

"When we've got a bad situation like this on our hands," Bear keeps on going, barreling through my warning, "the last thing we should be doing is acting like a bunch of babies in a thunderstorm crying for our mamas. Jesus." He stands up and heads for the door.

"I don't know about the rest of you, but I got work to do. I don't have time to be scared."

"What a prick," Davy mutters when Bear's disappeared through the doorway. "I'm glad he's gone, Sheriff."

"Me, too," echoes Chugger. "Maybe now we can really talk."

Frank doesn't say anything, but judging by his expression he's right there with Davy and Chugger. And it seems to go deeper for them than just being glad Bear left this meeting. The rift in my tiny force is bigger than I suspected. I was wrong to think that they weren't bitter about how close I am to Bear. Jealousy is a powerful emotion. In my opinion it sits right beside money at the core of all evil.

"Finish what you had to say," I order. I don't agree with Bear's delivery but I agree with his message. We don't have time for this crap. "Hurry up."

"We think you should call in the state guys and let them lead this investigation," Davy explains. "Let us step back into a support role. It's not that we don't have faith in you, Sheriff. We're just not sure we have the technical resources to handle the case."

I shake my head in disbelief. "Peter Schmidt's over at the Mattress right now. He's the best guy around for what we need."

"He's good," Chugger agrees. "But investigating the scene is only one piece of the puzzle. We need more resources in the field."

Their dialogue is so scripted and rehearsed it's painful for me to listen to. I'll bet that whole thing with Davy crumpling up the piece of paper was part of the act, too. I bet there's nothing on it at all. I ought to look at it. I ought to demand it right now. "What do you mean?"

"More feet on the ground with experience in this kind of thing," Frank chimes in. "Come on, Sheriff."

My deputies are driving at two possible concerns as indirectly as they know how. Either they think I can't figure out who murdered Cindy and Clements on my own, or they think I don't want to figure it out. Whichever one it is, it's a pretty terrible indictment of my ability as a police officer—or my morals.

I tap the table nervously. I'm losing control of these guys, I can feel it. "Gentlemen, I think we need to—"

The storage room door opens and I expect it to be Bear coming back to the meeting because he's realized how stupid it was of him to storm out the way he did. If only because when he's present he can have some control of what's said—and what isn't.

But it isn't Bear, it's Cam.

"Sheriff Summers, there's an urgent call for you from the precinct. You can take it in my office."

I stare at Cam, wondering why Mrs. Erickson didn't call my cell phone directly. It's probably because she wanted to tell him something before she spoke to me. After all, Cam's the one who decides what her raise is every year. He's the one who approved of her getting extra options on her phone before I did. He's really her boss, not me.

"I'll be right back, gentlemen."

"Thanks for coming," I say to Davy as we whip past my house in the Cherokee. The urgent message was that Lewis Prescott wants to see me at his estate on the Boulder as soon as possible. "This is a tough time and I need everybody's support right now." Vivian is supposed to be at work, and though I don't have to worry about Darrow Clements anymore, I check the driveway. I'm still worried about someone breaking into my house. "I heard what you said back there at Cam's place." I buried the strongbox back in the woods last night after I got home from watching the Jenkins tape at the precinct. But people could still plant incriminating stuff in the house to frame me, and maybe they could follow my prints back to where I buried the box. Especially if they know I'm going to be busy for a while. "I know you guys are worried about the investigation, but it'll be all right." I breathe a shallow sigh of relief when I don't see anything suspicious at the house. Of course, that doesn't really mean anything. "I just want you to understand that I trust you, Davy. Very much."

He looks over at me with a hesitant grin. "Thanks, Sheriff."

Davy's suddenly busting with pride and I semiregret what I'm about to do to him, but it has to be this way. "So let me tell you something," I say as my voice gathers strength. "Don't ever pull a stunt like that on me again." I actually hear him swallow hard over the whine of the tires on the road. "No more sneak attacks in front of the other guys. You hear me?"

"Sir?"

He's gone from a high to a low in record time, which is exactly what I wanted. "What the hell got into you? To put me on the spot like that. If you've got a beef, you come to me on your own. Now what was all that really about back there?" He swallows hard again. I glance over and see his Adam's apple go up and down like a piston inside an engine. *"Huh?"*

"Um, just what we said it was about, sir. We're scared. We've had two murders in Dakota County in just a few days. Ritual murders at that, and we're scared that we can't stop what's going on. We're scared for our families and our friends. The guys and I think we need to call in as many people as possible. You know, get as much experience as possible on top of the situation as fast as we can."

"Is it that you guys don't think I can handle the investigation myself? Or that for some reason I really don't want to find out what's going on in our county?" I can be direct when I have to. A lot of people can't, but I don't have any problem with confrontation when it's necessary. "Because I have a conflict?"

"Oh, God, oh, God, no," he stumbles. "It's ah, it's just that . . . I mean this is a—"

"What if I told you I was about to make an arrest, Davy? Would you believe me?" I know that second question's a tough one for a subordinate to answer, especially if he doesn't, but too bad. I'm actually more interested in his tone and his demeanor when he answers than in what he says. I know what he'll say. He has to.

"Yeah . . . I believe you. I, I mean *of course* I believe you, Sheriff."

His answer was purely predictable, but his body language isn't giving me much of an endorsement.

"How long you think before you make the arrest?"

"A day or two at the most." I pull out my cell phone when it starts ringing. "Hello." I'm on the phone for less than thirty seconds and the news is terrible. "All right," I mutter, pursing my lips. "Thanks for letting me know." Unfortunately, I sort of expected it.

"Who was that?" Davy asks as I bury the phone back in my jacket.

He seems nervous. He's fidgeting like mad with the zipper on his jacket, and he isn't the kind of guy who fidgets. "What's the problem?" I ask, trying to make him even more uncomfortable. "What's wrong?"

"What do you mean?"

I point at his hands. "What's wrong with your zipper? Is it broken?"

Davy looks down at it. "What? Oh, no," he says, letting go of it. His hands rest in his lap for all of two seconds, then he goes for the Velcro on one of his pockets, ripping it open time after time. I've never seen him like this before. "Who was that on the phone?" he asks again.

"A nurse from the hospital over in Superior." I hesitate, not certain I should tell him what I just learned. But I do anyway. "The boy I found out at the cabin the day after the storm died this morning."

Davy lets out a long, sad sigh. "God, that's awful."

I stare at the road ahead, thinking about carrying the kid back to my house over those snow-covered ridges. How at one point during the trek I thought I was going to pass out from exhaustion. How I wanted to reunite the boy with his mother so badly, but now that'll never happen. The worst part for her is that she'll never have closure. She'll never know what happened to her son, because there's no way we can figure out who he belongs to. For a long time she'll hold on to a desperate hope that a miracle will happen and her son will come walking back through her door one day, as any mother would. But then she'll finally accept it. We put a picture of the boy out on several missing person websites, but we've gotten no responses.

Davy and I ride in silence until we pull up to the Prescott estate.

"Do you know why Lewis Prescott wants to see you?" Davy asks as we climb out of the Cherokee.

"No." Davy's anxious. It's like his head's on a swivel he's so nervous. Maybe it was my imagination, but for a moment it almost looked like he was reaching for the pistol on his hip. "He didn't say."

"Maybe I should stay out here," Davy suggests, his eyes flashing around as he stops in his tracks. "Outside, I mean. There aren't any cars in the driveway. That makes me a little nervous, you know? Why don't you go in and I'll stay out here? Just in case, Sheriff."

Jesus Christ. Davy thinks I brought him out here to kill him. I can't believe it. This is insane. "Now look, Davy, I'm getting—"

"Sheriff Summers!"

My eyes zip to the front door and there's Lewis Prescott. "Yes, sir."

"Come inside, Paul!" he orders. "Hurry up!" He points at Davy. "You stay where you are, son. The only person I want to talk to right now is the sheriff."

Davy clearly isn't insulted by the snub. In fact, he looks relieved. Like the governor just called and he's gotten a reprieve from the chair. He hustles back to the truck and pulls out a pack of cigarettes as I head toward the front door. I didn't have a clue that he smoked. I guess I really don't know him very well at all.

When I'm through the mansion's doorway and into the foyer, Prescott actually shakes my hand. I'm shocked. I don't think we've ever shaken hands before. At least, I can't remember it.

"Thanks for coming to see me on such short notice," he says. "I know you're busy."

It occurs to me that Prescott might not even know about Clements. That he might think I'm just busy in general. He seems stressed. He seems like he's under the crushing stress of a man whose fortune is crumbling around him. Not the shock-stress a man who just heard about an associate being murdered by a cult of devil worshipers is feeling. It was one of his assistants who called Mrs. Erickson, and I didn't ask her if she told the assistant about Clements.

"Do you know about Darrow Clements?" I ask. "Do you know what happened to him?"

Prescott looks at me like I just climbed out of a UFO. "Of course, I know. Why the hell do you think I'm here? I left Minneapolis as soon as I heard about it." He puts both hands up and a frustrated expression comes to his face. "Sorry for the tone, Paul," he says. "It's been a difficult couple of weeks."

It's hard to believe that this is the same man who manipulated, tortured, and controlled me for more than twenty years. Who often seemed to take pleasure in the pain he caused me. Like the night he wouldn't let me into his Edina compound. I heard him chuckling on the other end of the line with the guard and I could tell the guard felt bad for me.

"What's going on?" I demand. "Why'd you want me to come out here?"

"I didn't want to be seen with you in town."

I raise one eyebrow. He must have realized how bad that sounded, because he groans and puts a hand on my arm.

"I didn't mean it like that. God, what's wrong with me today? What I meant was that I didn't think it would be good for either one of us if we were seen together in Bruner. You know, given what's going on."

I don't have a clue what he means by that but I don't ask.

Prescott takes a deep breath and gathers himself. "I need your help, Paul."

"Help?"

He gazes at me for several seconds without blinking. "Look, I can't have it get out that my daughter was killed by a cult. I can't have people think Cindy died that way, especially her mother. I don't want my wife going through the agony of remembering how her daughter was tortured to death every time she thinks of Cindy. It would destroy her. And I don't want the newspapers down in the Twin Cities to pick up on the story and drag Cindy's name through the mud by speculating that she was somehow involved with the cult. We all know how those God damn beat reporters can be. They're just trying to write stories that'll sell as many copies as possible."

It's my turn to stare back at him. I understand exactly what he's saying and I hate that I do. What's wrong with me? Why can't I treat him like the bastard he is? Why do I have this flaw that makes me have sympathy for people who've caused me so much pain? Maybe it's because I'm impressed that he'd care about his wife's feelings at all, and it reminds me that Mrs. Prescott was always pretty nice to me. A mother having to cope with the loss of a child is bad enough. She shouldn't have to think about her daughter's throat being slowly cut open inch by inch as she's nailed to the floor—which is how Schmidt told me it probably happened. The uneven sawing serration marks on Cindy's throat indicated to him that the killer took his time and that she suffered for a while.

"It's already out there," I say quietly. "I mean, I think some of the locals may know that Cindy's murder at least appeared to have been ritual killing." I grimace. "The woman who works for me is a huge gossip and she's been spilling it."

"Then you've got to deny it." Prescott's eyes are suddenly burning. "Hold a press conference or something."

"That's a double-edged sword," I point out. "If I deny it, people might dig into it even deeper, they might ask even more questions, especially the reporters."

Prescott points a trembling finger at me. "I don't care what you have to do, Sheriff Summers," he says, his attempt at a bedside manner evaporating, "but I want you to head off any rumors that Cindy and Clements were murdered by a cult. Do whatever it takes but do it. Lie if you have to, I don't care, but do it. Do you understand me?"

I'm sitting at my desk at the precinct in the dark, with only the glow from a few computer lights faintly illuminating the office. The screen's dark because I haven't used the computer in a half hour. In fact, I haven't used anything in the office. I've just been sitting here staring straight ahead, contemplating my life. It's after eight o'clock and, though I told Vivian on the phone that I'd be home late tonight while I was on my way back from the Prescott estate with a visibly relieved Davy, I'm surprised she hasn't called to see where I am.

I've been sitting here for thirty minutes reflecting on my career as a law enforcement officer, thinking about how I've been going backward ever since I dropped out of the University of Minnesota. How I could look at it the other way around if I wanted to delude myself. I mean, I went from a city force to a state force when I went from Minneapolis to Madison. In most people's minds that's a step up. And when I came to Bruner I went from being a captain to sheriff. Again, a lot of people would say that was a promotion. The thing is, I know better. And the worst part about that backward career track is that I've been controlled the entire way. I've been a pawn for a long time, shoved into this north-country closet by a bully. And the desperation of being completely controlled is finally catching up with me.

A rap on the precinct door finally distracts me, and I rise from my chair and steal into the reception area. "Who the hell can this be?" I mutter. I glance through the window beside the door. "Sara?" I open the door a crack, and I'm met with a rush of cold air from the darkness. As the weather people had predicted, the temperature is diving. "What do you want?"

"I need to talk to you."

Sara and I haven't spoken since we "happened" to meet in the woods and she led me to the cabin. As the hours have gone by I've become less convinced that our meeting was coincidental. I know it would have been difficult for her to find me out there, even if she'd gotten some help with regard to which direction I was headed, but I'm not putting it past her. She has abilities most people couldn't understand. I don't fully understand them, but I accept the fact that she has them.

"Let's do it tomorrow," I suggest.

"No, it has to be now."

It sounds like she's slurring her words. "What's in that?" I point at the Pepsi bottle she's clutching like a preacher clutches a Bible.

She laughs. "Pepsi."

"What else?"

A smirk lights up her face. "Just let me in."

And I do. I don't know why, but I do. "Let me see that." I reach for the bottle when she's inside the precinct and the door's closed behind her.

But she pulls it away with a giggle and a whoop.

"Come on, give it to me."

"You know what I've always liked about you," she says, holding the bottle out for me and tilting her head down seductively, "other than those beautiful eyes and that wide chest?"

"What?" I take a sniff of the bottle and cringe. It's just like I thought. The bottle's full of rotgut, homemade moonshine. Three or four swallows of it and you're on your ass.

"You treat me with respect; you don't treat me any differently because I'm a Chippewa." Her expression turns mean. "Everyone else thinks they can dis me and call me nuts whenever they want to. Even your wife."

Sara's very drunk. "My wife doesn't even—"

"Your wife better watch her step," Sara interrupts, holding up her hand.

"Why?"

Her sneer turns sinister. "Because maybe Cindy Prescott wasn't her real rival. Maybe your wife shouldn't assume she's taken care of all of the women who might steal you away from her."

"My wife didn't take care of anything."

Sara stares at me for several seconds. "You sure about that, Paul?"

"I'm sure."

"Sure you aren't protecting her somehow?"

"What do you mean by—"

"I hear Caleb Jenkins is missing some videotapes," she cuts in, flipping her long black tresses with a sexy shake of her head. She unzips her jacket. "You know anything about that?"

"Why would I know anything about it?"

Sara takes off her jacket and drops it on the floor, then pulls her sweater over her head with one quick move and drops it on top of the jacket. She's not wearing a bra.

"Put your sweater back on."

"What'd you see on that tape, Paul?" she asks, taking a step toward me. "Did you see someone look back into the camera real quick?"

"Maybe."

"Well, did you or didn't you?"

"Okay, I did."

Her eyes are flashing. "You saw me," she whispers, "didn't you, Paul?"

I hesitate for a few moments, then nod. "Yeah, I saw you, Sara. I sure did."

"I bet you liked it, too. I bet that mind of yours conjured up all kinds of silly things about me, didn't it?"

I move close to her, so our faces are just inches apart. "Tell me something."

"What?"

"Do you remember Bill Campbell's son coming into the Saloon one night a few years ago before I got to be sheriff."

A curious expression comes to her face. "Maybe. Why?"

As I turn to head to the Cherokee after locking the precinct front door, a hulking figure looms out of the darkness in front of me. *"Jesus!"* I almost go for my gun as I step back against the door, then I realize it's Bear. "Are you trying to give me a heart attack?"

"Just the opposite, Professor. I'm trying to make sure you stay alive."

"What's that supposed to mean?"

"I saw Sara leave here a minute ago."

"Huh?" I ask innocently.

"Don't play dumb with me. I saw her come out."

I glance up and down Main Street. It's a little before nine o'clock. The shops are dark and the sidewalks are deserted. "Okay," I admit, "she was here. She was drunk and I tried to sober her up. I didn't want her going home and getting into it with Ike."

"Did you screw her?"

"What?"

"Did you screw her?"

"Of course not. Why would you ask—"

"Because she wants you to."

"How the hell do you know that?"

"I just do."

We stare at each other for a few moments as the mist from our breath rises and disappears into the air above us. "You're out of your mind," I say. "And I don't care if she does want me. You know I'd never do that."

"Mmm."

"I *wouldn't.*"

He nods. "Good. Stay the hell away from her. She's poison."

"Yeah, yeah." I pull the collar of my jacket up around my neck. It's colder out here than I thought it would be. "Hey, thanks for giving Davy an earful at the meeting this afternoon. He deserved it."

Bear snorts. "He's a little prick and so are the other two. We ought to replace all of them. I've been telling you that for a while."

"And it was good to see Karen." Bear might be right about making some personnel changes on the force, but I don't want to give him even the slightest clue that I'm thinking about it because he'll shove it right in their faces. It's better just to avoid the issue right now. "Thanks for having her come to Bruner. I know that was tough, but it helped me."

"It was," he admits.

I shouldn't bring this up, I should just let it go. But that's not my nature. "I need to ask you something, Billy."

"What?"

"Today at your place . . ." My voice trails off as I second-guess myself.

"Yeah, what?"

Here I go again, suspecting my best friend in the world of something terrible. It's crazy and I wish I could stop. Pretty soon he's going to give up on me and I won't be able to blame anyone but myself.

"Come on, Professor," he urges. "What's up?"

"I saw that big new television in the other room." I could tell he was trying to keep me out of there when we were meeting with Karen but I saw it. It was impossible not to. "Christ, it takes up half the room."

"So?"

"So where'd you get the money for it?" I've got my suspicions, but I want to see what he says. I want to see if he can come up with a credible answer. "The thing must have cost ten grand."

He stares at me intently for several moments and I'm sure he's about to take a swing at me, or at least tell me to mind my own damn business. But then his eyes drop to the steps and he gets this defeated look on his face.

"It's all part of the thing with Karen," he explains, his voice low.

"How do you mean?"

He swears under his breath. "I took out a life insurance policy on her a while ago with an agent down in Madison."

"With Mickey?"

"Yeah, Mickey." He looks at me with a curious smile. "Didn't I introduce you to him?"

"You sure did." It was about a year ago and Mickey reminded me more of a loan shark than an insurance salesman. After he left my office all I wanted to do was take a shower. "He was an interesting guy," I say sarcastically.

Bear rolls his eyes. "Which is Professor-speak for you couldn't stand him."

"I couldn't."

"Anyway . . . well . . ." Bear hesitates. "This is tough."

"Tell me, Billy. Come on, it's freezing out here."

He clicks his tongue against the roof of his mouth a few times. "Okay, here's what happened. Mickey and I reported that Karen was dead to the insurance company. It was a fifty-thousand-dollar policy, and I gave her ten grand of it to change her name when she left me. Mickey and I split the other forty thousand down the middle."

I put a hand to my head and take a deep breath. Bear just admitted to me that he's committed insurance fraud. It's a felony; he could go to jail for years, and I should arrest him for it right now. I'm a police officer, for Christ sake, and he just admitted to a crime. But he's saved my life twice and I still feel guilty as hell about suspecting him of killing Karen. What am I supposed to do, blow the whistle on him? Of course, I should. That's easy to say when you're not involved. But when it's your best friend in the world it's different. At least the money didn't come from where I thought it did.

"God damn it, Bear, why the hell'd you do that?"

He rolls his eyes. "Why do you think I did it?"

"Don't they need a death certificate or something to give you the money?" I ask.

Bear chuckles. "Mickey's got friends in the morgues. I don't think it's the first time he's pulled this one."

I wave a finger at him. "You're gonna get—"

"I'll deal with that when the time comes."

"God, I worry about you."

We stand there in the darkness for a few moments, then Bear does something that takes me completely by surprise. He hugs me. And it isn't a quick lean-in that could be taken as one of those shoulder-to-shoulder things men do at clubs as they're shaking hands. It's a real, both-arms-all-the-way-around-me hug that nearly takes the wind out of me it's so hard. I don't think a man's ever hugged me like that before. It feels strange and I feel stupid for feeling strange.

"You're my brother, Paul," he says when he finally pulls back. "I love you. I really do, like a brother."

I shake my head, the fact that he just called me Paul hitting me hard. That he told me he loves me hitting me even harder. Those awful moments in the barn are careening back at me, too. After my father had made his final confession and put the gun to his head. When he looked at me and told me he loved me so damn much. I was only sixteen but I knew what he desperately wanted was for me to tell him that I loved him, too. But I couldn't, the words wouldn't come. When it was obvious I had nothing to say, my father pulled the trigger and that was that.

Ever since, I've wondered whether I could have saved my father if I'd just told him I loved him back. The question has haunted me every day now for twenty-three years.

Maybe Bear is searching for the same compassion. He's a much tougher man than my father was, but you never know.

25

VIVIAN'S WAITING FOR me in the kitchen when I come through the back porch door. She's standing by the stove and she looks nice. She's done her hair and she's wearing a pretty dress. She's trying hard and I appreciate it.

"Hi, there."

"Hi." She smiles sweetly and trots to me, then slips her arms around my neck and kisses me. "I should be suspicious of where you've been, Sheriff Summers," she murmurs when her lips fall from mine, "but I'll try not to be. I guess this is the new me."

It all feels and sounds good, which is why I can't believe what I'm about to do. It's like when I asked Bear how he got the money to buy that big new television. I shouldn't get into this with her, like I shouldn't have gotten into it with him. I should just leave well enough alone, but I can't. Along with the husband I have to be the sheriff.

"You don't have to be suspicious. You know that."

"Uh huh." Vivian forces a wary smile to her lips and nods at the oven. "I made some dinner for you. Ribs just the way you like them. Lots of barbecue sauce."

I smelled them when I walked through the back porch door and my stomach's already grumbling. But when I have something as important as this on my mind I have to get right to it. I wish I had more patience. Maybe life wouldn't have turned out much different if I did, but the ride would have been a lot smoother.

"Let's go into the living room, Viv."

She was headed to the oven to fix me a plate, but she turns around and gives me an aroused look. "What's wrong?"

She can hear that tone in my voice, I know it. "Come on," I say gently, taking her hand and leading her to our couch. "Sit."

"Okay," she says hesitantly.

I ease down next to her, trying to figure out how best to start this. I tried to figure out how to do it all the way home but I didn't come up with anything good. Any way I do it this conversation could send her into outer space. "Viv, I want you to listen calmly to what I have to say." Right away I see fear in the crow's feet at the corners of her eyes. I knew this would happen. "Please don't overreact."

"What are you going to tell me?" She grabs my arm. "Oh, God, Paul, are you going to divorce me?"

"No, no, honey. This isn't about divorce." It never crossed my mind that she might think this was the beginning of a divorce conversation. "Don't worry."

She lets out a heavy sigh, almost a sob, and puts a hand to her chest. "You scared me to death. I really thought you were going to—"

"Are you in the cult?" I ask her directly.

"*What?*" Her mouth falls open and her hand goes quickly from her chest to her lips so I won't see her teeth. It's such a natural reaction for her after all these years. "How could you think I was part of that awful thing?"

She took the bait. "Well, how did you know it actually exists?"

"Well, I guess I . . . I mean . . . well, you've told me."

"I've never said anything to you about a cult in Dakota County." I'm sure I haven't, too. I've been careful not to all this time so I could have this moment with her. In the back of my mind I've always worried that if there really was a cult there was a chance she might be in it. "Never."

"Then I must have heard about it at work. Janet must have told me."

Janet Carlson manages the Bruner Washette for Charlie Wagner. I seriously doubt Vivian would have heard anything about the cult from Janet. Last I heard they hadn't spoken more than a few words in a month.

"I know you and Janet don't talk. How could she have told you?"

Fire dances in Vivian's eyes. "Do you know everything about my life?" she snaps.

"Don't blame me." I never miss an opportunity to drive the wedge deeper between Vivian and Mrs. Erickson. "Blame Mrs. Erickson. She told me about you and Janet not talking."

"That bitch. I ought to—"

"You ought to what, Viv?" For several seconds after I ask the leading question I'm sure she's about to explode. But then she shuts her eyes, inches closer to me on the couch, and puts her head on my shoulder. She's trying hard, and all of a sudden I get a warm feeling in my heart. I really love her again. It's crazy. "You ought to what to Mrs. Erickson?"

"Nothing, Paul," she answers in a soft voice. "Nothing at all. What I ought to do is be glad you're home."

I love her very much but I have to press, I can't let it go. That's just who I am. "If I called Sheriff Wilson down in Brower County and asked him to go out to Loon Lake to see Heather and Marty, would they tell him you've stayed at their house as many nights as you've told me you have? I've kept a record of the times you've told me that, Viv. I have it all written down. Or were you somewhere else a lot of those nights?"

"Why are you asking me this, Paul? Why don't we just relax and have a nice night?" Her hand slides to my knee.

"Vivian, I—"

"I love you, Paul. I love you so much."

As I stare down into her dark eyes I don't think I've ever felt so guilty, I don't think I've ever been so sorry for something I've done. Why did I have to go back out to the Prescott estate that last time? "I love you, too."

26

A N HOUR AGO I dropped off a copy of all that financial information that was crammed into the box Chelsea gave me with a friend of mine named Doug Cooper. Doug's an accountant who should be able to confirm with authority exactly what all those numbers in the Prescott Trading annual report really mean and, more important, what the implications are for Lew Prescott and Jack Harrison. Doug's got an office in St. Paul, and since I needed to be down in the Twin Cities again anyway, I didn't have to make an extra trip. I told Doug a little about what was going on when I gave him the stuff, but only what I felt I had to tell him to get him on board and get that bloodhound nose of his in gear. It's better if he doesn't have the full picture right now. For his own good. Just in case this thing turns out to be even bigger than I already think it is.

I got to know Doug while I was on the force in Minneapolis, when I helped track down the killer of his thirteen-year-old daughter. He wanted justice any way he could get it, and I worked overtime finding the guy so Doug wouldn't turn vigilante and get himself in big trouble. Doug and his wife seemed like a nice couple, and I know cops aren't supposed to get emotionally involved in cases, but I couldn't help it. I pored over the evidence and the clues time after time during my off-hours. I even went to the murder scene four times after the crime scene guys were finished with it. Then it hit me one night at two in the morning like a hurricane, as I was watching an old movie in my barely furnished apartment. Suddenly I knew who the murderer was. It was like an epiphany, because it all came to me in a few seconds. Everything. The how, who, and why, and suddenly the case was solved.

The next morning I went to see the detective in charge and I laid it all out for him. He gave me a quick thanks and a pat on the back that was more of a shove out of his office and that was the last I heard from him. That afternoon he and his partner arrested the guy I named as the killer and by nine o'clock that night he'd confessed to the murder. The following day the detectives called a press conference and explained in detail to a mass of reporters how they'd broken the case wide open. Thing was, I called Doug at two in the morning, right after I figured out who the murderer was. So when the detectives took all the credit for solving the case, Doug was so mad he couldn't see straight. He told me he was going to make it right with the higher-ups on the force, but I told him not to. I told him the most important thing at that point was for his wife and him to get closure with what had happened to their daughter and not to worry about who got credit for solving the case.

Doug's never forgotten what happened, how hard I worked on the case. As thanks he's done my income taxes for free every year since. It's not like filling out my return is any big deal—only a few of the lines on the form require ink from me—but it makes me feel good to know a professional is doing it, and maybe what's even more important to me is that he still appreciates how I helped him. He's been a CPA for thirty-two years, the first twenty-two with one of the big national firms working with several large corporate clients in Minneapolis. So he's eminently qualified to look at the Prescott Trading stuff, and I know he'll never say a word to anyone about it.

After I left Doug's place it was still early, still a little before daybreak, because Doug's a night owl. He always has been. So I got another cup of coffee at a 7-11 before I drove over to Edina Engineering. I tossed the empty cup from home in the trash can outside the 7-11 doors as I was going in, and it was then that I realized it was the first cup of coffee I'd finished in a long time. I actually stood there staring down into the can for a few seconds looking at how empty the cup was. The clerk saw me doing it and figured I was crazy, because she gave me that look when I got to the counter, but I didn't give a damn. I realized that for the first time in a long time I was going in the right direction.

Now I'm standing off to one side of the Edina Engineering parking lot behind an SUV waiting for Henry Steinbach to show up—I parked my Cherokee down the street so it wouldn't create a stir with its Dakota County Police Force down each side. Last night I went to the "People" section of the company's website to see what Steinbach looked like, and it was easy to find him. He's got his own page because he's one of the senior executives, and he was in the company-wide picture, too. He's a bald, middle-aged-looking guy with a dark beard and mustache who I recognize right away when he climbs out of his minivan after parking in the spot marked "H. Steinbach." It's the same van that was parked in that spot last week when I came here and was so trusting of Mrs. Driscoll, the firm's receptionist. I figured one of the other nonexecutive employees must have used Steinbach's spot that day since he was traveling. I guessed wrong.

"Good morning, Mrs. Driscoll." The receptionist looks up from her keyboard and I can tell I'm the last person in the world she wants to see standing in front of her desk right now. "Remember me? I'm Sheriff Summers from Dakota County, Wisconsin."

"Uh, yes, I remember."

I watch her fingers carefully as I give her a friendly smile. There won't be any secret alarm delivered to the executive offices with the push of a hidden button. Not if I can help it. "I was here last week looking for Henry Steinbach, but you told me he was in California."

"I remember."

"I never did get a call from him."

"Well, I gave him the message."

"I'm sure you did." I lean over her desk so no one else can hear us. "I just watched Mr. Steinbach park his car in his personal spot outside. It's the same van that was parked in that spot last week when I was here. I know it's the same van because I remember the license plate. JKT-719." I nod at the credenza behind her desk. "I'm sure you have a record of that somewhere in your files, Mrs. Driscoll. You probably help the personnel department with all of that kind of information, right? That's probably one of the things you do here."

She's staring at me now as though she's hypnotized, as though I'm swinging a pocket watch on a chain back and forth in front of her eyes. I know it's not just because of what I'm saying, but because of how I'm saying it, too. See, I'm using this certain tone I've perfected over the years. I don't use it often but when I do, people listen.

"Now," I continue, "just because his van was here last week doesn't necessarily mean *he* was here. I understand that. But I can check out your story pretty easily, can't I? And if it was wrong in any way, you could be in some trouble because you would have knowingly made a false statement to a police officer." I have no intention of making trouble for this nice lady, but one way or another I will see Henry Steinbach in the next few minutes. "I want you to take me back to his office right now. No, *no*," I say quickly when she reaches for her phone. "I don't want you to call him. I just want you to take me back to his office."

She stares at me a little longer, then slowly rises from her seat. "Follow me, please."

She leads me out of the reception area into a quiet corridor. The men and women beyond the open office doors lining the corridor are staring at their computers or have their noses buried in reports and don't look up. I'm glad. I'm wearing my uniform and I don't want to create a stir, because I want the element of surprise on my side. I considered wearing civilian clothes today, but I wanted the uniform on me when I came face to face with Steinbach. I wanted all the intimidation it and the badge bring.

Steinbach's got a typical midwestern executive office. Everything's big. The office itself, his desk, the sofa, the chairs around the coffee table the sofa sits in front of. And there's a lot of dark wood in it as well as tasteful prints of wildlife scenes and pictures of him hunting just about everything you could hunt, along with other executives of the firm. I know they're other Edina Engineering executives he's hunting with because they're all wearing Edina Engineering hats in the pictures as they kneel side by side proudly behind their kills, guns resting on their knees.

"Mr. Steinbach."

"Yes, Mrs. Driscoll," Steinbach answers in an aggravated tone without looking over from his computer screen, "what is it?"

"Uh, sir?"

"What the devil—Oh, Good Lord."

When he catches sight of me his face tenses right up. As he rises out of his chair, his eyebrows knit together and his mouth twitches on one side. Yup, I'm damn glad I wore the uniform.

"I'm Sheriff Paul Summers," I say as I move to where he's standing to shake hands with him. Then I make myself at home by sitting down in the chair in front of Steinbach's desk without being asked. "I'm the sheriff of Dakota County, Wisconsin," I say, pulling out my badge and giving him a good, long look at it. "That's up north, east of Duluth and Superior," I say, stowing the badge back in my pocket when he finally takes his eyes off it. "I just want to ask you a few questions."

He motions for Mrs. Driscoll to leave and to shut the door as she goes. She can't get out of here fast enough. "What kind of questions, Sheriff?"

"What were you doing up in my county last week? And who were you doing it for?" I'm pretty sure I know who he's working for but I want to hear him say it.

"That's confidential."

"Mr. Steinbach," I say evenly, "I will get the answers to my questions one way or the other." I hate to be mean to this guy, because he hasn't done anything wrong. He's just trying to do his job and not get screwed in the process, but at this point I don't care about his feelings. I can't. Time is of the essence. "If you make things difficult for me, I will—"

"Will you promise to keep our conversation completely confidential, Sheriff?"

"Yes."

"I mean *completely* confidential. Will you promise me that no one will know how you got your information?"

"Yes."

He takes a deep breath, as though he's trying to figure out if he has any options other than to talk to me. "Look, I'm sure you already have a good idea of who my client is."

"Lewis Prescott?"

Steinbach nods. "That's right."

"Well, what are you doing for him?"

Steinbach stares at me for a long time. I've heard how deliberate engineers can be, but this is ridiculous. "How did you find me?" he finally asks.

"Bat McCleary."

"Who's—"

"Bat owns the Exxon in Bruner. You filled your car up there last week."

"But—"

"We checked Bat's credit card receipts. Your name jumped out at us real fast, since you used your corporate card to pay."

Steinbach curses under his breath. "I'm a pretty good geological engineer, but I don't know dirt about covering my tracks, do I?"

He breaks into a chuckle at his own joke. As corny as it is, I laugh right along with him, because I want him to feel as comfortable as he can with me.

"It's tough to cover your tracks, you know? You think you have," Steinbach says, "but there's always a way to slip up."

"Especially these days," I agree. I give him a few moments. "Now tell me what you're doing for Lewis Prescott."

Steinbach's expression turns grave. "Sheriff, are you aware that Lewis Prescott owns a lot of land in Dakota County?"

"Yes."

"I'm not talking about just the land his estate is on. I'm not talking about his part of the ridge overlooking the Boulder River. The ridge all those mansions are built on." Steinbach takes a deep breath. "Prescott owns a lot more than just that. I'm talking thousands and thousand of acres between the bottom of that ridge and something you all call River Road up there in Dakota County."

My mind flickers back to the morning Cindy called and begged me to come to the estate to fix a broken pipe. To when I pulled up to the Prescott estate after barreling down 681 and gazed out over that sea of pine trees at the bottom of the ridge. That's all his. "I know," I murmur. "So what?"

"So what?" Steinbach asks, both eyebrows raising. "*So what? I'll* tell you what, Sheriff. All that land is filled with taconite, which is the stuff they turn into iron. The same stuff they're mining in the Iron Range up in northern Minnesota as fast as they can. Except that Prescott's taconite is high grade. The stuff up in northern Minnesota is typically 25 to 30 percent iron ore, but Prescott's stuff is almost 40 percent. That's what my work shows, anyway." Steinbach shakes his head. "Seems like the rich just keep getting richer, doesn't it?"

He keeps on talking, but I'm not really listening, because this hurricane just hit me out of nowhere. The same way it did the night I figured out who'd murdered Doug Cooper's thirteen-year-old daughter.

Lew Prescott stands in front of me. After all of these years, I've finally made it into his compound. He called me back within three minutes of the call I placed to him after I'd walked out of Henry Steinbach's office, and he told me to come right over to those three huge mansions I've never been allowed into until today.

"What is it?" he asks. "What do you want?"

"Why are you so concerned about the cult in Dakota County? Why are you so worried about reporters' picking up on that story?"

"I told you," he snaps. "I don't want my wife thinking Cindy was tortured. I don't want them inferring that she was part of the whole mess."

I shake my head slowly. "That's not the reason and we both know it. Now tell me the real reason."

27

THE SNOW WE were supposed to get over the weekend never materialized. Temperatures got cold, down into the single digits last night, but we didn't get any accumulation. A few flurries Saturday night but that was it. I was glad because I had my heart set on making it to the Twin Cities this morning. If we'd gotten a new blanket of white in the north-country, I might not have seen Doug or been able to startle my new acquaintance Henry Steinbach in his office until the middle of the week. No snow over the weekend, but now the weather people are talking about another big storm that's supposed to hit us hard tomorrow night or Wednesday morning. It's amazing, but the big storms don't end here until late April, some years not until May.

I ended up having a decent discussion with Steinbach after I was able to refocus on what he was saying, after I got over that hurricane that hit me. Turns out Lewis Prescott is a jerk to almost everyone, including business associates, and I think that's a big reason that Steinbach was so willing to talk to me. He told me Prescott's been as demanding and arrogant a client as Edina Engineering's ever had, and that the old codger's behind on his bills, way behind. I wanted to tell him why I thought Prescott was a slow payer but I didn't. I kept that to myself. When I stood up to leave, Steinbach seemed disappointed that all I wanted to do was find out about taconite. I think in the back of his mind he was hoping that I was trying to put the old man behind bars. And I'd sure like to, but I didn't say that.

In ten minutes I learned a lot more about taconite than I really wanted to know, but I appreciated the cost of the education so I listened patiently. Apparently, taconite is a Precambrian sedimentary rock—whatever that means—which is usually made up of about 25 to 30 percent iron ore. That I do understand. I mean, it's pretty simple. And iron is in a lot of what we use in the world, so taconite equals money. Again, that's a pretty simple concept. Steinbach told me how most high-grade iron ore had been mined out of the United States by shortly after World War II, so the world turned to taconite as an alternative. It just so happens that there's a mother lode of it in northern Minnesota, in something called the Iron Range. And, I learned from Steinbach, there's more of it tucked into a pocket of Dakota County, Wisconsin, just southeast of the Iron Range that's owned by Lewis Prescott. The most important thing I learned was that taconite isn't mined by drilling deep into the earth through a hole in the side of a mountain. It's extracted by blasting the earth's surface wide open with massive amounts of dynamite. It's a deafening, dirty mining technique that leaves the landscape looking like a war zone. And somehow Lewis Prescott has all the permits he needs to start blasting away.

I'm almost to Bruner when my cell phone rings. It's Doug, my accountant friend. "Hi there."

"Paul?"

Doug doesn't sound like himself. "Yeah, it's me. What's wrong?"

"Are you sure this stuff you gave me is authentic?"

I never thought about that. I never considered the possibility that Cindy might have paid some cheap, unethical accountant to create numbers out of thin air because she hated her father so much. Of course, I never would have thought she'd recruit Caleb Jenkins and his crew to make like they were harassing her on 681 that snowy afternoon, either. "Yes, I'm positive." The incident on 681 was one thing, but forging documents would be quite another. I don't think her penchant for drama could reach those heights. I don't think she could have hated her father that much.

"Well, based on the numbers you gave me, Paul, I'd say Prescott Trading only has a few weeks left before the banks take it over. Unless, of course, something incredible happens."

Doug's words echo in my mind as I speed past my house. *Only a few weeks left before the banks take it over.* They sound almost exactly like the words penned in longhand on the memo in the box Chelsea handed me. I didn't give Doug that memo, just the numbers. I didn't want him influenced by what Jack had written to Prescott. I wanted his unbiased opinion. "How incredible?"

"Fifty million of cash at least," Doug answers, "based on the blood pouring off these pages spread out on my desk. If Prescott puts fifty million of cash into this company, I think he buys himself another six months from the banks." He hums to himself for a few seconds. He always does that when he's thinking hard. "That might even buy Prescott out of the whole mess if oil gets to triple digits a barrel by July or August. If it doesn't, he'll need to put more money in by the fall." Doug chuckles harshly. "Jesus, they really screwed up on that oil bet. This company's a hundred years old and a couple of stupid bets on oil could bring it down. It's really a shame."

I don't know how the hell Doug figured everything out and came to his conclusions so fast, and I'm not going to ask. I don't care how he did it, just that he did and that I have complete faith in his analysis. "I'll call you later, Doug," I say, racing past the entrance to the Campbell estate on my left. "Thanks for your help."

As soon as I hang up with Doug, I call Edina Engineering and ask for Henry Steinbach. It's Mrs. Driscoll and she doesn't sound happy when she hears who the caller is. I can't blame her; I caused her some stress today. I'm on hold for a while and I'm worried that he's going to start dodging me again, but, just as I pull up to the stop light at Main Street, he answers.

"Hello."

"Hello, Mr. Steinbach."

"Look, Sheriff, I can't be talking to you all the—"

"Just one more question," I say, checking both ways before going right. "That's it, I promise."

He hesitates. "All right, one more answer. Maybe," he adds, "depending on the question."

"What's all that taconite Lewis Prescott controls worth? What would a mining company be willing to pay for that tract of land now that he's got all the permits and licenses he needs to start dynamiting?"

"It's impossible to—"

"Ballpark. That's all I want. Just your best guess."

"Well, based on all the tests we've done," Steinbach answers, his voice dropping way down, "on the low side, a hundred million, and on the high side two hundred."

The pieces of the puzzle are falling neatly into place. "Thanks," I say, pulling into Bat's Exxon station. "Thanks a lot."

Bat's out of the office to greet me at the pump before I'm even out of the Cherokee. Jesus, it's freezing. It's at least ten degrees colder up here than it was in the Twin Cities. But Bat still hasn't traded in his grimy Milwaukee Brewers baseball cap for a ski hat.

"Howdy, Sheriff."

"Hey. Fill it up, will you?"

"Sure thing. You doing okay?" he asks as he slides the nozzle into the truck.

I catch his eye. "What do you mean?"

He shrugs. "The meeting tonight. You know, over at the church. You okay with all that?"

"What meeting?"

The nozzle clicks loudly and stops pumping for some reason. "The one Davy Johnson called," he answers, resetting it so gas starts flowing again. "The one Mrs. Erickson's telling everybody about."

One of Bat's sons comes out of the office. I start to wave but he turns around as soon as he sees me. "What's the meeting about?"

"You mean you don't know?"

"No."

"You won't shoot the messenger, will you?"

"No."

Bat pulls his cap down tight over his scalp, as tight as he can get it. "Davy, Chugger, and Frank want you out." He spits. "They don't think you're doing enough to find out who killed Cindy Prescott and Darrow Clements."

So that meeting in the storage room of Cam Riley's hardware store was about my morals, not my skills. It wasn't my imagination at all when I thought Davy was scared on the ride to the Prescott estate. He was terrified. "What do you think, Bat?"

He pulls the nozzle out of the truck. "I think you're a good man, Paul, but I think you may have some conflicts, based on what I've heard over the last day or two. I hate to say that."

I hand Bat fifty bucks for the gas. "We all have conflicts," I remind him in a steely voice.

He nods. "Yeah, but some are bigger than others."

I'm about to get into the Cherokee when I feel his hand on my shoulder.

"Sheriff?"

I don't feel very good about Bat right now. He's always been a local I could count on no matter what, but it seems like even he's deserting me now. "Yeah?"

"I don't know if this is important or not, but Bill Campbell was up here this morning."

I turn back around. *"Again?"*

Bat looks up Main Street toward the precinct. "Yeah, that's what I thought, too."

"Did he come in here? Is that how you know?"

"No. One of my boys said he saw old Bill out east on Route 7 this morning real early. Near where Gus and Trudy died. He said it looked like Campbell was talking to a cop, and it looked like one of your guys, based on the uniform. But he couldn't tell which one it was and he didn't see a police car. I guess they were all back off the road a bit and behind the cars."

It feels like I've just been kicked in the gut, like the wind has suddenly been knocked out of me.

I need to talk to Sara right away.

The meeting Davy Johnson called for tonight has me mad, really mad. Madder than I've been in a long time. Even madder than I was at Lewis Prescott the night he wouldn't let me into his home and laughed about it with the guard at the gate. I can't believe Davy went behind my back like this, I can't believe he's this much of a traitor, especially after what I said to him on our way out to the Prescott estate the other day. I thought I'd gotten to him, I thought I'd dug down to his sense of honor. Apparently I was wrong. He called this town meeting to have me cut loose without even telling me. It's a shock, I have to admit.

I can't believe Mrs. Erickson, either. I can't believe the way she's putting news of the meeting out on her network and obviously editorializing about it during her broadcasts. I know we haven't seen eye to eye since I got to Bruner four years ago, but this kind of disloyalty is unforgivable. If I'm still standing when it's all said and done, if I still have a job when I've brought the murderer to justice, Davy Johnson and Mrs. Erickson won't be members of the Dakota County Police Force any longer. And if Cam and the rest of the town council won't support me on that, they'll have my resignation and Vivian and I will start new somewhere else. Maybe flipping burgers wouldn't be so bad after all, and maybe I'll go back to L.A. to do it. The cold and gloom of these Wisconsin winters may finally be getting to me. Sunny and warm year-round is starting to sound very good.

The fact that one of my guys was talking to Bill Campbell this morning is driving me crazy, too. My gut tells me it was Davy—and my heart hopes it was. Of course, I'm still wearing that big, broad-brimmed paranoia hat, so at this point I'm suspicious of everyone. Not lost on me is the possibility that Bat could be involved in all of this, too. I really feel like it's me against the world at this point, and that's a terrible, terrible feeling. Never knowing if someone's around the next corner aiming at you wears you down quickly. Even if it's just insults and accusations they're shooting.

Sara wasn't at the Saloon when I stopped in there fifteen minutes ago and Ike claimed he didn't know where she'd gone. He was back in the kitchen making hamburger patties and he was in a foul mood. I don't know if it was me and the meeting tonight or because he and Sara had an argument, but he barely said a word and he wouldn't look me in the eye the entire time I was there. His face looked bruised, but I couldn't tell for sure if it was. After I left the Saloon I headed west out Route 7 to their house. I didn't like Ike's answer when I asked him where she was, and I have to talk to her as soon as possible, anyway. So going to their place seemed like the best thing to do.

Their house is two miles this side of Bickerstaff Lane and Shawmut Lake, and it's always seemed odd to me that they live west of town when the general store and the Saloon they own are on the east side of Bruner. It's a quarter of a mile off Route 7 down a rutted, gravel road that snakes through some thick stands of hardwood trees—mostly poplars and oaks with some maples mixed in there, too.

Ike and Sara's home reminds me a little of Caleb Jenkins's place, because there's junk strewn all over the front yard. Old car bodies, tractor tires, snowmobile parts, and tools lie on the ground like dead soldiers after the suicide charge of an epic battle. They're everywhere. Right now it's all covered by four inches of ice and snow—all that remains of the massive storm that hit us since the warm spell that followed up got to it.

Ike and Sara's yard looks like Jenkins's yard, but their house is much nicer than his. It's two stories and though it could use a fresh coat of paint and a few bricks at the top of the chimney, it's in pretty decent shape. As I climb out of the Cherokee I spot Sara's ATV beside a tree to the left of the house. The four-wheeler is on its side, which strikes me as strange. You leave it like that for long and gas and oil go places they shouldn't in the engine. Sara knows that.

"Sara!" There are three other homes on the same gravel driveway this house is on, but they aren't visible from Ike and Sara's place, even in winter. The trees grow too close together here. "Sara!" My voice echoes through the forest. Most of the time Sara rides that ATV to town on the side of the road—it goes up to twenty-five miles an hour—but sometimes she uses a red pickup that's parked on the other side of the house from the ATV. She likes the ATV better, she says, because she can go anywhere with it any time she wants and therefore bother anyone she wants to any time she wants to. Point is, both of her standard modes of transportation are here, so she should be here, too. Unless Ike's done something very bad. I hate to say it but it wouldn't surprise me. I don't think it would surprise anyone around here. Sara can be a damn tough woman to deal with, and Ike isn't the most stable soul around. *"Sara!"*

As my call to her fades into the cold air, I hear something that sounds like footsteps crunching through the snow. The noise is coming from behind the house, and it sounds like two separate sets of steps. I pull my 9mm out from beneath my coat and take off. As I race past the pickup I spot Sara and another figure—a man—

heading away from the house. One moment they're in the backyard and the next they're beyond the tree line. I only saw them for a split second before they disappeared, but it looked like the guy was holding a pistol to the back of her head. And it looked like Caleb Jenkins.

I turn and head for the nearest point of the tree line. I'm out in the open here and I'm very vulnerable. I expect Jenkins to start shooting at me as I race for cover but he doesn't. I roll behind a tree and come up on one knee with my gun aimed at the place where the tracks cross the tree line. I'm only fifty feet from that spot, and I can see the two sets of footsteps in the snow disappearing into the forest.

"Sara!"

There's still no response.

I sprint along through the brush just inside the tree line, hunched over like a running back barreling through the line of scrimmage as I tear through the briars and the brambles that claw at me. It reminds me of my high school football games when I was trying to avoid tacklers. And the lack of visibility reminds me of the other day when I was following that girl and the two guys who were chasing her through the thick stuff out on the Campbell estate. Of how vulnerable I was then, too.

I'm getting close to where Sara and Jenkins disappeared into the forest. He could be waiting for me behind any of the trees ahead with his gun drawn and I wouldn't have time to react if he took a shot at me.

So I stop. And listen. And hold my breath. And listen some more.

But I don't hear anything, not one damn sound. It's as if I've gone completely deaf it's so, so quiet in here. I don't hear anyone breathing or moving. There's still snow on the forest floor and the top layer is icy, so I ought to hear Sara and the guy crashing along if they're moving. But I don't.

I may not hear Jenkins—but I feel his presence. He's close, I know it. He hasn't gotten far. Sometimes I just know these things. It's a good trait to have as a lawman.

I take several deep breaths, then stand, with my back to a sturdy oak tree and my gun pointed toward the sky. I take another breath, then bring the gun down and swing around the big tree in one smooth motion. Sure enough, there he is. He's just twenty feet away across a small clearing, staring at me with his stringy hair, bad teeth, and that hungry look in his eyes. It's Caleb Jenkins all right, and like the awful coward he is, he's using Sara as his human shield. He's aiming a .50 caliber Desert Eagle pistol at me and grabbing Sara tightly and roughly around the neck with his left arm. Sara's eyes are wide open and there are tears streaming down her face.

I've been in a couple of close-range shootouts in my life, and I was able to survive both times because three things happen to me all at once in these situations. First, my mind goes clearer with a gun pointed at me than at any other time; second, everything in my field of vision seems to physically slow down except for me; and, third, my hand goes dead still so my aim is deadly accurate. I don't try to turn these things on, they just happen automatically. And they give me an amazing advantage over my opponent.

What a lot of people don't realize is that the most important things to remember in a close-range gun battle are: stay calm, think clearly, and take your time aiming. Don't fire wildly, just make each shot count. The reality is that Jenkins's only real chance to hit me is with his first shot, because after that Sara will be dead or running, he'll be naked without his shield, and I'll put him down. He's trying to seem calm to throw me off, but I know his blood's pumping so hard and fast he can barely see me. As long as I have faith in myself and all those things that happen, I'll win. It's that simple. He should have taken a shot at me as soon as I came out from behind the tree, but he didn't, and that's when he lost any advantage he might have had. The very fact that he didn't take that shot tells me a lot about his confidence—or lack of it.

"I've been waiting for this," Jenkins says in a raspy voice. "I've heard all about how good you are in a gunfight, how you stay so calm." He grins defiantly. "Well, we'll see about that."

The barrel of his huge pistol is shaking hard and he sees that I've noticed, which makes it shake even harder. A .50 caliber pistol packs one hell of a punch and the Desert Eagle is an awesome gun. If he hits me I'm going down, there's no doubt about it. But that gun's heavy, and not only do you have to be strong but you've also got to be practiced with it to be any kind of accurate. Plus, hitting a target twenty feet away with any pistol is tough, and though Jenkins handles guns a lot, they're mostly rifles and shotguns. Based upon what I saw at his shack, anyway.

The thing is, I don't want to kill Jenkins. I want to take him in alive, because I've got a lot of things I want him to tell me about the cult. Plus, he could end up being an excellent witness later on, since he strikes me as the type who'll cut any kind of deal he can to save his own ass. "I guess we will see about that, Mr. Jenkins. Probably a lot sooner than you'd like to."

Jenkins tightens his grip on Sara's neck and she whimpers. "Before I kill you, Sheriff," he says, "I want to tell you something."

"Oh, yeah?"

"Yeah." His smile turns into an arrogant smirk. "I watched that little blond bitch you love so much die. I watched her clothes come off and her hands and feet get nailed to the floor and her throat get sliced open real, real slow with the knife from your kitchen drawer. I watched her blood pour out all over her papa's mansion, and I listened to her try to scream with her neck all cut open like that. Then I watched the life seep out of her." He chuckles. "How does that make you feel, Sheriff? Huh?"

It ought to make my blood boil and thus the gun I'm holding shake—which is exactly what Jenkins wants. But I already came to grips with everything he just told me when I watched the video I took from his house. They taped her murder—it's the last thing on that second tape—and I forced myself to watch it even though it made me physically sick to my stomach for thirty minutes afterward. "It makes me sure I don't want to kill you out here," I answer evenly. "See, if I can take you in alive, then the state of Wisconsin can lock you up for the rest of your life and they can tell your prison mates that you're a child molester."

"I'm no child molester," he snaps angrily.

"Oh, no? Well I carried a seven-year-old boy back from that cabin you all burned down the other day. He died because you left him in the cold to suffer. I'd say that's molesting."

"Hey, I didn't want to—"

"You know what happens to child molesters in prison?" I watch the fear push his eyes wide open. "That's right, Mr. Jenkins, those big boys inside the pen will torture you every day you're in there. It'll be hell on earth, and every morning when I get up I'll think about you and I'll—"

He squeezes the trigger, but right before he does he moves slightly, exposing his shoulder. I shift to my right, making my shot at him a little more difficult for me, but his shot much more difficult for him. The big .50 caliber round blows past me into the trunk of the oak tree a foot to my left, and it's almost like I can actually see the bullet fly by because everything's slowed down so much in my field of vision. A millisecond later his shoulder explodes in red with my shot and the Desert Eagle flies into the air as he tumbles backward. The moment I see he's hit, everything around me accelerates to normal speed.

The gun lands in the snow a few feet from where Sara's crouched, and she's on it in a heartbeat. Before Jenkins even starts screaming in pain as he lies sprawled in the snow.

"Don't do it," I warn her. "I mean it."

But she doesn't aim the Dessert Eagle at me like I thought she was going to. She points the barrel of the huge gun down at Jenkins and cocks the trigger.

"What the hell are you doing, Sara?"

"He knows everything." The fear's gone and now her face is twisted in rage, and what is obviously a desire for revenge. "He knows I took you out to the cabin. He knows I saw you the other night. He knows *everything*. I don't know how he knows but he does. I can't let him live."

"I don't understand," I say, giving Sara a wide berth as I hustle around her to where Jenkins is writhing on the ground. I don't want to do anything that might make her squeeze that trigger, but I have to make sure he doesn't have another weapon on him. I kick him a few times in the right spots, and I'm confident he's unarmed, so I holster my weapon. Then I'm careful to back off a few steps so he can't lunge at me if he's faking about how bad the pain is. Now I'm only a step away from Sara, who's still pointing that Desert Eagle down at Jenkins, both hands wrapped so tightly around the big gun's handle her Native American fingers are almost white. "Sara, this guy's going to be locked up for the rest of his life. He can't—"

"You just don't get it," she whispers. "You just don't get it, do you?"

"Talk to me, Sara, tell me why I don't get it."

"He'll have me tortured. Whether he's in jail or not he'll get a message to them and they'll find me. They'll chop off my fingers, my toes, my hands, my legs." She shakes her head. "You can't understand how terrible it would be."

"*Who?* Who's going to do all that to you, Sara?"

"If I'm going to die, I'm going to decide when and where. I won't let them torture me to death. Not like they did to Cindy."

"I'll protect you, Sara." For the first time since Jenkins went down she moves her gaze away from him and she looks at me. She looks at me the same way Cindy did at the mansion when I followed her home from 681 that afternoon Jenkins and his gang played their parts in her drama of the day. Sara looks at me like I'm her knight in shining armor. "Just tell me who's behind all this."

"You'll protect me?" The gun drops slightly. "You promise?"

"Of course." She moves to where I'm standing, so she's right in front of me and she's staring up at me with those big, mahogany, almond-shaped eyes. God, she's beautiful. The skin of her face is perfect and her jet-black hair glistens in the sun. "I'll always protect you, Sara. You know that."

"But will you love me?"

Somehow I knew she was going to ask me that. "Did you kill Cindy?"

She blinks and lets the gun fall to her side in her right hand. "I love you, Sheriff," she whispers. "I've always loved you."

"Did you tell Ike that?"

She nods slowly and her eyes close halfway, as if she's suddenly been drugged. "Of course I did," she says. "I had to. I had to tell him the truth."

No wonder he wouldn't look at me back at the Saloon. "Did you kill Cindy?" I ask again. It wasn't clear to me who was doing the cutting on the tape. They were all in robes and all I could see was a woman's hand committing the unspeakable crime. "Did you?"

She reaches out and takes my hand in hers. "What do you think?"

My question clearly didn't surprise her. I guess I have my answer. "Tell me, Sara. Did you?"

"I'm a Chippewa, Sheriff. When I want something, I get it. And I want you. I've always wanted—"

I go for the gun. I lock the fingers of my left hand tightly around her right wrist and try to shake the weapon loose. But it doesn't happen, and instantly I know I'm in trouble. As slim as she is, she's strong. I can feel the power of her passion surging through her body. I've underestimated my opponent and I don't usually do that.

The gun goes above her head as we struggle, then we fall to the ground and flail in the snow. She's screaming so loudly in my ear as we struggle it almost busts my eardrum, but I'm finally able to slip my finger behind the trigger and fire over and over until the clip's expended. When it starts clicking, she slams her forehead to mine, jumps to her feet, and bounds away.

Just as Jenkins makes it to where I am, and instantly I'm in another battle for my life, because he's yanking at the Glock in my holster. Despite the shooting pain in my forehead, I'm able to cover the holster with one hand and hammer his shoulder with the other. Then I give him a swift knee to the groin and he's writhing in the snow again. This time he's down for the count.

I struggle to my feet and search for Sara, but she's gone. The forest has swallowed her up and even if I follow her tracks I know there's no way I'll find her now. This time she's gone for good.

28

"SHERIFF SUMMERS. *Sheriff Summers!*"

Maggie Van Dyke hurries toward me along Main Street's darkened sidewalk as fast as she can, as fast as her sturdy legs will carry her, calling out my name over and over. I'm still two blocks from the church, but at least fifteen people who are heading to the meeting as well are within earshot and I cringe at how loud her voice seems. It sounds like the wail of a fire truck on a clear, cold night and I want to stay anonymous as long as I can, at least until I walk into the church. Even when I get there I'm going to stay in the back until I absolutely have to say anything. And I will have to speak, I will have to defend my actions—if I expect to survive.

I just got back to town from Ike and Sara's place after a long afternoon. Jenkins was no help at all, not that I really expected him to be. All he wanted to do was get into the ambulance and be whisked off to the hospital in Superior. I tried to interrogate him even as the EMTs were tending to him inside Sara's house where I'd helped him walk from the clearing. And I used the old line that if he shot straight with me right away, I'd try to reduce his charge from the attempted murder of a police officer to something less serious. I mean, I really pressured him. But Jenkins just kept repeating that he wouldn't say anything until his lawyer was present—and maybe not even then. It was like his mantra, like someone had schooled him on what to say and how to react if he was ever arrested. Even the bit about my leaking word to the prison gang that he was a child molester wasn't working, though I reminded him of it twice more.

Finally, I had to let the paramedics take him away. Jenkins shouted at me as they lifted him into the back of the ambulance on the stretcher that he was going to sue the county and me personally for waiting an hour to call for medical attention. I almost shot the bastard again.

"Yes, Maggie." Even though it's dark and I can't really see them staring, I feel the eyes of the people on the street boring into me. Davy Johnson and Mrs. Erickson have screwed me royally. I sense a wave of sentiment building against me even though I'm still two blocks from the church. "What is it?"

"Sorry to bother you, Sheriff, I really am. I know this is a bad time for you and all, but have you heard anything about Karen, anything at all?"

As I stare down at her, I realize that it's beginning to snow. I feel the fine, icy crystals hitting my face and see the glow of the streetlight over in front of the washette.

"Sheriff?"

Bear begged me not to say anything about what's going on with Karen and him. He's breaking the law, he's defrauding an insurance company out of fifty thousand bucks, but he's my best friend and he saved my life. *Twice.* How can I break that trust or walk away from the greatest debt anyone can owe? How can I destroy a friendship that's lasted twenty-five years and put my best friend in jail? "Maggie, can we talk after the meeting?" I suggest. "Or maybe first thing tomorrow morning at the precinct?" I hate to dodge her, but I don't want to talk right now. Bat was right. I'm conflicted, *so* conflicted everywhere I look. "I haven't had a chance to check for anything that might have come into the precinct today. You know, calls or emails from any of the other counties or the state boys." Which isn't true. I just went to the precinct to pick up a vitally important envelope I haven't had the guts to open yet because I'm afraid of what might be inside. It's information I requested late last week that's tucked beneath my jacket right now, and what's inside the envelope could have awful ramifications. "Is that all right?"

Maggie looks down dejectedly. "It's just that I'm getting frustrated," she says. "It's been—"

"I know, Maggie," I interrupt, getting frustrated myself. I don't mind being a little curt with her at this point because I know Karen's all right, and maybe Maggie should have given her sister a little more of what Gus and Trudy left behind after all. "Tomorrow morning. Okay?"

"Sure, I guess." She wags a finger at me. "You just promise me that—"

"Sheriff! Sheriff Summers!"

My gaze flashes past Maggie and into the gloom at the person who's yelling at me now. As I search the darkness I have to shield my eyes because the snow is really starting to come down. Then I recognize the face. It's Lewis Prescott. Maggie scurries off as soon as she looks over her shoulder and sees who it is. Christ, the whole town is afraid of this guy.

"What do you want, Lewis?" It's the first time I've ever called him by his given name and it feels especially good because I can tell I've surprised him. "And make it fast, damn it." I nod up the street. "I've got to get to this meeting."

"Don't talk to me like that, boy," he snaps. "You better show me respect, because I can have you—"

"What the hell do you want, Lew?" He stares at me from beneath his fur hat like he doesn't recognize me, like he doesn't believe what he's hearing. "Come on, out with it."

His eyes narrow. You don't surprise Lew Prescott for long, even in the desperate state he must be in right now. "Remember what I said about any talk of a cult," he warns. "Put it down right away if anyone even whispers anything about it in this meeting. Be firm on the fact that there is absolutely no cult." He takes a satisfied breath, certain he has me where he wants me. "Or else."

I stare down at him. We didn't get anywhere when I went to the compound in Minneapolis to talk to him about why he wants me to squash any talk of a cult. He wouldn't come clean with me even though I gave him every opportunity. "Or else what?"

"Or else you can kiss your job bye-bye," he warns. "Tomorrow morning you'll be out on your ass, and I promise you won't get a job as a cop anywhere else in this country. My people will follow you wherever you go and make the authorities in that jurisdiction aware of your less-than-exemplary record."

I don't even bother arguing about how he's made everything up. I just gesture toward the church. "Chances are I'm going to be out of a job in an hour anyway, Lew."

"Well, if you just do as I say, I'll find you another job. And I'll put you on the payroll at Prescott Trading until that happens. At the same salary you have now." He holds up a finger. "Plus, I'll pay for your move to wherever the new job is."

"If you can. Well, if Prescott Trading can." I've hit him with another howitzer, and it's registering all over his face. For the second time in a few seconds I've shocked this man I've hated most of my life, and it feels almost too good to describe. Better than eating a dozen chocolate-covered doughnuts in one sitting. Even now as I'm headed for one of the most difficult situations I'll ever face. "Pay for it, I mean."

"What are you talking about?"

"You know exactly what I'm talking about, Lew. The fact that Prescott Trading is going under unless you come up with a lot of money real fast." Prescott takes two steps back, like I've actually hit him. "Otherwise the banks are going to foreclose on you and take everything you have including the estate up here and the compound in Minneapolis. I mean they're going to take *everything*. Everything your family has built for over a century. It's all going to be gone like *that*," I say, snapping my fingers loudly right in front of his patrician nose.

The old man grabs his chest. "My God, how did you—"

"But then there's all that bloody taconite in the ground behind the estates." Prescott's eyes roll back in his head when he hears that one, and I keep the pressure on even though I know the meeting's about to start and I want to be there for everything. "That could save you, couldn't it? And *that's* the *real* reason you don't want anyone to start talking about a cult in Dakota County," I barrel on. "Because it might scare off the two mining companies you have bidding for all that taconite. Not because of how Cindy will be remembered, or how your wife will feel. You don't give a damn about either of them. You never did, you bastard. That's why you don't care that Jack was beating Cindy, that's why you didn't care about screwing old Bill Campbell's wife seven years ago."

"Oh, my God," he whispers, overwhelmed by what I've said.

"You're worried about this cult maybe killing someone from Edina Engineering or somebody from one of the mining companies who's looking at buying the taconite from you." I put a finger in his face. "Because maybe people in the cult like Dakota County the way it is, maybe they like the way it's isolated from the rest of the world and they don't want a lot of strangers coming in here and messing it up. Maybe they don't want all that land ripped up between the ridge and River Road."

"Paul," Prescott gasps, "how did you find out?"

I lean down so our faces are close. "What you really need to worry about isn't how I found out. What you need to worry about is my telling everyone in the meeting what's really going on here."

"I'll pay you," he blurts out. "Whatever you want. *Whatever*."

I stare at him for several moments. It's an odd feeling when you realize you've finally beaten a man you've always wanted to take down. A man who's manipulated you for years, and now the situation is suddenly reversed. Suddenly you hold his fate in your hands. "I'll let you know, Lew. I'll let you know."

I turn and head for the church, and as I do my cell phone rings. It's a number I recognize right away. I stop fifty feet from the church door when I end the call and slip the phone back into my pocket. Then I shake my head for a second and put my face in my hands. Finally I pull the envelope from inside my jacket, rip it open, and gaze at what's inside in the dim light coming from the church. It's even worse than I thought.

29

"EVERYBODY PIPE DOWN!" Davy shouts over the hum of voices inside the packed church. He's standing up on the pulpit with his arms outstretched. *"Please!"*

On Sunday mornings you can hear a pin drop before the processional. Before the choir members follow the cross and Father Hannah down the narrow center aisle to the altar, then break away to their special section of pews. Hardly anyone in the congregation even talks before the service begins. And when they do it's in a low whisper only to the person next to them and almost directly into that person's ear.

Right now it's like being at a Saturday night dance at the fire hall up Main Street from here. You can hardly hear yourself think. Mostly the same people who come to Sunday service are here now, but I guess they figure God's gone to bed or something. That or it's flat-out impossible for them to control their anticipation and excitement at the prospect of what might happen in this meeting, and they're all speculating wildly about how it's going to go down. The bad thing is that they're probably right. It probably will be a Fourth of July fireworks show worthy of New York City's harbor or the Mall in Washington.

The other thing that's different tonight is that the church is brightly lighted. That occurred to me as soon as I walked in. It's almost always dim in here on Sunday mornings in the winter because Father Hannah doesn't like using anything other than candles during his services. And it's usually gloomy outside, so not much light gets in through the windows.

"Enough!" Davy yells, banging a gavel on the tilted piece of lacquered dark wood that's bolted to the banister on which Father Hannah places the yellow pieces of legal paper he preaches his sermon from. Finally the crowd begins to settle down. "Thank you."

"I can't believe this is happening," I mutter to myself, casing the crowd from my corner in the back near the double doors. "It's not right."

The entire town council, including Cam Riley, sits in the pew directly in front of the pulpit, and Lewis Prescott sits two rows behind them. His seat was taken when he got here, but the townspeople who were in that row when he showed up scattered like lambs from a butcher when they saw him coming. All except Mrs. Erickson, who didn't budge an inch and gave Prescott a smirk when he eased into the spot vacated by Janet Carlson, the woman who's Vivian's boss at the washette. Bear's standing up front against the wall on the opposite side of the church from the pulpit with a scowl on his face. The same ugly scowl he has on his face the morning after a Badger or Packer loss. Bat McCleary sits a few rows in front of where I'm standing, flanked by his two boys. And Frank and Chugger—the other two traitors on my staff—stand in front of the pulpit with their arms folded tightly across their uniform jackets.

I'm about to look back at the floor, at the spot of red carpet I've been focused on since I came in, when someone else's presence catches my eye. At the back of the other side of the church stands Bill Campbell. He's a big man with a barrel chest and a shock of white hair. With him is a young Turk I don't recognize who looks like Bear except that he's wearing a stylish blue sweater and cuffed flannel pants and his hair is shorter and neatly combed. He's not quite as big as Bear, but almost. I'm amazed that Campbell and his guy would show their faces at this thing, but I guess the outcome of it is that important to him.

"Let's get to it," Davy says.

Davy glanced at me when I first came in but he hasn't made eye contact with me since.

"In the last two weeks," he continues in a dramatic voice, "we've had two terrible murders in Dakota County."

I see Lewis Prescott's shoulders pinch together at the sides of his neck. He's afraid that Davy's going to get graphic with his description of the murders. Maybe he's even more afraid that if Davy does, I won't respond, that I won't deny the existence of the cult as he so desperately wants me to. After all, I walked away from his offer. Something he probably has no idea how to handle. I wonder if he knows Bill Campbell is here. If he doesn't, I have a feeling he'll find out soon enough. If what I've deduced is right.

"The first was Cindy Harrison," Davy says in a melancholy tone with a deferential nod to Lewis Prescott.

Which tells me something right away.

"And the second was Darrow Clements." Davy takes a deep breath. "Ladies and gentlemen, I have the deepest respect for Sheriff Summers." He hesitates and nods toward me now. "Who's standing in the back of the church."

The entire congregation looks over their shoulders at me in unison and my gaze falls to the carpet again. I can't stare down a hundred and fifty pairs of eyes. It's impossible.

"He's a good man but he's over his head in this situation." Davy motions toward me. "I'm sorry, Sheriff," he says in front of the crowd, "but I have to say it. Frank, Chugger, and I believe—"

"You don't have to say anything!" Bear shouts out of nowhere.

There's a collective gasp from the crowd. You just don't see this kind of thing happen in the north-country. People may be thinking nasty thoughts, but they rarely shout them out in a public forum. Usually it's the stiff upper lip for Lutherans on the south shore of the Big Lake.

"You don't know what you're talking about, you little punk!" Bear yells, taking several steps toward the pulpit. Frank and Chugger make their moves at him, but he points a finger and it's as though he's got stun-gun powers, because they go motionless. "Touch me and I'll kill both of you," he hisses loudly enough for everyone to hear. "Even if this is a church."

"Tell us more about the murders, Deputy!" a voice thunders from the back of the church.

My head swivels left as Bill Campbell takes the floor. Of course he does. It makes so much sense. It's a perfect forum for him to do this in.

Lewis Prescott shoots up out of his seat at the sound of Campbell's voice and turns around. His face goes pale when he sees who's yelling. It's like he's actually going to have a heart attack.

"There's a cult involved!" Campbell shouts. "A cult of devil worshipers! Isn't that true, Deputy?"

Davy Johnson suddenly looks like a man who'd rather be any place in the world other than where he is now.

"There's no cult!" Prescott shouts back. But his voice doesn't have the same thunder to it that Campbell's does. He's like a mouse against a lion. "I saw my daughter's body!" he yells as loudly as he can. "There weren't any pentagrams or other ritual carvings on her body. She was murdered by someone who wanted to take her away—"

"*Liar!*" roars Campbell.

"By a man who wanted to take Cindy away from her husband," Prescott yells back. "A man who's wanted her for years. The same man who killed Darrow Clements because Clements was getting close to figuring out who killed my daughter."

"It was the cult!" bellows Campbell.

"It was Paul Summers!" Prescott shouts back.

Suddenly the church goes even quieter than it does on Sunday mornings just before the cross begins its journey down the aisle toward the altar. A pin hitting the carpet would seem like a volcano going off right now. I swallow hard as those hundred and fifty pairs of eyes stare at me again. Apparently, Lewis Prescott thinks he figured out how to deal with my turning down his offer of money.

"It's not true," I say calmly. It's time to begin my defense. It's time to tell everyone what's really going on in Dakota County. "You all know me, you know I'd never do something like that. It's not in me." I glance at Prescott, then point at him. "That man over there has a terrible problem. His company, Prescott Trading, is about to fail. It's about to be taken over by the banks that lend to it." I assume Prescott is about to start yelling anything he can think of to silence me, but to my surprise he doesn't. "Unless he can come up with a million bucks in the next two weeks."

"You're out of your mind," Prescott finally snarls. "You're just trying to—"

"So he's going to sell all that land he owns between the Boulder River and River Road," I shout him down quickly. "Those thousands and thousands of acres that stretch out behind all the River Family estates up and down Dakota County. He's going to sell it to a mining company for lots of money because there's taconite in it." I see jaws drop and hear shrieks of surprise all around me. "Lots and *lots* of taconite. Then he's going to use the money he gets from the sale of the land to save Prescott Trading.

"It all sounds wonderful," I keep going, "nice and tidy." I hold up one hand. "But there's a big problem. Something Mr. Prescott is very afraid of because it could break his deal. If word gets out about us having a cult of devil worshipers here in Dakota County that's murdering people, the companies bidding on his property might give him a lowball offer or back off completely. Especially if that cult kills somebody from one of the mining companies bidding on the land who came up here to inspect the site. And that's something Mr. Prescott simply cannot have, because then he and his family lose everything." Prescott sinks slowly down into the pew and puts his face into his hands. He knows there's no way he can deny what I'm saying. I've got him dead to rights. He thought he knew how to deal with my turning down his money, but he really didn't. See, I'm not in it for the money, and he doesn't scare me, because ultimately I know the truth always wins out. And maybe I just don't care whether I live or die anymore. Which can be a powerful thing when you're in a fight, because it lets you take actions you'd otherwise be too scared to take. "Let me say that again, people. Mr. Prescott will lose *everything*, and he'll probably go to jail." My eyes shift to Bill Campbell. "The thing about getting taconite out of the ground is that it's basically strip mining. It's a nasty, loud, dirty process. You dynamite the ground open, then you haul away the rocks you blew out of the ground and process them somewhere else." I point at Campbell. "Isn't that right, Mr. Campbell?"

Campbell looks around like he can't believe I'm talking to him. "How the hell should I know?"

"Oh, you know. You also know that Lew Prescott has all the permits he needs to go ahead with the mining and that the permits he has are transferable to any buyer. He did that before you could stop him."

"I can't believe I'm saying this," Campbell snaps, "but for the first time in my life I agree with Lewis Prescott. You're out of your mind, Sheriff Summers."

"Sure I am, Bill." I like using their first names. Suddenly I don't feel so inferior anymore. "I'm sure you'd just love to sit on that huge back deck of yours at your estate on a nice summer afternoon sip-ping your gin and tonic and listen to the soothing sounds of dynamite. Inhale the lovely scents of oil and gas exhaust as they waft gently through the air up the side of the ridge. Taste the dirt and sand in your mouth along with that gin and tonic while you try to read a book or listen to music." I take a few steps toward him— and the door. "It'd be even better if you were having a party with your family and all of that blasting was going on right down the hill. Wouldn't it, Bill?"

Campbell looks around helplessly at the crowd that's staring at him. Like Prescott before him, he knows he can't deny what I'm saying. I've got him dead to rights, too.

"Throw on top of that the fact that you out-and-out hate Lew Prescott, and have for years, because of what happened with him and your wife, and you see this as a chance to bury him like he's never been buried and we're at case closed. Aren't we, Bill?"

"What's your damn point?"

I rub my eyes for a few moments. I'm very tired. "A man from Brower County named Caleb Jenkins tried to kill me this afternoon out at Ike and Sara's place." Gasps of shock and amazement race around the church. Evidently a lot of people know who Caleb Jenkins is. It's a small world up here in the north-country when you're a true local. "He could tell us who ordered the murders of Cindy Prescott and Darrow Clements, because he's in the cult. But he won't talk. Not yet anyway. He's at the hospital in Superior with a bullet in his shoulder because I shot him. He was trying to kill Sara but I got to him first. He was trying to get information out of her before he killed her because she was in the cult, too, but I got there in time." My eyes flash around the big room. "She believes she'd be tortured if she told me what was going on, so she ran away this afternoon, and I'm sure I'll never find her." I'm standing in front of the double doors leading to the outside. "There's one more person who I'm sure can tell us who the leader of the cult is. Who can tell us who's carrying out these horrible murders and for whom all of this is ultimately being done. That's an important thing I just said, if you didn't hear me. She can tell us for *whom* this is all being done." I hesitate as I stare intently at that individual for whom all of this is being done for several seconds. Then I glance at the individual who I'm almost positive is carrying it out. "There's one more person I'm sure can tell us everything." My eyes narrow. "And I'm going to go save her right now."

With that I'm out the church door and sprinting through the blizzard for my Cherokee. I may not care anymore if I live or die, but I care that she does.

30

I'M HALFWAY HOME, racing down 681 through the gale and the whipping snow, when headlights appear in my rearview mirror. It's him, I know it is.

He's coming after me because he understood exactly what I meant before I dashed from the church. He knows which person could tell me everything about the cult, which person could pull back the black curtain for all to see it, which person could be my star witness. It's Vivian. That's why he's tearing down 681 after me as I race for home. He needs to do away with both of us if he's to have a chance of surviving. There's no death penalty in Wisconsin, only life without parole, which for him would be even worse. If he kills both of us, maybe he can make it look as if it's a cult killing, as he's made the other murders appear.

According to Sara, Vivian's been in the cult for several months. Sara told me that the other night when she came by the precinct clutching her pop bottle full of rotgut moonshine. She told me a lot of things that night. She told me that Vivian was forced to bring the knives from our kitchen drawer for the sacrifice of Mel Hopkins's goat and for Cindy's murder—which was the knife I found at the cabin after Sara took me out there. Using knives from our drawer and planting that Bruner Washette ticket at the scene of Cindy's murder were meant to keep Vivian in line, to keep her from telling me or anyone else anything about the cult. If she did, if she broke ranks with the cult, she knew she'd be implicated in the murder. Or, worse, she'd be executed before she could tell anyone what was going on. According to Sara, Vivian was told all that over and over by the man who's running the cult, by the man who's chasing me now.

Vivian joined the cult because it fascinated her, and because it gave her a sense of belonging as well as the companionship she's been wanting so desperately. Companionship I haven't been giving her, but I will now—if we survive. Apparently, when she understood the murderous path the cult was headed down, she tried to quit—but she couldn't. Once you join this cult you join it for good—or you die.

Sara told me how Vivian cried while Cindy was being murdered and wasn't actually present when Darrow Clements was killed at the Friendly Mattress. Vivian could still face prosecution for witnessing Cindy's murder and not going to law enforcement immediately to tell us what she knew. But if I can prove she was in danger of being murdered herself if she told anyone, she might not be prosecuted.

I still can't believe Sara killed Cindy. I guess she is crazy, just like everyone always said she was. You'd have to be insane to kill someone the way she killed Cindy—inch by inch across the throat with a knife. That was one thing she didn't tell me the other night. I had to find that out this afternoon.

I glance in the rearview mirror. The headlights are closing in on me even though I'm pushing the Cherokee as hard as I can. The road's already slick with fresh snow and I'm constantly fishtailing along the pavement. I can't go any faster.

A few hundred yards from my driveway he reaches my bumper

and nudges me with his. For several fleeting seconds I'm able to hold the road, I'm able to stay in control. But then the front wheels go hard left and I'm hurtling toward the pine trees lining the side of the road. Then I'm able to wrench the wheels back to the right. But the change in direction is too sudden and the Cherokee flips. The truck rolls over and over down the narrow strip of grass between the road and the forest before it finally comes to rest upside down against several trees. Thanks to the seatbelt and dumb luck, I'm alive. I'm banged up and bruised, but as far I can tell, nothing's broken.

Somehow I'm able to unbuckle the seatbelt, drop down to the roof, and shove the door open. As I crawl out of the Cherokee, I see that he flipped over, too. He's just pulling himself from his vehicle, so I take off for the house, limping. Something's wrong with my left knee. It feels like ligaments.

"Vivian!" I shout as I burst through the back porch door. "Viv!"

I don't have to look far. She's standing in the kitchen by the stove and there are literally hundreds of candles lighted everywhere.

She smiles at me sweetly. "I love you, Paul."

I race to where she's standing. "Vivian, we've got to—"

But I'm too late. I whip around as the back porch door flies open and the man chasing me bursts into the kitchen with his gun drawn.

Billy Brock stands in front of Vivian and me, chest heaving, blood dripping down his face from a gash over his eye.

"Why'd you do it, Professor?" he mutters. "Why couldn't you just leave well enough alone?"

I move beside Vivian and take her hand in mine. "Because I'm the sheriff, Bear." It's the first time I've called him that in a long time and I think it's because he isn't Billy to me anymore. "It's as simple as that." He's someone I don't know now. "You turned into a killer for hire and you used the cult as a way to do it. You had Sara kill Cindy and you killed Darrow Clements yourself and you took money for the murders from Bill Campbell. The money for that new TV in your house didn't come from some insurance scam. I talked to that agent of yours down in Madison tonight, right before I went into the church, and he denied everything."

"Of course he did, he—"

"He said he'd let anyone I wanted come to his office and look at anything they want to!" I shout, "and I got your bank records, Bear, for that account of yours over in Superior." His eyes open wide. "I looked at them right before I came into the meeting tonight. You've been putting cash into that account for the last few months, lots of it. You've turned into Bill Campbell's hired gun. He hates Lew Prescott from a long time ago, and he hates the thought of his backyard turning into a taconite dynamite range, so he hired you to stop it by scaring people away from buying the land. He hired you to set the cult up and make it seem like you were killing animals and people because you were devil worshipers when all you really worship is money. Maybe the rest of the people in it, people like Caleb Jenkins, maybe they think it's real. Or maybe some of them are in on the money, too. I don't know, we'll have to find out. But my bet is that your next target was going to be a senior executive of whatever company showed interest in buying the land. Or maybe it was going to be Henry Steinbach." I can tell I've struck a nerve by the way Bear's looking at me. Like he thinks I must have planted a listening device on him somehow. Apparently, I couldn't be more right about what I'm saying. "I bet Bill Campbell had no idea before tonight how bad the situation is for Lew Prescott at the family company. Campbell was going to luck into that one, wasn't he, Bear? By getting in the way of the taconite deal he was going to put Prescott into bankruptcy and probably ruin Jack Harrison's political career. But he didn't know that when he first talked to you, did he?"

Bear shakes his head. "You can't prove anything, Professor. You can't—"

"Have you told anybody else in the cult that you're taking money for the murders? Have you told anyone else what's really going on?"

"They don't need to know—"

"Is that why Karen left you? Because she found out what was going on? But you couldn't bring yourself to kill her, could you, Bear? Despite all the fights and the yelling, you couldn't kill her, could you? So you paid her off." I shake my head. "And she took it." A strange smile plays across Bear's face and a horrible thought flashes through my mind. "Oh, no. You didn't, did you? You didn't kill Karen."

He nods. "After we met at the house the other morning. I couldn't risk it any longer."

"Oh, my God."

"You'll never find her body. No one—"

In one smooth motion I pull the Glock from my holster and fire—but not before Bear gets off a shot that grazes my left shoulder. Vivian screams as Bear clutches his gut and keels over. I hit him right in the stomach, exactly where I was aiming. I grab Vivian's wrist and hobble quickly through the house to the front door, pulling her along. Then we're down the steps, onto the front lawn, and into the storm.

While we were in the house it turned into a raging blizzard out here. Sustained winds must be at least forty miles an hour and the gusts have to be whipping up to fifty, maybe even sixty. The snow's blowing sideways and the tiny ice crystals feel like missiles blasting my face. I can see Vivian shrieking right next to me but I can barely hear her.

When we've only made it twenty feet onto the lawn I turn to face the door, putting myself between Vivian and the house. I feel her fingers clinging to me as the door opens and Bear staggers onto the porch and stops directly beneath the overhead lamp.

Bear stands there, one hand on his gut as his jacket whips crazily around him. He gazes at me for a few moments, then slowly raises his gun and aims. Vivian's screaming at the top of her lungs, begging me to run. But I won't. I have to see if Bear will take another shot at me, I want to see if he'll actually try to kill me. I want to give my best friend one more chance.

A flash of fire spits from the barrel of his gun, but he misses. As I knew he would. But now I have to shoot back because he's staggering down the porch steps. I can't let him get off another round, because he's getting too close. I can't put Vivian in that kind of danger.

Everything goes into slow motion as I raise my gun, aim, and squeeze the trigger. Then it all speeds up again when Bear tumbles to the ground. He's dead, I know it. I hit him right in the heart, right where I was aiming. I had to kill him this time, I didn't have a choice. If he'd gotten any closer he might have actually hit me. Worse, he might have hit Vivian.

As I stare at his body lying on the ground, I realize that this is what he wanted. He didn't want to live anymore; he couldn't handle the guilt and maybe he'd found out that having a little money wasn't as great as he thought it would be. Not enough to become a killer. So he came after me because he wanted to die. He didn't race out of the church to kill me, he raced out of the church so I'd kill him. He knew everything was over and he didn't want to go to jail.

For several moments I gaze at the ground, what I've done sinking in as I stand here in the raging blizzard. I've killed my best friend, the man who saved my life twice. Finally, I turn around to hold Vivian.

And behind her is Sara. She's ten feet away pointing a revolver at us. She's screaming that if she can't have me, no one will.

There's no way I can get my gun up in time and she's a damn good shot. Better than any of my deputies. Vivian and I are about to die. Sara will put us both down with the first shot, then finish us off with a few more rounds as we lie on the ground helpless.

Just as Sara squeezes the trigger of her revolver there's an incredible blast of wind that seems to shake the ground we're standing on. It rushes down from above with a great roar, knocking a huge limb off a pine tree that crashes onto Sara. I don't even feel the pain in my knee as I climb over the limb and grab the revolver from Sara's hand. But as I do, I realize that there was no need to worry about her shooting us.

Sara's dead.

Epilogue

I<small>T TURNED OUT</small> that somehow Bill Campbell knew Prescott Trading was in trouble. How he found out was never clear to me, but in the end it didn't really matter. All that mattered was that Campbell had, in fact, approached Bear about starting the cult and using it to destroy Lew Prescott. Campbell had never forgotten what Prescott had done after that cocktail party seven years ago—and apparently several other times as well—and he didn't want to listen to the sounds of dynamite exploding down the ridge from his mansion for the rest of his days. So he hatched a plan.

I could believe it of Campbell, given all the stories I'd heard about how he'd created his business empire. What I couldn't believe was that Bear agreed to help him. That Bear gave in to the lure of money in return for killing. You think you know someone—but you never really do. It's a horrible truth.

When the trial was over, Vivian and I moved to Montana, to a little cabin on the Bitterroot River. We don't have much money, but we found our happiness again. I do private security up in Missoula, and Vivian waits tables at a little restaurant not far from our cabin.

A year ago we got an incredible surprise when Vivian visited her doctor. She was pregnant. Three months ago she had a little boy and we named him Paul, Jr. Someday I'll build a canoe with him in the barn out back during a long Montana winter—and we'll name it *Intrepid.*

Acknowledgments

Thanks to Cynthia Manson, Peter Borland, Judith Curr, Louise Burke, Jack Wallace, Barbara Fertig, Andy and Chris Brusman, Kevin Erdman, Jeanette Follo, Steve Watson, Bart Begley, Jim and Anmarie Galowski, Gerry Barton, Pat and Terry Lynch, Nick Simonds, Skip Frey, Tony Reinhardt, Jeff, Jamie and Catherine Faville, Baron Stewart, Mike Pocalyko, Bob Carpenter, Mike Lynch, Matt Malone, and Chris T. and Gordon Eadon.